I BLINKED, TRYING TO SEE, panicked by my

I blinked, over and over, but the light would

Then the fingers holding me tightened so mu

"Jurekil'a u'hatre davos!"

The man behind me was breathing hard, almost as hard as the people panicking around us. He spoke right near my ear. I couldn't see him through the light, but his panic slammed into me, making my eyes close, making me nauseated.

"Gaos… di'lanlente a'guete… you're a fucking manipulator!"

I couldn't make sense of anything he said.

I wasn't thinking about the gun anymore. Or about the dead guy by the wall.

I wanted to get the fuck out of there. I wanted to go home.

Then another thought hit me.

A rush of panic brought pain to my heart, my heart to my throat.

Jon.

Jesus Christ.

Had I hurt Jon? What happened to Jon? Where was Cass?

Terror hit me.

"JON!" I raised my voice as loud as I could. My words sounded rough, blurred. "JON! ANSWER ME! CASS! CASSANDRA! WHERE ARE YOU?"

I still couldn't see.

An arm wrapped roughly around my waist.

It wrenched me back against a hard, muscular body.

I gripped that arm in my hands, still fighting to see, to find Jon or Cass with my eyes. I didn't really struggle against the man holding me. I doubted I could have budged that arm even if I tried, and I could barely make myself try. I couldn't remember ever being so drained.

I was fucking exhausted.

I could barely keep my eyes open.

Before I could wrap my head around what he was doing, the feelings coming off him, he was carrying me.

I couldn't see, but I knew we were heading towards the door.

That's when I first heard the sirens.

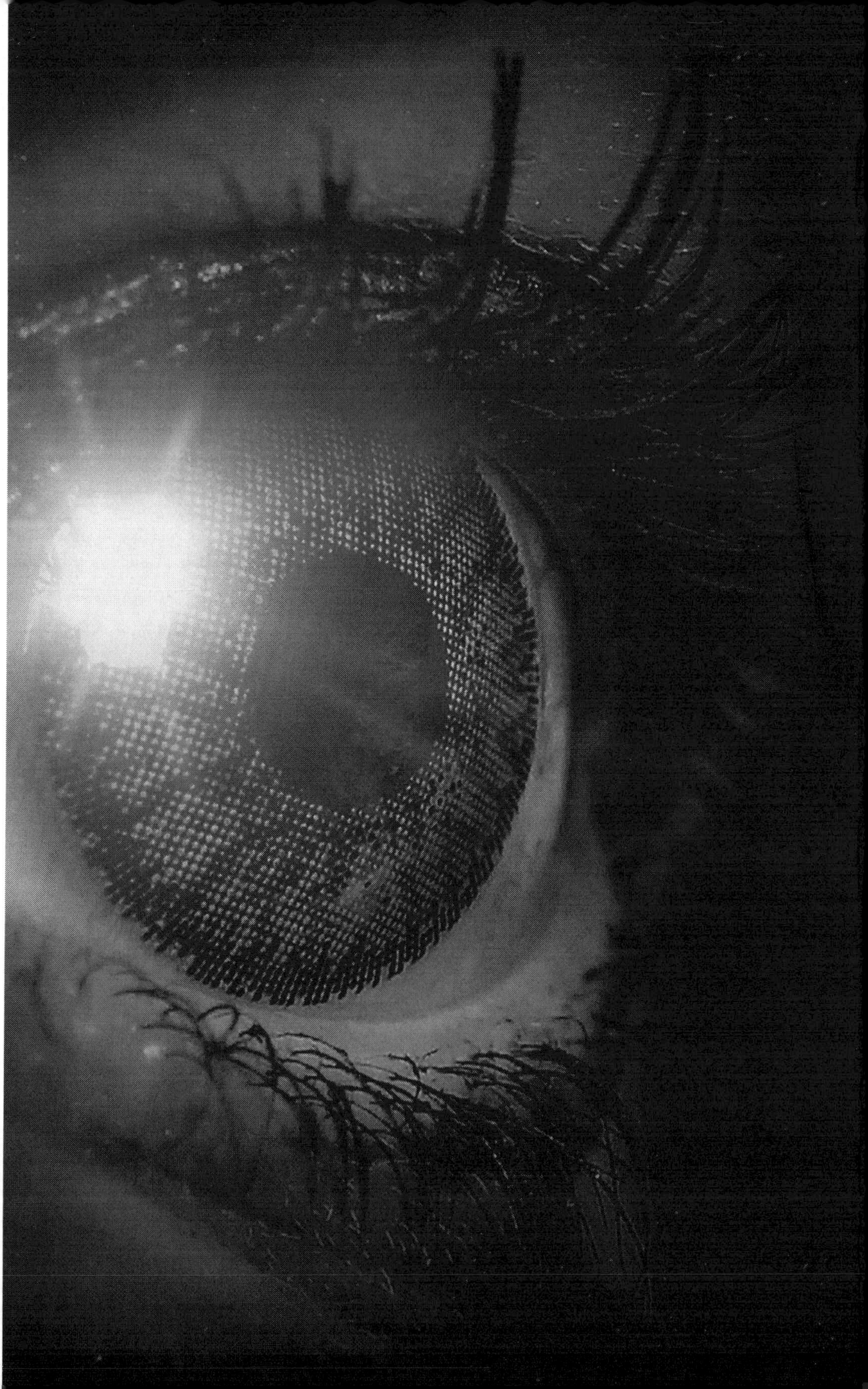

DARK SEERS

BRIDGE AND SWORD: BOOK ONE

JC ANDRIJESKI

Dark Seers (Bridge and Sword: Book One)

Published by White Sun Press

First Edition

ISBN: 9798829350475

Cover Art & Design by Camila Marques

2022

Link with me at: https://www.jcandrijeski.com

Or at: https://www.patreon.com/jcandrijeski

Mailing List: https://www.jcandrijeski.com/sign-up

White Sun Press

Printed in the United States of America 2022

Dedicated to Maya, Samantha, Naomi, Keeley and Allie and all of the other lights that came to build us a better world.

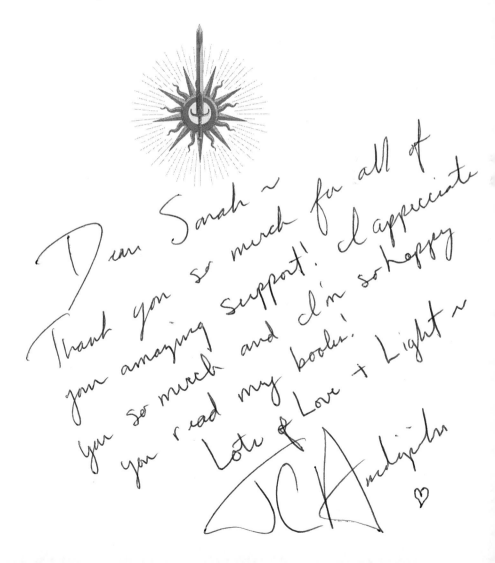

Dear Sarah ~
Thank you so much for all of your amazing support! I appreciate you so much and I'm so happy you read my books!
Lots of Love + Light ~
JC Andrijeski
♡

"The meaning of events is the supreme meaning, that is not in events, and not in the soul, but is the God standing between events and the soul, the mediator of life, the way, the bridge and the going across."

~ Carl Jung, *The Red Book, Liber Novus*

CHAPTER I
ALLIE

"He's baaaack..." My best friend, Cass, grinned at me from where she leaned over the fifties-style lunch counter, her butt aimed at the dining area of the Lucky Cat Diner where we both worked.

Given that our uniforms consisted of short skirts and form-fitting, low-cut blouses, Cass was giving an eyeful to at least a few of our regular customers.

Oblivious to that, and to the men sitting at the counter, pretending not to stare at her ass as she stuck it up in the air, she grinned at me, her full lips more dramatic than usual with their blood-red lipstick.

"Did you see, Allie? Your buddy? He found your section again."

I muttered something.

I might have rolled my eyes.

Mostly, I continued my personal, ongoing battle with the diner's decrepit espresso machine.

"What's the pool up to now?" Cass asked. "Seventy? Eighty?"

"It's over a hundred now." I used the metal stopper to compress finely-ground espresso beans into a metal filter. I tried to be careful, but still managed to spill a small pile on the linoleum counter.

"Sasquatch threw in twenty yesterday," I reminded her.

Thinking about that, I grunted.

"He must really want the cash. He walked right up to the guy. Asked him his name, point-blank. Said he wouldn't leave until he told him."

Cass's eyes, with their thick black eyeliner, widened. "What happened?"

"Same thing that always happens, Cassandra. *Nada.* That guy could stare down a professional killer. He probably *is* a professional killer."

My best friend laughed, kicking up her high heels, which were red-vinyl platforms, more seventies than fifties, not like it mattered. Again, the nearby men pretended to sip their coffees as they surreptitiously checked her out.

Cass had a red thing going lately.

Her long, straight black hair had dark red flames coming up from the tips, the color matching her lipstick, eyeshadow, fingernail polish, and the five-inch heels.

Two months ago, everything was teal.

She could get away with just about any color or style she wanted, though. She just had that kind of face, not to mention a gorgeous body. Cassandra Aria Jainkul was, and probably always would be, one of the most physically beautiful women I'd ever seen in my life, even compared to feed avatars and movie stars.

I hated her a little for that, sometimes.

Looking up from where I was still doing battle with the diner's antiquated espresso maker, a machine I was convinced had it in for me, personally, I blew strands of my much less dramatic dark brown out of my face.

I glanced at the man in the corner booth.

I didn't tell Cass, but I'd seen him walk in.

Hell, I *felt* him walk in.

It was weird being so attuned to the guy.

He'd never said a damned thing to me either, apart from relaying whatever single-item purchase he wanted off the diner's menu. He never came in with anyone else. He flat-out ignored my few attempts at small talk. He never made eye-contact.

He generally stared out the window, or down at his own hands.

Mr. Monochrome took the practice of ignoring other human beings to the level of art.

The extremes he went to avoid conversation didn't just verge on rude.

They *were* rude.

Yet he didn't exactly come off as a dick, either.

My mind superimposed various stories—undercover cop, international fugitive from justice, spy, private detective, terrorist for the seer underground.

Serial killer.

Of course, this was real life, so the reality was likely a lot less interesting.

Jon, my brother, simply referred to him as "Allie's current stalker."

Which wasn't totally fair, to be honest.

This guy didn't give a shit about me. Apart from eating at one of my tables every day, Mr. Monochrome ignored me along with the rest of humanity.

He likely worked at one of the tech companies nearby and came to the Lucky Cat because we still accepted cash. Most places in San Francisco didn't.

So yeah, a tinfoil hat weirdo, maybe.

But likely a harmless one.

I glanced at the monitor on the wall.

The news feeds still played up there, showing the reaction to the latest terrorist attack in Europe. I watched the President of the United States give a speech from behind a podium, but the volume was too low for me to hear his actual words. His blond wife stood beside him, hands clasped, a solemn look etched on her face.

I knew neither one of them really looked like that, of course.

According to the Human Protection Act, both were required to wear avatars to avoid being targeted by seers working for enemy governments.

The rules against real-time images kept getting stricter, too.

Even the landscape around them had to be digitally altered now.

I told myself I didn't need to hear the President's actual words.

I'd listened to dozens of Caine's speeches already, just like everyone else. President Daniel Caine was the most popular president we'd ever had. There was already talk of adjusting the presidential term limits a second time, to allow him to run for a fifth term.

Opposite Caine's wife stood his Vice President, Ethan Wellington.

Wellington's avatar showed him to be a handsome black man in his late forties, roughly the same age as Caine. I remembered reading somewhere that they'd gone to school together. Both were young, energetic, articulate.

Both of them bothered me.

I honestly couldn't have said why, exactly.

Hell, even *Jon* liked Caine, and he hated most politicians. Objectively, I got it. I even agreed with Jon's reasons whenever we talked about it.

Caine had done a lot of good.

My distrust of him felt practically physical, though.

I glanced at Mr. Monochrome again, wiping the counter off with a wet rag where I'd spilled the espresso grounds. If I was right about my tinfoil hat theory, he likely believed a lot of the same wild theories my brother did. Jon had a whole paranoia thing about seers, in particular. He was convinced our government used seers to spy on our own domestic population.

To be fair to my brother—and possibly Mr. Monochrome—I *had* noticed a lot more seers on the streets lately.

Of course, rich people had been importing privately-owned seers to San Francisco for decades. The difference was, they used to hide it. Owning a seer had become a status symbol in recent years—a way to mark yourself as part of the uber-wealthy, or an executive in a forward-thinking corporation.

I'd read in the feeds somewhere that a highly-trained seer could go for more than the cost of *buying* an apartment in San Francisco.

So yeah, being a peon myself, I couldn't get very close.

A few times, I got within a dozen yards of one, though.

Like most people, the closest I'd likely *ever* get to a real-live seer was a glimpse of one on the street. All my knowledge of the seer race would come via online feeds, movies, stories from my friends. The seer sex-fetish bars were way out of my price range too, even if I'd been into that kind of thing. No amount of tips, tattoos, digital renderings, or coffee-shop gallery paintings would ever buy me access to that world.

So yeah, unless I had a rich relative somewhere I didn't know about, I would have to appreciate the beauty of seers from afar.

I was curious, though.

Most people were curious, I suppose.

Cass poked my arm, pulling me out of my reverie. When I looked over, she raised her eyebrows suggestively.

"What'll you give me if I go over there right now?" she grinned. "... and offer to blow him if he'll give up his name?"

The man at the counter next to her coughed, spitting out some of his coffee.

Glancing at him, I grunted.

I looked at Cass, only to realize I'd completely forgotten the cappuccino I'd been making. I turned my back on her briefly, and hooked the metal filter into the corresponding threads on the machine. After a bit of a struggle, I got it locked in place and stuck a wide-mouthed coffee cup under it, hitting the red button.

When I heard the tell-tale hiss, I turned towards her.

"What'll I give you to blow my stalker? Hmmm." I folded my arms, pretended to think. "How about a grilled cheese sandwich? You like those, right?"

She smacked my arm. "Cheapskate."

"What were you hoping for? I'm basically offering you my dinner."

"Right. I'm thinking you just don't want me to blow your new friend." Grinning faintly, she gave me an exaggerated wink. "I guess I'd better let you blow him instead. If you do a good enough job, maybe he'll tell *you* his name."

When I smacked her with the counter rag, she laughed.

"Hey, starving artist." She nudged my arm. "We're going out tonight, right? You're still in your *I'm getting even with my lousy, cheating, fuckwad, loser ex-boyfriend by going out to clubs, getting rip-roaring drunk with my best pal Cass* phase, right?"

I grunted. "I think that phase has run its course."

"Aww." She pouted. "One more night. It's Saturday."

I shook my head. "I'm supposed to work at Spider's new shop tomorrow. He and Angie wanted to see a few more designs... so that's what I'll be doing tonight. I can't draw drunk, so partying's out, sorry."

She frowned, and that time it looked real. "Boring. At least call that Nick guy. Get him to come over and screw your brains out when he gets off work."

I grimaced. "Ugh. No. I had to end that."

"What?" Her mouth puckered disapprovingly. "Why? He was cute!"

"He started getting weird."

"Define 'weird,' Allie."

"I don't know." I shrugged. "Just weird. Clingy, I guess."

Staring at me in disbelief, she snorted.

I heard real irritation in her voice.

"Jesus. The magic pussy strikes again." Leaning her ass on the counter, she frowned. "You'll have to give me your secret one of these days, Al. I think I have the opposite... the anti-magic, dick-repellent pussy. They all want to bang me, then... *poof!* They're gone. You get marriage proposals. I get vomit-stained notes on my bedstand."

I let out an involuntary laugh. "You have bad taste in guys, Cassandra. That's not the same thing as being dick-repellent or whatever. If I slept with those guys, they'd leave me crappy notes, too."

"Sure, they would."

"They would," I insisted. "And you know it."

Mollified slightly, she propped her jaw on her hand, looking down the bar.

"Maybe," she admitted, glum. Perking up slightly, she glanced over. "Hey, is Jon coming in today? After his morning kung fu class?"

"Far as I know." I jerked my jaw towards the cat clock with the eyes that flicked back and forth. "He should be here any minute."

"Now, *he's* someone I'd blow for free," she said wistfully.

I grimaced. "Seriously? Can you just... not? Talk about him like that? He's my brother."

"Your brother is seriously fine. And he's your *adoptive* brother. No reason to get all skeeved hearing me lust over your *non*-blood relative."

I flung the rag over my shoulder. Bending down, I looked under the bar for almond milk. "You know he's gay, right? I mean, it's not like we haven't known that since kindergarten."

She sighed wistfully. "A girl can dream."

Internally, I sighed.

Cass had always oscillated between *bad for her* and *completely unattainable.*

Her entire sex-partner-picking meter was broken.

"You're sure he's not bi?" Cass asked hopefully. "Even a little? Like a secret bi?"

"You're welcome to ask him."

"Maybe I'll just show up at his place in a trench coat and a teddy. See how he responds to real-life stimuli."

The men sitting there all looked away as her eyes turned in their direction, trying to hide the fact that they were staring at her.

"Yeah," I grunted. "Good luck with that."

Walking the cappuccino over to the guy at the counter who'd ordered it, I walked back to her, shrugging. "Personally, though, if you're going to start going after guys who aren't card-carrying members of the bag-of-dicks crowd, I'd suggest trying with males of the species who actually like sleeping with, you know, *women."*

"Where's the fun in that?"

Still thinking, I added, "Jon has good taste in guys. Instead of playing 'scare the hot gay guy,' maybe just ask him for tips on how to pick up, you know, men. With an emphasis on guys who aren't anything like your father or your bag-of-dicks brothers."

She laughed, but I saw my words reach her, even as she shook her head ruefully.

"Yeah," she conceded. She dumped part of a saltshaker on a napkin and spread the granules around with a finger. "How's your mom doing?"

"She's okay."

"Really?"

I looked up from where I'd been rearranging a stack of paper napkins.

Seeing the probing look in her eyes, I exhaled.

"Let's see. Her last bender was two weeks ago, so she's probably due for another one. Last time I went over there, she was watching old tapes of us with my dad, when me and Jon were kids. She yelled at me when I tried to turn it off, then started crying."

"Jesus Christ." Cass winced. "You need to get her help, Al."

"And pay for it how? My stellar blow jobs? I already had to drop out of school." I grunted, dumping the old almond milk carton in recycling and straightening. "Even if I added blow jobs to my repertoire of gigs, I doubt I'd pull in enough to pay for a week of rehab, and she needs more like a year, plus counseling."

Frowning, I found myself thinking through it for the thousandth time, despite my own words.

"Jon would help, but he doesn't have any money, either. He'd have to hit up one of his tech partners, and I don't want to ask him to do that, not until he's more established. Then there's the little problem of her flat-out refusing to go. We tried to get her to a grief therapist and she wouldn't even do that. She won't even *talk* about Dad. She watches those videos of him, you know, before he got sick... I swear she wants to pretend it never happened. Like he's on a business trip or something."

Cass frowned, watching my eyes. "I really like your mom."

I nodded, my chest tightening. "Me, too."

A throat cleared.

A male throat.

I turned, startled at how close they were.

Pale, glass-like eyes met mine.

A narrow mouth hardened under high, sharp cheekbones and an angular but handsome face. He was tall as hell. I'd known he was tall of course, but somehow I hadn't fully realized *how* tall, not until now, with him standing right in front of me.

His coal-black hair hung longish, cut in a way that struck me as expensive.

His watch looked expensive.

An expensive-looking coat hung from his broad shoulders. His headset looked expensive. The rest of his clothes were black and nondescript, but they looked expensive, too.

It was Mr. Monochrome.

And he was staring straight at me.

CHAPTER 2

MR. MONOCHROME

He cleared his throat again. I heard impatience that time. Annoyance.

"May I speak with you?" he asked. "It's important."

I blinked.

Nope. He was still there.

He was also definitely talking to me.

I glanced at Cass, who was staring up at him, too, her red-lipsticked mouth ajar where she leaned over the lunch counter, her short-skirted butt in the air. When I glanced back at Mr. Monochrome, he hadn't followed the direction of my gaze.

Those pale eyes remained on me.

"Now, Alyson," he said.

I wasn't someone who generally had to listen to people who spoke to me like that. One benefit of working jobs I didn't care about.

Even our boss at the diner, Tom, didn't go there with me.

Then again, Tom didn't exactly carry this guy's presence.

Also, my head only came up to about the middle of this guy's chest. He had one of those frames that made him appear more lean than bulky, more of a runner type than a weightlifter. Now that he stood in front of me, though, I decided that might be deceptive, too. Up close, he looked more like one of Jon's martial arts buddies.

The muscles this guy wore definitely looked functional, not purely decorative.

The weirdest part was definitely that stare, though.

His piercing gaze stunned me in some way I couldn't articulate to myself, maybe in part because his eyes weren't at all what I expected. I'd known his irises were on the light side, but I hadn't realized *how* light. Looking at them now, they appeared to have almost no color at all. I supposed technically they must be blue or gray, but they reminded me more of crystals I'd seen in New Age rock shops. Their lightness was made stranger by his pitch-black hair, but I didn't see how they could be contact lenses.

Maybe they had a virtual component?

Maybe he'd gotten some kind of augmentation surgery?

Mr. Monochrome stared at me while I drank him in.

Then, without warning, he moved.

Before I could get out a single word, he caught hold of my upper arm. His fingers felt like flesh-wrapped steel; they closed around my bicep and I immediately panicked.

He gripped me tightly enough that I let out a surprised yelp.

I fought him, jerking back…

…when something slammed into my chest.

Liquid heat, reassurance, presence, light… I don't know what the fuck it was, but it confused me, calmed me, and completely wiped out my ability to think.

I didn't tell myself to stop fighting him.

I just… stopped.

When my vision cleared, he was watching me, wary.

"All right?" he asked.

Thinking about his question, I nodded.

He gestured with a hand.

I followed the motion with my eyes.

He moved oddly. I liked it. Every movement contained grace, an effortless fluidity. An animal quality, I thought… like a big cat. Everything about it precise. The small, vague but expressive gestures, those little adjustments of his body and face.

The way he stood there. His angular features.

Precise. Interesting. Sensual.

It pulled at my eyes, at some other part of me.

The fascination felt visceral.

I tried to think what it reminded me of.

I realized it didn't remind me of anything.

It was new.

"Come," he said, gruff.

Before I'd made sense of the word, he was leading me through the opening in the linoleum-topped counter.

I followed the tug of his fingers.

I couldn't think of a single reason not to.

Cass followed behind us. I was aware of her, but I didn't look back.

Her voice grew increasingly frantic.

"Allie! Wait!" She reached for me, catching hold of my arm. "Wait!"

The man holding my hand didn't wait. He scarcely glanced at her, scarcely paused his steps. Focusing on the diner's front door, he continued to walk us in that direction. He dragged Cass along with us until she was forced to let me go.

"Hey!" Cass burst out. "Wait! What are you doing with her? STOP! STOP!"

I heard the fear in her voice.

It didn't alarm me.

It just felt… irrelevant.

The man holding my hand remained silent.

Despite his silence, I felt tension vibrate his presence, all the way down to his fingers. Aggression wrapped in stillness, a hard line of thought moved precisely in the background, calculating things. Time. How much time was left. Distance. Documents needed. Law enforcement. Weapons. Car.

He needed a car.

A different voice took my focus off him.

It was hard, loud, and it came from right in front of us.

It was also extremely familiar.

"What the fuck do you think you're doing, man?"

My mind wavered…

…then it clicked back, sharpening.

My brother, Jon, stood in front of us. His long, dirty-blond hair was up in a half-ponytail, probably because he'd just walked here from the martial arts studio where he worked.

He stared from my face to the man holding my hand.

Jon's hazel eyes focused on that hand, the one gripping mine, right before they slid up, measuring the man attached to it.

He seemed to make up his mind.

"Let go of her, man," Jon said. "Now. Or I'm calling the cops."

My brother's voice was blunt, with no hint of empty threat.

He spoke without emotion, his eyes matching the steel underlying his words. It was his martial arts voice, the one he used with his students. I knew that voice. I'd seen it in action when I'd gone to his fights and other events.

I'd never seen it used like this.

Something about it brought my mind back, marginally, at least.

I tugged on my hand in the tall man's grip, trying to retrieve my fingers.

The man glanced at me, his grip tightening.

Calm down, I heard distinctly in my mind. *Now, Alyson.*

That time, it didn't calm me.

I still couldn't quite force myself to speak. I frowned at him instead, gritting my teeth as I fought to clear my mind, to understand what was happening, what I was doing.

The man in front of me faced Jon. "I won't hurt her."

Jon frowned. He looked at me. "Are you all right, Al?"

Answer him. Tell him you're fine.

I frowned, looking at the man holding my hand. For the first time, it crossed my mind to wonder what was wrong with me.

Why did I want to do as he said?

Tell him, the man's mind prodded, insistent. *Tell him you're fine, Alyson.*

"I'm fine," I blurted.

My voice sounded doubtful.

Jon's eyes never left my face.

He didn't direct his next words at me, however.

"What's going on here, Cassandra?"

"I don't know!" Worry sharpened her voice. "He just fucking *grabbed* her and started walking for the door. They didn't even talk. It was like he drugged her or something… she just *went* with him…"

Jon's mouth hardened.

He glared at the man holding me, then held out his hand.

"Come here, Al." Jon motioned towards me, a brief flick of his fingers. "Right now. Get behind me."

No.

I bit my lip. "No."

"Alyson!" Jon's voice hit into me. "COME HERE. NOW."

I started to move forward, but the man holding me tightened his grip.

"No." He looked at Jon, then at Cass. "There isn't time for this."

His voice was deep enough to shock me.

He also spoke with an accent. I don't know if he'd been hiding it before, or if I just hadn't heard him speak enough words to catch it, but I heard it clearly now.

It sounded European to me.

Really, it sounded German.

Jon stared up at him. "Excuse me? You need to let go of her. Now."

"Don't make me force the issue, Jon." The black-haired man glanced at Cass. "Cass. I'm trying to help her."

Jon's light eyes widened. For the first time, his voice grew openly hostile. "Do we *know* you, man? How do you know our names?"

There was a silence.

Then Mr. Monochrome turned his head, fixing that cold gaze on me.

Tell them you're coming with me willingly, his mind sent. *Tell them we're going outside to talk. Tell them it's all right… that they can watch us from inside.*

"What?" I stared at him, bewildered. "That's my brother."

"I know who it is," the man growled out loud. "Either you deal with this, or I will."

Abruptly, he tensed.

Holding up a hand to silence me, he turned towards the diner's front door. Every muscle in his long body clenched. His arms, chest and shoulders grew taut.

His grip on my hand tightened.

Before I could turn to see what he was looking at, he moved, sliding his free hand into the jacket he wore. When he removed it, his fingers held a gun.

He wrenched me closer to him and aimed the barrel of that gun at my head. I let out a gasp when he flicked a metal bar on the end, and pressed the barrel firmly to my skin. Everything about the gesture was smooth, practiced, expert.

My heart jackhammered in my chest. Adrenaline flooded my limbs.

He pressed the gun tighter to my temple.

Don't fucking move, Alyson. Do what I tell you.

Cass screamed.

I heard other people, diners probably, reacting around us.

I heard Jon yell at Cass to get back, to go behind the counter.

I felt strangers panicking, their minds crashing into mine. I heard chair legs screech as they moved back, as everyone got out of the way.

But none of them were why Mr. Monochrome pulled the gun.

None of them even registered on his immediate radar anymore.

He didn't plan to shoot Jon, or Cass.

He barely noticed they were there.

He stared only at the new man who'd just walked into the diner.

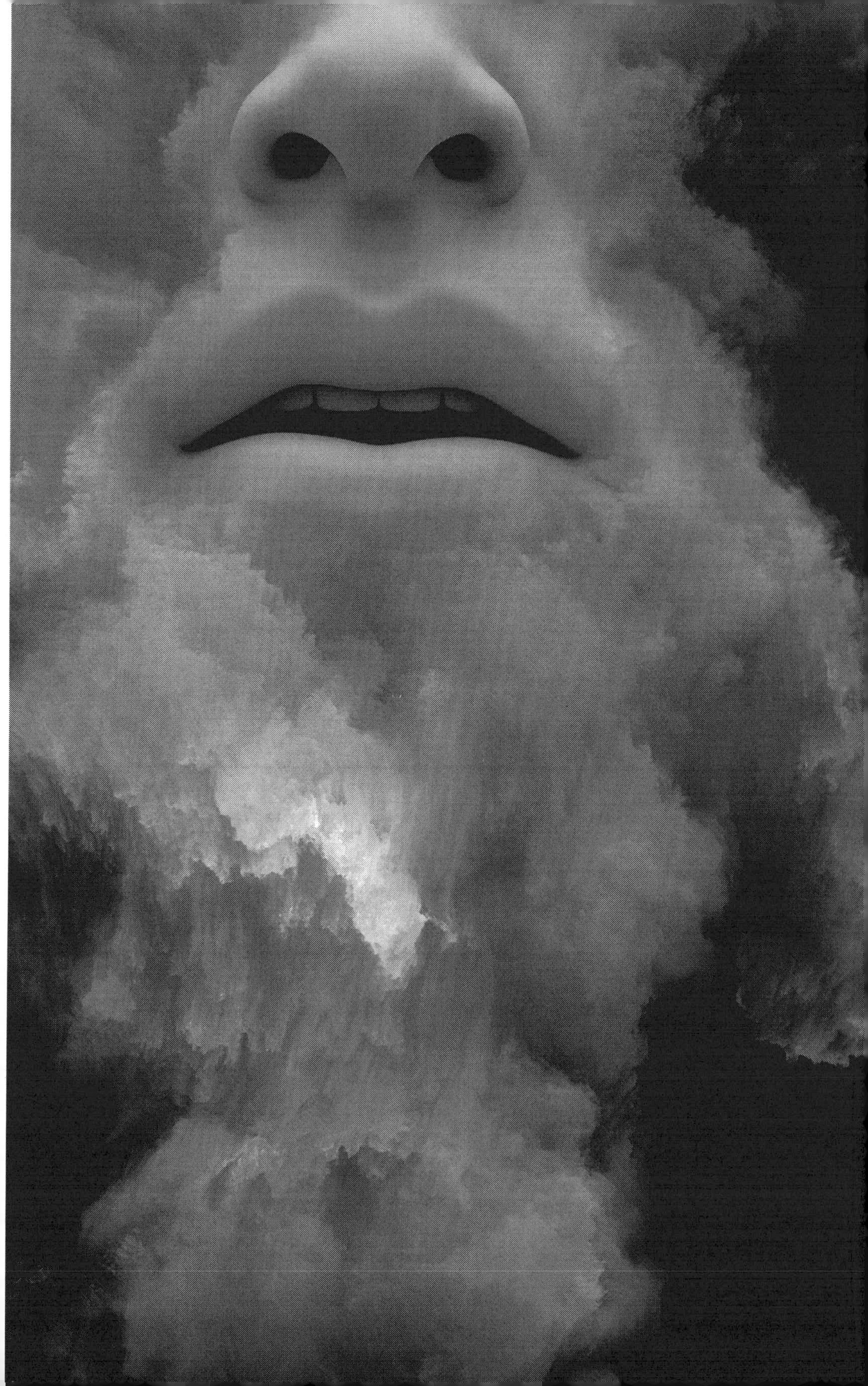

CHAPTER 3
GLOW-EYE

I stared at that man, too.

He walked in smiling, his long arms swinging, his saunter casual.

Yet it was all camouflage.

Behind that slow, fluid walk, he moved like a predatory animal, stalking in through the glass doors and winding around Jon like he was little more than a pebble in a slow-moving stream, a scarce hindrance to reaching his destination.

The new man was handsome.

Shockingly handsome.

Auburn hair fell on either side of perfect bone structure, light eyes of pale amber, dark brows, a well-formed jaw, full, beautifully-shaped lips. Those lips quirked in a faint smirk as I watched. His eyes never left the gun, or the man holding the gun to my head.

The smirk was definitely aimed at him.

"Now, now, Revi'," the auburn-haired man said. "Let's not get overexcited."

Mr. Monochrome jammed the gun tighter to my head.

"You can't possibly think I won't do it." The German accent grew more prominent. His voice was cold as metal. "Turn around. Leave. Now.

I looked at Jon, who was staring between the man holding a gun to my head and the one he'd called "Terry."

Jon and I were clearly superfluous now, mere props in whatever this was.

I could tell Jon was struggling to make sense of that same thing, the way he'd been shunted aside even as things escalated.

Still, Jon recovered faster than I did.

He held up a hand to Mr. Monochrome.

"Put the gun down, man," he said, his voice shaken. "Please. Don't hurt her."

Mr. Monochrome's eyes never left the auburn-haired man.

"Leave, Terry," he growled. "Right now. My orders are clear. I *will* kill her."

"No, you won't."

The man holding me gripped me tighter.

He held me around the chest now, his free hand gripping my shoulder. Long, iron fingers dug into muscle, practically holding me by my collar bone.

"The *fuck* I won't. Walk out of here. Now."

Jon turned, staring at the auburn-haired man without lowering the hand he held up towards Mr. Monochrome.

"Are you a cop?" he snapped.

The auburn-haired one didn't give him so much as a glance.

Jon tried again. He raised his voice sharply. "What are you *doing*, man? Leave! Don't you see he means it?"

The auburn-haired man didn't glance at Jon that time, either.

"This is so childish, Revi'," he said, clicking his tongue on his teeth. "We both know you will not kill her."

"Terry—"

"The police are already on their way." He shook his head, that smile still playing around full lips. "So is SCARB. Are you really so willing to wear a collar again? Do you miss Asia so much, you'd be happy to return there to live in a work camp?"

Clicking his tongue in that oddly expressive way, he held out his hand. "Give me the gun, Revi'. Give it to me, and release her. I will let you leave before they arrive."

He took a step towards us.

Mr. Monochrome took a longer step back.

He angled us closer to the door, still holding the gun tightly to my head. As he did, he maintained his distance from the other man by walking in a careful circle. I felt each sideways step in small nudges from his hands, arms, feet.

Those nudges caused us to move almost in tandem.

Jon turned with us, his hand still up.

He was pale now, and I saw his eyes dart towards the door, then back to the gun pressed hard to my temple. He glanced at the auburn-haired man, without taking his eyes off the gun for more than a millisecond.

"You a cop?" Jon asked again.

The auburn-haired man smiled, his eyes following the man who held me. "In a manner of speaking. Yes."

"He's not a fucking cop," the man holding me said. His accent grew harder. "Jon, you don't want her to go with him. Trust me."

Jon gave the man holding me a cold look, then shifted his gaze back at the auburn-haired man. Despite the look, and the anger I saw in it, for some reason, I found myself thinking Jon believed him. He believed the guy holding a gun to my head.

I believed him, too.

It was entirely irrational, but I would rather leave there with Mr. Monochrome than with the handsome man who lied about being a cop.

Mr. Monochrome continued to maneuver us towards the door.

The auburn-haired man took a step nearer. Then another.

He walked cautiously, his eyes on the man holding me.

"Revi'," he warned. "Be reasonable."

He held up a hand, as if to calm a wild animal--one he'd cornered and now snarled at him. His voice turned matter-of-fact. "You've lost this round, old friend. You waited too long. Let her go. If your people want to negotiate getting her back—"

The man holding me let out a humorless laugh.

"Go fuck yourself, Terry."

The auburn-haired male smiled. He shifted his gaze to look solely at me.

I couldn't make myself look away from those amber, light-filled irises.

I'd never seen eyes quite that color before.

They really seemed to glow with their own internal light.

"Has he told you, little sister?" the man asked. "Has he told you who you are?"

"Shut the fuck up, Terry."

The auburn-haired man never took his eyes off me.

"Of course he didn't." He broke out in a disarming smile. "Why would he tell you something so important about yourself? Something that alters the entire fabric of our civilization, the entire future of the races of this world? Why indeed? It's far easier to simply club you over the head and drag you with him by force."

Chuckling mildly in amusement, the man kept those disconcerting eyes focused on me. "We have been looking for you longer than you've been alive, Alyson dear—"

"Shut up," the man holding me growled.

The man ignored him.

"Do you have any idea how important you are, Alyson dearest?" he asked me. *"Gaos di'lalente...* the Thousand and all their powers above. How the elders managed to hide you here, all this time, allowing you to play human... it is beyond words. It has truthfully upped my respect for their abilities a fair bit. I would never have guessed them capable of such a—"

"Terry. Quit with the fucking games—"

"Hush, Revi'." The auburn-haired man held up a hand, his eyes still locked on mine. "You had your chance to speak to her. You squandered it. Clearly."

His focus remained intently on me.

"You are the Bridge, Alyson. Do you know what that means?" A faint smile returned to those full lips. "Do you learn anything of our people in your human schools? Do you learn anything of yourself?"

"Leave her the fuck alone, Terian."

I glanced sideways at the man holding the gun to my head.

It occurred to me again that I was less afraid of him than the man with the auburn hair.

The thought made no sense. It was borderline nuts, but the feeling persisted.

The auburn-haired man seemed to take my silence as an answer.

"The Bridge is sent to *save us,* Alyson..."

His voice grew a denser quality. It vibrated my skin, making me grimace.

"…You're here to return your people to their rightful place. You're going to burn the human world… burn it right to the fucking ground, Esteemed Sister. You're going to set us free."

I stared at him.

Despite the smirk, he meant those words.

I *saw* it in him, somehow.

He meant everything he'd just said.

He meant it with the fervor of a religious fanatic.

Silver lights flickered around his aura. Above his head, I glimpsed a pyramid made of the same metallic light, rotating in the darkness over his head. Something about that glimpsed vision brought a spike of pain to my temples.

White-hot, shocking, it blinded me briefly

It also made me nauseous.

I closed my eyes, leaning against the man holding me.

He clutched me tighter. Concern bled through his fingers, coupled with a darker anger. For the barest instant, I really felt him there. The feeling was familiar—so damned familiar it crushed something in my chest. He breathed with me, holding the gun to my head, and briefly we felt like a single being, a single heart and set of lungs.

Pain twisted through me at the thought.

It was nothing like the pain I got from that pyramid.

The man holding me turned his head, looking at me.

I felt that denser, more animal pain on him, too.

God, longing.

Grief.

Some sense of time.

Too much time.

Years and years of time.

Lifetimes of time.

I felt all of those things intensely, without understanding any of it.

I was about to speak—

—when the man with the auburn hair lunged at us.

He moved without warning, without sound. He must have been

waiting for an opening, any opening, and made his move the instant the other man turned his head.

Yet somehow, I still saw it coming.

I saw his attack unfold in the abstract, a blurred motion of aggression and intent. It came straight at me, so fast I didn't have time to think about any of it.

Maybe that's why it happened.

Maybe that's why I could do what I did.

I felt every inch of expanding heat as adrenaline shot through my veins, every millimeter of those iron-like fingers gripping my shoulder, every increment of my heart hammering, the man holding me breathing. I felt every piece of his breath. I felt his blood vibrate my body.

I saw my brother's face as he watched, terrified, from a few feet away.

As if he could see it coming, Jon stared at me, his hazel eyes wide.

I don't know how to explain what happened after that.

Something in me just… let go.

A fist I'd held clenched, somewhere in the middle of my chest, abruptly loosened.

Whatever it was, I'd held it for so long, I hadn't known I held it at all.

When I let go, it started a chain reaction.

A folding sensation, like a telescope being collapsed in segments. A ticking film in the background of my mind with an oddly mechanical, utterly beautiful precision. A rush of power hit me somewhere in the middle of the chest…

I breathed it out.

It was as natural as…

Well, breathing.

Power slammed out of me. It felt like if I'd held it in, even a second longer, it would have burnt me to ashes from the inside.

Then it was gone.

I watched it go, fascinated.

A slow-motion millisecond unfolded outward. It moved with the same precision I'd seen when that part of my mind collapsed.

A wave of pure light, pure energy left my chest.

It hit the man who'd lunged for me first.

He was a big man.

It didn't make any difference.

The light slammed into him and he flew back, like a baseball smacked hard with a precisely-wielded bat. The auburn-haired man's feet left the ground. He'd already begun to fly through the air, reaching the place where Jon was, when Jon got hit by the still-expanding wave.

Jon's feet left the ground, too.

I watched in that moment of timeless silence, seeing their bodies fly through the air, going in the opposite direction from where I stood. I saw that same force that came from my chest, only now it looked like a pale green light in the darkened spaces behind my eyes.

My own eyes were light—only light.

Somehow, I saw through that light anyway, for those few seconds at least.

I watched Jon fly partway over a tabletop where two college-aged kids were eating pie and drinking coffee. They'd been watching the exchange between the four of us, I realized—everyone in the diner had been staring at us.

But no one had left. They stared, riveted, but they didn't leave.

The screaming had stopped.

Although a number of people had backed off, moved to other tables, they hadn't escaped into the bathroom or through the kitchen.

No one left even after Mr. Monochrome pulled the gun.

That should have struck me as strange.

It did later. At the time, I scarcely noticed.

Now I saw the two college kids' faces alter in slow-motion. Their eyes widened. Their mouths opened. They sat there, paralyzed, as my brother headed straight for them.

His back slid over their pie and coffee, only an inch or two above the surface. His legs and tennis shoes hit the edge of the chrome tabletop, knocking their plates and glasses sideways and back, causing the girl sitting there to throw up her arms, also in slow-motion.

Jon kept going. He didn't stop entirely until he crashed into a second table. That one had no people but three trays covered in dirty soda glasses and coffee cups. The other waiter, Corey, must have left them there when he went on his smoke break.

Glasses and coffee cups flew towards the wall.

Some shattered on the floor, some careened sideways, smacking across chairs and tabletop, some broke under Jon's arms and hands.

Jon ended up half on the second table, half on the floor.

I saw him gasp, his hands, face, and forearms cut and starting to bleed.

The auburn-haired man flew further.

Unlike with Jon, there were no tables. There was nothing to stop him, nothing standing between the onslaught of the pale green light and the diner's far wall.

I don't know how I was able to watch him and Jon at the same time.

Both unfolded simultaneously, in fractions of a second.

Yet somehow, I saw every detail.

I watched the auburn-haired man fly through the air, amber eyes wide, the handsome face contorted in disbelief as his arms pinwheeled, his hands and fingers actively looking for purchase. One of his hands sought something else, too. It dug into his jacket, reaching for the gun there, fighting to get it free of the holster he wore under the suit.

I watched him struggle with it as he flew all the way to the wall.

It was a testament to him, really, that he even tried.

Both struggles abruptly ended.

He slammed into a row of glass shelves covered in fifties knick-knacks and Lucky Cat souvenirs. An old radio, metal lunch boxes, Elvis Presley records, a letterman's jacket, coffee mugs with the Lucky Cat logo, all crashed to the linoleum floor.

He shattered the shelves with his shoulders, head, and arms.

When he did, the sound seemed to come abruptly back on in the diner.

Screams were the first thing I heard.

Then breaking glass.

Then gunshots.

I flinched, violently, sure I was dead.

Something whizzed by me.

I felt it pass, felt the air move.

The man holding me grunted, half of his body jerking back.

More gunshots broke the quiet. That time, they were deafening, seeming to happen inside my head. The man holding me fired past me, his arm and shoulder absorbing each discharged shot. For the first time, it hit me that he was left-handed.

He wasn't firing at me.

When he stopped, I looked back. The end of his gun was smoking.

I followed his stare back to the diner wall, back to the auburn-haired man.

He was dead.

He still gripped a gun in his hand, only now that hand and gun had fallen to the floor. He'd done better with pulling out his weapon than I'd initially thought. He somehow managed to unholster it right before or right after he impacted the wall.

He also shot first.

The man holding me answered him.

Now the auburn-haired man was dead.

The round, black hole in his forehead was so precise it didn't look real.

My vision slanted out.

Light took its place. That light blocked my view of the surrounding room.

Gasping in panic at my sudden blindness, I found myself acutely aware of everything else happening around us. I heard people scrambling to their feet, knocking over chairs, moving tables. Screams followed. I felt fear—of the guns, yes, but not only the guns. Some of that fear felt aimed at me. People were trying to leave for real now. I heard and saw them disappear into the kitchen, shouting.

Nearer to me, loud speech and frightened gasps confused me.

I felt their panic like a physical force. It made me wince, then grimace from the pain of it—but I couldn't see them, or anything else.

My eyes wouldn't work.

Everything was light. Just light.

Green light, like what my mind conjured around that force in my chest, just before Jon and that other man flew across the room.

I blinked, trying to see, panicked by my blindness.

I blinked, over and over, but the light wouldn't dim.

Then the fingers holding me tightened so much I let out a gasp.

"Jurekil'a u'hatre davos!"

The man behind me was breathing hard, almost as hard as the people panicking around us. He spoke right near my ear. I couldn't see him through the light, but his panic slammed into me, making my eyes close, making me nauseated.

"Gaos... di'lanlente a'guete... you're a fucking manipulator!"

I couldn't make sense of anything he said.

I wasn't thinking about the gun anymore. Or about the dead guy by the wall.

I wanted to get the fuck out of there. I wanted to go home.

Then another thought hit me.

A rush of panic brought pain to my heart, my heart to my throat.

Jon.

Jesus Christ.

Had I hurt Jon? What happened to Jon? Where was Cass?

Terror hit me.

"JON!" I raised my voice as loud as I could. My words sounded rough, blurred. "JON! ANSWER ME! CASS! CASSANDRA! WHERE ARE YOU?"

I still couldn't see.

An arm wrapped roughly around my waist.

It wrenched me back against a hard, muscular body.

I gripped that arm in my hands, still fighting to see, to find Jon or Cass with my eyes. I didn't really struggle against the man holding me. I doubted I could have budged that arm even if I tried, and I could barely make myself try. I couldn't remember ever being so drained.

I was fucking exhausted.

I could barely keep my eyes open.

Before I could wrap my head around what he was doing, the feelings coming off him, he was carrying me.

I couldn't see, but I knew we were heading towards the door.

That's when I first heard the sirens.

CHAPTER 4
RUNNING

He gripped my legs, holding me in a fireman's carry.

I still couldn't see.

I couldn't make sense of where we were.

My body wanted to shut down.

I was so weak I could barely hold onto him. My vision remained blank, lost in that green and white light. The images that came through in fits and starts didn't make any sense.

For the same reason, I mostly ignored them.

I tried to grip his back, but the dark jacket he wore eluded my fingers.

I had no idea where we were going.

I felt his urgency, his fear for himself, for me, so I didn't try to fight him. I tried to talk to him a few times, but I couldn't form words, even when they made sense in my head.

Meanwhile, those glimpses of sight started growing stronger.

The sky went dark.

Not dark-dark. Not devoid of light entirely.

But yeah, weirdly dark, like we were in a sudden eclipse.

The world returned to me in a blurred, underwater painting, tinged with purple and rose, filled with auras and other strange lights. I'd seen auras around people before, but nothing like this. These were so bright, I could barely make out their physical forms. Some of the lights

I saw didn't seem attached to a particular human at all; they flickered and swirled in that twilight space unmoored from physicality altogether.

Yet somehow, they were still alive.

The man holding me ran past those dizzying lights and auras, dodging pedestrians and cars. Eyes stared at us out of those lights, watching as we passed, following us.

I can't tell if all of them are really there.

Are we being surrounded? Followed?

Hunted?

Hunted, yes, his mind murmurs.

Are all of those beings really there?

No, he answers simply.

This stumps me.

They aren't here, on the street, but they're watching us?

Yes.

From where?

He doesn't answer that.

Am I dead? I wondered.

No, is all he says.

He continued to run.

The walls of buildings glowed at me as we ran past, filling my eyesight with oddly invasive lines. I wondered again if I am dead.

You're not dead, Alyson. Impatient that time. Annoyed.

No… worried.

His fear leaks through to me, too.

Sirens. I hear sirens again.

It hits me that I'm hearing a lot of this through him.

He's still running with me down the street, moving shockingly fast, given he's got me slung over his shoulder like a sack of flour. I can still feel his fear. I can feel his thoughts through his fingers, where he grips my calf.

I feel them through his arm where it circled my thighs.

Craning my neck, still gripping his sides, I looked for more of those glowing shapes.

Whispers and glimpses flicker at me in that dark space, there and gone.

I look down at the man holding me, looking for the cloudy light-shape around him.

His light is different, though.

He isn't cloudy at all.

Under my hands, light bones and skin stand out, crystal-clear where other people are blurry and gray. I can only see the vague outline of the jacket I grip awkwardly in my hands. Gold and pale-blue light runs through tiny veins inside light-bones and light-flesh. I clutch tighter at his back, staring at those vibrating strands in bewilderment.

Something about them pulls at me; I get lost staring at him.

What the hell is he?

Seer. I hear the German accent inside my head. *We look different. It is how you can tell those others are watching us from afar. If they were here, they would look like me.*

"Seer." I forced out the word with an effort.

When he didn't say anything more, I looked down at him again.

I bounced rhythmically against his back, clutching him to hold on.

That's when I noticed my own hands.

Letting go of him with one of them, I raised it to my eyes.

Crystal-clear light bones glowed under translucent skin. Those same, pulsing, liquid veins covered my fingers, arms, palms.

I look like him. I look like *him.*

My mind grappled with that, tried to make sense of it.

Lowering my hand, my fingers clenched into fists on his jacket. I watched them do it that time. I followed the trails of light up my arms. His are white and pale blue, tinged with gold. The colors that make up my light-skin and light-bones and light-blood are different—gold and sunset-orange, pale flickers of green and turquoise blue.

We are the same, but different.

Again, my mind returns to what he said.

Seer.

He said he was a seer.

Of course. It was the only thing that made sense.

It made sense, but it brought my whole world crashing down on my head.

Terrorist. He had to be a terrorist.

I felt like I must be losing my mind.

Why had a terrorist been coming to my place of work every day? Why had he singled me out? Why had that other guy, the dead guy?

It hit me he had to be a seer, too.

That explained everything. The language. The weird religious crap.

The weird eyes.

I'd been hearing this asshole in my head since he first came up to me.

"Are you really a fucking *seer?"* I spoke out loud that time, my voice deafening in my own ears. "What the fuck? What the fuck is happening?"

Honestly, I'm not sure I said it aloud at all, not until he answers me.

QUIET! he snarls inside my mind. *You're shouting, Alyson. Do you want to get us both gunned down? Or just me?*

I press my lips together.

I hadn't known I was shouting.

I didn't want to shout again.

I could feel his fear tangibly again.

"We have to go back," I manage. "Jon. I have to see if Jon—"

His mind cuts off my words.

Are you out of your gaos d' jurekil'a mind?

His mental voice is intense as hell.

It slams into me, making me flinch.

Do you really not realize what you fucking did in there? If you go back now, they'll put you in a goddamned cage. They'll put a collar around your neck. You'll be disappeared into a military black site, where they'll do god knows what to you. Probably for the rest of your natural-born life. You just performed telekinesis in a restaurant full of human witnesses...

His thoughts turn to an angry mutter, barely aimed at me.

A fucking manipulator. Gaos d'jurekil'a. A fucking manipulator... *and no one tells me.*

My mind blanked.

Maybe I just really wanted it to.

He slowed his pace out of nowhere.

My heart jerked into my throat as my stomach rammed sharply into his shoulder. He skidded as he slowed. Then he made a sharp turn left. Within seconds, he'd built up his momentum again, working up into another sprint down a narrower street.

This isn't a dream. I am sure of it, suddenly.

I'm not about to wake up from this.

My nausea abruptly worsened.

"Where are you taking me?" I blurted.

He didn't answer

I have no idea if he even heard me.

When he shifted my weight on his shoulder, I gripped him tighter, startled.

Then he was bending down, depositing my feet back on the ground.

I clung to him briefly, as much in confusion as anything, but he disentangled my arms and hands, his motions businesslike. I'm still exhausted. I still feel completely drained. I realize that's probably the real reason I can barely think.

His eyes shine at me in that dark space, diamond-like, a pale green-gold.

"Stay here," he said aloud. "Don't move, Alyson."

His voice is a command.

It never occurs to me to disobey it.

I stand there, in the middle of that open space.

I watched him walk around the faint outline of shapes that stand in rows all around us. He looks over a number of them, and I fight to remain vertical, panting, trying to decide what to do. I hear sirens again, somewhere in the distance.

It occurs to me again that I've been hearing them for a while.

I can't run. I can barely stand.

Panting, staring around, I try to decide if there's anything I can do.

I can barely see, though. I can't make sense of the landscape around me, the blurred shapes, the man's crystal-clear outline…

I look up at the sky, and gasp.

Giant, winged creatures swim through the darkness overhead. Some look like whales. I see one flap enormous wings, a mouth full of glass-like, glowing teeth. It trails a long, flicking, coiled tail, screaming silently into the night.

The man grabs my arm again and I jump, letting out a little shriek.

I jerk my eyes back down, towards him.

I can practically see him frowning at me. *Allie. Calm down.*

My vision flickers—dark to light, then back again.

For an instant, I see him.

Meaning, I see him as he really is. Mr. Monochrome. I'm still with him. Somehow, the sheer reality of that manages to penetrate.

"Come on." He pulled insistently on my arm.

Again, I don't fight him. Following the tug of his fingers, I stumble over the asphalt, fighting to blink my eyes again, to see past that dark.

He has to help me walk.

He has to steady me with a hand. His muscles keep me upright.

The next thing I know, I am being pushed to sit.

He has his hand on the back of my head. The angle forces me to bend my neck forward. He guided me into a seat; I realize I'm sitting in a car.

Something cold circles one of my wrists.

Before I can make sense of that, he's gone.

He closed a door between us. Then he leaned down through the open window, tugging on my cinched wrist. I hear the rattle of metal.

Before I could react, he caught hold of my other hand.

That same cold feeling cinched over my other wrist.

I tried to move. My hands stopped abruptly, only a few inches from the door.

The metal rings around my wrists.

Handcuffs.

He just handcuffed me to his car.

It took another second or two for that information to penetrate.

While I stared down at my light bones and veins, the faint outline of handcuffs around my wrists, he walked around the front of the car.

It hit me again.

He shot that man. In the diner.

He *killed* someone.

A seer.

That was... really, *really* illegal.

Like he'd likely be put down by SCARB if they had it on record, which of course they did since there was surveillance everywhere.

I heard the door open to my left.

A creak of leather and rustle of clothes, then his weight hit the driver's side seat, moving the car under me. I turned my head, squinting and blinking to see him. His crystal-light outline, the liquid glow in his veins, his mouth, cheekbones, even his hair, flash between glimpses of his physical face.

"We have to get you out of the Barrier," he muttered. "You're calling every seer from a few thousand miles away right now."

It hit me again that he really *was* a seer. He had to be.

He was a seer, and now he had me handcuffed to his car. I could barely breathe.

I am breathing too much.

If the man noticed, he didn't react.

I watch him bend down, feeling around for something. He feels above him then, moving things around. There is the sudden, sharp jangle of keys. He bends over the thing in front of him and I remember again that this is a car.

He's starting the car.

He turns the key.

The engine rumbles to life. It's a deep, heavy sound. Whatever kind of car this is, it has a big engine. Likely a V-8. It might even be one of the enhanced race cars they had nowadays, the ones that weren't really street legal but sometimes showed up on the roads anyway.

But if it had an actual *key,* it must be old.

Damned old.

"Where are you taking me?" I practically yell the words. That time I hear how loud I'm speaking. I realize I'm trying to compensate for all the interference in my head.

I was about to try again, when he shocked me by answering.

"You're making way too much noise in the Barrier, Alyson. You're too visible. You're too loud." That deep, Germanic-sounding voice vibrated my chest along with the V-8 engine. "I'm going to have to knock you out."

His voice is so calm, I can't comprehend his meaning at first.

Then his words penetrated.

My fingers tightened around the chain holding me to the door.

"You're not going to knock me out."

The way I say it, it's close to a threat.

He turns, looking at me. His eyes are as empty as glass.

"I'm sorry, Alyson."

It's the last thing I remember.

CHAPTER 5
DRIVE

I didn't question the motion of the car at first.

The steady vibration and hum relaxed me, even if I struggled finding a comfortable resting place for my arms. A bump in the road brought my eyes abruptly open. The sky through a dirty windshield showed the faint pink and gold of pre-dawn.

I'd missed the night. All of it.

Maybe that's why it took me so long to remember anything about where I was now.

The silhouette of a saint statue broke my view. It was glued to the dashboard above an old-fashioned FM radio with silver knobs.

My eyes traveled left, meeting an angular profile framed by black hair matted to a pale neck. Sharp, light-colored eyes sat above high cheekbones, taking in the road. He had the beginnings of five o'clock shadow.

Flecks of a familiar-looking brown substance stained his shirt. A lot more of it decorated his arm and shoulder, which bulged from a crude, homemade bandage.

Feeling my stare, he turned. His eyes appeared cold, even in the morning sun.

I tried to raise a hand—

—and my arm jerked to a stop.

I turned slowly. I stared at the handcuffs on my wrists for a full minute before the reality of them penetrated. I looked at my ankles next, found them bound with hard plastic, like those tie-binders they use on reality cop shows.

Leaning back, I leveraged my weight to try and budge the only object I thought I had some chance of influencing, namely the plastic armrest. When it stayed firmly affixed to the door, I looked over at him again, watching him stare at me.

I translated his expression as disinterested puzzlement.

He didn't try to stop me as I continued to test my limits of motion.

My whole body hurt; I felt like I had a tequila hangover, complete with the head-splitting migraine. I felt weak, hungry, nauseated. I also felt weirdly exposed, even under the dog-smelling blanket someone—probably him—had draped over my legs and lower body.

I still wore the same clothes I'd had on at work.

My throat hurt. I was insanely thirsty.

My neck crimped from where I'd slept against the car door.

I thought about my mom in a kind of blurred panic. I struggled against the door's armrest again, only pausing when my headache bloomed hotter, forcing me still.

I tried to think past the pain.

I wondered if I could reason with him.

"I can hear you," he informed me, his words flat. He turned, staring at me with those glass-like eyes. "You know that, right?"

His words jarred me. I'd forgotten about the German accent.

I'd forgotten how deep his voice was.

I'd also forgotten that he'd said he was a seer.

He shifted in his seat, as if uncomfortable. "Don't force me to knock you unconscious again. I would rather not. There are things we need to talk about."

I looked out the windows.

I knew he could hear me. He just told me he could hear me.

I tried to think my way out of this anyway.

I tried to replay everything that happened in that diner.

I saw Jon in my mind as he crashed into that table. I heard gunshots, heard the man cursing in a foreign language in my ear. I remembered people in the diner screaming. I remembered Cass trying to stop this man from dragging me to the door. My mother's face flashed in my mind's eye. I imagined her reaction when police knocked on her door, when Jon came in, limping and injured, saying I'd disappeared.

My friends, co-workers, and old school-mates would see my face on the feeds. However this turned out, I'd be marked as having been wanted by the cops and Seer Containment. I'd come up in criminal and terrorist alerts for anyone who searched my name.

Probably for the rest of my life.

Staring at the scenery flashing by, the mist-covered ocean out the window past the man in the driver's seat, I realized I recognized none of it.

We had to be well outside of the Bay Area already.

"Maybe forty minutes to the Oregon border," he affirmed, glancing at me. "I had to take the coastal highway most of the way, which slowed us down. They don't have as many flyers out here. The camera posts are mapped, so easier to avoid."

I turned over his words. In the end, I shook my head, unwilling to follow the trails they wanted to lead me down.

"My mother is suicidal," I said, turning towards him. "She drinks, and she's suicidal."

He didn't answer. He didn't even look at me.

"I can't just disappear," I said. "Whatever this is, you can't just take me out of my life like this. It may seem like nothing to you, but people depend on me. I take care of my mom. I go there every day to make sure she's okay, and—"

"I know all of that." He cut me off without looking over. "I also know you remember what happened in that diner. Which means you should know there's nothing I can do about it, Allie."

I flinched when he said my name.

He didn't take his eyes off the road.

I watched him rearrange his hands on the steering wheel. He wore one ring. It was silver, without any markings I could see.

"Are you going to tell me what this is?" I said, when he didn't say more.

I watched his face in the silence, biting my lip.

"Look. I get that you're seer. I get that. But whatever this is, it doesn't make any sense. I've never done anything to you people. I was always supportive of seer's rights. I was never one of those people who—"

He let out a low, humorless laugh.

It startled me into silence.

I was still fighting to think through my mind's cocktail of anger and panic and migraine when he turned, his eyes like two flat stones.

"I'm sorry for your mother. Truly. But as I said, there is absolutely nothing I can do about it." He made an odd, graceful gesture with one hand. "When we get somewhere safe, it is possible I can try to influence things. But right now, I have no way to get word to anyone who could help your family."

I touched my ear, looking for my headset, and he frowned in my direction.

"I threw it out. Before we left the city."

"What?" I stared at him. "Are you serious? That was a registered headset. I could get fined for that... not to mention it being totally fucking illegal."

He shook his head, making an odd clicking noise with his tongue. The sound again conveyed a kind of cynical humor, like he couldn't believe what I was saying.

He went on like I hadn't spoken.

"The second I go into the Barrier, we would have SCARB all over us..."

Despite the humor I'd heard in that sound, his voice was stripped of emotion.

"...Any attempt to communicate via headset would also immediately put the authorities onto us," he added. "In either case, we'd be picked up, likely within minutes. We'd be separated, collared, and stuck in a World Court black site. I'd be questioned and probably beaten to death. You'd likely end up in a genetics lab. Until the Rooks extracted you, at least." Another flat stare. "None of these scenarios would help your mother, Allie."

Again I flinched when he used my name.

He continued to watch me, gauging my expression with those glass-like eyes.

"Your brother appeared to be all right. He will be questioned by SCARB, and likely Homeland Security. They might detain him for some time... and your mother, too... but they are both human, so they will likely let them go after conducting scans to ensure they knew nothing about your racial status. They will put your family under surveillance, of course. They would hope you might contact them, so they would want them outside a cell anyway."

He made another graceful gesture.

"You did not hurt him badly. He can help your mother. Cass will help, too."

I absorbed his words.

He definitely knew way too much about me.

I felt the blood slide from the veins in my face as the rest of what he was saying sank in.

Glancing out the dusty windows, I fought through the limits of my options.

We drove on in silence while I massaged my wrists around the two handcuffs. I watched out the window as he passed a semi-truck.

We passed another a few minutes later.

I considered yelling out at them, banging on the windows, but the more I thought about it, the more the possibility struck me as not just futile, but dangerous.

The sun was getting higher in the sky.

Seagulls and pelicans winged over diamond patterns of sunlight flickering over waves. It was beyond strange to be looking out over that perfect view with my wrists handcuffed to the door of a stranger's car.

When I glanced over at the seer next, he was staring at my bare thigh, which had shifted out from under the ugly, gray blanket. Seeing the denser look rising to his eyes, I retracted my leg, hiding it back under the coarse wool.

I'd forgotten all those other stories about seers.

Frowning, he averted his gaze.

"You are safe with me, Alyson," he said.

I let out a low snort. I couldn't help it.

When he gave me a sharp look, I made my expression blank. I stared out the side window at sandy cliffs and windswept grasses. My fingers clutched the chain between the metal bracelets as I tried to think if there was any way I could talk him into unlocking the cuffs.

I remembered he could read my mind.

That pretty much limited my options.

"Yes," he agreed neutrally.

I faced him, my jaw hard.

"Are you really *not* going to tell me why you took me?" I stared at him, biting my tongue when he didn't answer. "What? Are you a religious fanatic of some kind, like your pal in the diner? A terrorist? One of those 'unaffiliateds' who want a seer nation?"

Still watching his face, I bit my tongue until I tasted blood.

I fought to control the emotion that wanted to rise, but mostly failed.

"I'm a *waitress,*" I snapped. "Did you miss that? Do you really think anyone's going to think twice about blowing my head off to get to you?"

He made that soft clicking noise with his tongue.

I watched him do it, briefly dumbstruck at how alien it sounded, how alien he looked as he did it. I'd read somewhere about seer language, how they used sign language in addition to verbal and telepathy. It hit me again that he really wasn't human.

He looked human.

But he wasn't.

I don't know if he heard me thinking that, too, but his next words bled impatience.

"Alyson," he said. "You need to work with me. You need to get over this view of yourself as a victim in this. Try, anyway." He glanced at my face. "You cannot afford to indulge in this much denial. You understand far more than you're pretending right now."

"The hell I do," I snapped. "Who *are* you? Are you going to tell me?"

Again, his expression tightened.

He glanced at me. His eyes looked uncomfortable now.

"You were seven when I began watching over you."

When I let out an angry sound, he cut me off, his voice hard.

"Yes. It is true." He made that shrugging motion with his hand. "There is a term for it. It is seer, though. It won't mean anything to you. I was not around much in the physical. My job was to keep an eye on you. To assist in keeping you hidden."

Grunting, he gave me a flat look. "That became increasingly difficult these last two years. Your behavior has been… erratic. It is why I came in person."

"Erratic?" I stared at him. "What do you mean, my behavior has been 'erratic'?"

Turning, he quirked a dark eyebrow at me.

His lips twisted in a kind of cynical humor.

"You stabbed your ex-lover's girlfriend," he reminded me. "In public. With a broken wine bottle." Grunting, he looked back at the road. "You got arrested, Alyson. That's not something I could cover up. Even with our contacts in law enforcement."

I stared at him.

For a moment, I fought with how to argue with that, how he even *knew* about it.

In the end, I shut my mouth.

"I'm not judging you," he added. Giving me another sideways glance, he clicked his tongue. That time I heard real amusement in it. "Truthfully, it was a very seer thing to do. But it was also very conspicuous. Too conspicuous."

"Seers stab people a lot?" I said, sarcastic.

"When it comes to infidelity, yes." Again he turned, staring at me with those crystal-like eyes. "Usually we're a bit more thorough, though."

I clenched my jaw.

I was still staring at him when something else occurred to me.

"If you're seer, can't you make me believe anything you want?"

He turned, aiming a cold stare at me.

"Of course," he said. "But why would I? You are nobody, as you said."

I didn't have a good answer for that, either.

I looked out the window.

"He called me something," I said. "The guy in the diner. He called me a name—"

"The Bridge, yes. That is not a name. That is your title."

"Title?" I looked at him, bewildered again. "So this Bridge thing is… what? Some myth of yours? Like a Dalai Lama kind of thing?"

When he didn't answer, I sharpened my voice.

"You have to know how completely crazy that sounds. You're a seer. You have to be able to put yourself in my shoes a little, right? Empathy comes with the territory?"

The man's mouth hardened to a line.

When he didn't say anything, I bit back another surge of anger.

"If you want me to work with you, you have to tell me more," I said.

I waited.

He didn't speak.

"You sound German," I added. "I didn't think any seers even lived in Europe anymore. I thought you were all in Asia, with the exception of a few who worked directly for—"

"Alyson." His deep voice held a warning. "Just stop."

"Stop?"

He nodded, eyes on the road. "Stop talking. Stop trying to make this go away. This is shock. Denial." He waved a hand at me vaguely. "You know the truth. Your human life... it is over. You are talking at me, saying things you know are not true, or know are half-true. You are trying to convince yourself that this is not real, that you don't understand. It is better to remain quiet. To allow the truth to sink in."

I stared at him.

Realizing there was at least some flicker of truth in his words, I clenched my jaw.

When he didn't say anything else, I bit my tongue.

"Look." I flipped my arm over. I showed him the lighter skin of my inner arm. I pointed at the "H" tattooed there in black ink on my skin. "I've been tested. Literally *hundreds* of times. I was adopted, so I got tested every time I registered. Whatever you're trying to do, framing me as some kind of sleeper seer agent, *Syrimne*-wannabe, I don't appreciate being the fall guy for whatever takeover trip you've got planned..."

I trailed as he hiked up the sleeve on his own left arm.

Seeing the barcode there, on a lean, olive-toned arm, my eyes locked on the black "H" tattooed on his skin.

He watched me long enough to make sure I understood.

Then he tugged down his sleeve. He placed both hands back on the leather-wrapped steering wheel.

"It's ink, Alyson," he said. "It's fucking meaningless."

I lapsed into silence, that sick feeling in my gut worsening. After another pause, I shook my head, remembering my last visit to the doctor, what he'd said—

"Are you really going to pretend you didn't do that thing?" The seer turned on me, his narrow mouth curled in a frown. *"Gaos d'lanlente.* Alyson! Your name is likely all over the news feeds by now. Your name. My face. Your face." He continued to glare at me, anger tingeing his voice. "You want to blame *me* for this? I would have gotten you out *quietly.* I would have gotten you past him, if you'd just—"

"Yeah," I snapped. "You were doing a bang-up job getting me out 'quietly.' Stellar. I particularly enjoyed the gun you aimed at my head."

He frowned, looking away.

Staring out the windshield, he twisted his hands on the steering wheel's leather grip, not speaking as he clicked under his breath.

I sat there silently too, scowling as I stared out the window.

Even so, both of our words began to sink into the deeper recesses of my brain.

My hands grew suddenly cold.

Had I really done that? Had I really thrown people across the room?

"Yes," the man next to me growled. "You did."

Barely pausing in my thoughts to give him an angry glare, I clenched my jaw, not answering. Still, that sick feeling in my gut was getting worse.

Telekinesis was not a common thing.

Fuck. That was the understatement of understatements.

It was practically unheard of.

Apart from Syrimne, who'd been dead something like eighty years, I was pretty sure another telekinetic seer hadn't been discovered since seers were first found on Earth.

It certainly hadn't happened in *my* lifetime.

Syrimne was a unicorn.

To humans, he was also the bogeyman, even now.

During World War I, he'd wiped out half of Europe.

He'd blown up planes, igniting fuel tanks with his mind. He'd exploded bombs, ignited the gunpowder in bullets before they left their guns. He smashed bridges covered in troops, destroyed water mains and supply lines, set fields on fire.

He'd killed millions.

According to one account I'd read, he'd even set the air on fire.

In the end, it took an elite team of seers and humans, working together, to bring him down. If not for them, Syrimne likely would have gone on to destroy Russia and the Middle East, maybe the United States and Asia, too.

Germany would run the world now.

Or, more likely, seers would.

I remembered reading debates around Syrimne's probable motives in my race history classes in college. They all agreed he was one of a kind, though, that the telekinesis thing was a total fluke. All of my race history professors, too. They all seemed to think he was some crazy genetic anomaly, that something like him would never happen again.

Thinking about that now, and about what little I remembered from the diner, I felt sick.

That sick feeling worsened, the longer I stared out the window.

"You are understanding now?" That gruff, German-sounding voice broke into my thoughts. "You see why I had to get you out of there, Alyson?"

That time, I heard a faint sympathy in his words.

I stared out the window without seeing anything.

That nausea I'd been feeling was bad enough now that I thought I might puke all over the gray blanket. I tried not to think about Jon, or the fact that the diner was wired with cameras. Every building in San Francisco was wired with cameras.

It was part of the racial codes.

SCARB would have access to all of those feeds.

So would the San Francisco Police Department.

And Homeland Security.

"I won't let them take you, Alyson," he said. "Not if I can do anything about it."

I couldn't look at him.

He cleared his throat. In my peripheral vision, I saw him gesture in that way that reminded me of a shrug.

"There are several... oddities... in your make-up," he said. "Some of these will aid us in getting you out safely. Your blood is undetectable as Sark." He glanced at me. "Seer, I mean. The lack of discernible markers for your blood is an extremely rare condition. Only one in several hundred thousand seers have this. I have it, too. It is part of why they assigned me to look over you. It will make it easier for us to get past any attempts they might put in place to keep you from leaving the country."

I stared at him. I couldn't help it.

"Leave the country," I repeated.

"Of course. We can't stay here."

His voice was so matter of fact, I had no answer.

He went on in a measured tone.

"As to what the Bridge is, that will be explained to you, as well. I am perhaps not the best-qualified person to do so. In short, however, we believe you to be the reincarnation of a being that appears within the seer pantheon." Glancing at me, he narrowed his gaze, then adjusted his words. "Well. Not precisely a *pantheon.* Not in the human sense. It's not believed you are a 'god.' You are instead seen as the reincarnation of a particular light frequency, or impulse, only in a manifested form—"

"What?" I blinked. "What?"

Exhaling, he shook his head.

His words and speech-patterns grew oddly academic-sounding.

Like he was one of my professors, teaching a class.

"As I said, I am perhaps not the best person to explain this," he said. "The bottom line is, you are important to seers. You were hidden among humans for that reason. You are a being who only incarnates on Earth prior to a major shift in the historical timeline. Your arrival here signals that change is coming. It also provides a catalyst to that change."

He glanced over at me.

"Meaning you, Alyson. *You* are seen as one who would help facilitate that change." Still thinking, he shrugged. "Or possibly cause it, as I said. Depending on which interpretation of the myths you believe to be the most—"

"What is your name?" I cut in.

He glanced at me.

Then he frowned.

"Dehgoies," he said. "Revik."

"Your name is Dego-ees?" I pronounced the strange name slowly. After another few seconds, my brow cleared. "Revi'. That man called you Revi'. That's short for Revik?"

He nodded, once.

"Revik is my given name. In seer naming conventions, the family name comes first. That other seer is called Terian."

"Terry," I said. "Short for Terian."

"Correct."

"That's a pretty chummy way to refer to a guy who's threatening your life," I observed. "Were you two friends? Ex-boyfriends? What?"

The man turned to stare at me.

He shook his head, but not in a no. Instead, he exuded irritation.

"In a manner of speaking, yes, we were friends. Colleagues, as well. We aren't now."

"That's the second time you've done that," I said.

He looked at me. "Done what?"

"Referred to him in the present tense. You *killed* him, right? Why do you keep talking about him as if he's still alive?"

The black-haired man frowned. "That's complicated, Alyson."

"So he *is* still alive?"

"Yes."

I pursed my lips, wanting to know how he could possibly know that. After a few seconds where he didn't elaborate, I shook it off.

"All right. We'll come back to that, Degho-ees—"

"Revik," he said, giving me a look. "I just told you. Dehgoies is my family name."

Staring at him, I bit my lip, clasping my cuffed hands together.

I could feel the part of me that wanted to go off on him.

I wanted to yell at him.

Truthfully, I wanted to do more than that, but I knew that wasn't exactly going to help my situation, either.

I forced myself to stay silent, but only just.

As if feeling that, too, the man exhaled, leaning back in his seat.

"As I said, the elders are better equipped to talk to you about the spiritual aspects of your role here." Running a hand through his black hair, he gave me a sideways glance, his mouth grim. "My purpose is simpler. I am to bring you to them. Alive. There are things you need to understand, to better help me accomplish that. The news feeds are not..."

He tilted his head, making another vague gesture with one hand.

"...accurate. Particularly in terms of their portrayal of relations between humans and seers."

Once more, he sounded more like a professor than a criminal.

The contradictions were odd enough to frustrate me.

I wanted to categorize him, and I couldn't. Not really.

He resumed in that same lecturing tone.

"There are things I will need to teach you about your people. Because of all the misinformation out there, not to mention the intentional *dis*information, you should assume most of what you *think* you know about seers is wrong. For one, seers are not a single, unified entity. That seer in the diner. Terian. He represents a different faction than I."

I let out a humorless snort.

I felt him glance over, but didn't look away from the window.

He waited a beat, then shrugged it off.

"It is in the interests of both human and seer governments to keep this more complex reality from civilians," he continued. "There has long been a sort of 'cold war' happening between seers and humans on many levels."

As if feeling something from me, he glanced over.

"A trained infiltrator can eliminate their frequency from regular perception in the Barrier, mainly through blending with the lights that make up their environment. I am doing this for us now, but the human and seer governments are aware of this ability. They still have means of finding us, so we will have to be careful."

He glanced over, probably feeling he was losing me.

"...Anyway," he continued, waving off his own words. "My point is, you will need to be trained. And educated in these things. I can perhaps help with the beginnings of that. It is certainly a more practical way to spend our time together."

I clenched my jaw.

He glanced at me again, then cleared his throat.

"Free seers, meaning those who were not sold into slavery at birth or in childhood... or forced into it in some other way... we have only three real options."

He went back to staring at the road.

I watched as he steered us precisely around a curve that hugged a steep cliff.

"Our first option is to live with traditional, religious seers in seclusion," he went on in that college-y voice. "It is not a bad life, but not all of our people are suited to it, just as not all humans would be. Our second option is to be contractually owned. To sell our sight to humans. This path provides some freedoms, assuming one is skilled enough to get such a contract in the first place, and has an employer who is fair. But it is risky… a kind of voluntary slavery. And it is not open to all seers, depending on their sight rank."

He adds, "The third option is to join the Rooks… or 'The Org,' as they call themselves. Or sometimes 'The Brotherhood.' The Rooks are an underground network of seers with an anti-human agenda. They are everywhere. Many of them have infiltrated human institutions. The seer you met, Terian, is one of these."

I noticed he used the present tense again.

"I am also what is known as an infiltrator," he added after another pause. "That means I am a seer trained to find things behind the Barrier. It is a trade. One that is learned, often at a young age. We work in various capacities in the human and seer worlds."

"A spy?" I said, looking at him.

He frowned. I got the impression the term irritated him.

"A human equivalent might be espionage," he said diplomatically. "It is how my human employer sees it, certainly. For Rook infiltrators, the designation of espionage is probably more accurate. They do not follow Code and operate under a quasi-military structure, as you see reflected in the spatial representation of their network of seers."

Again, he seemed to feel he was losing me.

He glanced in my direction.

"The Pyramid, Allie. We call their network the Pyramid."

I stared at him.

I felt the blood slide from my face.

Shrugging, he cleared his throat. "In your art, you have painted representations of the Pyramid, have you not?" He glanced at me, his voice carefully polite. "Those depictions were quite accurate, as I recall. The fact that you saw so much about this is something that has been a bit of a curiosity among the elders of our kind. It is also another reason the decision was made to pull you out of hiding. There is some question as to whether you have some ability as a prescient. You were drawing them with increasing frequency."

I didn't answer.

Remembering that strange, hallucinatory pyramid image I'd seen over that Terian seer's head, I felt my stomach do another flip. I bit my lip harder.

I watched the scenery flash by through the window.

"So you have an employer?" I said, not looking over at him. "Where are they? And how are they letting you walk around without a collar?"

He turned, staring at me.

After a pause, I turned, too.

That time, his colorless eyes were hard as metal.

Pausing a beat, he looked away.

I could almost see him fighting to control his temper. His expression grew taut, right before he went on in that academic-sounding voice.

"Different permit levels and security designations exist for seers, Alyson," he said. "I hold a classification above that of most seers you've seen discussed on the news feeds. Because of the kind of work I do, and for whom, I have virtually unlimited rights of assembly and travel. That includes the ability to move freely without a collar. I can carry a gun, and—"

"What?" I stared at him. "You can carry a gun?"

He gave me an annoyed look. "I shot someone, Esteemed Bridge. Right in front of you."

"Don't call me that." I grimaced. "I mean legally. You can *legally* carry a gun? How?"

He gave me another irritated look.

"There's a lot about this world you don't know, Esteemed Bridge," he said, his voice polite on the surface, but colder underneath. "It's what I've been trying to tell you."

There was a silence.

In it, he went back to staring at the road.

"It would help," he added, his voice even colder. "If you would make a conscious effort to remember that you are speaking of your own brothers and sisters when you talk about things like collaring and enslaving seers." Another brief stare. "You might remember, as well, that you can no longer exclude *yourself* when talking about such things."

Those glass-like eyes studied mine.

I frowned right back at him.

"So far," I retorted. "The only person enslaving me is you."

He shrugged. His eyes flickered away.

He made his voice academic sounding again.

"You should know, in our mythology, humans are the third race," he said, focusing back on the road. "The first is Elaerian. The second Sarhacienne, or Sark, which is us… the name 'Sarhacienne' means 'Second' in the seer tongue. The third is human."

He glanced at me.

"Each race is said to destroy its own civilization at a certain point in its evolution, as a means of moving to the next level. Elaerian, the first race, no longer exist outside of the Barrier. It is said that we Sarhaciennes did not have sight before the Second Displacement."

He paused again, giving me a narrow look.

"According to seer history, every race has risen in power, reach, and technology until a critical period is entered in their development," he continued in that deep voice. "There have been two Displacements so far… one Elaerian and one Sark. We believe a third Displacement is coming." He looked at me. "A human one."

Images hit at my mind at his words—sharp, shockingly clear.

In them, I could see bombs falling.

Storms raging on the sea.

A blue-white sun burns cold and bright over the Earth.

A brilliant, silver sword intersects the middle of it, blinding me…

When that light fades, I see San Francisco in ruins.

I see the White House empty of people, window frames blackened from fire, parts of the domed roof collapsed inward and missing, the white walls peppered with machine-gun holes. My breath stopped. I gripped the chain holding my wrists together as pain stabbed at my chest.

I fight to block it, to force the images from my mind.

Red starbursts flash behind my eyes, exploding over a dusty Asian city.

I let out another, sharper gasp—

—when warm fingers clasped my forearm.

"Hey."

He gripped me tighter when I turned.

I blinked at him, unable to see him clearly at first.

His face is strangely close to mine, those glass-like eyes watching me with a sharper scrutiny. For the first time, it hits me how intelligent he is. I can see it in those clear eyes. I can feel it on him; it's like a tangible shimmer around his form.

He is lonely, though. He is almost painfully alone.

It hurts me, that aloneness.

"What is it?" His voice is sharp. "Are you all right?"

I can only shake my head.

He pulled on me more insistently with his fingers, nudging me with his mind to snap out of it, to come back to the car, back to the present.

When I tried to do as he asked, his face clicked back into focus, its angular lines hard, almost predatory. That hardness didn't seem aimed at me, but it made me reappraise him yet again. That time, I couldn't help but see him as dangerous.

I still wasn't sure if he was dangerous to me.

I noticed again how tall he was.

His head nearly scraped the roof of the car.

Still, I could see more than just anger there.

I felt concern, visible behind his scowl.

"What the fuck was that?" he growled. "Don't do that again."

I blinked. The image of him righted.

"Do what?" I said. "What did I do?"

"Your light… *aleimi*…" he said, pronouncing the unfamiliar word carefully. "Your seer's light. You did something with it just now. Whatever you did, it made your *aleimi* flare. A flare like that makes you visible inside the Barrier, even when you're outside of it. You cannot do that right now. You cannot. Even with me shielding you."

His voice was stern, as if he were talking to a disobedient dog.

Again, I could only stare at him.

How he thought I could have done something like that knowingly, much less on purpose, was totally beyond me.

He might have heard that, too.

Letting go of my arm, he put his hand back on the steering wheel, clicking softly with his tongue. When he returned his focus to his driving, his expression remained taut.

After another pause, he cleared his throat.

"The Rooks are undoubtedly looking for us," he said, his voice subdued. "They will send many seers after us, Alyson. More than I could handle. When I asked you just now, to keep your light dim… it is this that worries me. Not anything you did, per se."

He glanced at me.

That time, his voice bordered on apologetic.

"Normally, such flares are perfectly fine. I did not mean to imply that you did anything wrong intentionally. I'm simply asking you to *try* and control such things. Do whatever you can to stay grounded, to keep your emotions in check… at least until we reach somewhere safe."

Leaning against the car door, I frowned.

Turning over his words, I decided it wasn't worth trying to argue the point, especially when he was obviously trying to meet me halfway.

Instead, I found myself battling another wave of exhaustion.

I closed my eyes, listening to the thrumming of the car's engine.

"So they really want me dead?" I said. "These Rooks?"

When I opened my eyes, looking at him, he frowned.

"Yes." Pausing, still watching my face, he made another of those tilted wing gestures with one hand. "Well. Dead, perhaps. More likely they want you with them."

Remembering the Rook's words in that diner, I nodded.

I thought again about how well the two men seemed to know each other.

It hadn't only been their words, or the nicknames they'd used with one another.

I could practically feel that connection between them.

"You worked for them, didn't you?" I asked. "The Rooks. You used to be one of them."

Another silence.

He exhaled in a clicking sigh. "Yes."

"Yet you still think it would be so terrible?" I said, my voice cautious. "To go with them? Obviously you left. You're not dead."

I practically felt his annoyance that time.

More than just annoyance.

Other emotions lived there. Embarrassment. Confusion.

A kind of conflicted frustration rose in him, one that told me the issue was likely complicated, and he didn't wish to explain. I even felt something that might have been shame. Of course, I couldn't be certain about any of that.

I couldn't be certain if any of what I'd just felt was even real.

"We should talk about this later, Alyson," he said.

Glancing at the rough bandage on his shoulder, I frowned.

"So what is a Rook?" I said. "Can you at least tell me that? Are they just renegade seers? One of the terrorist groups the news is always talking about?"

He looked at me, his pale eyes catching another slanting ray of light from the sun.

"They are the enemy," he said simply.

CHAPTER 6
TERIAN

The corpse of a man who died in his early twenties lay with artistic precision on a stainless steel table.

Clear tubes protruded from his throat, from veins in his arms, legs, stomach.

He was additionally fitted with several color-coded sets of electrodes that dotted patches of his bare skin, a computerized headband, and the more conventional saline I.V.

The organic-looking headband with its soft, skin-like texture blinked rhythmically; it was the only light not coming from one of the four monitors that dominated the walls of the bone-white room.

A technician adjusted settings on a rolling console beside the steel table.

He utilized a standard interface and keyboard that projected data and findings to a portion of the organic-coated wall. Fluid coursing through the clear tubes disappeared into the same wall. It changed color subtly soon after each adjustment the technician made. Electrodes on the corpse's head flashed dark blue once the fluid stabilized.

That signaled another piece of the organic transfer had been completed.

Fogged pupils stared blindly at the ceiling.

The irises and whites were both the same milky gray.

As tubes carried the genetic virus to their host, the irises changed to an opaque yellow, the color of daffodils.

Or strong urine, the technician thought.

Over time, that yellow began to brighten. The skin looked different, as well. It wasn't flushed with life, not exactly, not yet, but it somehow appeared less dead.

That much took twelve hours.

It would have taken longer, but they'd prepped the body in advance.

Day one came and went.

The technician's boss came to the room, several hours past the first signs of real change in the body's animation markers. An older scientist, she checked the readouts on the monitor, making more and infinitely more subtle adjustments before nodding a stiff approval to the junior tech. He watched her every move in undisguised tension.

She was not known for being tolerant of errors.

"Now," she said, nodding once, decisively. She had the barest hint of a German accent. "Now, we wait."

TERIAN LAY ENTIRELY STILL.

His new body's only hint at animation lived in an elusive attempt to focus his eyes.

New eyes—to him, at least—they looked out from the foreign planes of an unfamiliar face. He hadn't gotten a good look at the thing, yet.

It didn't matter. It belonged to him now.

At least until he managed to trash this one, as well.

He gazed up at a flat, dead ceiling, wishing he'd thought to have them put a monitor there. The dull shimmer of organics in his periphery weren't enough to distract him.

He had plenty to think about.

Unfortunately, none of it was particularly illuminating.

Even if he managed to figure out something important, he couldn't do much until he got his range of motion back.

His mind ground on anyway.

The basics of his condition filtered into his awareness slowly.

A period of adjustment always awaited him on the far side of one of these little "deaths." He should be used to it by now, but the very nature of the change made familiarity with its workings impossible. To ease his confusion, Terian had imparted a program into the transfer process that reminded him of that fact, even before bringing him fully awake.

The disorientation would not desist entirely until the process was complete, however.

He hated the quiet.

He disliked the emptiness that lay between states of active consciousness. While every death remained unique from the one before, all instances shared certain similarities in physical sensation and mundane forms of psychological stress.

In the beginning, silence always met him.

Therefore, whatever the desirability of said state, the most intelligent course of action lay in accepting this fact with some attempt at grace. Philosophical musings should accompany death, Terian thought, no matter how temporary. Death, like life, should not be viewed as being without consequence. The mental ritual contained a vestigial superstition and yet, Terian liked the idea of taking a moment to appreciate his ample gifts.

It felt borderline noble.

Gradually, memory began its stealthy return.

Pieces of his past filtered through Terian's consciousness like leaves falling in cold wind.

Some stuck, eliminating gaps.

Technically, all of his memories had been connected to this new body since the raw technique of transfer, but with every body came a new set of nonphysical structures, a combination of Terian's mind and the mind of whomever's body he now wore. Gaps remained while his *aleimi* relearned pathways to access the material world.

More time passed.

He applied pressure to the process of his rebirth.

He tried to access his previous body's final moments. This early remembering took work, mainly in the form of separating his own, multi-life memories from those of the body he now wore… which of course carried only one mortal life's worth.

Well, really, not even that.

Terian liked his bodies young.

When those final memories surfaced, the images and sensations came with no warning, a movie that began and ended without prompt or fanfare.

Light flashed outward.

Terian heard screams, felt his body flying through the air.

He flew through empty space, lost in no-time as he fought to unholster his gun. Pain exploded in his head and spine as he slammed into something that shattered under his back. He raised the gun, saw a dull flash of light as it went off.

Then another flash, from the other side of the room.

Dehgoies.

Of course.

Terian should have brought more than one body.

The rest of it filtered back.

He rewound the mental tape to earlier in that confrontation.

Dehgoies hadn't been the one who threw him across the room. The baby seer had done that, the one Revi' had been clutching in his arms, pretending he'd be willing to kill, if only Terian didn't leave them alone.

The Bridge.

I'thir li'dare.

She was telekinetic.

She could manipulate matter.

An intense flush of emotion hit him, enough to slant out his sight, to stop his virgin mind in its tracks. He struggled to think past it, lost in wonder.

Gaos. It changed everything. Everything.

An earth-shattering, Barrier-shattering discovery.

It was beyond anything he'd dared to let himself hope.

He should have shot Dehgoies through the window of that diner. He should have killed him before the goddamned traitor and defector even knew he was there.

Then again, Revi' had always been one for following rules, for sticking to protocol.

Maybe he really would have exterminated her, if he'd felt cornered enough.

Her being telekinetic only increased that likelihood. After all, it made her about a million times more dangerous than anyone in the Org anticipated.

No, shooting Dehgoies likely would have gotten the female killed.

As it was, she made that decision for both of them.

A shadow fell over him, blocking the white, pock-marked ceiling.

"Sir?" a voice said. "It is too soon. You must rest."

He fought to move his mouth, to speak… then to use his light.

They needed to know.

They needed to *know* about her.

Fatigue encumbered him before he could figure out his vocal chords or how to use his new mind. It was too much for him—the stress borne of birthing, of straining back to life—even as drugs aided his return to a blissfully dreamless sleep.

Does he remember? A FAMILIAR VOICE SAID OVER HIM.

Terian cannot open his eyes.

He floats over himself. He watches them speak within his mind as if it was a conference room on one of Galaith's many private planes.

He remembers his death, the female scientist said.

It was Dehgoies, was it not?

The female's thoughts turn affirmative. *The images we've pulled indicate that, yes. Would you like to see?*

The other's light indicates yes.

She plays the memories, as one might play a video from the feeds.

Ah. The voice sighs as its owner watches, but the emotion behind it feels complex, a flavor of pride mixed with regret. His words remain all business. *She truly is exquisite, is she not? To see the two of them together… I admit, it touches something in me.*

The female scientist does not answer.

Galaith sighs again, right before his mind grows business-like.

You are still checking for anomalies each time our Terian returns to a new body? Each and every time, Xarethe? No exceptions?

Yes. Her voice is stiffly certain. *He is not resurrected without a thorough examination, father Galaith. There are no anomalies. No irregularities of any kind.*

Another silence fell while he thought about her words.

She broke it, her voice cautious.

Sir, if you don't mind my asking…? Dehgoies. Is it strictly necessary that he remain a part of this equation? It is clear he is no longer a friend to us, nor to—

I do mind, Xarethe, Galaith's voice holds the faintest of warnings. *Ensure that our friend Terian remains stable, happy and free of any disturbing thoughts. As is appropriate for any good and loyal friend of the Org. Ask him to contact me as soon as he is able.*

Of course, she sent diplomatically. *There are some tests I'd like to recommend. For her, I mean. For when we have her in custody…*

The voices begin to fade from Terian's hearing.

He drifts from his consciousness like a boat blown further and further away by a cool breeze.

THE NEXT TIME HE WOKE, THE OLD DOCTOR WAS THERE IN PERSON.

He opened his eyes to find her bent over the main monitor.

She smiled at him when she saw his eyes open, the deep lines of her aged face making the expression something more akin to a grimace. As always, there is something reptilian reflected in her black eyes and strangely flat nose.

How long have I been out? he sent to her.

She made a few final adjustments before glancing at him a second time. Her thin lips curved in another faint smile. "Approximately forty-six hours in total, brother."

Terian blinked. He tried to move his jaw. It remained sore.

You know about her? he sent.

"That our new Bridge is telekinetic?" That narrow-lipped smile. "Of course. The news hit the public feeds, brother. SCARB could not contain it. There were black market broadcasts with footage of the event. Her name is public, too."

We are still tracking them?

"We are looking for them, yes," she corrected. "Dehgoies sent out a number of decoys when he left the city. We are not sure which of them is him yet."

How many?

"Three squads on our side. And we are now leveraging the human media."

How many decoys? he sent.

"At least eight." Her voice remained emotionless. "We are still compiling the last set of your memories. There are those who think you botched this assignment, brother." When she looked over next, she smiled. "Galaith is not one of them. Nor am I. None of us could have anticipated she would turn out to be a manipulator."

I want to go after them. As soon as possible.

"Your diligence is noteworthy, brother. But your recent imprints of Dehgoies' light will have to be collated before we will have a real-time track. Until then, the usual channels are being utilized." She patted his arm reassuringly. "Do not worry, Terry. Another day should not matter. He cannot get out via the airports. That limits his options."

You still have no idea where they are. Terian stared at the ceiling. *Did anyone recover the body? My body,* he clarified.

"Of course. The team is already working on it, brother. Estimate 91 days to clone and reconstruct." The old doctor sat in a chair beside the bed, looking oddly anachronistic as she squinted at readouts over cat-shaped bifocals. "Full re-load in 106 days." She smiled at him again, taking the glasses off her veined nose, exposing pressure marks from the frames. "You won't be disappointed, Terry."

Is this one a temp? Terian sent. *I don't remember it.*

"A temp," the woman said. "Yes." She smiled at him in a grandmotherly way. "Would you like the same personality structure as the body he killed? It is no trouble at all. I have the base characteristics loaded now."

What's available?

"This is a seer's body, so you have access to that biology and the requisite skills—"

Intelligence? Problem-solving? Can I boost them at all?

The doctor made a low clucking sound, a modulation of the sharper, more aggressive clicking common among seers.

"There are limits, Terry. You are fairly well dispersed right now."

I can't lose any of the others?

The old woman chuckled, even as she gave him a sharper look. "All are on assignment, *Mein Herr.* If you remember, you are using a significant amount of your problem-solving skills with body number nine already."

Terian frowned inside his mind, staring up at the ceiling.

He could see no solution, and it bothered him.

The doctor offered, "I can add creativity. A slight warning, however... it would be associated with a form of sociopathy that can be a bit unstable."

Terian didn't hesitate. *Do it,* he sent. If he could have moved his lips to smile, he would have. *And if he kills me again, I'll blame you this time, Xarethe.*

She smiled.

When she turned towards him, however, her eyes were empty of warmth.

"Whatever story keeps you hard at work, my fragmented little friend." Rising to her feet, she adjusted her glasses back on her nose, peering again at the machine. "I may have some words for you, at that, if you ruin another of my bodies so quickly."

She glanced down over the bifocals, giving him a harder stare.

"I will deny I said this," she said. "But do us all a favor, Terry. Kill that son of a bitch already. I am tired of this cat and mouse game with him."

Terian's lips twitched in humor.

I don't think that would go over well with the big boss. His face creased painfully with another attempt at a smile. *I would have liked to see you in your prime, Xarethe.*

The old seer looked at him.

For an instant, her eyes flash hard white, her lids falling to half-mast, making them appear even more reptilian.

No, she told him. *You wouldn't.*

CHAPTER 7
APOCALYPSE

I stand alone, on top of a high glass building overlooking a smoky city.

An angular, steel and glass structure reaches up on two legs from the edges of the skyline, barely visible through a veil of smog and smoke.

More skyscrapers reach up like jagged teeth, standing in rows like metal soldiers as far as I can see. A low building made of watery domes, bulging shades of blue-green and blue-white, like giant raindrops, crouches near the edge of an enormous park.

Already, lights are coming on, although the sun isn't yet above the horizon.

People emerge from apartment buildings and single-dwelling homes with briefcases and backpacks. Some jump on bicycles or mopeds, or patiently wait for buses and trains, drinking hot tea and reading feed marquees. The whisper of car horns grows audible as others crawl along a jam-packed freeway, fighting to get downtown.

I recognize this skyline. I've seen it on the feeds.

I search for landmarks, trying to identify it, when a booming sound erupts over the city, followed by a silence so profound my heart stops beating.

Wailing sirens start up.

They grind into the morning light.

Then I see them.

Trails of smoke follow bullet-like shapes over a curve of amber sky. I feel powerless. Worse than powerless.

I feel responsible.

I did this.

I have no idea how, or why, but I did this.

This is because of me.

The first bomb hits. Then another.

I hear the echo of concussions as they pelt the Earth, one by one.

I hear the scream of metal as it rips through steel, just before—

I JERKED AWAKE.

My face hurt from being ground into a wrinkle in the cloth seat. Drool connected my lips to the cushion until I raised my cuffed hands, wiping my mouth clumsily with the back of my hand.

I gazed through a dirty window.

Seeing the light pink of another pre-dawn sky, I felt my heart clench.

But I wasn't in that city anymore.

Here, pale blue sky rested above a row of two-story Craftsman homes.

Our car was the only one in the parking lot.

I glimpsed ocean through the trunks of trees on the other side of the road, on a street that sloped downwards, probably leading straight to the beach. A seagull sat on a dimming orange parking lot light, stabbing at something with its beak it held between its toes.

Next to me, he shifted position, drawing my eyes.

His long body stretched across the driver's seat, his head and neck cramped in the crack by the driver's side door. Despite the awkward angle of his body, he was asleep.

His face, even his hands lay open as he breathed.

I watched him sleep.

I remembered the gun he'd put to my head, the feelings I'd gotten off him in that diner, and nausea slid through my lower belly. Somehow, that feeling made everything worse. The sheer intensity of it caught me off guard. A sharp pain stabbed through my chest.

It felt disconcertingly intimate.

It also hurt like hell, and made my skin flush.

Fuck.

I rubbed the center of my chest. I frowned as I watched his face tighten.

He'd uncuffed me from the door somewhere around Crescent City.

That was right before we'd crossed over into Oregon. He stopped somewhere to siphon gas, probably to avoid the cameras required at all refueling stations. He'd also found us food, and me a toilet. I'd had to deal with him standing there while I used it, but at least he'd listened to me when I told him I needed one.

Afterwards, he left me cuffed, but not to the car.

He used a new plastic band for my ankles, killing my hope that he might leave my feet free, at least.

I continued to watch him sleep.

That pain-nausea feeling didn't go away.

It deepened in another slow wave, making my skin flush, my pulse come faster. The pain in my chest sharpened as I broke out in a sweat.

It rose over the next few seconds, crested.

Only then did it begin to recede.

I was just starting to relax, to breathe normally, when I felt a returning pull from him.

It slid stealthily into my awareness, a slow, sensual tugging below the navel that brought another flush of heat, an even denser wave of that discomfort. Shocked, I gripped my lower belly, then went back to rubbing the spot in the middle of my chest, my breath coming harder when he didn't stop whatever he was doing.

I was still watching his face as he shifted his weight uncomfortably, lowering a hand to rest on his thigh.

When that feeling didn't lessen, a soft sound left his throat.

I waited to see if he would wake.

When he didn't, I let out my held breath.

Forcing my mind off him, I bent forward, testing the binders on my ankles.

The hard plastic had already cut into my skin. I tugged on the ring anyway, feeling the connecting points for how to unlock the plastic knot. I fumbled with the end, realized a key fit in there, albeit a small one.

I opened the glove box, moving papers and the oil rag as quietly as I could, looking for something sharp. All I found was a broken pen that leaked ink, a used up book of matches and a condom so old the wrapper had cracked in the heat of the engine. I felt around under the seat, looking for anything that might saw through the thick plastic.

"Does it hurt?"

I jerked back.

My head slammed into the open glove box lid.

When I glanced up, rubbing my head, his pale eyes shone orange in the fading streetlights.

"Yes," I said, my voice openly cranky.

He didn't answer.

I watched him lean forward. He reached for his back pocket.

My eyes followed his hands as he pulled out a rectangular piece of featureless, black metal. He unfolded the blade housed inside. Before I could fully absorb the reality of the knife, he bent to my ankles.

Without warning, that pain and nausea leapt.

Holding the plastic off my skin, he cut through it with a single tug.

I was still reacting to the relief of that pressure being gone when he pulled off the hard coil, letting it drop to the floor of the car. Once he had, he traced the red line on my ankle with his finger. When he did, that dense feeling in my gut surged.

Jesus fucking Christ.

Whatever that feeling was, it made me want to grab a fistful of his hair.

Other images tried to insert themselves. The nausea feeling rose, even as my throat closed, my tongue thickened.

I forced my eyes off his downturned head.

I looked out the window, my jaw clenched.

"Is it all right?" His voice was gruff.

"Yeah." I drew my feet away from his fingers. "Thanks."

"I should have taken it off," he said.

"It's fine. Forget it."

I watched him look at me.

Studying his clear eyes, I couldn't help remembering what he was.

Even in early adolescence, one of the main things I'd heard about seers was that they had, well, *issues* with sex. We were cautioned about that even in school. They told us the males would rape or manipulate us into sleeping with them, that the females couldn't say no, no matter who asked. Supposedly, they didn't have sexual preferences.

I was told they would basically fuck anyone... or anything.

I guess I always figured it was b.s., a way to scare girls off the males at least.

Looking at him now, I wondered.

There was definitely something weird about him. If that was his sexuality I was feeling, it came with an added component of some kind.

Whatever that added component was, there seemed to be a lot of it.

Averting his eyes, he sank back to his seat.

After he refolded the knife and replaced it in his back pocket, he shoved his hand in his front pocket, extracting the keys.

"Did you sleep?" I said. "Or were you faking before?"

Ignoring me, he started the car, gunning it to blow out the exhaust. "Are you hungry?"

"Yeah," I said. "Can I call my mom?"

The look in his eyes flattened. "No."

He put the car in gear. The wheels crunched through gravel and garbage as he drove to the edge of the parking lot. We bumped over the low curb as he pulled onto the road.

"Where are we?" I asked.

"Washington."

I stared at him. "Washington? What the hell happened to Oregon?"

"You slept through Oregon. I took us to the main highway."

I gazed out at the gray-looking town, feeling my stomach start to cramp.

"Why?" I said finally.

"I'm more familiar with the cameras up here. And I wanted to make some time. There is a safe house in Seattle. I thought—"

"No," I said, looking at him. "Why can't I call my mother?"

His fingers tightened on the steering wheel.

"You must know of a safe way to make a call," I added. "You seem like you know these things." Remembering my dream, the fire-red mushroom clouds over the glass and steel structures, I swallowed. "Can't I call her just once? Tell her I'm alive?"

"No. The Rooks will have infiltrators with your people by now."

It took a few seconds for his words to penetrate.

Not seeming to notice my silence, he exhaled, clicking in a dull anger. "They will use them to gather imprints on you. To track you." He pointed to a sign with missing marquee letters. "I could get us food there. It's off the camera grid."

I stared at him.

My mind turned his words over in disbelief.

"You said they'd let them go," I said. "My brother. My mom. What do you mean the Rooks will be there? What does that mean for them? Are they safe?"

He focused on a field beside the road, a stretch of waving grasses dotted with wildflowers. Cows grazed there, in the early morning light.

"Revik!"

My tone jerked his eyes over.

His fingers tightened reflexively on the steering wheel.

"What does that mean?" I asked. "Are they going to hurt my mom? My friends?"

After a flat beat of time, he looked back towards the window. He glanced at me as he shifted the car into a higher gear.

"We will eat later."

He turned onto the ramp for Highway 5 North.

The Plymouth made a growling noise as he accelerated from the base of the hill.

In my defense, I didn't know I was going to do it.

I didn't plan it, which is probably why he didn't look over until I already had my fingers on the handle of the car door.

By the time he lunged, I was in mid-motion.

My weight followed with a hard lurch as my fingers snapped the latch.

His foot slipped on the clutch. He miscalculated where he aimed his hand as a result, snatching at the edge of my ripped shirt, getting the blanket instead. I slid off the seat and into cold, rushing air as the blanket unraveled around me…

There was a silence.

In it, I felt free, an odd rush of joy.

Then my body smashed inelegantly into the ground.

I hit, bounced, rolled, scraping arms and elbows and face as I tumbled down a rock and weed and garbage-strewn slope beneath the ramp.

My cuffed wrists smacked against my chest, then my face.

I finally used them to slow my fall. I dug the metal rings into the dirt as I slid on my stomach, my legs partly splayed.

Coughing gravel dust, I stumbled to my feet at the bottom. My ankles and knees hurt like hell. I didn't have a plan. But that dream mixed with the thought of my mother being surrounded by terrorist seers more or less made up my mind.

I had to turn myself in.

I had to.

Not only for my mom.

The dream still colored everything behind my eyes, even more than the image of my mother's face, or my brother's. On the faint chance Revik was right, I was better off being dissected in a lab somewhere than living with seers who wanted me to help them blow up the damned world.

I might not be a saint, but I wasn't about to go down in history as the greatest mass-murderer of all time.

I wouldn't be the next Syrimne.

I wouldn't.

I limped barefoot towards the main road.

I gritted my teeth as I reached the asphalt. I winced again as my feet landed on sharp rocks and small shards of glass.

On the ramp above, the GTX had come squealing to a stop.

I glanced backwards right as another car slammed into it from behind, knocking it further into the middle of the ramp. Cars careened in angled stops, making a rough line behind the first, and promptly began to honk.

Revik got out.

Ignoring the other drivers, he walked to the edge of the ramp and looked down the slope at me. A young guy in a stained shirt and cap got out of a rusted pickup and started walking towards the Plymouth.

"He's a seer!" I screamed, pointing at Revik. "He kidnapped me!"

I didn't do it to get him caught.

I knew he wouldn't get caught.

After what I'd seen him do with his mind already, I doubted anyone could catch him.

Well, not unless SCARB got here a *hell* of a lot faster than I thought they would.

My goal wasn't to get him locked up; I wanted him to run away. I wanted him to climb back in the GTX and leave me there.

He didn't, though.

He stared down at me, his long form making a black silhouette against the sky.

The guy in the baseball cap looked at me, then at Revik. His voice rose in excitement. "Call the cops, someone! Terrorist! *Bona fide* terrorist here!"

Revik turned his head.

The guy with the stained baseball cap stopped in his tracks.

His face went into a childlike slump.

After the barest pause, he turned around and shuffle-walked back to his truck. He climbed into the cab and sat there without moving. The two other people who'd gotten out of their cars also returned to them.

Come back to me, Alyson. Immediately.

His mental command jerked my eyes up and back.

I felt my breath stop.

I fought the compulsion there, the power I felt behind it.

"Just go!" I shouted the words up at him. "Just go! *Go!* They won't catch you if you leave now. I *have* to do this."

His mental voice rose in a cold snarl.

You would give yourself over so easily to the dark? His pale, glass-like eyes locked on mine. *You're so willing to become a pawn of the Rooks? Do you know how many have died, Alyson, to keep you from that fate?*

He was angry.

Really damned angry.

My throat constricted as I took in the expression on his face. I hadn't been afraid of him before. I probably should have been, but I hadn't been. I was genuinely afraid of what I felt off him now, even as my physical vision slanted out.

"I never asked anyone to do that!" I yelled. "I never asked for this!"

Do you think any of us ask for our fate?

"I CAN'T LEAVE THEM!" I shouted.

His mental voice came through harsh, unfiltered.

You don't have the luxury of being this selfish, he sent. *And you cannot save them. Not like this. The Rooks would only use your family more viciously. They'd use them to force you to cooperate. They would torture them until you obeyed. Then, once they had broken you completely, they would make you kill them with your own hands. It is how they train seers. I know this. I have seen it, Allie.*

His mental voice grew colder.

I have done it.

I shook my head, feeling my own anger rise.

Something in those words echoed in my mind though, making me doubt suddenly, what I'd been about to do. When I looked up the hill, I saw Revik coming after me, taking long strides through the sliding shale covering the slope.

I felt myself wavering, trying to decide what to do, when—

Everything around me disappeared.

CHAPTER 8

BARRIER

Darkness descended.

I see Revik through that darkness, flickering in and out, outlined in pale sky, shadowy and lean at the rise in the road, then stark in the negative, a brilliant light against indigo clouds. Gold and red sparks meet and pool through lines that make up his arms and chest.

I know I'm in that place he calls the Barrier, even as I take in his sharp, structured form.

I have barely wrapped my mind around this, when…

His arm surges with a fire-like light.

The light brightens, turns blinding, right before it leaves his fingers.

Before I can question what it might mean, the starburst spins down upon me, aiming straight for my chest. I don't think, don't form a single conscious thought.

Instead, I step aside, even as a part of me reaches up, takes the fire-like ball and sling-shots it back at him in one smooth, reflexive motion.

I realize what I've done.

I watch, bewildered.

It's going to hit him, I think.

I have no idea what it will do to him. Just before the fiery burst touches his outline, a white density of light materializes around him.

The starburst hits the shield, glances off and dissipates.

It all happens so fast.

When it's over, I feel something off him.

Surprise, yes—but another feeling follows close behind.

It's not quite pleasure, but a sharp flicker of interest, like a part of him wakes up.

The predator raises its head.

He focuses on me intently, like a wolf meeting its own kind.

I see him in the physical again. His pale, light-filled eyes are watching me, and I see the predatory stare there, too.

"Hey!" I hold up a hand. "You threw it at me! You fucking *started* it!"

He starts walking faster down the hill.

I feel my anger build as I watch him. It slides through me as sharp waves of heat. I watch him walk, and I want to hit him back, for real that time. I want to do what he tried to do to me. I want to throw one of those fucking balls of sparking, electric light.

I want to do it without warning him, the same chickenshit way he did to me.

Asshole.

That predator's interest flares in him again when he feels my anger.

That time, I feel him deliberately rein his instincts in.

His stride lengthens, and he is coming towards me faster now.

You are not going to get the outcome you desire, doing this. His light flashed back to gold, exuding reassurance. *If you give yourself to the Rooks, you will kill countless more people, Alyson. You will do exponentially more harm. More than you ever could under the elders of your kind. The elders love peace, Esteemed Bridge. Not war. They are not like me. They are not killers.*

He is still walking when he adds,

I apologize for this, Esteemed Bridge. This is my fault. I told you too much. I am not qualified to talk to you about your role here. The elders should do this, and I am tasked to bring you to them. Walk to me, Allie. I will take you to people who can help you understand. Then, with full knowledge of your options, you can decide what part you wish to play in this.

I backed up to each of his steps, but I was doubting myself for real now.

I believed him.

I believed what he was saying.

Come to me, Allie. He held out a hand. *Please, Allie. Let me take you to your people.*

He came to an abrupt stop, mid-step.

His expression grew taut.

His head cocked, as if he listened to some far off voice.

When he focused back on me, the predator was completely gone.

Allie, I am not playing anymore! Come to me, now! There is no time!

The fear in his words disarmed me.

Making up my mind, I started to walk towards him, then to run, even as another negative image of him inside the Barrier fills my vision.

I stumbled, stubbed my toe on a rock.

I caught myself before I could fall.

Then I was running for real.

My limbs moved muddily but I forced them faster. Sickness rose in my gut as his light reached for mine. He was trying to dim my light now, to make me less visible, to hide me. I felt the good intention behind it, I knew he wasn't trying to hurt me. Even so, I felt a whisper of fear as his light slid into some part of me I can't see.

I made it to the road.

The scene around me vanished again.

Blind, I fought to manage my limbs, couldn't.

Out of nowhere, a hard thud collided with the meat and bone of my physical body. Pain rocketed up my leg, pooled in the point of contact.

The pain brought me abruptly back to my body.

My eyes snapped open.

The Barrier is gone.

I find myself staring into the chrome grill of a car, on my knees, holding my stomach. Nearby, a car door opened, and the sound is so loud it deafens me. I stared at the dotted dividing lines in the road, garnished with yellow reflectors.

"Get out of the road!" a man yelled at me. "Are you crazy, girl? Trying to kill yourself?"

Fear lurched me back to my feet.

The light must have changed. The road was full of cars now.

My knees were bleeding but dread eclipsed all of it. I could feel it somehow, even as the throbbing in my temples worsened.

Something bad was coming.

Whatever it was, it was coming fast.

It was almost here.

I pushed past the old man with the angry face and bushy eyebrows, seeing his expression change as he took in my appearance, my hair matted with blood and dirt, my cut feet and hands, the ripped up waitress uniform and handcuffs.

"Girl." He called after me. "Hey… girl! Are you all right? Where are you going?"

I didn't look back.

I looked only at Revik now.

He'd reached the bottom of the hill.

He slid down the last of it on leather boots through dusty gravel and broken glass. I ran towards him, feeling each bare foot hit hard at the pavement. I darted into traffic, and again cars honked, swerving to avoid me.

I slammed into the bumper of a red compact and it screeched to a stop.

The woman inside stared up at me, wide-eyed.

I ran on. People on the sidewalk reacted slowly, staring as they realized something unusual was happening, something they probably shouldn't ignore.

Then, right when I began to think I was going to make it, something took me down.

REVIK WATCHED HER FROM THE BARRIER. HE WILLED HER TO RUN FASTER.

He has totally fucked up.

He frightened her, broke her trust with his honesty about the Rooks, or at least his refusal to lie. He confused her with his clumsy explanations on what it means to be the Bridge.

He is glad he chose to tell her less, rather than more, about Terian, and about what the Rooks truly are.

He does his best to shield her light, to keep her in her body, out of the Barrier.

When she runs into the street, he sees interest dawn on the faces of watching humans.

It is too many for him to push.

Worse, her light sparks in panicked waves that remind him that she is the Bridge, not just some fledgling seer with poor light control.

When she is hit by the first car, he starts after her, his heart in his throat.

He splits his consciousness, leaving a lesser part to steer his physical body.

He jumps the rest out.

A silver-white cloud descends over both of them.

A darting, lightning-like bolt comes out of it, aimed at her.

It knocks her completely out of her physical body.

Right in front of a speeding truck.

No! he yells at her through that space.

She can no longer hear him.

She collapses in the middle of the road, even as the truck heads her way.

HE THREW HIMSELF IN FRONT OF HER, BETWEEN HER AND THE VEHICLE.

The driver saw him and then her and slammed on the truck's brakes, careening cab and cargo to a slanted halt a few feet from them both.

By then, Revik crouched over Allie, arms outstretched, protecting her, his eyes glowing a pale white the human wouldn't see.

The driver leaned his bulky form out the driver's side window.

"Hey! Wiseass! Get your damned girlfriend out of the road, unless you want to scrape her off the pavement with a spatula!" He paused, looking down. "And put some clothes on her, while you're at it! What the hell do you think you're doing, with the…"

Trailing, he took in Allie's crumpled form.

Her handcuffed wrists had welts from two days of driving, made worse by her fall down the hill. Her small hands folded together in a neat gesture of prayer. The ripped-up uniform with its low-cut blouse and short skirt was now decorated with splotches of blood and caked in dirt, as were her hair and feet. She had a bloody nose from hitting the pavement, fresh cuts and scratches from the fall, and she looked pale and overly thin without her light.

He looked at her, took it all in.

It hit Revik that she looked bad.

Really bad.

He was struck again by how small she was physically.

She moaned. He felt her regaining consciousness slowly. His body reacted from the sound, enough that he had separation pain to deal with on top of everything else.

Gaos. The way he reacted to her… it was unnerving as hell.

"Help me," she murmured. "Help."

It wasn't loud, but Revik heard it.

He saw the truck driver watching her moving lips. The man's eyes widened, as he seemed to put two and two together.

"What in the holy hell—"

"Police!" Revik pulled a flip ID with badge from his pocket, miraged it into a local configuration from memory. "Stay in your vehicle! This woman is in my custody!"

Revik felt the worst of his tension dissipate as the man's face calmed.

He had blundered, but he'd contained it.

He could still get her back to the car.

He felt other humans around him start to relax as well, as soon as they saw the badge and heard his words. She'd gone from fleeing kidnap victim to suspect fleeing police custody.

Even so, Revik knew he didn't have a lot of time. He shoved the ID back in his jacket pocket and bent his knees, crouching down beside her.

When he glanced up next, the truck driver's eyes looked utterly blank.

Something about the expression there made Revik pause.

Then Revik saw the man's eyes roll up in his head.

His irises flashed with a silver light.

Fuck.

Revik looked at Allie.

He shoved his arms under her jointed limbs, lifted her to his chest. As he straightened to his full height, he saw the truck driver reach behind him. He glimpsed the wooden stock of a worn, pump-action shotgun.

Seeing that much, Revik didn't wait.

He gripped her tightly and ran, flat-out for the car.

CHAPTER 9
ROOK

Revik sprinted down the sidewalk, holding me against his chest.

Unerringly rhythmic, his feet impacted the sidewalk as if he counted steps alongside his breaths. He held me close, and that felt calculated too, as if he knew exactly how to hold me so I would slow him down the least.

When he reached the gravel-strewn hillside, he vaulted up the steep bank, sliding in its shale folds. He didn't stop once as he fought his way upwards.

I felt sick, dazed, useless to him.

Images around me flashed in negative, then back to positive.

In the dark, silver threads shone like bright wires in rose-lit clouds. Tarnished silver entangled the lights of people all around us on the sleepy Washington street.

Laughter brought my gaze higher.

A face hovered below a bright silver Pyramid.

I recognized it as a ghostly version of the auburn-haired man from the diner. His handsome face morphed in Barrier winds, distorted by silver light. There is symmetry to those flickers of light, like film stuttering in a projector. The Pyramid's shifting cells split and reconfigure, moving on gliding rails.

The crushing weight of the silver light suffocates me.

I see you! Pretty bird! Do you know who carries you on such swift wings?

My chest clenched.

My mother calls me her bird. She has since I was a kid.

I felt Revik again, his arms around me, the steady beating in his chest.

No one has ever felt so much like me.

Terian's laugh rose higher. *I could tell you such stories about your new friend! Do you know what he used to like to do for fun?*

Images started to coalesce in my mind, movies that began as soon as I focused directly on them. They draw me in, until I cannot help but look. I feel Revik there, and know part of my fascination comes from him.

He and Terian stand in a cell-like, windowless room.

On the floor sprawls a young girl with blond hair and inhuman, gold eyes, a beautiful face and Revik is watching her, his own eyes hard, calculating.

The predator is there, but here, he lives in silver light.

A jarring contact met my head and back.

I groaned. My breath escaped in a rough gasp.

Pain brought the physical world back into focus.

Staring down at me is Revik's sweaty face.

His eyes are still glass shards, but the silver light is gone. The predator is gone, too. Fear lives there instead, faint but visible.

I understood suddenly, where we were.

He'd set me roughly on the hood of the GTX.

My back hit the protruding air vent on top, snapping me out, hard enough that I wondered if he'd done it on purpose.

Either way, the pain yanked me away from Terian's mind.

I struggled to sit up as Revik walked to the rear of the car, opening the trunk with the keys and pulling out a black gym bag filled with something heavy. He reached inside the driver's side window to unlock the door.

"Allie!" he said, jerking it open. "Now!"

I rolled over the top of the hood to the passenger side while he leaned over and opened my door from the inside. By the time I got in, he was ripping open the black nylon bag.

The line of cars behind us had resumed honking.

I watched Revik jam the key into the ignition, holding a gun against the steering wheel.

"Put on your seat belt!" he said.

I fumbled with the strap as the GTX's engine rumbled to life.

I couldn't quite work the seat belt with the handcuffs.

Revik put the car in gear. A voice emerged above the sound of the car's motor. It took me a second to realize it was real.

It wasn't his, or something from inside the Barrier.

"What in the name of Mary's tits..."

Jerking my head around, I forgot the seat belt and crouched down, looking past Revik and through the driver's side window. Two cops stood there. Behind them, a black and white slanted down the bank beside the fisherman's truck.

The cop who'd spoken stared at the gun in Revik's hand.

"You got balls, buddy," the second cop said, unholstering his sidearm. He raised the gun, aiming it at Revik's face. "Toss it out the window. Real slow."

"Sleep," Revik said. "Now."

Both cops collapsed on the on-ramp without emitting a sound.

I sucked in a breath, shocked at the clean indifference of the act.

I didn't have time to think about that, either.

In the rearview mirror, I caught movement in the space by the fisherman's truck. I turned my head right as another policeman emerged.

My voice burst out of me.

"Revik!" I yelled.

The third cop pulled his sidearm.

I saw the brown eyes flash silver as he raised the gun.

"Seer!" I yelled.

"I know," Revik growled.

His hand clamped roughly around the back of my neck, forcing me down past the bottom of the seat and under the windows. He took his foot off the brake in the same instant and the car lurched forward as the cop squeezed off his first round.

The sound of the shot seemed to come late, a second after the soft plink as the bullet went through the rear driver's side window. I turned my head, staring at the hole in the upholstery until Revik shoved me down even further on the seat.

I crouched on the mat when I heard the GTX's engine roar back to life.

Revik threw the car into reverse, slamming into the truck behind us.

He aimed the handgun, fired at cop number three.

The sound of the gun filled the car, making me wince. He hit the cop in the chest on the second shot. It knocked him backwards into the police car so that the man's arm and shoulder broke the passenger side window.

The cop's partner emerged. He fired wildly, his red face contorted in a furious mask.

Screams erupted on the street below.

I peered over the edge of the window. I watched people run in fear, eyes wide, and for a moment, I saw them through Revik's eyes, a flock of birds scattering. Revik swiveled the gun towards the fourth cop. He narrowly missed the man's head.

I felt him go deeper into the Barrier, and that time, either I am too close to him with my mind, or something else drags me in right along after him.

REVIK HEARS TERIAN'S LAUGHTER.

He hears it before he locates him among the crowd of glowing bodies.

I feel his attention shift before it occurs to me I'm in the Barrier with him.

I'm also halfway inside his mind.

Terian throws a clusterfuck of silver, spinning lights at Revik's head, a Barrier structure that makes the orange sleeper Revik lobbed at me earlier look like a blown kiss. Revik makes his energy flush with the background and disappears, something he can do even with a part of himself operating on the ground.

He melts sideways and reappears, too late for Terian to redirect.

The silver spinners disappear into the empty nothingness of Barrier space.

I'll kill her, Revik tells Terian.

No, Terian says. *You won't. That's the beauty with you, Dehgoies. By the end of this, we will have not only her, but you as well. You're a half-step from falling willingly, my friend. We can be brothers again.*

Revik focuses on me.

He knows I am with him, somehow, but he can't see me here.

You will help us train her, Terian says to him. *Breaking in newbies was a particular talent of yours, as I recall. Especially the females.*

Terian sees Revik starting to withdraw and calls after him.

I will let you have her, my brother!

In that heartbeat of Revik's hesitation, Terian lobs another cluster, this time of images, sensations. In it, Revik sees my body under his, our lights merged. He feels me as I open to him. That pain I felt in the parking lot worsens exponentially, for both of us.

It grows unbearable as he imagines himself inside me.

He imagines me wanting him there.

It is a mirage—the whole thing is a lie—but it catches both of us off-guard and briefly, he is forced to untangle it.

He snaps the connection and is met with another liquid surge of... *separation pain,* he calls it... that dense pain and nausea I've been feeling with him. Whatever it is, whatever it means, it makes me want to touch him. Everything about that pain makes me *really* want to touch him, and it's worse now.

All of it is worse, and not only for him.

Gaos. Stop. Fucking stop.

Unlike with me, the feeling is familiar to him.

It is something he understands.

It bothers him, though. It bothers him that he should feel it with me. He shouldn't, he thinks. The realization that he does, even after all this time, angers him. It creates a resonance with some younger version of himself, a place and time he wishes to forget.

That anger briefly suffuses his light, until he replaces it with reason.

He simply let it go too long, he thinks.

He will remedy that, in Seattle.

At the thought, heat flushes his belly, a flicker of sensual memory. I glimpse bare skin, a seductive smile. That time, it has nothing to do with me.

The Rook laughs. *You lie, Revi'! I know you... even if your clan friends do not! I see how empty this new life of yours is!* Terian's smile turns friendly, and Revik recognizes that too. *You can do better than unwillings, my brother. Or have you forgotten?*

I feel the part of Revik that succumbs to the pull.

Memories war there.

A place and time when Terian was his friend.

She will be my gift to you! the Rook calls out. *Do you think your clan elders would offer you such a prize? Access to their precious Bridge? Do you, Revi'?*

There is only the barest pause.

When it ends, Revik makes his light disappear, but Terian's laughter follows him out of their connection.

I saw you thinking about it, my brother! I saw you!

The clouds fade as Revik wills himself back.

Back to the car.

Back to me.

I SAW HIM COME OUT OF IT.

Crouched on the floorboards of the GTX, I watched him warily, wondering how much of what I'd just witnessed really happened.

My handcuffed wrists rested on the seat in front of me.

I watched his face as he fired the gun out the window, his light focused on his targets. I heard the crash of breaking glass, felt him hit something he'd aimed for.

I wondered why he wasn't driving away.

Even as I thought it, he slammed his foot on the gas.

His hand holding the gun fell to the manual gear shift.

Once more, his eyes phased, but it was gone as soon as I saw it, leaving only a tension around his eyes, a quick glance at me. The GTX leapt forward, throwing me into the edge of the seat. I heard more shots and peered back through the rear window.

I glimpsed the cop in the road, firing steadily at us.

"Get your head down!" Revik barked.

Before I could react, he caught hold of the chains between the handcuffs, yanking me down forcibly. I crawled back below the seat to the floor.

"Was that Terian?" I looked up at him, panting. "The guy from the diner?"

Revik gave me the barest glance.

"Yes," he said.

"How is he alive? How the *fuck* is he alive?"

Revik jerked the wheel sideways. The tires thumped up over a curb, bounding me high enough to pass the armrest.

"Put on your fucking seat belt!" he snapped.

"I can either stay down or wear a seat belt… pick one!"

He didn't answer.

When I realized I didn't hear any more gunshots, I slid carefully back up the seat, peering out over the dashboard past the plastic statue of the saint.

Still holding the gun, Revik gripped the steering wheel with his other hand, edging it hard and soft as he maneuvered us across a pit of gravel towards a field that stood between us and the freeway. I looked back at the onramp.

He'd bumped us over the curb to avoid the line of police cars heading for us on the frontage road beside the freeway entrance.

Slamming his foot on the gas once he cleared the gravel, he bounced us across a weed-choked stretch of grass dotted with broken bottles, plastic bags and scrub brush. I glanced at the speedometer, saw it edging towards sixty, then glimpsed a large rock and cried out, but Revik already jerked the wheel to clear it, jumping us into oncoming traffic.

"Jesus! Revik—"

"There are things I haven't told you," he said, over the screech of tires as he straightened the car out from a skid. For the barest instant, his eyes glinted silver. "About me. About Terian."

I swallowed as his eyes faded back to clear.

"Is he here?" I said. "In the physical?"

Revik barely looked at me. "No."

I glanced over as he wiped his nose. I didn't notice the blood until his fingers came away covered in it.

"What happened?" I said. "What's wrong with you?"

"Nothing. I'm losing light." Reaching into his pocket, he dug something out and tossed it at me. Small and bright, it landed on my lap. It was a key.

"I'm not chasing you anymore," he said.

I snatched the key off my leg just before he swerved again.

Revik rammed the GTX over the path of an eighteen-wheeler, sliding past as the driver honked angrily, laying on the horn.

I unlocked the cuffs from around my wrists, dropping them to the floor.

"Thanks," I said.

He nodded curtly.

He didn't look over.

CHAPTER 10
MORTAL PERIL

My seat jerked sideways when something crashed into us without warning.

I heard a loud screech of metal grating on metal.

I glanced out my window and flinched back, seeing a truck driver in a blue flannel shirt staring at me, a shotgun resting in the crook of his arm. His eyes looked manic, not quite at home, and I sensed more than saw the silver flicker of light that lived there.

He aimed the shotgun down at the hood of the GTX.

Before I could make a sound, Revik hit the brakes.

His sudden stop slammed us abruptly into the car behind us, making me cry out. He created enough space to slide the GTX behind the bigger rig, pulling us out of range of the crazy guy with the shotgun.

Taking a breath, I gripped the armrest under the side window. I stared at the blurring trees, half in disbelief at the view out the windshield.

He spoke up as he weaved between cars.

"We don't have much time," he said. "There's a safe house in Seattle, but if we lead them there, it won't do us much good." Clenching his jaw, he glanced at me. "Any ideas?"

I gripped the dashboard, not looking at him.

"Do *I* have any ideas? Don't you have a contingency in place for this kind of thing? Someone you can call?"

He gave me a grim look. "You would not like the contingency, Allie."

Before I could respond, he swerved again.

He caused another car to slam its brakes too hard.

I glanced back as it swerved off the road.

I watched through the rear window as that same car veered into a metal guard rail past the gravel shoulder, stopping so violently, the rear of the car rose in the air. I looked to my right, saw the truck driver pacing us from a few lanes over. The driver glared at us, now from the other side of the cab. I couldn't help wondering if he'd wake up tomorrow and wonder what the hell he'd been doing, shooting at two total strangers.

Or maybe he simply wouldn't remember any of it.

"I am keeping them out of your light," Revik said, loud over the wind from the broken windows. "If something happens to me, they will try to take over your *aleimi,* Allie. You won't have much time." He gave me a hard stare. I realized his nose was bleeding again. "If I pass out, hit me. Hit me hard… as hard as you can. Pain can sometimes snap us out. If the body perceives itself in mortal danger, the light will return."

I stared at him, bewildered.

I was still watching his profile when he wrenched the wheel.

He swerved into the shoulder briefly to get around a pickup truck, then aimed us back at the center lane. Once we hit a relatively open patch of road, he jammed his foot on the gas, and the car leapt forward.

I didn't look at the speedometer.

"Your presence here complicates things for both sides," he went on, his voice loud. "The leader of the Rooks is a being called Galaith. He is *obsessed* with collecting sight skills. I know him. Your being telekinetic will change everything for him. He will move any mountain… do anything in his power to bring you in alive, Alyson. He will kill anyone who gets in his way. You cannot let that happen, Esteemed Bridge. No matter what happens to me—"

I shouted over the engine and rushing wind.

"Shut up and drive, Revik!"

The GTX swerved around another cluster of cars.

I smacked my head against the passenger window, bit my tongue against the pain. We were back in the left lane.

"Hold the wheel," Revik said.

"What?"

He turned to look at me…

…and his eyes are pure silver, a hard metallic sheen of light.

Inside, pictures flicker in an organic projector, a war happened and happening and about to happen in shadows and exploding lights. I see vultures around his head, raptors…

His eyes clicked into focus.

They were crystal again, clear like glass.

I could see *him* in them again.

He looked at me, briefly, then turned away, coughing.

Blood speckled the glass of the driver's side window. He wiped his mouth, but when I started to ask him if he was okay, he grabbed my wrist.

"I need you to drive," he said.

He was already moving out from behind the wheel.

Gripping the steering wheel, I considered protesting, but realized it was too late.

He was crawling into the passenger seat to my right, pushing me into the driver's to take his place. I slid over and jammed my foot down on the gas in a kind of panic. I was barely situated when I saw him lean over into the back seat.

He retrieved the black gym bag.

He placed it on the floor between his legs.

Watching him, I perched on the edge of the driver's seat to compensate for his long legs, wrestling back control of the car.

Only when I had it going straight did I fumble for the knob to move the chair forward.

I forgot about both things when a booming sound vibrated the sides of the car.

I ducked. I felt nicks and cuts from shards of glass. I turned my head, looked at the ragged hole punched through a rear side window.

The trucker accelerated from a few lanes over, leaning out of his cab.

Revik opened the black gym bag. He pulled out a shotgun that looked like law-enforcement issue. He dug around the bottom of the bag for a box of shells. Cracking the cardboard open one-handed once he found it, he dumped a pile in his lap, then began methodically loading the Remington 870 with deft fingers.

He paused, giving me a quizzical look.

"How do you know that?" he said. "About the gun."

I looked at him, blank, then at the gun. "Old boyfriend." When Revik went back to loading, I said, "What are you going to do? You can't just shoot them all."

He continued loading the gun.

He didn't answer me at first.

Once he'd fitted the last shell, he glanced at me again. His voice went flat. "You have the right to lodge a formal complaint regarding my methods with the Council once we arrive. They will hear you, and with a great deal of sympathy, I assure you. But reminding me of the damage I'm doing to my soul won't help either of us *right now,* Allie."

I stared at him uncomprehendingly.

I saw no hint of sarcasm in his expression.

When he seemed to be expecting a response, I could only nod.

"Okay. Sure."

He chambered the first shell with a smooth jerk of his hand, then leaned out the window. I watched in the mirror as he aimed at the truck. He fired the instant he'd leveled the barrel.

The truck swerved and his shot went wide.

Revik aimed again.

He hit the grill that time.

The truck swerved behind another 18-wheeler.

Revik sat back, his pale eyes locked on the mirrors. I heard a bleep of loudspeaker and turned, saw a Washington State police car pull up alongside us.

Inside, a red-faced officer leaned back stiffly in his seat, driving and glaring at us while his partner aimed a shotgun at Revik.

"Pull over!" the driver yelled. "Right now!"

I caught the barest whisper of Revik's thoughts.

We are not the criminals. It is them. Help us.

The cop driving glanced at his partner.

Confusion softened both of their faces.

We are in danger. Protect us. Please.

The officer nodded to Revik, indicating the highway ahead. He shouted, "...Go on. We'll take care of this, sir."

Thank you, officer.

The driver tapped his brakes, picking up the police radio mouthpiece and speaking into it as the car fell dramatically behind.

I looked at Revik, dumbfounded.

"Go faster," he said. "They will do the same to us."

I muttered something about free will, hammering my foot down on the gas. My fingers whitened as the scenery started to blur.

Revik shrugged in answer to a question I hadn't asked.

"I thought you would prefer that to my killing the driver," he muttered.

I followed the direction of his eyes through the rear-view mirror. I saw the vibrating reflection of the cop car slow beside the truck's cab, right before I heard the same blare of loudspeaker and warning tap of siren.

A second later, Revik turned to me.

"It is done. Faster, Allie."

The Washington cops' siren blared back into life.

I already had the pedal down hard. Now I pressed it to the floor, feeling my chest constrict as the GTX leapt forward. We were definitely past my comfort zone in terms of my ability to navigate at high speeds. I was on the verge of being out of control when I felt Revik with me in the Barrier.

I felt him directing my hands. I resisted at first—

Let me. You will learn.

A grid appeared over the landscape and road, a maze of bright lines that overlaid the scenery and cars. The grid showed me how the drivers interacted with one another and the light of the Barrier. I could almost see what each driver would do—

Another blast hit the back of the car.

My eyes snapped to focus.

Revik's mind left mine.

He leaned out the window, propping the stock against his shoulder and firing. The sound boomed inside the car, deafening, right before I saw the cop car swerve to avoid being hit. The black hood erupted in smoke after Revik's third shot penetrated the engine block.

The police car swerved again, then rolled.

I heard a squeal of tires, a sound like an explosion, but the crash sounds were rapidly receding. I swallowed back bile.

He was right. There was no time to be squeamish.

I had to focus.

A shot hit the back of the car with a loud plink and groan of metal. Revik leaned out again, returning fire.

His mind felt closed to me now.

I stared out the windshield at the thickening traffic.

We were getting closer to the city. This was going to get harder.

I couldn't think about that, either. I could only focus on two things: getting us past the line of cars and not crashing from the speed.

I barely noticed the second police car pull up alongside us.

I glanced over in time to see the officer in the driver's seat reach for his sidearm. I sucked in a breath, ready to duck, but the man unholstered his weapon and held it out to Revik through the window, the handle pointed towards us.

I worried Revik had told him to shoot himself, but…

…the gun simply left the officer's fingers.

It clattered to the road, bouncing behind us.

"Watch the road!" Revik snapped, glaring at me. "*I* am doing this! You drive!"

I turned back to the windshield.

But his anger had allowed me to feel him again, at least in part.

The gun was as far as he would get with that particular human; the Rooks already had control over the cop's mind. The knowing of that fact reflected a bitterness in Revik that surprised me.

…bastard's doing it on purpose, forcing me to kill as many as he can.

When he looked at me next, anger still hardened his features.

Swallowing, I nodded, trying to let him see that I understood.

WE WERE APPROACHING SEATTLE.

I glimpsed the familiar skyline to my left, then flashes of nearer buildings through a maze of overpasses dripping with dark green plants.

I recognized landmarks from being here with Jon, but couldn't read signs with how fast we were going. Anyway, slowing down wasn't an option, much less taking one of the off-ramps. I'd stopped looking at the speedometer by then altogether.

Revik was doing something in that other place.

For the same reason, I couldn't ask for his help, or use his grid thing.

I saw people point and stare at us from the other cars as we passed. I saw other vehicles hitting their turn signals and pulling over, moving out of the way of the line of cop cars screaming behind us, clearing the freeway for the chase.

I felt it when yet another cop's mind ceased to be a pull toy between Revik and whoever else.

I felt Revik let go just before the cop accelerated, coming up on us blaring light and sound from his overhead siren. I glanced over in time to see the dark-skinned cop smile at Revik, making an odd flowing up and down gesture with one hand that had the flavor of a taunt.

Whatever that gesture meant, it definitely didn't look human.

Then, whatever held the cop's body let go, leaving the cop sweaty-faced, determined, and completely focused on the two of us. From his eyes, he fully believed we'd killed his whole family with baseball bats then lit his house on fire.

Revik turned to me, his pale eyes hard.

"Stop the car," he growled.

I thought I'd heard him wrong. "What?"

Behind him, I saw the Seattle cop raise a shotgun.

Before I could react, Revik grabbed the wheel, jerking it sideways to slam into the cruiser. The cop dropped the shotgun, and I heard his partner yelling excitedly.

"Revik, Jesus! What are you—"

"Take that exit! Now, Allie!"

He pointed and I veered, braking to slide across lanes.

I saw the truck driver in the blue flannel shirt, who was, amazingly, still behind us.

He saw me, too.

He saw me head for the exit and began the turn to follow.

I glimpsed faces as other, noninvolved drivers reacted. Their eyes widened in fear as they tried to get out of my way. By some miracle, I slid behind the Washington cop car, in front of a different trucker who honked madly at us.

Then we were past.

I winced from the final scrape of metal as the GTX grazed his grill.

Revik leaned out the window.

Now he fired at the Seattle cop from behind.

He blew out a rear tire with the first shot, smashed the back window with his second. He chambered another round and aimed again, blocking my side view when he climbed up to sit on the passenger side window.

The Seattle cop cut across multiple lanes and again I felt the difference; it was no longer a human driving, but one of those things with lightning-fast reflexes and 360 degree vision. I was forced to brake. I saw Revik clutch the window frame as he lost his balance.

The Seattle cop swerved, just making it onto the exit off-ramp behind us.

A sign flashed by, too fast for me to read clearly.

I glimpsed white words spelling "Mercer Island."

Revik slid back in through the window. He landed heavily on the seat. When I looked over, his shoulder was bleeding again. A dark, spreading stain grew under his shirt.

"You are trained in basic firearms use?" he said.

"Right," I said, loud over the wind and engine. "Dad taught me to shoot cans. I'm practically Special Forces."

"Good." He propped the gun up on the seat between us. "Use it if they get too close." He added, "Or if I don't come back."

"What? Revik, that's not funny, I—"

His body slumped against the seat.

I cursed, swerved into a guardrail, and the GTX threw up sparks as metal grated metal. I gripped Revik's bare arm, digging in my nails, hard enough to bruise his skin. I shook him, then wondered if I should hit him, like he'd told me to before.

"Revik! You've got to be kidding me! REVIK!"

Something smashed into the back of the car.

We were merging into the main sprawl of traffic on the new highway. The truck driver with the blue flannel shirt was in the next lane over. Pulling up alongside the GTX, he aimed the pump-action shotgun out his window.

I hit the brakes like Revik had done, and another cop car hit us from behind. That same police cruiser forced me along until I accelerated.

Then the guy was honking, waving at me to pull over.

A rush of panic made me wonder what would happen if I did.

Even as I thought it, the first Seattle cop drew up next to me on my other side.

...and for an instant, I see him.

A metal thread cage ensnares his light. Behind his eyes breathe the orbs of the Rook controlling him. They shine coal red, and he makes his thumb and index finger into the shape of a gun, pointing it at me as his lips stretch in a corpse's smile.

Bang, bang, little girl.

I snapped out. I still, miraculously, gripped the steering wheel.

But I feel them in me now. They drag at me and I shriek, as if the sound of my own voice might keep me in my body.

But I can feel myself separating out, losing control of my limbs.

Lowering my head, I bite down on my fingers. My teeth clamp on skin and bone and my light rushes in like a rubber band snapping back.

Pain came with the light.

Clarity, too.

I un-clamped my jaw from the red crescent on my knuckles. Blood dripped over the steering wheel once I'd extracted my teeth, but all I could feel was relief.

Just then, everything went dark.

We'd entered a tunnel.

My foot mashed down harder on the accelerator.

Orange lights streaked by in irregular lines as cars cast shadows on tile walls. Surrender no longer felt like a good idea. The Seattle cop's eyes flash red a second time, and I realize I am still inside the Barrier, just enough that they are all around me.

I slam my head against the driver's side window, hard enough to crack it.

My head leaves an impact mark surrounded by spider web lines.

I'm starting to lose it. I feel sick, anemic—like my blood is being leached out of me as they pull on me.

I keep my foot jammed on the accelerator as I lean over and snatch at Revik's seat belt.

I miss it the first time, grab for it again.

That time, I manage to hook it with my fingers.

A car slams the GTX from behind, and I lose the silver buckle, curse.

The third time, I dragged the nylon belt over his body and hooked it into the clasp at his side. His skin glistened with sweat, but he looks overly pale.

I hit him with my fist, hard in the chest.

I hit him again on the side of the head, trying to wake him.

In doing so, I lost control of the car. I slammed us into the guardrail, leaving more paint and metal. Sparks flew until I dragged the GTX off the rail again.

Sunlight rushed into my eyes. It slanted in a bright angle through the windshield as we flew out of the second tunnel. Before me stretched a long bridge with water on either side. The ramp aimed straight for the lake's surface where the bridge floated on top of the water.

I glanced at Revik.

"Mortal peril," I muttered. "Mortal peril."

I didn't think.

I saw every flash of metal and sunlight as I swung the wheel.

Veering behind a green Jetta, I made a straight line for the right guardrail. Beyond that lay nothing but sky and the waters of Lake Washington.

A thick, protective rail stood between us and the water…

…but my mind seems to clasp it, fold it. Or maybe it's not my mind at all, but whatever it is, however it happens, suddenly I can see through it…

…and we are through.

Exhilaration lifts me as the car soared.

Then gravity clutched the GTX at the top of the arc. Its nose tipped.

As my stomach lurched, the view through the windshield abruptly changed. The sky spun, replaced by water. I watched it turn. I could only hold onto the steering wheel.

Strangely, I flashed to being on a runaway horse as a kid. I'd clutched the mare's black mane, screaming in fear and hysterical laughter.

Back then, as a kid, I'd been sure I was going to die.

Now, nothing so concrete reached my thoughts.

There was just a long, slow silence as the water rushed to meet.

THE GRILL SLAMMED INTO THE SURFACE OF THE LAKE WITH AN ENORMOUS splash.

On the bridge, cars swerved, honking, slamming into one another.

An 18-wheeler's brakes screeched as it followed the GTX's trajectory towards the gap in the rail. A woman in a Toyota glimpsed round, rough-cut holes in the grill and front fender of that same truck as the metal trailer skidded past her view.

It seemed about to follow the GTX over into the lake, when the driver swung the wheel, throwing the cab perpendicular as it slid towards the gap in the wall.

The truck's trailer rammed metal, bending it outwards.

When it finally came to rest with a shudder, the cab faced north, like a dog peering over its own shoulder.

In a daze, people exited their vehicles.

Several walked to the rail overlooking the blue-gray water.

The scream of sirens could be heard approaching from the other side of the tunnel. The dull thud of news and police helicopters grew audible overhead.

Onlookers and law enforcement alike stared down at the lake's depths, at the rings of wavelets forming a perfect circle in an otherwise calm surface. They all looked at that same spot in the water, searching for the thing they'd witnessed smash through a two foot guardrail and fly out into the early morning sky.

But the GTX was nowhere to be seen.

CHAPTER 11

SURFACING

Cold green shimmered around me, clouds of sand and rising bubbles.

Dazed, I grappled with the car door until fingers gripped my arm.

I turned to see Revik through the green water.

His eyes were open, his long fingers so white they looked drained of blood. The knuckles of his hand bled in soft red clouds. The dashboard in front of him bled upwards into the water from an odd-shaped smear as well.

Watching the blood was like watching a film happen in reverse.

No Barrier, he sent, so softly I barely heard him.

My mind, everything about me, remained oddly calm.

I squeezed his arm to let him know I understood.

Revik hit the locking mechanism of his seat belt clumsily. He immediately rose to thump up against the roof of the car as the belt slid off his chest. It was only then that I realized the car was still sinking. Blood swirled around us from his head and hand. He pedaled his arms to reach me. He grabbed for the strap of my seatbelt.

He fumbled with the clasp. He hit the button to unlock it from around my body.

He got it undone, then held me to keep me from rising too fast

My body hurt—badly enough to bring the first real flickers of fear.

My limbs only half-cooperated as I jerkingly tried to swim. At the prompting of his hands, I aimed for the open driver's side window.

I've always been able to hold my breath under water for a long time.

I've always been able to see well underwater, too.

My dad called me a fish.

He would time me at the community pool, taking bets for French fries and beers from the other parents on how long I could stay under.

We usually won those bets.

But now I was starting to worry about air.

I had no idea how far down we were.

I pedaled clumsily through bubbles, aiming my body at the window.

Shards of glass nicked my cheeks and arms, then grated on my leg until I jerked away from the edges of the window. I let out a garbled sound as I kicked my way through.

Then I was on the other side, in open water.

I watched the car roof and hood as the GTX sank below me.

Revik swam past me and I felt his fingers on my arm, pulling me to follow.

Above us, I glimpsed rays and sparkles of light through chunks of green plant matter. I remembered anti-drowning training and followed the bubbles. The tugging on my arm grew less once I was swimming alongside him.

Then I saw clouds and patches of blue sky through a window of clear water.

Right before we would have breached, he pulled me roughly sideways, guiding me under the surface before I could reach the open air.

I fought panic, trying to trust the feeling I got off his hands, the sense of purpose I felt there. By the time he let me rise, I'd lost that battle entirely. I was panicking for real, fighting to pry off his fingers, and the sunlight was gone.

He didn't let go until we breached the surface together, gasping.

Once I'd filled my lungs with air, choking out the water I'd inhaled, I looked up. We were under the bridge. Land lay roughly a hundred meters behind where I watched Revik tread water. I glanced at it, then looked at Revik himself, watching him gasp to regain his breath.

Massive cement pillars stood to either side of us. The thundering sound of cars on the bridge overhead echoed over the water.

The sound touched a memory in me.

Something about that memory brought a wave of fear.

I was still staring up at the underside of the bridge, when Revik's fingers circled my arm a second time. I felt an apology there, but also fear, enough to take my breath. He looked different with his hair slicked back, and for an instant, I could only stare at his face. I almost didn't recognize him with how pale he was, exaggerated by the wet hair and the blood on the side of his head.

Only his eyes and mouth looked the same.

"Don't go into the Barrier." He was having more trouble than me regaining his breath. I watched him struggle to speak. "Not even a little, Allie. If they find us—"

"I won't." I clasped his arm. "I won't go in, Revik."

Hesitating, he nodded. That fear never left his eyes. He didn't let go of my arm, either.

I stared at his face, worried. He didn't look good.

"Can you swim?" I asked.

He looked over his shoulder, towards shore. He still held my arm, only now it felt like he was using me as a flotation device. I felt him hesitate, as if thinking about my question.

"Come on," I said.

I let him continue to hold my arm as I started heading for shore.

I used slow, strong strokes of my arms and legs.

I pulled him with me, and he didn't try to let go.

WE REACHED THE ROCKY SHORELINE, STOPPING AT EACH SET OF CEMENT pillars to let him rest. As if by mutual assent, we didn't get out of the water right away but traveled south, sliding from one private dock and mooring to the next in a slow procession down the shoreline.

The morning sun disappeared behind cloud cover, which helped turn everything gray when police boats skimmed the water on their way towards the bridge.

I heard the *thwup, thwup, thwup* of rotary blades, and couldn't help but follow them with my eyes. Some of the helicopters looked military. I wondered if they were SCARB, one of the other military branches of the World Court, anti-terrorist forces from our own government, or naval troops on loan from down the coast in Tacoma.

We hid under one dock and the next until our teeth chattered.

We waited for them to circle and pass.

We didn't speak, and I tried not to worry as Revik's breathing grew ragged. Just as the activity really exploded around the bridge and the submerged GTX, we climbed out into a public park, wading over and through thick vegetation that surrounded the last bit of water before it dumped us out on a wide, manicured grass lawn.

I helped him into the trees.

I was likely more conspicuous with my tattered waitress uniform and bare legs, but he looked worse than me, and not only because of the blood still running down one side of his face. I could only hope no one saw us as we entered the forested park, where the trees made us at least as inconspicuous as your average homeless person.

Once we were well out of sight of the shore, I helped him lean against a tree, then slide down to sit.

He was shivering by then, so pale he looked dead.

I looked around for something I might cover him with, then decided speed mattered more. At the moment, the cops were focusing on the submerged car.

Once they saw it had no one in it, that would change, and fast.

The adjoining neighborhood didn't look rich enough to have a grid along the entire coast. If it did, we were screwed, since our presence would have been recorded and sent automatically to SCARB and local law enforcement already.

For now, I had to assume regular, mid-grade, upper-middle class suburban security, which meant towers on the streets that took timed images and maybe flyers at night, depending on how paranoid the neighbors were.

Still thinking about this, I squatted next to his legs.

"Hey." I grasped his arm, tightening my grip until his eyes opened. "Don't go to sleep. You can't sleep, okay? I need to know I can trust you if I leave."

"There is a safe house—"

"You told me," I said patiently. "But we're not going to make it like this. You can't do anything in the Barrier, so we need to do it the human way. I need to find us clothes. And at least one local ident card, to get us past the gate."

I saw him look at the wet uniform clinging to my body, my blood-matted hair. He nodded.

"Okay."

"Okay," I said. "Don't fall asleep."

"I won't."

"Promise me."

He looked up. Something about his expression made my chest clench. After a bare pause, I realized the look in his eyes was trust.

He was trusting me to take care of this.

He gripped my hand as I thought it, his long jaw hard.

"I promise, Allie."

I SLID THROUGH A ROW OF BUSHES, TRYING TO AVOID THE ROAD WHILE staying on the edge of park that backed up against the nearest street full of houses.

I'd done the best that I could, given limited options.

Thank God, Seattle was nothing like San Francisco.

I found an open back door with no external cameras by about the fourth or fifth house I checked. From a slight rise overlooking a set of backyards that formed a gentle curve around that part of the lake, I'd spotted the clothesline first.

Looking out from behind the trunk of a tree, I scanned the area for people watching from windows, or hanging out in adjacent yards.

I heard feed stations blaring from a few places, but no other voices.

Men's clothing hung from the sagging cotton rope between two maple trees.

I saw sheets on another line that went to the other side of the Craftsman-style house. Women's clothes hung there in a more colorful line of blues and purples. I also saw what looked like a child's clothes, but that line was much closer to the back of the house. It was the men's clothes that drew my eyes. I hoped they were dry, even as I measured the length of the pant legs with my eyes, wondering if they would be close enough to fit him.

A few minutes later, I slid through a gap in the tall evergreen shrubs that hid the back of the house from the lake's shore.

Avoiding the footpath and its stone steps to their private dock, I kept to the fence, getting as close to the line as I dared without breaking cover. I only walked out to tug a pair of jeans and baggy sweats off the line. I grabbed a long-sleeved T-shirt next, and a slightly damp sweatshirt.

Taking my bundle back to the hedge, I didn't wait but pulled the bloody and ripped-up white waitressing blouse over my head and left it in the bushes. I writhed out of the black miniskirt and underwear.

Briefly, I was stark naked, and freezing my ass off.

I quickly pulled on the long-sleeved tee and jeans. The jeans were way too big. I rolled up the cuffs so they rested on the top of my feet and folded over the waist to keep them up without a belt. I swam in the shirt, but that mattered a lot less.

I left the sweats and sweatshirt in the hedge and looked back at the house.

The back door was open.

My first thought was panic.

I wondered if someone had seen me.

When I didn't hear or see anyone after a few minutes, I decided the door had already been open.

Thinking again about what we needed, realistically, to get out of there without being noticed, I crept forward reluctantly, my heart pounding in my chest. If I was seen, this would be all over, and fast. If they were watching the news feeds, it wouldn't take long for anyone living here to put two and two together.

I made it to the back door in a crouch.

I peered into a large but dated kitchen with oak cabinets and white-tile counters. On a butcher-block cutting board, I saw an actual home-made pie. Staring at it, seeing the dark berry puree bleeding out of the crust, and smelling the sweet tang of cooked fruit, I felt my stomach grind into a hard knot.

Tiptoeing around the pie to the refrigerator, I opened the door softly.

I glanced quickly over the contents before grabbing a container of milk and quaffing a few swallows. Setting it down carefully so as not to rattle the shelf, I pulled out a package of bread, then another plastic bag of what looked like real cheese, probably from one of the local farmer's markets.

I closed the door just as softly.

I looked around until I caught sight of the entryway table.

On it sat a leather purse, worn to a pale beige. It looked like something my mom would wear, and suddenly I felt a little sick.

Shoving aside my lingering guilt, I walked quietly down the hall, conscious of any loose floorboards as I lifted and placed my bare feet. I reached the purse and opened the snaps, wincing at the faint click before I tugged it open.

The woman's wallet lay on top, a faded Gucci with a white and brown pattern.

I opened it and found an ident card. Breathing a sigh of relief, I tugged it carefully out of the plastic protector, shoving it into the front pocket of the stolen jeans.

Closing the purse, I hesitated again, seeing the woman's headset on the counter next to the purse. It was a private version, non-government.

After the barest pause, I snatched up the headset, too.

I turned for the back door.

...and found myself facing a little boy. Maybe three or four-years-old, he stared up at me with wide dark eyes, his curly black hair a rumpled mess. His mouth fell slightly open. He clutched a stuffed alligator in both hands.

I held up a hand. My heart leapt to my throat.

"It's okay, kid," I whispered. "Tell your mom I'm really sorry."

The kid stared at me. His almond eyes grew wider.

Then, abruptly, his mouth opened.

"Mom!" he shrieked. "Mommy! There's a dirty lady in here! She has my sammich bread! She has my sammich bread!"

My heart stopped for a half-beat.

Then I bolted, leaping over and past the boy.

I landed off-kilter on one foot, picked up my weight, stumbled for the door, limping on the ankle I'd just twisted. I knocked into the door frame as I ran by, smacking my shoulder and making a loud clattering noise that echoed into the small clearing.

A screech of lake-rusted hinges followed me as the door swung behind my erratic path. I glanced over my shoulder and saw that the door hung crooked on its wooden frame.

I didn't look back again.

At the small opening in the hedge, I scooped up the clothes I'd stolen for Revik, then ran behind the denser vegetation and through the next backyard.

Minutes later, I was back in the wooded park above the row of homes.

Panting, I ran up to the tree and cluster of roots where I thought I'd left him.

He wasn't there.

My heart stopped.

...until I realized I'd gone to the wrong tree.

Running to the next set of dark trunks, I skidded on the grass, nearly tripping over his long legs before I realized it was him lying there. I'd barely regained my balance when I focused on his face. His eyes were closed.

Panic bloomed in my chest. I was sure he was dead.

His eyelids fluttered open as soon as I crouched beside him.

"I didn't sleep," he said, his voice gruff. "I didn't."

Relieved beyond words, I kissed him on the mouth.

I swear he kissed me back.

Even so, when I looked at him next, his eyes registered a dim surprise.

"Sorry I took so long." I fought embarrassment, then grinned. "But hey, look!" I showed him the headset. Fitting it over my ear, I switched it on, even as it occurred to me to hope it didn't have a DNA encryption key.

Some of the newer ones did.

Luckily, it wasn't that new.

Even so, I had to use it now. Before she reported it stolen.

I scrolled through the woman's cached numbers until I found one labeled "taxi."

"Yes," I said when the dispatcher picked up. I waited for her to trace our location. "Yeah, now." I glanced at Revik, watched him fumble with the sweatshirt I'd brought him. "We'll be in the parking lot." I hung up, crouching in front of him again. "You up for this? We can't go door to door. We'll have them drop us near a bus stop, or downtown. It's in Chinatown, right?"

He nodded, unbuttoning his shirt.

I continued to stand there as he struggled out of it. Looking down at his exposed neck and shoulder, I found myself focusing on a question-mark scar curling up from his back to his throat. It was pale white, faint enough that it had to be old.

I hesitated, wondering if I should offer to help.

I thought better of it a few seconds later and walked off a few paces instead, sitting on the grass with my back to him.

Twisting off the clasp ties, I reached into the first plastic bag. I pulled out a piece of bread and began munching on it. It was soft with a crunchy, chewy crust, and at that moment I decided it was the best damned bread I'd ever eaten.

I tried to make myself look remotely normal while I ate, combing fingers through my hair to get as much gunk out as I could, pausing occasionally to try to clean up my face on the long-sleeved tee. I tried not to think about Revik getting dressed behind me.

I knew I was overly aware of him though.

I decided it was shock.

Shock, or just that almost-dying, intimacy-forged-in-adversity thing.

I'd read about that—those insane situations that make you feel abnormally close to someone you don't really know, all because you barely escaped death together. That had to be the reason I'd kissed him, too, and the reason I was conscious of him undressing behind me.

I didn't want to think about that strange, distinctly sexual pain I'd felt around him a few times now. Or the fact that I could have sworn he was hitting on me when we both first woke up in the GTX that morning.

"Stockholm syndrome," I muttered.

I let out a humorless laugh, knowing that was at least partly shock, too.

I stuffed another piece of bread into my mouth and chewed. I couldn't afford to be light-headed from lack of food, not given the shape he was in.

Anyway, whatever my problem was, in the immortal words of Scarlett O'Hara—I would think about it tomorrow.

CHAPTER 12
SEATTLE

The sun was dipping into afternoon when we finally stood in front of a red-painted basement door.

By then we'd taken the taxi, three buses, and we'd walked for roughly a mile.

I looked up the cement stairs to the street, where a woman leaned against a telephone pole covered with stapled-on band flyers. Nylons torn, makeup running down her cheeks under a slightly askew wig, she swayed drunkenly on high heels, staring at Revik with half-hearted interest. She saw me looking at her and gestured in a dismissive wave.

"Enjoy yourself, girlfriend." She burst into a laugh. "That one's too drunk to fuck, so you best be nice. I find him in the gutter tomorrow, I'll remember your face, honey."

My eyes found Revik's.

He continued leaning against me, his hand on the wall.

He was having trouble breathing.

I asked him, "You're sure this is the place?"

He didn't look at the woman, who called out again, trying to get his attention.

"Yes," he said.

"Hey, lover! Be careful! That one looks like a predator." She burst into more drunken laughter. "Wanna come home with me? I'll take good care of you, baby. Hey! Tall and dark!"

"This doesn't look very inconspicuous," I muttered. "From the sign out front, it looked like a whore house. A seer one. You're sure we're at the right—"

"This is it, Allie," he said. "I've been here before. Seers have photographic memories. And a lot of the seers you're going to meet have worked as unwillings." He gave me a flat look. "Trust me. It is here. Be polite."

Noting the exhaustion in his eyes, I just nodded.

Even so, I found myself turning over the "unwilling" word in my head a few times. I gripped him tighter, but still hesitated, staring at the chipped, red-painted door. I knew the real reason I was hesitating. I was about to walk into a building full of seers.

Seers who would probably think I'd done this to him.

Remembering how I'd jumped out of the GTX in that town, I winced.

They wouldn't be that far off, really.

"Knock, Allie."

I raised my hand.

The door opened before I could touch the wood.

A woman stood there with stunning dark-red hair. It hung in precise ringlets down either side of a perfect, heart-shaped face. Bare, pearl-white shoulders shone in the shadow by the door. My eyes took in that flawless face, the dark blue eyes that shone almost violet and perfectly drawn lips. Everything about her, from her clothes to her figure to her hair, reminded me of a sex siren from the forties or fifties.

The clothes she wore fit so well they must have been made for her.

Or painted on her, perhaps.

She smiled, and the smile drew me like a caress.

"Can I help you, friend?"

I glanced at Revik.

"Been here before, huh?" I queried.

I meant it as a joke, but my nerves were audible.

Revik clicked at me softly, a sound I still didn't have a precise meaning for.

That time, it sounded almost chiding.

He remained outside the circle of light, but I felt him relax when he saw the woman. Clearly, he knew her, recognized her, at least. Turning away from the relief I could see on his face, I looked past her, glimpsing a wider space behind her with more people.

But her eyes must have followed mine to him.

"Revi'!" The violet eyes widened, all trace of coyness gone. "Gods, Revi'! What has happened to you?"

Before I could say a word, she stepped forward, not moving me aside so much as sliding into the gap between me and Revik. She encircled his waist with one arm.

She took him from me before it occurred to me to resist.

I found myself just standing there, strangely lighter without him to prop up, watching her bring him inside.

I had to force myself to follow after them.

Once I had, someone stepped behind me, swinging the door closed.

More people rose from chairs, their faces showing different amounts of surprise. None spoke—not aloud, anyway. Looking around at all of them, I glimpsed satin dresses and long jackets, faces heavy with make-up, a variety of skin tones and hair textures.

The first woman I'd seen appeared to be in charge.

She gestured with her free hand to the others, speaking an odd mix of accented English and that language I'd heard Revik speak a number of times now.

"Mira, lock the door! *Il'letre ar enge.* Ivy, set up the room. Yes, *ugnete.* Make sure Sharin knows. Tell her to open the back entrance to customers for now—"

The woman with the long red hair stood at a decent height, maybe five-nine, but still looked small where she supported Revik with her shoulder and side. I saw her caress his back with a ring-adorned hand and felt more than that pass between them.

"That was you on the news!" she said, looking up at him. "I should have known. They intimated terrorism. But we didn't expect you so soon."

As if remembering, she looked back at me.

Her eyes glowed, catlike, taking me in.

"Is this her?"

Revik glanced at me, too. He turned away an instant later, speaking only to her, using that other language, interspersing his words with a series of clicks.

"Arente ar mulens, sarten," he said softly. He glanced at me again. *"Il en, yet. Igre ar ulen.* Bridge," he added.

The woman stared at me. *"Ar li ente u?"*

"Ur et estarn. Alyson... *ut te* Allie."

The woman looked at me more intently.

Her irises blurred just enough that I suspected she was reading my mind, what there was left of it, anyway. I saw Revik nod to her perceptibly. He gestured fluidly with one hand, ending on a downward slash.

I stood there, feeling helpless, fighting back emotion that felt more and more like anger. My eyes found his fingers entangled in the woman's dark red hair, caressing the bare skin of her neck and shoulder.

A pulse of warmth reached me.

I jumped, my face hotter when I realized who had sent it.

Then it hit me.

He had access to his abilities again.

He met my gaze. *Ullysa has a construct over this place. It will keep us hidden from the Barrier. We are safe here... for now.*

Ullysa made a soft clicking sound that held a trace of amazement.

It drew my eyes.

"She is *young,* Revi'," she said. *"Gaos.* I pictured an old man from the Elders' impressions. Is she trained at all?"

Revik made another of those downward slashing motions.

No, he translated for me.

Ullysa looked up at Revik's face. "And how did they find you? We were told you got away from San Francisco cleanly."

"It was my mistake—" Revik began.

"No," I said. "It wasn't."

Ullysa looked at me in surprise.

Her expression suddenly grew much more difficult for me to read.

She bowed formally to me, as if remembering herself suddenly, and I saw her cheeks bloom with a bit more color. Indicating around the room with her free hand, she bowed to me again. I couldn't help but notice her other hand was now under the sweatshirt Revik wore, caressing his bare back.

Realizing I was staring, I looked away.

"Wait here, please," she said politely. "...Esteemed Bridge. I apologize for making you both stand here. And for my staring."

I held up my hands, not hiding my annoyance. "It's fine. Whatever."

She left the room with Revik, whose eyes I avoided, only to meet other stares aimed at me from different parts of the room. Ignoring those stares pointedly, I plopped down on one of the plush chairs to wait. Once I had, I realized that was probably a mistake, too. A number of seers had risen to stare at me. Most of those stares felt benignly curious, but I felt shimmers of distrust and hostility from at least one.

From another, I also felt fear.

"Are you really telekinetic?" a tall woman asked me, with curled black hair.

I blinked at her.

Looking away, I didn't answer.

I met another woman's gaze, almost by accident. Her eyes were predatory, but beneath that, I felt a lot of anger. That anger felt aimed at me.

Specifically at me.

Great. This woman actually felt dangerous.

"Should we call his owner?" a different, young-sounding woman asked from another part of the room. She sounded worried. "He'll be in trouble, won't he?"

"What is the point?" The predatory woman's eyes remained on me. Her accent was thick, and sounded Slavic. Russian, maybe. "His owners will have declared him rogue by now. They will cut a deal with SCARB to avoid being fined."

"But I thought his job was classified. Even among the humans, don't they—"

"Well, they may not tell the human news crews what he did for them," the Russian said, rolling her eyes in an exaggerated way. "But that does not mean they will not shoot him down like a dog now."

Her eyes returned to mine.

"What do you think, little girl? You were raised human."

Her full lips curled, but it wasn't really a smile.

"Would you kill him?" she taunted. "...Or play with him a while first?"

A few of the other seers snickered.

I tried looking from face to face openly, the way Cass would have done.

I'd always sucked at those games, though.

When most of the seers only avoided my eyes, I focused back on the Russian. The woman had her hair piled in braids around an angular but striking face with caramel-colored skin. Her coffee-colored brown eyes shone with so much light that I found myself fighting a kind of fear reaction just trying to hold her gaze.

Her full lips curved higher, so I knew she must be reading my mind, too.

She stood beside a short Asian woman with a wide face and dark hair hanging down the center of her back. Both wore silk robes that covered only the top of their thighs.

"Does it bother you, that we are whores?" the Russian asked me, folding her arms. "Would it bother you less or more to know he sells it, too? But then, we seers are all 'big sex,' yes?"

Anger colored her voice.

After she studied my face, her predatory smile returned.

"Ah, you do not like what I say. But Revi' *is* a whore... of many kinds. Offer him money. See what he says." She grinned around at the others. "We seers always need money!"

More laughter rose in nervous waves.

A few others held my stare now too, smirking at me knowingly.

Their expressions and bodies seemed to shift around me, a sea of hair and skin and glowing eyes. They looked like animals to me—I couldn't help it. They gestured to one another and their voices echoed in my head, seeming to come from all sides.

Has she tasted him yet?

No. I do not see him in her.

No wonder she is so angry.

Laughter rings, in my mind and outside.

My head pounds, but my body feels far away, like a shank of meat on a hook. I close my eyes, trying to block them out.

Do you think it was she who beat him half dead?

Knowing Revi', he liked it.

A few more of them laughed.

He was hungry. Even under all that. Do you think she refused him?

Not this one. She is hungry, too.

Did he ask you for it, little girl?

This last is directed at me, and comes from the Russian with that angular face and light-filled eyes and long, brown legs.

The rest of the prostitutes fall silent, waiting for my answer.

I look around at them, knowing there is no good answer, no good not-answer.

Exhaling, I fold my arms, sinking deeper in the chair.

Still, I'm annoyed. What the hell is it with all their "young" references and the "little girl" crap? I'm almost thirty, for crying out loud.

The laughter is louder that time.

A few of the seers grin at me in open amusement, and this time, I feel decidedly out of the loop on the joke.

The room is half in darkness now. Their faces flicker, in and out, negative to positive.

The Russian, who is still nearest to me, smiles.

I am Kat, and I have tasted him. Would you like to know how often? In what ways?

Before I can answer, images swirl briefly, cutting off my train of thought. I feel him, taste the flavor of him, as she said, feel a sense of his skin and touch. My body reacts involuntarily.

A thick surge of that nausea brings heat to my face.

Kat laughs, and the images recede.

Yes… she is hungry for brother Revik. Kat looks around at the room. *But is it him in particular, I wonder? She is new to our kind, after all. Maybe she would like one of her other brothers just as much? Who will break her in for the rest of us?*

My fists curl.

I don't turn my head towards any of the males I now feel looking at me with interest. If they're not just having fun with me, there's no way for me to know.

I see a wine bottle, half full on the table.

I let my hand wander closer—

Stop! A voice breaks through the others. *You are going too far. She thinks you mean it!* The short, Asian female steps closer, and I realize it is her voice. She looks at me with curiosity, but also sympathy. *She can't help what she's been taught. She's scared, Kat. You're being mean.*

Kat snorts. *I am educating her. What does she think he's doing with Ullysa right now?*

Don't be stupid, says another. *He's wounded.*

He is never that *wounded,* a male voice remarks humorously.

Another roll of laughter twangs strings of light, this one warmer, more genuine. I blink, try to focus my eyes.

A more mature-sounding female voice rises next.

My head turns; I can almost distinguish them now. An African-looking woman stands in the back, smiling at me with dark eyes.

Retract your claws, Kat. She's only a cub.

She wants to know. Look at her!

She doesn't want to know. You are angering her, Kat. And you are jealous.

Jealous? Of what? Why would he play with a half worm, when there is no money in it?

He wants anything with a pulse, a different male voice laughs. *And her soul may look like an old man, but she is beautiful. Her light pulls. Of course he wants her. I want her. The paradox alone is intriguing. Even without those eyes.*

I am exhausted.

I'm fighting to stay awake when another presence enters the room. The others fall silent, and it is a schoolyard silence, children caught tormenting a wounded animal.

Even Kat steps back, looking defensive.

"What is going on in here?" Ullysa says.

I am standing. When had I gotten to my feet?

Just having a little fun, big sis, Kat sends, smirking at me.

I look at Kat, and the woman's eyes pulse, more schoolyard politics, this time a warning from the head bully to remain silent. But I don't care anymore. I feel sick, more tired than I can remember feeling. I want to call my mother, make sure she's all right, and Jon. I want to talk to Cass. Then I want to sleep, pretty much anywhere but here.

To hell with these people.

I know I can't leave, though. I have no place to go.

The thought brings another surge of anger, directionless that time.

Grief starts to rise in its wake, but I suppress that, too.

"You are right," a voice says, cautious. "You cannot leave, sister."

I glance over, and Ullysa's eyes reflect alarm, maybe at my thoughts, or maybe at something she sees in my face.

"I am sorry about your family," she says, her voice still careful. "Did you not watch the feeds?"

I shake my head, but I can't let myself think about her words. Putting out a hand like a zombie, I lean my weight on the chair I'd been sitting on, moments before.

"Is my mother all right?" I ask.

Silence is my only answer.

Shaking my head, I realize I can't deal with whatever that means.

Fuck it. If they want to screw with my head, or rape me or whatever, there isn't a hell of a lot I can do about it. Maybe I wouldn't even remember.

When I glanced up, Ullysa was staring at me again, disbelief in her eyes.

Then her expression hardened. Her eyes turned to glass, reminding me of Revik's before they swiveled to face the rest of the room.

Her anger flared, a red streak in the dark.

She was begging for it! Kat said, before Ullysa could speak. *Her sad, human eyes on our brother's ass…*

Ullysa fury pulsed higher. "Do you know who this is? Do you have any idea what you are doing right now?"

Stepping towards me, she ignored my flinch and took my arm.

I stood there, not liking her hands on me much, but I didn't try to pull away. She spoke quietly, warmly. At each word, I felt more calm descend over me. I knew that calm wasn't real. I knew she was manipulating me, using her seer powers somehow to force me compliant.

I couldn't fight it.

Not right then, anyway.

"I am very sorry to have left you alone, Esteemed Sister." She glared around at the seers filling the rest of the room. "…I would never have done so, if I knew my own people would *shame* me in such a way."

Her eyes returned to mine, and softened.

"I wanted only to look at the nature of his wounds. Right now, more than anything he requires sleep, and that is better done in pairs." She glanced at Kat. "He asked for you," she added pointedly. "He wishes for you to join him."

I didn't know which of us she meant, me or the Russian.

At that point, I didn't much care.

When she looked at me that time, Ullysa smiled. A flicker of relief shone in her violet-tinged eyes. She stroked my arm again.

"He is very weak. Did you feed him at all, sister?"

I had to think about that. I shook my head. "No. I stole some stuff. He wouldn't eat it..."

I trailed, hearing the prostitutes snicker.

Ullysa's voice remained gentle. "Sister, I meant light. Did you give him any of your light?"

I blinked, trying again to think.

Finally, I could only shake my head.

"I don't understand."

Kat broke out, "You see? She acts like one of them. Thinks like one of them!"

Ullysa's eyes flashed fire. "She is only recently awakened, and you should know why that is! You are embarrassing me, Kat!" She turned back to me, her fire dimming back to that warm ember. "I will show you, sister. Please come with me."

I followed her, giving a last glance at Kat, who was staring at me, her brown eyes glowing in anger. I turned away once I saw the fury reflected there. I pushed it from my mind a second later, focusing on the hallway itself.

Plush, dark-green carpet cushioned my bare feet. It felt heavenly after our walk here, over rough ground and dirty, trash-covered sidewalks.

Tapestries hung on the walls to either side, depicting colorful dragons belching fire. People in Asian-looking costumes floated on clouds, surrounded by fantastical-looking animals that may have been lions, only with curling blue and green hair.

I touched the face of a giant white dog with bared teeth.

Ullysa smiled. "They are Chinese. Given to me before the Cultural Revolution."

I nodded, but didn't speak.

We turned down a few more forks in the hall. I realized the apartment must be huge, not really an apartment at all but more like a floor, or perhaps they owned the entire building. After we'd crossed what felt like the length of a football field, I followed Ullysa into a square room with a white door.

The building must be set in a hill, I thought.

The side I was now on faced the downward slope, as windows showed us to be aboveground, rather than on the basement floor, like before. In front of those same windows, rust-colored drapes hung from rods below a low, red ceiling. An even thicker, gold-white carpet sank under my bare feet.

I glanced towards the bed, and over the headboard saw another painting, this time of a round-eyed god riding a lion. He spat fire below an elaborate headdress of looping tongues of flame. Next to the god, I saw an image of what might be a buddha.

A stack of buddha-like heads rose up in a graceful cone from his torso.

"She likes the paintings, Revi'," Ullysa said. "Especially the *thankahs.*"

I glanced down, and saw him watching me from the bed. The sweatshirt was gone, but he didn't look like he'd been doing the big sex, like Kat said.

He was pale, sweating, and looked at me with transparent relief.

He gestured delicately to the woman who sat next to him in a chair. That same woman was halfway through stitching up his shoulder.

As soon as he finished the hand-gestures, she pressed a palm to his forehead.

When she took her fingers away, his eyes were closed.

Seeing him lying there, so still and pale, I stepped closer to the bed. I shoved my hands in the pockets of the oversized jeans, but didn't take my eyes off his face.

"He will sleep now." The woman stitching up his shoulder—girl, really, now that I stood closer—smiled. She couldn't have been more than sixteen. Her bleached, platinum blonde hair stuck up in curled tufts around an elfin face. "I let him stay awake until he saw you. But he must sleep now. His light is very depleted."

I hesitated, not sure I was ready for more bad news.

"Is he all right?" I asked.

"The shot was clean," she assured me, tugging the thread up by the needle, pulling his skin taut. "Physically, he will recover well. He has lost a lot in structure, though," she said more somberly. "That will take longer." The elfin face turned to mine. "Will you hold for him?"

My mind puzzled over that for a few beats.

I glanced at Ullysa.

"We will all provide light," Ullysa explained to me. "But one person serves as a conduit. Ivy is asking if you will take that role."

I still didn't get it.

I nodded anyway.

"Okay. Sure."

Ullysa's smile warmed. "As in many things, the best way to learn is by doing."

But that rubbed me the wrong way. My jaw tightened as I forced my eyes off him. I looked at Ullysa. "I'd rather not use a dying guy as my test case. You're his friends. Shouldn't one of you do it? Not the 'half-worm' raised by humans?"

Ivy glanced up at me in surprise. "He asked for you."

My cheeks warmed. "Fine. Okay. I didn't say I wouldn't. I'm just not sure I'm the best choice."

Ullysa took my arm. She guided me gently towards the bed.

"You must be very, very tired, Esteemed Sister," she said, her voice a low purr. "This requires no strength or effort, I assure you. Merely structure, and you have that in abundance. We will do the rest."

I stared at Revik's body sprawled on the dark orange comforter.

Ivy was knotting the stitching on his shoulder now.

I watched until she glanced up, smiling as she bit off the excess thread with her back molars. A pulse of warmth reached me from the girl's light, like what Revik had done to me in the other room. It seemed to be a form of affection—reassurance maybe?—like a hand on the arm at hello.

The simple gesture brought emotion surging back to my throat, however.

"Is my family all right?" I asked. "Is anyone going to tell me?"

The warmth from Ivy increased.

After a beat where she and Ullysa exchanged looks, she turned back to me.

"Interviews were released by SCARB. They have all said you are innocent, that you would not hurt anyone." Ivy clicked softly. "No avatars, of course, but we will protect them. We believe the Rooks were behind that, the showing of their real faces."

"No avatars?" I frowned. "What did they look like?"

Ivy rolled her eyes up in thought. "A very sad and worried woman with dark curly hair and large eyes who they say is your mother. A handsome man with streaked hair, Chinese writing on his arms, and broad shoulders who is your brother. A Thai girl with hair like Ullysa's and who wears dark lipstick..." Ivy held her hands out to approximate Cass's generous chest, and I laughed, in spite of myself. Ivy smiled. "They seemed very nice."

I felt myself take a breath. "Then they're okay."

Ivy smiled. "They are fine, Esteemed Bridge."

I hesitated, staring at her.

Esteemed Bridge.

I shook it off. I wasn't ready to know what those words meant to these people. I couldn't handle any more dreams about falling bombs, or about me murdering whole cities.

Ullysa pushed gently at my back until I sat on the edge of the bed.

She very efficiently removed the jeans I'd stolen off the clothesline earlier that day, leaving me with the long-sleeved T-shirt and nothing else. I slid my legs under the quilt, not caring. Lying down was followed by unspeakable relief.

I sank between clean sheets.

I watched Ivy continue to work over Revik, bandaging his shoulder. If I'd known him even a little better, I would have curled up on his other side, maybe even wrapped my arm around him.

I was tempted to do it anyway.

I turned to Ullysa, but she held up a hand.

"Shhh, Esteemed Sister. Do not talk. I apologize profoundly for the lack of warmth in your greeting here. Revi' has already told us you saved his life several times."

I opened my mouth, about to argue, then decided she probably wouldn't care.

"What do I do?" I asked. "The holding thing, I mean."

"Relax," Ullysa said.

This time it was a command.

My eyelids immediately closed.

CHAPTER 13
GERMANY, 1941

I stand in a field.

I recognize this place.

It is a part of me, somehow.

While he was in the hospital, dying, my father asked for a painting of this. I'd done it, crying the whole time. I hung it above his hospital bed, so he could see it when he was lying down. In one of his drug-induced deliriums, he told me it was the Fields of Peace. He told me it was the place of heaven in Egyptian mythology.

My father, engineer and amateur anthropologist.

After the funeral, I'd put the painting in my mother's garage.

I couldn't bear to look at it, not even to imagine him there after he'd died.

The place itself lives on, though.

I cannot escape it.

Grasses pool at my feet, flooding down the hill like ocean waves. A cold wind stirs them into rippling patterns, woven wildflowers creating a mosaic of dusty pinks and purples in the sharp, clean air. I am awake, more awake than I can ever remember being. Snow-covered mountains loom above where I stand, jagged and coarse, and incredibly still.

Those mountains have their own presence. I feel different just looking at them.

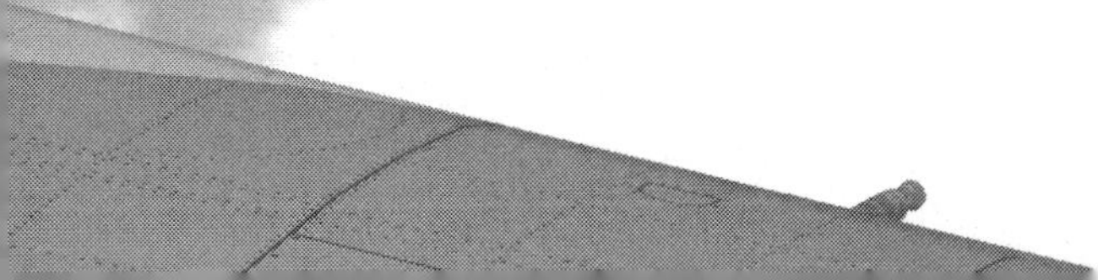

It is as if my mind moves faster here.

He pulls on me, turning my head.

He stands there, alone, staring up at those same mountains.

His form is utterly still.

He belongs here, too. Like my father did—like I do. They are his, as much as they are mine. He doesn't seem to see me, but I feel him all around me.

This place, it is a part of him.

I am a part of him, too.

...I WALK A HIGH-CEILINGED CORRIDOR.

The scene shifted so seamlessly, so utterly without fanfare, that I don't question where I am at first. I don't wonder how I got here.

The corridor is carpeted, lined with dark wood paneling that looks antique, oiled to a lustrous shine. Lamps hang down from the ceiling at regular intervals, made of crystal and iron. They flicker as I walk past, but I am a ghost here; my hands slide through walls.

Brightly-colored paintings garnish the dark wood walls.

I trace them with my eyes.

White men on muscled steeds, Wagner-esque with a hint of Valhalla. The riders' expressions mirror one another, stern but wise, unintentionally cartoonish.

Through an open doorway, a harsh, emotional voice speaks over the crackle of an ancient radio.

Servants stand over it, listening.

They don't notice me, but I recognize the voice. I even understand the words, although in the real world I don't speak German.

"God knows that I have indeed wanted peace..."

Ahead, the muted sounds of a cocktail party beckon.

The man's strident words pull at me, inexorable.

"...We were forced to fight. In the face of such malice, I can do nothing but protect the interests of the Reich with such means as, thank God, are at our disposal..."

Voices grow louder from the room at the end of the corridor. I hear laughter interspersed with the murmur of conversation, some of it tinny and off-kilter, drunk-sounding.

The door bangs open.

The sounds grow louder briefly, then fade as the door swings slowly shut.

A cluster of men walk towards me, wearing uniforms.

The radio is still audible to my ears.

"...They were bound to regard this action as a provocation emanating from the State that once had set the whole of Europe on fire and had been guilty of indescribable sufferings. But those days of using seers and Jews to fight the battles of men are now past. An error we regret, one we will not repeat..."

Four men approach me. Soldiers.

I recognize the color and shape of their uniforms and what they mean. In my world, they symbolize an almost cartoonish evil, the worst impulses in mankind, but here, the clothing feels mundane, ordinary.

They speak German, like the radio.

"The *Fuhrer's* speech is not finished," a tow-headed boy of maybe seventeen says. He shoves a cap back on his head, rubbing his forehead. "We shouldn't have left."

The man next to him throws an arm over his shoulder.

"Aw, read the text in the papers. I need something stronger to drink... and something prettier to look at. There are nothing but dogs in that pen." Drunk already, he grins, eyes bleary. "...At least that I could bark at without getting shot!" He laughs, slapping the tow-headed one in the back of the head. "Dogs! Ha!"

A third looks over, a giant with dark hair and thick lips.

His arm, when he raises his flask, is the size of my thigh.

"My God. You didn't have the view I did. Did you see Rolf's wife? Holy Christ."

"What an ass on her!" tow head says, smiling. "And those tits!"

"And she has that look—" the drunk one leers.

"—Like you want to surprise her," the giant says. "Yes, I saw. Lucky bastard."

The fourth one listens intently.

Of them, his eyes shine clearest. They are dark blue, the color of brushed steel, in a ferret-like face. His uniform is the least rumpled, the least sweat-stained. He also wears a slightly different insignia at his collar.

"He should not have brought her here," he says only, into the silence.

Tow-head takes the flask from his giant friend. "He's in love. It's romantic, isn't it?"

The ferret-faced man's German remains clipped.

"It is no excuse for stupidity. Blauvelt was not subtle in his attentions. I would not want the assignments Rolf pulls after this meeting." He mutters, softer, "...Especially with his pedigree."

"What?" the giant asks. "What did you say?"

"Aww, who cares?" the drunk one says. "He'd cut our balls off if we breathed on her. Let's go find our own tail. Some that doesn't have a Luger attached to it."

They walk through me and past me down the corridor from which I've come, as if I were a puff of smoke. I watch them leave out another door, but my feet compel me to continue in the other direction.

The sounds of the party grow louder.

I follow the clink of glasses, the low murmur of voices, but above that, the rise and fall of the emotional speech dominates. Occasionally the words are broken by wild applause, both by those in the room ahead of me and by a crowd far bigger that carries through the loudspeakers.

"...The training of our officers is excellent beyond comparison. The high standard of efficiency of our soldiers, the superiority of our equipment, the quality of our munitions and the indomitable courage of all ranks have combined to lead at such small sacrifice to a success of truly decisive historical importance. What need have we of homo fervens? Of Syrimne? Should we weaken our humanity further by dependence on foreigners and half-breeds...?"

Another swell of thunderous clapping drowns out his words.

I enter a room with ceilings two or three times the height of the corridor.

A giant banner cascades down a fireplace of river-polished stones. I stare up at the black swastika riding the center of a white circle on a blood-red background.

The sight of it should shock me, but somehow that is ordinary here, too.

Away from the crowd gathered under metal speakers, men in uniform talk in small clusters, eating and drinking with women in party clothes that make them look like gaunt, long-necked birds. My attention is drawn to a group standing off by itself.

An older man in a medal-covered uniform smiles, listening to a beautiful woman with thick, dark hair and wide eyes, who looks embarrassed as she answers a question of his in a low voice. Her curved body is draped in a glittering blue dress and pressed into the side of a harder body next to hers. Her nearly-black hair is piled in elaborate curls on top of her head, studded with diamond-like pins that match her dangling earrings and the stones on her dark blue shoes.

She clutches the hand of the man next to her, who is tall, who wears a German infantry uniform that is at least a few cuts above the rank and file.

As I focus on the three of them, I hear their words.

"...We will have these English scum routed in no time, do you not agree, Rolf?" The older man takes his eyes off the dark-haired woman, staring up at the tall man at her side. "What have you to report from the front of late?"

The taller man takes a drink from a glass half-filled with ice and amber liquid.

I can't flinch exactly, nor feel real surprise, not in this place.

Even so, I stop walking when I see Revik's profile.

Except for the clothes and haircut, subtleties in his expression and posture, he looks exactly the same as when I last saw him, minus the bruises and with a bit more weight on his long frame.

He glances at the woman, his light eyes as still as glass. He tugs her closer before he looks at the man across from them, who frowns.

Revik's voice is low, familiar in all but its tone, which is not quite insolent, but close to bored. Although he looks the same, he sounds younger, somehow.

"With all respect, Commander Blauvelt," he says. "These British are stubborn. It will be months yet before they fall. And if the Americans become involved—"

The man waves a hand, irritated. "They will not."

"Fine," Revik returns evenly in German. "But Churchill has been astute in cultivating a friendship with the American President. We would be fools to discount his charms entirely." He smiles, shaking his glass towards the loudspeakers. "Especially when our *Fuhrer* does not."

Blauvelt frowns in disbelief.

Revik's gaze takes in the rest of the room, his light eyes narrow.

"The American taste for isolationism may run out," he said thoughtfully. "Or the ability of their arms manufacturers to quell the outcry over the distress in Europe. If they were to feel themselves threatened by any of our incursions on the sea, or if we were to let our gaze go too far East..."

He trails as the dark-haired woman tugs sharply on his hand.

Her eyes hold a warning when they meet his.

Shrugging, Revik leaves off, but I see the hardness that touches his mouth.

Blauvelt notices none of this.

He waves a gloved hand, having decided to dismiss the alternate view, rather than honor it with anger.

"You are saying I must tremble in fear over a fat old man on a tiny island because of his cripple friend? Bah! They warned us about France's mighty armies as well! And the legion of seers supposedly commanded by the English!"

Blauvelt smiles at the dark-haired woman, who glances to Revik with worried eyes.

"Your husband would have us fear the gypsies next, *Frau* Schenck! What do you make of this poor display? Or are you merely wondering how he and I could be such tremendous bores in such enchanting company as yourself... and when you are wearing such a lovely gown?"

Frau Schenck smiles, still clutching Revik's hand.

There is a moment where husband and wife look at one another, and I cannot help but see the intensity that comes briefly to his light eyes, or how her expression softens.

Blauvelt, watching them look at one another, frowns.

...AND I BLINK, FLINCHING VIOLENTLY AGAINST A GUST OF ICY WIND.

I clutch my body, shivering as I look out over a bleak landscape of dark and torn earth, winding, muddy ruts cut through iced-over snow.

The horizon seems to go on forever.

It is broken only by heavy carts drawn by shaggy horses who stomp and paw at the icy ground. Their ribs press out against their thick winter coats. They huddle with the humans for warmth, and the humans do the same with them.

A man lies in the snow not far from me, features blurred by a thin layer of water frozen over his face. His ice-filled hair sticks up like fine grass. Dark, rust-colored streaks stand out on his chest and one upraised hand, soaking the wool coat wrapped around his emaciated frame. His eyes are stuck in an expression of agony.

I look to the endless plain of white and black.

I see more bodies, a line that stretches to where land meets a heavy, dark-gray sky. Columns of smoke hang in wind-rent patterns below the clouds.

As if the sound comes back on, an explosion breaks the quiet.

It is loud, but I can tell it is still some way in the distance.

A soldier approaches, stepping around bodies.

Behind him, more wagons are stuck in the mud. Men lean against them to shield from the cold. Some are wrapped in heavy coats, rubbing hands together and blowing on fingers, faces obscured behind gray scarves. One works over a body while I watch, trying to pry a wool coat off stiff arms, stomping and cracking ice and bone with his boot.

The approaching soldier speaks from within a few feet of where I stand.

"*Heil* Hitler," he says, raising his hand.

I look back, flinching when I see how close he stands to me.

Revik lowers his hand from the returning salute, wrapped in a winter coat, wearing a cap of the German *Wehrmacht*. Breath comes out of his narrow lips in thick clouds. He has a beard, and his eyes reflect back the sky in darker tones.

With one boot, he prods at a body frozen in the snow below where he stands.

"They have found more, then?" he says in German.

"What? Found what, sir?"

"Glow eyes." Revik's own eyes shift up. "Jews. Communists. Are they bringing them back alive, or just shooting them?" He half-smiles, his voice bitter. "Because we could use the bullets."

I stare at him, more shocked by his eyes than his words.

I have never seen that expression before—on anyone.

"Sir." The soldier takes a breath. "Sir, we cannot remain here. Russian infantry traveling south from Rostov, moving fast. The panzers are stuck in the mud a few miles up—"

"Pull them back," Revik says. "Those in the town, too. I imagine their fun is spent. Or their tolerance for the smell of burning flesh, at least." The bitterness edges towards what lies under it now, something more raw, something painfully real. Grief comes off him in a dense cloud, along with a heavier despair that goes beyond all of those things.

"Do as I say, Lieutenant," he says, when the other hesitates.

When the soldier turns to go, however, Revik's voice stops him.

"Any news on von Rundstedt?"

I cannot tear my eyes from Revik's face, lost in the unhappiness I see there.

"Sir." The man hesitates again, turning. "The advance divisions were forced to turn back. Von Rundstedt has been, well… replaced, sir. For health reasons is the word of the office."

At Revik's harder look, the soldier's face reddens. "We are to be led by General von Reichenau in the next attempt. You are in charge of the Eleventh until von Reichenau can evaluate our status."

Revik nods. Stomping snow off his boots, he turns, gazing out over the body-strewn field. The feeling in his eyes is gone by the time he completes the motion.

He clasps black-gloved hands at his back.

"And my recommendation to Berlin?" he says. "We could be helping them in the West."

"Denied, sir. Blauvelt felt—"

"Blauvelt?" Revik's eyes turn to ash. "Is our *Fuhrer* no longer deciding strategy on the Eastern Front? It is fallen to his swine, instead?"

The other hesitates. Stepping closer, he lowers his voice.

"Sir, when I spoke to his man, he had news, sir. A message. He claimed to know you, and recommended me to assist him in this…"

The man's voice trails as Revik's eyes narrow.

"Well?"

The man takes a breath. "It's about your wife, sir."

Revik's face grows whiter than the snow flurrying around them in dry bursts.

He is reading the man's mind now. He no longer hears the words coming from his lips.

The world fades around the wind-chapped face of the unnamed soldier speaking to him earnestly. Details remain with me briefly, the smell of rotting corpses and unwashed clothes, burnt flesh imprinted permanently behind his eyes, knowing that friends and even relatives burned in those ovens, that the humans are no longer simply doing it to one another.

Then, all of it is gone.

...I JERK VIOLENTLY.

I am somewhere else.

Indoors now, warmed by a fire blazing in a grate, its light casting flickering shadows over a dated room that doesn't feel dated here.

A mirror hangs over the fireplace.

Fresh flowers bloom over a flower-patterned vase with wing-like handles. I gaze into reflective glass, see a room washed in dusty pinks and rosewood trim. Lamplight warms a stained-glass shade from a table beside a heavy wardrobe.

For a moment, the sounds of wet wood crackling distract me.

Then I hear breathing—the heavy, half-expressed breaths of a rhythm I recognize.

I look towards the bed.

Tufts of gray hair stand unevenly across a man's bare shoulders and in patches along the sides of his thick back. He lets out a low grunt.

The woman under him, I recognize. Her thick, curled dark hair lays in an artful fan on the bed. She smiles at him, but the smile is painted on, practiced. A shiver of revulsion reaches me as she stares up at his face; it's gone before I realize it's not mine.

The woman is tired. I feel her unhappiness like a shroud.

The door slams open.

The sound is loud, but I can only watch, unsurprised to see him, although he looks different to me now, older than he's ever looked to me.

His eyes shine, appearing nearly black as he stands in shadow by the door.

My gaze drifts to his white, long-fingered hands.

I see them clutching the wooden handle of an ax.

The woman has seen him, too. Her voice is filled with terror, but not for herself. Her words come out in a near wail.

"Rolf! Rolf, no! Darling, no!"

He is walking to them in a straight line, his long legs moving with a quiet grace I recognize.

"Rolf! They know what you are!"

He doesn't look at his wife, but at the stretch of white skin and tufted gray hair. Blauvelt has turned his head, eyes wide in shock, but he hasn't pulled out of Revik's wife.

Revik swings the ax before he completes his last stride, embedding it between the man's shoulder blades. It sinks down to the thickest part of the blade.

Blauvelt screams.

Revik slams the wooden stock forward, ripping it out with a thick, wet sound and Blauvelt screams and screams and screams…

Revik's wife screams with him.

Unflinching, his face a mask of emptiness, Revik raises the blade and swings again.

…I AM LOST. I AM LOST.

A farmhouse lays buried in snow.

I lay with him and Elise, two forms huddled in ratty blankets, a man and a woman. The woman is pregnant, at least seven months, and she is asleep, though the man is not.

Revik lays on his back in the dark. He watches snow fall through the square window at one end of the hay loft. His face looks half-dead to me now.

His eyes sharpen with a sudden flash of light, and he raises his head.

His skin is whiter, his weight less.

His beard is shorter, and unevenly cut.

He is listening. There is a resignation in his eyes as he looks down at his wife. She has lost weight also, and her dark hair is matted with dirt, limp on the straw by her hollow cheeks. Her eyes are bruised with fatigue. When the doors burst open below, he hesitates, then shakes her gently awake. Hearing the sounds in the barn, she stiffens, clasping his arm.

"We are caught," he says quietly. "They know we are here."

Her eyes widen like a frightened animal. "No—"

"You need a doctor, Ellie."

She starts to argue, but he puts a finger to her lips.

He is just sitting there when the SS Commander lifts his head above the lip of the hayloft, holding a Lugar. Before the man can speak, Revik sits up, raises his hands so they are visible.

"Rolf Schenck?"

Revik nods. "That is me."

"You are under arrest."

His wife, still half-lying beside him, bursts into tears.

…DARKNESS FILLS ME, COLD. I HEAR HER LAST WORDS TO HIM. SHE THINKS he let himself be caught. She thinks it is some thinly disguised revenge, an excuse couched in fake nobility.

There is some truth in what she says, he knows.

Yet he did not do it for the reasons she thinks.

He has no place to take her, not anymore.

You want to die so much? I hope they torture you! I hope they beat you half to death…

She bursts into tears, clutching at him.

I hate you! I hate you! You do not love me!

…then she is gone, too.

There is nothing to push against, nothing with which to push. A faint whisper of voices speaks softly, a tinge of warmth he cannot quite feel. He knows that is his fault, too. He will not let the voices near enough to feel them. He does not want their false assurances. He does not want them to tell him things he cannot yet bear to hear.

The soldiers come to tell him his wife is dead.

They tell him Blauvelt's child killed her.

When he attacks them, they laugh.

He attacks again and again, until he hurts some of them, until they beat him down to the stone. He continues to fight, until his body will no longer function.

The light is gone.

It is gone.

...I WAKE ALONE IN THE DARK.

I wonder if it is sleep I came from, or simply another place. A place of numbness, of dark, of unending silence. I don't feel alive. I don't remember what alive feels like.

The only hints I continue to exist live in emotions too painful, too wrenching to ignore.

Anger lives here. Not only anger. A wanting of—something.

That something is death, but death alone feels empty, unsatisfactory.

His muscles hurt from disuse, and of all things belonging to him that he would like to use now, it is them.

He amuses himself with their minds instead, if they are foolish enough to be alone with him. He flexes the only muscle he can. He ignores the voices that grow fainter and fainter as he learns new trails in the light.

They know what he is.

His marriage is void. He was never married.

He gets the followers, too. They leave him notes, send him scriptures. Some believe him an angel and some think him a devil.

He doesn't discriminate; he hates them all.

His wife gets her wish, too. They beat him when they're bored, but it's never enough—for them, or for him.

He has forgotten the reason that brought him here, the thing that once seemed so important.

It is a story to him now.

It strikes him as juvenile, childish.

In any case, his own people will not come for him. Not anymore. Perhaps not even before he became a murderer.

This will all end soon.

He knows enough to allow it to happen. He sits, leaning on a stone wall. His hands crumple together in his lap, his wrists encased in iron chains. His face is covered in bruises. His skin twitches when a fly alights on a cut, but he does not brush it away.

It happens again. And again.

A clanking emerges from outside.

The door opens and Revik squints as two men enter.

Surprise touches his light; his internal clock tells him it is too soon. But these are not priest and guard. The first man is of medium build and wears expensive clothes. Where his face should sit, I see only a blur, a movie screen on which several movies are being projected at once.

The second man I know from a diner in San Francisco.

Like Revik, Terian does not appear to have aged.

He wears the black uniform of the Gestapo. On him, it looks like a party costume.

"Rolf Schenck?" the man who is not Terian says.

Revik looks the two men over. He does not know either of them.

"I've answered all of your… questions," he says. "Or would you like to hit me some more?" He raises his bound hands. "Maybe you could take these off? I could use the exercise."

Terian laughs, nudging the man with no face.

"I'll hit him, sir," he says. "He seems to want it so badly."

"No." The new man's focus remains on Revik. "No. I think we could find better ways to spend our time together. Perhaps, as Terian here believes, we could be frank with one another, yes?"

Revik gives Terian a dismissive look, looking at the man with no face.

"Does he make you feel safe, worm?" he says only.

The faceless man smiles through his shifting countenance.

"You are operating under a misconception, Rolf. I do not speak for the Reich, nor for any of the human governments. I would like to offer you a job. One you'll find interesting, I think, even apart from your current lack of options."

Revik uses his mind to scan the human in the expensive clothes. He cannot read this faceless man. He assumes the seer with him shields them both.

He lets his hands fall to his lap. He shrugs.

"I'll be otherwise engaged. Or hadn't they told you they plan to cut off my head?"

Terian laughs.

Revik's eyes flicker back to his.

"I told you, sir." Terian smiles, looking at Revik like he's his new favorite toy. "This one will be well worth our time. Once we've honed the snarl a bit."

The faceless man acts like he doesn't hear.

"I think we can help you with your little problem, Rolf," he says. "Or should I just call you Revik? Living amongst us hasn't made you forget your true name entirely, I hope?"

Revik's eyes swivel to Terian, this time in utter disbelief.

"Yes," the faceless man says. "I know who you are. Not only Rolf Schenck, German patriot, but Dehgoies Revik, seer of clan Arenthis."

Revik continues to look only at Terian. He speaks to the other seer in their own language, the one filled with rhythmic clicks and rolling purrs.

Only this time, I understand him.

"What game is this?" Revik says. "You gave our clan keys to a human? The elders will *hang* you for this."

It is the faceless human who answers him, though.

He speaks the same language back to Revik.

"Rules were broken, it is true," the faceless man says.

He gestures smoothly, seer-like.

Revik follows the motion with his eyes, his expression stunned.

"...But you can be selective with rules as well, Rolf. Such as the one against choosing a mate from among the females of my kind."

The faceless man clucks his tongue ruefully.

"For these things tend to happen with humans, do they not? Sadly, my kind does not have the same respect for loyalty to their mates. Nor do most in my race understand the true repercussions of commitment."

His hands open as if in prayer.

I see a ring on his finger, what looks like an Iron Cross.

"She was lovely, cousin," he adds next. "I am sorry you lost her to such a vile representative of my species. Truly."

Revik's eyes change. For the first time, they belong to the Revik I know.

The anger and youth is leached out of them.

"What is it you want?" he says.

I glance at Terian, who is smiling. His gaze is predatory too, like he sees that thing in Revik, and wants it for himself.

"My name is Galaith," the faceless man says. "Perhaps you have heard it?"

There is a silence.

Then Revik snorts a laugh.

"*You* are the scourge of the seer world?" he says. "The one who downed Syrimne, single-handedly? You are lying."

Terian takes a step closer, his humor less visible now.

Galaith holds up a hand to each of them, like a teacher breaking up a fight at school.

"Who I *was* is perhaps less important than who I have become," the man says diplomatically. He asks Revik, "Why have you not simply walked out of this cell, cousin? If you wanted out, they could not hold you."

Revik lets his shoulders unclench.

Still eyeing Terian, he shrugs, folding his arms.

"Perhaps I deserve to die," he says.

Galaith nods. "Are you so tired of this life, then? You are young to feel this way. For your kind, I mean."

Revik stares at Terian. "Perhaps I am. Tired, that is."

The faceless man and Terian exchange a subtle smile.

Galaith's voice warms.

"I understand, cousin. More than you know. But, you see, there are many like you and I, Rolf. Tired of senseless death and war. Tired of the world being led by liars and old men, dreamers and fanatics. Those who feel the Codes, laws, bibles and prejudices of both species no longer represent the current realities of either. We would like to see these Codes…" He smiles. "…Modernized, as it were."

Revik closes his eyes, leaning his head on stone. "Approach my brother, Whelen."

"You have not yet heard my proposal."

"And yet I am not a fool," Revik says, opening his eyes. "Whatever game you and your pet Sark are playing, it is my family name you want. You picked the wrong son. Nothing I said would ever be heard in the Pamir, least of all by my own family. And I have had my fill of humans and your… 'modernization.'"

The faceless man holds up a hand, another gesture of supplication.

"I know your life has been hard, Revik. I know of the death of your parents. I know too that you were adopted by a family that did not want you."

When Revik's jaw hardens, Galaith's tone grows cautious.

"I also know of your current problems, as I have said. But women die in childbirth, cousin. Even among your own kind. It is pointless to throw away such a promising, young life for what is a relatively natural event. She was not seer. This suicide of yours cannot be inevitable."

He pauses, watching Revik's face.

"Was the child Blauvelt's? Or another's?"

Revik doesn't answer at first.

He gives a short laugh.

"You really want me to kill you. Perhaps I should oblige this wish of yours."

Galaith holds up his hand again. "You are wrong about me. My regret for your misfortune is sincere, cousin." He pauses, still watching Revik's face. "And I have already spoken with your blood cousin, Whelen," he adds. "I told him where you are. I told him of your predicament. Your family understands more than you believe, despite your decision to distance yourself, to live among my people and participate in this heinous war on her behalf."

"It was not for her," Revik said.

"It *was* for her, brother. You felt obligated—"

"I meant, it was not her fault." Revik is once more staring into the shadow-darkened corners of the cell. "Please go."

"Revik, your cousin, Whelen, doesn't interest me." Galaith's words contain a gentle pull. "We have no need of family names. That clan nonsense is of the past. I want your talent, Revik. I believe you will prove to be our most valuable asset yet."

Terian leans closer.

He holds up two fingers in a backwards V, wiggling them at Revik.

"Second-most valuable," he says, winking.

Galaith chuckles, patting Terian on the back with one hand.

"Yes," he says. "It was Terian here who petitioned hardest for your recruitment, Rolf. Brother Terian is most anxious to see what you can do. He may have created a bit of a reputation for you in advance, I'm afraid. One you may have to defend in not too long a time."

His smile grows more visible as he discerns Revik's involuntary reaction to his words.

"I, too, am anxious to witness these talents, cousin," he says. "Indeed, I am. Most anxious."

A flush of warmth grows in some part of Revik that doesn't need to feel much else.

He is still thinking, turning over this spark in his mind, when the walls around me fall once more into black.

CHAPTER 14
VOW

I choke… choked… am choking… caught inside a fisted clutch of light, an egg-shaped pocket that holds me unflinchingly in place.

Inside that heated glow, I birth.

Stars swim past me in a pale swath, sky broken by sharp eyes and lightning flashes, snaking charges of gold and orange and crimson, the late side of the setting sun.

I am with him again.

I have never left him.

Now we lie together on a bed, wrapped into and around one another, alone in a single room in a building full of seers. I know I am supposed to be like them. I know I'm supposed to be the same as those women I met when we came in off the street—yet he is the only one here who feels at all like me.

His breath warms my skin. His fingers wrap around me, stroking my face and neck and hair, stroking my arms and fingers and lips.

The pain between us worsens.

It is a spike that arcs, starting as a gentle pull before it keens steeply up, inexorable, becoming gradually more unbearable. In minutes, I am sure my insides will be ripped out, torn into so many pieces there is nothing left.

I've never wanted like this.

Never.

Beyond where I lay, a golden ocean beckons.

It is familiar.

Even more familiar than the mountains we share, the grief over our pasts.

He is there, too.

I'm sorry, he says. *I did this. I did this to you. I'm sorry—*

No. My voice is steady, somehow apart from the lights clashing, the ghosts winging over both of our heads. *No, Revik. You didn't. It's all right.*

Don't leave me, Allie. Don't leave me alone with this.

I feel confusion on him, confusion in his own words, what he means by them.

The feeling intensifies though; his hands tighten on my skin.

The pain worsens, making it hard to see.

Still, my own words come easily, without thought or regret.

I won't, I tell him. *I never will. I'll never leave. Not if you don't want me to.*

There is a question in this.

The question shocks his heart.

I am asking him for something. My light is, anyway. I can't say it's a conscious question, not fully, but the intensity behind it is real. It also feels entirely like me.

I am asking him for something.

I want a promise from him. A vow.

I want him to give himself to me.

It is nonsense, what I am asking of him, but I don't withdraw the question, nor try to qualify it or understand it in any way with words. I only wait, seeing what he will say. Before I've fully understood either the question or the possible answers he might give, he's agreed.

A surrender lives in that agreement.

I feel shame there, too, like he knows he should say no.

But he cannot—he will not.

I don't want him to.

He clasps my fingers, and I see tears in his eyes. They bewilder me, touch me sharply through the pain and he pulls me closer until…

He kisses me. It is a brief kiss. Clumsy. Awkward. Yet it is tender, too. Meaning lives there, more meaning than I can comprehend.

He kisses me again. That time, there is so much light in it, it cuts my breath.

He pulls away, even as the pain between us grows unbearable.

I feel him agree again, and it feels final that time.

It is absolute. He is certain now.

It feels like an ending and a beginning, all at once.

Even as I think it, the night sky disappears. Above us, light weaves in complicated patterns, in and out like a shuttlecock between silk threads. I have a fleeting impression of time removed. The weaving of the threads grows more and more complicated, more subtle, more beautiful and intimate.

I watch a painting form in that vastness of sky, a painting of fiery, diamond light, in a pattern too breathtaking for words. My struggle stops, even as the pain I felt before melts into warm breath, a feeling of ending, of beginning.

I know this, somehow. This is familiar to me.

I feel it in him, too, that surge of familiar.

The feeling is so heart-wrenching, so intense, I cannot see anything else.

He belongs to me.

He belonged to me before I asked the question.

A timelessness lives in that knowing, something so far from my conscious mind it feels alien. That deep sense of familiar is something I can't explain to myself, something I understand without words, without really understanding anything at all.

Something is… different.

I don't know it yet, but it will never be the same again.

CHAPTER 15

CHANGE

I sat in a window, balanced toe to heel on a white painted wooden sill.

My butt started to numb in the twenty or so minutes since I first fixed my perch.

But I didn't move from the narrow ledge as I looked out the rain-splattered window. Through the glass lived a world of gray, with charcoal streets and sad-looking trees breaking up long swaths of sidewalk.

A man walked by in a tarp of a raincoat, pushing a shopping cart filled with cans and covered with blue plastic. He glanced up at the window.

I held my breath, frozen as he stared at me, but his face looked resigned, his eyes blurred by rain. Gripping the cart's handlebars, he resumed pushing it down the street, his expression unmoved.

A long, slow, questioning tug slid through my belly.

My eyes closed. I grimaced in pain.

He was looking for me.

That tug grew urgent briefly. Filled with longing, it had an overt sexuality I found disconcerting, difficult to think past.

Gradually, it faded back, pulled somewhere else.

I glanced over at the bed, without turning my head.

Above him hung the tapestry where an angry-faced blue god rode a lion, tongues of flame circling its head in bright oranges and reds. My eyes shifted to the tapestry nearer to me, the one depicting a golden buddha with multiple faces. Crowning the stack of extra heads hung a delicate, androgynous face exuding golden light.

Revik moved.

My eyes drifted reluctantly down.

He slept on his back, arms and legs sprawled, his hands and fingers open. I studied the softness of his expression and felt that tugging, longing sensation return, urgent this time, enough to bring the nausea back in a warm flood.

I'd woken to the feeling, and him wrapped around me, half crushing me with his arms and body in sleep. I'd been careful of his hurt shoulder without thinking about it much, but I'd been wrapped around him just as tightly. My face rested in the hollow of his neck, one of my legs curled around and between his. My arm had been coiled around his waist, clasping his bare back, my fingers massaging muscles, caressing his skin.

I'd been pulling on him unconsciously, intensely, as much as he had with me.

It had felt completely natural that his fingers were tangled in my hair, that he'd tugged me closer with that same hand, his mouth brushing my temple in sleep. When I stroked his bare arm and chest, caressing his fingers, he let out a low sound, enough to wake me for real.

It was also enough to get me swiftly out of his bed when I realized parts of him were awake ahead of his mind.

Since then, he'd been looking for me with his light.

It wasn't enough to wake him, just enough to make me sick.

I still hadn't left.

I couldn't decide why, but my reasons for staying felt irrational, even to me.

I was starving. I needed a shower like I'd never needed one before. I smelled like filthy lake water and my hair had the consistency of matted straw. I wanted clean clothes. I also could be talking to the other seers, the friendlier ones, at least, trying to find out more about my mom, Jon and Cass, and what they'd been showing on the feeds about me and Revik.

Instead I was here, watching him sleep.

I couldn't make myself leave, even now that I had to go to the bathroom.

Feeling eyes on me, I turned.

When I saw that we weren't alone, I started, half-sliding off my window perch.

Ullysa smiled at me from the doorway, looking like an old movie still with her hair piled on her head and a powder-blue gown clinging to her hips. Turning away from me, she scrutinized Revik clinically.

Without thinking about why, I hopped the rest of the way off the sill.

I crossed the room, drawing the woman's eyes back to me.

Ullysa frowned, exuding a faint puzzlement.

That puzzlement didn't dissipate as she turned to study my light with the same narrow-eyed stare she'd trained on Revik.

"What?" I asked quietly when I reached her.

Ullysa's face broke into a smile of such sincerity, I was taken aback.

"He is better," she said, clasping my arm with warm fingers. "I am relieved. You did very well with him."

I blinked into the woman's violet eyes.

"Oh," I said. "Good. Yes, he seemed better." Glancing at Revik, I looked away, fighting embarrassment without knowing what it stemmed from precisely. Keeping my expression as neutral as possible, I met her gaze. "Look, is there any way I could borrow some clothes? I'm starving too, and a shower—"

"Yes! Yes. Of course!" Ullysa squeezed my arm, exuding more warmth. "You may have whatever you wish while you are here, Bridge Alyson! Anything at all!"

I smiled back, a little unnerved by her enthusiasm.

"Thanks. I'll pay you back, once I—"

"No. No, no, no." The seer waved this off, making a sharp line in the air with her fingers. "There is no need for that. The honor is ours. And Revi' is an old friend."

My eyes shifted involuntarily to the bed.

I found myself remembering some key details from the day before.

Things I'd managed to skirt in my mind all morning.

In particular, I remembered how the other seers had talked about him. I remembered the jealousy I'd felt on Kat. I remembered other things I'd felt on Kat, too—she'd clearly wanted me to know she and Revik had some kind of sexual relationship.

Watching his expression tighten briefly in sleep, along with the fingers of one of his hands, I sighed, more internally than on the outside.

"Yeah," I said belatedly. "I caught that. That you knew him."

When I glanced back, Ullysa was staring at me again, her odd-colored eyes bright with *aleimic* light. She didn't stare at my face; instead, her focus hovered somewhere just above my head, her eyes holding a kind of wonder.

The same intensity and precision shifted back to Revik.

I fidgeted with the doorjamb as she looked at him.

It occurred to me that I didn't want her getting too close to him, not even with her eyes.

Abruptly, Ullysa's violet irises clicked back into focus.

She bowed, her expression still holding wonder.

"Of course, sister. My apologies. Truly."

I wrapped my arms around my waist, shrugging.

It occurred to me I didn't know exactly what she was apologizing for.

Ullysa spoke before I could. "How is it that you are feeling yourself, sister?"

I noticed her accent had lost some of its human-like cadence. Maybe she had simply relaxed around me some. Or maybe it had something to do with whatever clearly bothered yet excited her about me and Revik.

"I'm fine." I tried to unclench my fists, to relax that reflexive but alien vigilance. I couldn't. "I'm fine. Just..." I glanced at Revik, stifling the impulse to step directly between him and the woman. "I'm fine," I repeated a third time, succumbing to the impulse by moving a half-step to my right. "Just tired, I guess. Hungry. In desperate need of a shower."

Ullysa smiled. "Please make yourself at home. We can supply you with anything you need during your stay."

"Stay?" I felt my face tighten. "How long will we be staying here?"

Ullysa smiled.

Her voice turned briefly business-like.

"You two are safe for now," she said. "But they found no bodies. In future, if you wish to fake your deaths, I suggest you consult Revi' first."

Her smile crept out wider, and didn't seem to have any relation to her actual words.

"The Rooks know you are here," she said. "They at least know you were seen together in Seattle. They know about the stolen headset. It is good you left that in the taxi." She added cheerfully, "It is better that we wait until they are not watching every route in and out of the city. We are sending seers starting today, to begin to create false trails."

Watching my eyes, she grinned again.

"Do you have a passport, Bridge Alyson?"

I shook my head. "No."

"That is easily fixed. Vash also suggested you might use this time to learn more about why you are here. To begin your training."

I glanced at Revik, feeling his light looking for mine again.

I pushed it aside gently, focusing back on the woman.

"Where will I go that I need a passport?" I asked.

"There are many places, Bridge Alyson." The woman's smile turned back to a grin. "Revi's home is not in this country."

I flushed, hearing the teasing behind this.

The woman must have felt his pull.

"Where does he live? Germany, or—"

"No," Ullysa said, surprised. "Not Germany. Not for many years. He lived in Russia also, I believe." Thinking, she brushed this off. "Currently, he lives in London. He has maintained a residence there for at least five or six years." She paused, smiling at me warmly again. "And it is no trouble at all to keep my light from his, Bridge Alyson. I completely understand."

My face grew hotter.

Succumbing to the impulse again, I stepped a little more firmly into the woman's line of sight to Revik.

Rather than causing offense, something in the gesture seemed to touch the other woman immensely. She startled me by touching my face, then kissing my cheek.

She turned as if to leave… then abruptly stopped.

I tensed before my mind supplied me with a reason.

Still polite, Ullysa glanced over my shoulder, a glimmer of asking permission inherent in the brevity of the peek.

"Revi', darling. Did we wake you?"

His answer was low. His deep voice made me jump, almost cringe.

"It's fine," he said.

"Are you hungry?"

"Yes."

I took a breath, turned—and found his eyes locked on me. The look in them was narrow, cold, with a veiled hostility that took me aback.

The hostility was unmistakably aimed at me.

Ullysa didn't seem to notice. "Of course you are." She smiled. "And congratulations, Revi'. I am touched. Very touched. Good hunting, friend."

Seeing that Ullysa was close to tears above her smile, I glanced again at Revik, feeling my nerves turn into actual fear when I saw his face. His skin had darkened; it was clear he knew exactly what Ullysa was talking about.

It was equally clear he didn't appreciate the comment at all.

He averted his gaze when it caught mine, folding his arms across his chest.

I couldn't take my eyes off his face.

Was he *blushing?*

He bowed slightly to Ullysa. "Thank you."

Wiping her cheek, the woman smiled, then turned to go.

I found I couldn't follow her out fast enough.

Before I made it through the door, Ullysa turned, looking at me in surprise.

"Alyson. Where are you going?"

I froze. "Passport. Eggs. Shower…"

"Why don't you stay here?" she suggested. "We will bring food for you both. It is too early for passports… and the shower can wait."

I felt cornered. I glanced at Revik. His eyes were trained out the window, as gray as the sky. I looked back to Ullysa.

"No, actually, it can't wait. The shower, I mean. Besides, I have to go to the bathroom. And I thought I might talk to you, and maybe some of the others."

Ullysa's eyes grew puzzled. "About what? We told you all of the news we knew last night. Nothing has changed since then."

My jaw tightened. "Well, about the Bridge thing, then. Maybe you can explain what that means to you seers. You know, before I accidentally kill everyone on the planet."

"I can talk to you about that," Revik said.

Startled, I glanced at him.

He continued to train his eyes out the window.

Mine fell involuntarily to his bare upper body, taking in the leanness of his long frame and the banded muscle of his arms, a pale lattice of scars that crept up over one shoulder. He had an armband tattoo just above one bicep, I noticed, something I'd glimpsed when he started taking off his shirt in that park, without really seeing it. It looked like some kind of writing in black and gold lettering.

I saw the edge of what might have been another tattoo on the shoulder of the same side. He also had the standard barcode tat on his right arm, along with the "H" mark he'd shown me in the car, designating his race-cat.

His body without clothes looked somehow older than the rest of him.

That definitely wasn't a bad thing, from my perspective.

I saw his fingers tighten on his upper arm, and looked away.

"Stay, if you want." His voice remained flat, formally polite. "Shower, then come back."

"No," I said. "You should rest. I can annoy someone else with my questions for a while." Seeing him about to answer, I said, "It's fine, Revik. And I know your friends will want to see you." I glanced down again. "Especially when you're not wearing a shirt."

His eyes seemed to flinch.

Staring at his long countenance, I found myself briefly lost there.

His eyes were still angry on the surface, but I could almost *see* the openness beneath, a vulnerability so much the opposite of his usual expression that I couldn't help but stare. Remembering him pulling on me moments before, the softness of his face as he held me in sleep, I blinked as the two images superimposed over one another.

I tried to reconcile them, couldn't.

My eyes shifted first, meeting Ullysa's in my attempt to escape his.

Her returning smile held amusement.

She folded her thin arms, quirking a pencil-darkened eyebrow at Revik.

Turning, I walked wordlessly out the door.

I saw Ullysa's eyes widen in surprise, just before she moved out of my way.

I didn't stop walking. I didn't even slow down enough to realize I didn't know where I was going, not until I'd passed another three doors. Then I stopped dead, standing in the darkened corridor.

By then, I was having trouble breathing.

Anxiety clenched my chest.

I held the wall with one hand.

I tried to turn it into anger, like he had.

The pull to go back to him was nearly physical in its intensity.

My mind fought to sift through details of the night before.

We definitely hadn't had sex. Anyway, hadn't those other seers said Revik was a prostitute? So was Ullysa, for that matter—so were all of the seers here. Sex wouldn't faze them; it certainly wouldn't have elicited such glee from Ullysa. Remembering what Kat said about Revik in that regard, what she'd shown me with her light, I fought with a hot flood of… God, *something*. Whatever it was, it briefly took over my whole mind.

It grew intense enough to scare me, past any semblance of rational thought.

A memory flashed inside me—of seeing Jaden in that bar, of finding myself suddenly holding a bottle decorated with a strange woman's blood.

Christ. Was it *jealousy?*

The stories I'd grown up hearing about seers started to come back, every feed broadcast I'd ever seen or heard about them and their sexuality.

Most of those made no sense to me now.

According to everything I'd ever heard, seers were incapable of relationships. They were sexually insatiable, and they didn't discriminate. Remembering those flashes of Revik and his wife, Elise, I found myself thinking those stories couldn't possibly be *less* compatible with what I'd seen and felt from him.

In those memories, Revik felt intense love for his wife.

He'd loved her to the point of insanity; he'd nearly killed himself over her.

The feeds also claimed seers were predatory with sex.

They said seers seduced humans by hooking into their victims' fantasies and delusions until they lost themselves entirely inside the seer's mind. Those stories always made it sound deliberate, though, and whatever happened between me and Revik the night before, it didn't feel like Revik had done it intentionally.

In fact, he seemed to blame *me* for whatever occurred.

As the thought sunk in, I remember more about the night before.

I remembered asking him for something.

I remembered a promise.

It was vague, though. I remembered a lot of light, Revik crying.

Was he angry at me for that? Had I broken some kind of seer etiquette, asking him for something he didn't want to give, something he didn't feel he could refuse, because of who I was? He hadn't seemed angry, though. Not last night.

He'd kissed me, hadn't he?

Or had I imagined that, too?

It definitely didn't feel like we'd had sex. No matter how battered my body was, I was still like 98% certain I would have noticed. Besides, I wanted sex. I could tell Revik did, too. Even in his anger, I could feel him wanting sex.

It occurred to me I might have been waiting for him to wake up for that very reason.

The admission made me feel a little queasy.

Images rose from the night before, confusing me more.

Whatever that had been, it hadn't felt like a dream.

My attempts to convince myself I'd imagined it rang hollow, too.

No, they were definitely memories. He'd been a *Nazi*... a married Nazi with a death sentence for murdering his commanding officer for screwing his wife.

That guy Terian had been there.

The pain in my stomach worsened.

I knew some of it was that seer pain I'd felt before, but now it was mixing with the stress of not knowing how to process any of this.

I stared at a nearby door.

It hung ajar, breaking the dark walls of the corridor.

For a long moment, I only stared, without really seeing it—then my eyes clicked back into focus. I realized I was looking at a pink tile wall.

It was a bathroom.

Pushing off the wallpaper, I made my way over to it, limping as my body's battered state grew more noticeable. I closed the door behind me, only to stand there indecisively, my back pressed to the wood. Finally, I turned around and sat on the toilet.

It wasn't until I'd relieved myself that it occurred to me that through that whole exchange with Ullysa and Revik, I hadn't been wearing pants.

Clasping my hands between my bare knees, I let out a strangled laugh.

I sat there for what felt like a long time.

My body was unbelievably sore.

Not sex sore—just run of the mill falling down a hill after being handcuffed to a car then driving off a bridge and smacking my skull sore.

The nausea worsened as soon as my bladder wasn't full enough to distract me. I gripped the edge of the pedestal sink, afraid I'd throw up if I tried to stand. It felt like some part of me had been broken and smashed, then reassembled with pieces missing—or maybe with new ones woven in with the old.

I still sat there, paralyzed, when Ullysa knocked.

After the second knock, she tried the handle.

Opening the door cautiously, she handed through clean clothes and a basket with soap and shampoo. I felt her concern. Once she'd placed everything on the tile, I felt her hesitate, about to speak. Preempting whatever thing she might try to communicate, I reached over with one foot to push the door shut.

Even through the door and intervening corridor, I could feel him.

His anger was still there, pulsing at me, but so was the other, unmistakable now, until the two wove together, impossible to separate as distinct feelings.

He wanted me to come back.

I felt it tangibly, if with a dim sort of confusion.

He was having the same reaction I was, and on more than one level.

For a moment I doubted what I felt, then a sliver of his pain hit me, weaving into some part of me I couldn't see. My body's reaction was immediate, and violent. My stomach hurt, but it wasn't just that. I felt my face flush, my chest and thighs warm.

I felt myself start to respond, to reach back in his direction.

I panicked, pulling that part of me back.

His pain worsened, turning liquid.

It was unmistakably sexual.

I was still sitting there when he dropped the pretense, asking me openly to return to the room. When I didn't respond, he pulled on me harder, letting me feel the want behind it, until I clutched the edge of the sink.

Stop, I thought at him, gasping. *Please, stop.*

After the barest pause, his presence receded.

I remained lost in his light. My skin flushed as I realized the flavor of his thoughts. He was having trouble not fantasizing. He wanted me to come back. He wanted it so badly he wasn't thinking rationally anymore. He wanted to fuck. The word hit at me; the desire behind it stole my breath, making me clutch the sink harder.

On the surface, he asked me again. Politely, that time.

When I let out a short laugh, his mind retreated. But not entirely.

I felt him thinking again. Then he started to open his light. I felt emotion expand off him, that vulnerability I'd glimpsed in the room, mixed with a hotter, denser desire.

Both things enveloped me, blanked my mind.

They grew stronger as his want intensified his pain.

He slid deeper into my light—

I panicked, pushing him back.

That time, he withdrew until I barely felt him.

Still flushed, I staggered to my feet, buying myself time by examining the bruises that ran all along my legs and arms. Limping to the tub, I bent to twist the porcelain shower knobs all the way to hot. I tugged the shirt over my head, dropping it on the floor. As water heated in the ancient pipes, I stood in the basin, shivering.

I tried to ignore the waiting I felt behind his silence.

Allie, he sent softly. *…please.*

The pull behind it cut my breath.

Gaos… please. Please…

Pain flickered around the spaces between us, and for an instant, I hesitated, staring at that void, feeling it with him. The lost feeling worsened.

Then I stepped under the hot water.

I let my mind go blank as the smell of steaming hot lake water rose off my hair, sliding off my body like a second skin. I lowered my head as the water beat at it, sending brown, brackish water down the sides of the tub and into the drain.

I felt him watch me as I continued to stand there.

His light flickered around mine, silent, waiting.

For a long time, it didn't move away.

CHAPTER 16

REJECTION

I stood before a silhouette target, trying not to feel foolish as I fumbled with the safety of the gun I gripped in both hands. Ullysa told me twice what kind of gun it was, but all I remembered was what Ivy called it—Baby Eagle.

Dad had been more of a rifle and shotgun kind of guy.

"Stop stalling," Ullysa said. "You have only perhaps a few more days before you and Revi' must leave here, Esteemed Bridge."

I nodded, only half-listening.

Being here, surrounded by seers, I forgot we were in Seattle most of the time.

I could barely remember it even as I watched the skyline change from day to night and back again through the windows of the upper floors. It was as though the building and all its contents remained disconnected from its physical location in the middle of the human city.

The one thread between it and us was the steady stream of clients for the prostitutes.

I still couldn't grasp the extent or prevalence of this kind of thing, meaning, seers living under the radar, smack dab in the middle of human civilization without any controls. I was curious about it, sure, but a little hesitant to ask questions at this point. I'd already made the mistake of mentioning SCARB once, and managed to silence an entire room.

It had been Kat, of course, who broke the silence.

"Why doesn't SCARB mind our lack of sponsorship?" The Russian seer sneered. "Well, perhaps, cub, we do them the courtesy of not killing them out of deference for the preciousness of living light? You see, what you call 'sponsorship,' we call *sla-ver-y*. Unless you know a way to own a seer's *aleimi* without owning the seer? If so, please share it with the rest of us. You truly will be our savior then, oh holiest of Bridges!"

Some in the room hid smiles.

I also felt pulses of anger aimed in my direction.

"Would *you* like sponsorship, cub?" Kat asked, her lips lifted in a cold smile. "Shall we call SCARB for you? Perhaps they mind *your* lack of sponsorship now, eh?"

Only later did I muster the nerve to ask Ullysa more about what *aleimi* meant.

As Revik had said, *aleimi* was the seer word for the light bodies I'd seen behind the Barrier, those structures and geometries I'd seen on Revik and myself, as well as on humans.

They also called it "living light," or, more commonly, just "light."

Ullysa further defined *aleimi* as, "the ability to carry light."

When I asked if this was like "soul," she shook her head. She said humans and seers were equal in soul, but they differed in this ability to carry and manipulate light.

No direct translation of the word existed in English.

It was strictly a seer word.

I was learning that even seer language had a Barrier component—meaning, the words contained meanings that required an ability to see them with the added structures in one's light. Generally speaking, their words carried more compound meanings and nuances in general.

One seer word often needed a sentence to translate into English.

Ullysa said more about this, about words being symbols and all symbols having unspoken layers. Since more than half of all shared seer culture came from Barrier-consciousness—a split consciousness unshared by humans—translation of many of their core symbols to human language remained literally impossible.

I even understood this, in part.

I'm not sure how much understanding it helped me, though.

Ullysa and I now stood in a cement, sound-proof bunker, complete with a firing range and rows of storage lockers that held everything from ammunition to plant seeds to casks of water and enough food for everyone in the building to eat for at least a few years.

Ullysa jokingly referred to it as their "ark."

She stood behind me, looking like a movie star even in protective glasses and with soundproofing mufflers over her ears.

"You should let Revi' help you with this," she said loudly over the sound-deadeners, repeating herself for the fifth time.

I nodded, staring at the target.

When Ullysa clicked at me, I glanced over at her face.

"Why will you not speak to him?"

"I really don't want to bother him right now, Ullysa."

"Why?" the woman said, exasperated. "Because of Kat? You *threw* her at him, and now you complain when he uses her to cope with—"

"Stop!" I held up a hand. "I don't need to know about his 'coping' methods. It's none of my business. Or yours."

With Ullysa, I'd given up pretending I didn't care where he slept.

Anyway, she was right.

It was my own damned fault.

That first morning I'd woken up in Seattle, I'd entered the kitchen after my shower, wearing borrowed clothes and following the smell of coffee and faintly burned toast.

There, Kat and two others, Ivy and the African-looking seer from the night before, looked up from where they lounged on barstools, leaning against a marble countertop next to platters of eggs and toast.

I avoided Kat's stare, focusing on the eggs and trying not to notice that I could still feel Revik. His presence coiled into me, wrapped into my light in a way that should have felt cloying, but pretty much did the opposite. I could feel the part of me pulling on him, too, not content with the amount we were connected now.

Briefly, hunger overshadowed the other thing I felt.

All three seers looked up when Ullysa entered the kitchen behind me.

It was the African-looking one who focused first on the empty space above my head. I realized she must be noticing the same thing that had so captivated Ullysa earlier. After scanning me thoroughly with a sharp gaze, she glanced at Ullysa with raised eyebrows.

When the same seer looked at Ivy, Ivy only smiled, making a shrug-like gesture with her hand before lifting a mug of coffee to her lips.

Kat gaped above my head in open disbelief.

"He's awake." I met Kat's eyes. "You can see him, if you want."

Ullysa stiffened. Shock wafted palpably off her light.

The African seer and Ivy exchanged looks as well. None of them spoke, but I felt their minds crackle around me. My words snapped Kat back to her usual hard demeanor.

Even so, her smile had the faintest bit of surprise in it as well.

"Thanks, worm. I accept."

Her choice of words hit me strangely.

Still, I didn't speak as she rose to her feet. She walked out of the room, not bothering to close her robe as she brushed by me on her way out. The African-looking seer left, too, but her eyes held as much puzzlement as Ullysa's.

It didn't feel as though she were following Kat.

Ivy stayed.

She and Ullysa remained silent as they piled eggs and toast on a plate for me and poured me a cup of coffee, shoving cream and sugar within my reach.

Ivy finally broke the silence.

"He might not like that," she said tentatively. "Even if the two of you have decided to wait to complete things. He might not like what you just did."

I halted a forkful of eggs halfway to my mouth.

"I just mean…" Ivy looked at me apologetically, shrugging with one hand. "You offering him to Kat. Even if you are trying to be generous, he might take it… wrong."

She hesitated, looking to Ullysa for help.

Ullysa was more direct.

"He will definitely take it badly," she said. "It is rejection. More than rejection. For a seer, it is an overt insult. Are you angry with him?"

I stared between them, gripping my coffee mug. I cleared my throat.

"No," I said.

Ullysa finished pouring herself a glass of juice. Not doing a very good job of hiding her puzzlement, she clicked softly, exhaling in a sigh.

"Bridge Alyson, perhaps the circumstances are not clear to you. Males are quite vulnerable after. Given his history, Revi', in particular, will have trouble with this. That would be true even without Kat there."

She studied my eyes and face.

Once she had, her expression softened.

"Please do not take him personally right now, sister," she said. "Or do anything rash. He agreed, the same as you. There are no 'mistakes' with these things. Give him time to adjust. He is perhaps not reacting to this in the way you imagined..." She gave Ivy a knowing smile, chuckling a little. "Revi' is not typical in some respects. But he is still seer."

At my silence, Ullysa glanced at Ivy.

Gesturing delicately, she added, "If he has asked you to wait to complete things, it is likely logistical only. He may wish for a construct in a more secluded location, away from other seers. Revi' can be quite traditional, in his way." She exchanged another wry smile with Ivy. "In any case, be assured, sister. The delay won't be for long."

I looked between them again, feeling my sense of unreality worsen, even as my pulse turned borderline painful in my chest.

Ullysa's smile faded.

She and Ivy exchanged another glance, this one worried.

Ullysa said, "Surely you must sense some portion of... what occurred?"

I felt my face redden. I was about to ask, when Ullysa cut me off.

"No," she said decisively. "No... *gaos.* I assumed the two of you had spoken about this. If you have not, this cannot come from us. It cannot. You must speak to Revi'."

I stared at her, feeling my jaw harden as that constricted feeling in my chest worsened. Still looking at me, Ullysa made a slash mark in the air with her fingers, the same gesture Revik told me meant "no" the night before.

"It is absolutely not our place to explain this," she said. "I apologize for saying anything at all to you, sister. He would be furious with us, if we discussed this with you before the two of you have spoken about it. And rightfully so."

I looked at Ivy, who only nodded, eyes serious.

"You should do it soon," Ullysa added. Her violet eyes met mine, hardening as her voice darkened. "Kat will not be able to help him with this for long, sister. And I won't have you retaliating, not in my home."

She gestured again sharply, as if in judgment.

"What you just did—it was an open offer. We both saw it. If you let it happen now, you have absolutely no recourse if he accepts."

At the serious look in both women's eyes, a kind of fear grew in me, but not one that impelled me into movement. I had no intention of chasing down Kat.

If he didn't want her there, he could damned well tell her himself.

As I pictured Kat in there with him, though, the pain came back in a sharp swell, along with fear, a sudden realization that I didn't really trust myself to go after her, whatever I told myself. The last time I got jealous, I'd nearly killed someone. What if Revik told me to leave? What if I walked in on them in the middle of... whatever?

I didn't trust myself to handle either of those scenarios well.

Remembering how angry he'd been when he first woke up, I wondered if he'd handle them all that well, either.

Even as I thought it, I realized I didn't feel Revik anymore.

He'd completely disappeared from my light.

When I didn't move, Ullysa sighed again.

That had been over a week ago.

When I'd finally returned to the bedroom with the orange walls, later that same day, Revik was no longer in it. No one came out and said anything, but it was pretty clear I'd committed some kind of major *faux pas*.

Ullysa's voice jerked my mind back to the present.

"Are you going to try?" Ullysa said, exasperated. "Or will you simply stand there? With all respect, I have other things that need doing, Esteemed Bridge."

I raised the gun half-heartedly, aiming at the dark human outline in paper hanging from a clip attached to a mechanized pulley about twenty feet away. Forcing my mind to a blank, I steadied the gun with my other hand and fired off three shots. Each one threw both of my arms back into their shoulder sockets.

When the sound died, I refocused on the target, lowering the gun.

Only one bullet even hit the white paper, and that was a tear in one corner even I had to admit was likely dumb luck.

Clicking at me, seer-fashion, Ullysa held out her hand.

"Give it to me."

I handed over the gun, swinging my arm to get the kink out of my shoulder. Something caused me to glance back as I did it.

Once I did, my breath caught.

Revik stood by the door. His long body leaned halfway against the frame. His eyes narrowed, focused on mine, then shifted to the paper target.

He raised an eyebrow.

I felt my face flush.

Wiping a few strands of hair out of my eyes, I found I didn't know what to do with my hands. I focused back on Ullysa, trying to listen to her.

"Watch," Ullysa said, raising the gun. "You are closing your eyes… and jerking every time you squeeze the trigger. You are not even looking at the target, Allie! There is no way you would hit it like that."

I nodded, swallowing. I felt Revik's eyes on me still.

"Revi' told me your father taught you to shoot—"

"Rifles." I heard the defensiveness in my voice. "I was a kid. I never took it up as a hobby."

"Well, fine. But with a rifle you must also *aim*. With your eyes open. And it is normal to flinch, but you must train yourself not to jerk."

I nodded again, then glanced back in spite of myself.

Revik had vanished from the doorway.

I felt a pang that made it hard to breathe.

I'd never been the mooning type, not even with Jaden, so it made me crazy how I found myself reacting to Revik now. Worse, it felt completely outside of my control. He was even starting to look different to me—and definitely not worse, unfortunately.

I felt Ullysa watching me, a curious look on her face.

I waved the weapon away with a grimace when she tried to hand it back to me.

"Forget it. I don't think guns are my cup of tea, 'Llysa."

"You must learn, Alyson."

"No. Not right now."

Ullysa frowned, glancing at the door.

For an instant, her eyes slid out of focus.

When they clicked back, she frowned again, muttering under her breath. She indicated toward the target with her free hand.

"Once more. I insist."

Sighing, I caved, taking the gun.

Once more. Right.

I raised the weapon to eye level, pointing it resignedly at the target.

As I concentrated on aiming that time, however, a grid appeared behind my eyes. It reminded me of the grid I'd seen while driving, the one Revik had shown me. I felt him with this one too, and flinched. He held me in place, almost as if he stood behind me, gripping my arms.

Just watch, he sent. *Trust me.*

I bit my lip, but forced myself to relax.

In the middle of that grid, a sharp spot of light hovered near the target.

I fought not to react as his presence retreated, leaving me standing there, shaking and a little sick-feeling. I stared at the grid and that sharp spot of light. Once I relaxed a little more, I saw that the grid originated from one of the geometrical shapes above my own head.

I aligned the grid and the sharp bright spot with the silhouette on the paper.

"Gently," Ullysa said.

I glanced at her in surprise.

I'd forgotten she was there.

I started to pull out of the Barrier, but a faint pressure told me to stay.

So he hadn't left entirely.

Aligning the grid once more, I forced a deep breath—and squeezed the trigger.

Inside the Barrier, there was no need to flinch.

Without clicking out of that calm state, I aligned the grid over a different part of the silhouette, firing again. I fired a third time, and a fourth. It all seemed to happen slow, like in a dream. But when I opened my eyes, the corridor between me and the target still drifted with smoke.

Ullysa laughed aloud, clapping her hands.

I stared at the target.

Four neat holes punctuated the head, chest and abdomen of the shadowy outline.

For a bare instant, I flushed in elation, tinged with a near relief that

I'd finally managed to hit something. Better yet, I might even be able to repeat the trick on my own.

Behind me, I felt his presence withdraw.

It left gradually, almost reluctantly, leaving a faint whisper of nausea in its wake.

CHAPTER 17
HORSEMEN

"Any more news of Jon or Cass?" I asked.

I didn't wait for an answer before plopping down on the enormous, faux-suede couch in front of the wall-length monitor. The feeds ran as a gentle hum on that same monitor, the sound low, text running beneath flickering and morphing images.

Mika flopped down beside me.

She gestured what I now knew to be a "yes" in seer sign language.

We had just come from the kitchen.

She handed me a glass of grapefruit juice and half a sandwich filled with something called *iresmic,* a chutney-like spread made by seers. Truthfully, it was weird-tasting in the extreme, but I could bear it, at least.

Most of the seer food they tried to give me, I couldn't get down at all.

Mika, who was the same, short, Chinese-looking seer from that first night I'd gotten there, gestured at the monitor.

"Your friends have been moved by the government," she said. "Your mother, too. It is good, Allie. It means they are handling it through the humans. The Rooks are leaving them alone." Mika rolled her eyes, smiling faintly as she finished swallowing her bite of sandwich. "It is the Rooks' new favorite toy, to call everyone a terrorist."

I tried to smile back.

I couldn't quite feel the same relief she did at the prospect of my mom and brother in a federal prison.

"I suppose breaking them out is out of the question?"

Mika laughed, poking me in the ribs with a finger. "You human-borns are all the same. It is all pow-pow with guns."

"Yeah," I said, exhaling. "That's me. Gun girl."

Mika smiled, but her eyes remained serious. "The Rooks have infiltrators all over the human government, Allie. And in every branch of law enforcement. It would be very dangerous for your family if we were to try such a thing. But do not worry! They will let them out soon. Our intelligence says your mother should be out in a few days. And in some ways, they are safer in there. The other humans may harass them once they are out."

I frowned, not reassured by that, either.

From above us rose a loud bang, like someone knocking a table to the floor.

I glanced up, then back at Mika.

When the seer didn't react, I forced a shrug.

"What about when they're out?" I asked. "Can your people pick them up then? Or do you think they'd be safer where they are?"

"We will monitor the situation closely." Mika hesitated, then added, "I know Dehgoies feels very responsible. He is talking to our infiltrators in California several times a day."

I looked back at the television.

I had to fight to keep my face neutral.

"He shouldn't," I said after a pause. "Honestly, I don't know enough about what he could have done differently to blame him for any of it. Anyway, he didn't make me a seer."

Mika patted my leg. "We will keep them safe. Do not worry, Bridge Alyson."

The banging above us started up again.

It grew louder, more rhythmic, broken by thick female cries.

I glanced up, then smiled wanly at Mika. "Someone's having fun."

Mika clicked in irritation, shaking her head. "Kat… always Kat. 'Llysa should give her a soundproof room, or at least one away from the common areas. Poor Ivy. Their rooms are right next to one another."

She noticed my expression then, and her irritation faded.

"Oh. Sorry, Allie."

I shook my head, taking another bite of the sandwich and chewing.

Mika sighed, staring back at the ceiling. "It's not *you,* you know. She would never admit to it, but she has always been weak for him."

I let the sandwich drop to my lap, suddenly not hungry at all.

Mika clicked her tongue. "It is no excuse. She would not be doing this if you had been raised seer. If it were me, she would wake up missing an ear."

I forced a smile. "Wow," I said. "Remind me not to piss you off."

Mika only made an irritated sound, aiming it at the ceiling.

Hesitating, I started to ask, but she gave me a direct look.

"I can't, Allie," she said. "I really can't. Please don't ask me."

I hesitated, then let it go, nodding. Still, everyone's silence on the topic of me and Revik was starting to feel pretty weird. It crossed my mind that Revik must have made them all take some kind of blood oath not to tell me anything.

But that seemed paranoid.

"No," Mika said, glancing at me again. "It's not."

I turned, staring at her. I opened my mouth to speak, but she cut me off.

"I can't tell you, Allie," she said, sighing with a soft clicking sound. "We all promised. You will have to ask him." Rolling her eyes, she added, "I think he's trying to force you to go to him. Or maybe he's just punishing you for offering his body and light to Kat."

Ignoring my stunned look, Mika gazed up at the ceiling when the banging started up again. Her voice grew apologetic. "It could be a customer."

I snorted. "At ten in the morning?"

"It could be."

I didn't argue. When the cries got louder, I glanced deliberately at the clock. Placing what was left of my sandwich on the ceramic platter, I nodded to Mika.

"I need to get going. Thanks for the food."

Mika looked at my barely-touched sandwich, then up at the ceiling. "You going to go play with guns again?"

"Sight training. Ullysa's turn to make me throw up while I try to block her and can't."

"You'll get better," Mika said, sympathetic. "It's like that for all of us at first. Only we're younger..." Flushing a little, she made an apologetic gesture with one hand. "You know."

I tried to ignore the sounds coming through the ceiling. "Even Ullysa says I'm learning slow. All those years of human conditioning screwed with my head, or something."

"She says that," Mika said. "And Ullysa acts like she is a novice, but she is *really* good at finding holes. She's an infiltrator, too, you know."

The cries above grew louder once more, even as the banging slowed, punctuated by more masculine groans.

I cleared my throat. "Can I practice on you later?" I asked.

"Sure. My first customer is at four."

Nodding, I rose deliberately to my feet.

I made a point of moving slow, but still felt like I walked too quickly from the room, heading for the nearest corridor without paying much attention to where it led. I was about two hours too early to meet Ullysa.

Biting the inside of my cheek, I decided to go to the compound's small temple. I could look at the paintings, read some of the old books they had lying around in there.

As I passed the industrial-sized kitchen, I saw movement and paused, peering through the swinging doors.

The kitchen was huge, even for the size of the building.

One wall consisted of an oven range with ten or so burners.

The room also contained two stainless steel refrigerators, along with rows of cabinets and counter space. A massive, wooden chopping block crouched by two porcelain sinks. In the middle of the room stood the high, marble table where I'd sat that first morning, polished to a mirror-like sheen and surrounded by barstools.

Revik stood by one of the cabinets.

His shirt hung open on his shoulders as he moved cans around.

I stared at him. I was still staring when he turned.

He flinched when he saw me there, then stared back, his pale eyes shining faintly in the kitchen's bright lights. I watched him reach for his own shirt. He buttoned it up while I watched, still not really looking at me.

"What?" he said finally. "What is it, Allie?"

I fought to suppress the feeling that rose in me, couldn't.

It was relief, but more than that. Grief. Frustration.

Something akin to despair.

From his face, I could tell he felt it, and that it startled him. His eyes flickered between mine, wary, but I saw something else there now.

"Allie?" His voice got lower. "Tell me."

For a second, I hesitated.

I glanced down the hallway, then back at him.

I *did* want to talk to him. I didn't know how, exactly, or even what I wanted to say, but I was more tired of the impasse between us than I knew how to express. I heard voices in the corridor, heading in our direction, and glanced at him again, feeling like the moment was about to pass. When I saw the wary look sharpen in his eyes, I found myself thinking about Kat, what I'd told myself about staying out of his business, leaving him alone.

He continued staring at me as the voices got louder.

I forced a smile, my nerves rising when it occurred to me he was probably reading my mind again.

I felt a whisper of anger on him.

Backing away, I shook my head, stepping away from the doorway.

"Sorry, I just…" I shook my head again. "Sorry."

I had just let go of the door when his voice rose.

"Alyson. Wait."

I came to a stop, in surprise as much as anything.

He exhaled when I turned, running his fingers through his dark hair. For a moment he only stood there. Then he looked up, meeting my gaze.

"Do you play chess, Allie?"

His voice was low, stiffly polite.

I stared at him. "Chess?"

"Yes." He motioned vaguely towards the marble bar, his accent thicker. "There is a board. We could play. Eat lunch."

I hesitated, but only for a few heartbeats. "Yeah," I said. "Great."

"Are you hungry? I could make us something."

I thought of the sandwich in the other room, then pushed it from my mind.

"Sure," I said. "Whatever you're having."

I just stood there as he poured a large can of soup into a pot.

He put it on the burner and lit the flame, then walked to a cabinet on the other side of the kitchen. I remained by the door as he pulled out a wooden chessboard that folded with hinges on the side, the black and white pieces housed within.

He opened up the box on the marble bar.

He started to pull out the pieces, to arrange them on the board, but I took another breath, and walked up to where he stood.

"I can do that," I said, feeling my cheeks warm. "You're making food."

He hesitated a bare instant, then put down the piece he was holding.

"Okay."

He retreated to the stove.

I set up the board. I toyed with asking him other things. Maybe something about the sight training with Ullysa, or the gun range trick he taught me, or more about me being the Bridge.

Finally, I settled on,

"You want to be black or white?"

When he looked over his shoulder, he surprised me with a faint humor in his eyes.

"You're the Bridge," he said. "You have to be white."

"Really?" I said, smiling back. "Why is that?"

"The White One," he said. "It is another name." Seeing my puzzlement, he gestured vaguely, facing the stove. "You know. There is the human myth. With horses. The Bridge is the white horseman."

He glanced back, bowing slightly.

"...Woman," he amended. "Horsewoman."

I smiled, but the comment stayed with me as I sat there.

"Do you mean the Four Horsemen?" I said. "As in, the Four Horsemen of the Apocalypse? The Bridge has something to do with that?"

He didn't look over, but continued stirring the soup as he nodded. "Yes. We call them The Four, though. Our myth is not the same as the human one." He gave me another wan smile. "The human one is based on ours."

I snorted a low laugh. I couldn't help it.

"Of course it is."

"It is," he insisted, but I heard the humor in his voice, too. "The Four are more like family. The Bridge is their leader."

Still smiling, I thought about it some more. "So there are three more like me?"

He made the "more or less" gesture with a hand. "Yes. Three more."

"And I'm the white one?"

He nodded again. "You are white. It is an *aleimi* thing. I do not fully understand it, but Vash could explain this to you. What the colors mean."

I nodded. Vash was the head of the Seven.

He was in India, with the other seer elders.

I remembered something about colors with the human myth, too, about each horse being a different color. White, red, black. Then there was the fourth one, the one I could never remember—

"Pale," he spoke up from the stove.

I nodded again. "Yes. Death, right?"

When he didn't say anything, I just sat there, trying to relax as he finished warming the soup. Pouring the contents of the pot into two bowls, he pulled spoons from a drawer and walked everything over to the bar, setting one of each beside me.

"You want anything to drink, Allie?"

"No," I said. "...Thanks. This is great."

When he nodded, his face still, I hesitated, wanting to say more. I tried to decide if I should ask him more about the Four Horsemen of the Apocalypse thing, or The Four, as he called them, or if I should leave that for another day. Somehow, pushing him back into his more academic, lecturing kind of mode didn't really appeal to me.

I picked up the bowl instead.

I was a little relieved to see it was regular old crappy human soup, like I was used to. Blowing on a spoonful to cool it, he motioned towards the board, using the fingers that held his spoon.

"White moves first," he said.

I swallowed my mouthful, nodding, then put down the bowl.

It crossed my mind that chances were good that he would kick my ass in this, too, given that there had to be a sight component to chess, just like there was with everything else. Still, a smile rose to my lips as I focused on the board, hearing the soft chink of his spoon as he ate.

When I glanced up, my eyes found one of the embroidered *thankahs* hanging on the wall, a golden buddha with peaceful eyes.

Under it, on a small shelf, stood a lit candle.

Incense sticks let off tiny lines of white smoke.

It crossed my mind that he must have done that, after Mika and I left.

I've never been a Buddhist or anything, or even religious, but for some reason, that touched me, too.

I moved my first pawn. Watching Revik's eyes narrow on the board, the bowl of soup balanced in his hand, I smiled again.

I didn't let myself think too clearly about why.

CHAPTER 18
LEAVING

He'd beaten me outside.

I stood in a doorway below the street, blinking against the tired rain of a Seattle afternoon. He threw a leg over the back of a motorcycle as I watched, and my nerves rose even more.

We were leaving.

Almost four weeks had gone by since I'd first woken up in bed with him.

I'd begun to wonder if we were ever going to leave Seattle.

But in monitoring the activity of the Rooks and SCARB, Homeland Security and whoever else, a group of seers somewhere in Asia finally decided it was safe for Revik and I to push on.

The main news feeds still ran "special reports" on who I was and my possible motives. Those reports showcased images of the car chase up Highway 101, along with scuba divers and scows dredging Lake Washington for the GTX and our bodies. While authorities wouldn't confirm or deny the rumors, some feeds still reported me as telekinetic, too.

I'd seen interviews of customers from the Lucky Cat, and a few of my old co-workers.

Cass and Jon weren't in any of the recent ones.

But I saw Sasquatch the cook being interviewed. I'd also seen interviews of Angeline and Corey, and a few others from the tattoo parlors where I'd worked.

Most of my friends looked pretty shell-shocked, even wearing virtual avatars.

Revik's face didn't appear in any of these reports.

Mine, on the other hand, was all over them.

They named me openly as a terrorist, using a non-avatar image of me from about three years ago, at one of my art openings. The only image I'd seen of Revik showed an avatar only, and called him a "potential accomplice" without using his name.

One thing in the plus column—my mother had been released from prison.

Mika assured me they had people watching her house to make sure she'd stay safe.

I hadn't heard anything directly about Jon yet, but Ullysa and Ivy told me he'd likely be released soon. Cass apparently had gone underground. They had no reports of law enforcement picking her up, so I had to assume she'd gone away on her own, or else left with Jack, her on-again, off-again boyfriend since we'd all gone to high school together.

Still, I never really relaxed.

It wasn't all Revik, or even the never-ending physical discomfort since that morning when he and I woke up in bed together. I was an outsider here, and I knew it. Most of the time, I couldn't forget it for more than a few minutes or hours in a stretch.

Even when they saw me as a fellow seer, I wasn't really one of them. I felt it in every word they said to me, saw it every time their expressions closed when I was around. It was less obvious with Ullysa, Mika and a few of the others, but it was still there.

I wasn't like them. I was something else.

During our frequent, if one-sided, chess matches, Revik told me as much as he knew about the mythology of the Bridge.

Maybe he was trying to get me more comfortable with the idea.

He also explained more about what I'd be faced with when we got to Asia.

Revik continued to make cracks about the Four Horsemen, too, which I think he meant mostly as a joke, although it was hard to tell with him. I sensed there was at least some seriousness to his teasing. He would drop things, here and there, that let me know he believed in the whole Bridge thing as much as the others, even if he seemed to see *me* differently.

Now I stood outside, feeling even more like an outsider.

In addition to the gun and sight training, Ullysa and her seers were extremely useful in one other regard—they taught me a *lot* about navigating the human world as a seer. I had new passports, visas, local ident cards. I even had a forged birth certificate. All of those documents said I was Yolanda Emily Paterson from Phoenix, Arizona, born a few months and four years before my actual birthday.

Which, to be fair, was probably made-up anyway.

I wore prosthetics on my nose, cheeks and forehead.

Contacts turned my eyes brown.

All of it was uncomfortable.

I also wore sunglasses.

My hair had been cut to jaw length and dyed burgundy, thanks to Ivy and the African-looking seer, whose name turned out to be Yarli. Both of them quizzed me about Phoenix the whole time they did my hair and make-up, until they felt I knew enough to be able to get past border control.

They asked me what languages I spoke, which was none apart from English and a smattering of Spanish and French. They asked me what countries I'd been to, which was nowhere but Mexico as a kid, a good ten years before the borders tightened.

Ivy, who was in charge of my paperwork, also asked Ullysa if we wanted to avoid "the usual places" for me, to which Ullysa said yes.

The usual places, I found out later, was a list of cities and countries in which the Rooks maintained a heavy presence.

That list turned out to be intimidatingly long.

Not surprisingly, Washington D.C. was on it.

Approaching the motorcycle warily, I stared at Revik's back.

Giving me a bare glance, he motioned with his head for me to get on behind him.

I stepped closer, then threw a leg over and eased onto the leather seat. My fingers touched his jacket for balance as he moved the bike upright. He clicked over the ignition, and I saw him wince as he stepped sharply down on the pedal.

He did it a few times before the motor caught.

My first thought was that it must be an old bike.

Upon closer inspection, however, it looked like it had been modified in a number of ways, so maybe it only looked old, or had been done up retro-style, with a modern engine.

"Are you okay?" I asked.

I couldn't be sure he'd even heard me over the revving engine. Picking up a dark blue helmet resting on the gas tank in front of him, he handed it to me.

"Revik," I said, fighting exasperation a little. "Is this really the best way to do this? You were half dead a few weeks ago."

"Put it on, Allie. Hold onto me."

Feeling sick already, I tugged my hair out of my face before stuffing the padding over my head. Arranging my new bangs so I could see, I fumbled with the straps under my chin.

I considered trying again with him, then gave up, realizing I'd have to focus at least half of my energy on not throwing up while riding with him anyway.

Finishing with the helmet, I slid my arms around him, gripping tighter as he shifted his weight back to center.

The nausea didn't get worse.

In fact, it was nowhere near as bad as I'd feared in gearing up for this.

Realizing it must be something he was doing, I went into the Barrier. I stretched out my light towards his. Carefully, I felt over the edges of a curved, glass-like surface around him.

He used some part of his *aleimi* to shove me off.

It wasn't subtle.

I kept my light off his as best as I could after that.

I watched him slide a handgun into a holster in his boot, covering it over with a pant leg.

Ullysa approached the bike, laying a hand on his arm.

"Be careful, Revi'," she said as he holstered another gun under his jacket. I knew she spoke aloud for my benefit. "My people will meet you at the airport, but you are alone until then." She looked at me, pointed at the space between my eyes. "Do not go into the Barrier, sister. Do what Revi' tells you. This is his job."

I nodded, not bothering to point out the number of times I'd heard this already.

Ullysa kissed Revik's palm in goodbye before he started putting on gloves. I focused on the line of seers standing outside in robes and shawls, a thin veil of moisture on each face.

I recognized Yarli, the African-looking woman with the kind eyes, and Mika under her hood. Then I saw Kat walking towards the bike, wearing nothing but a gold kimono and bamboo clogs. I watched her light brown eyes slide over Revik. A swell of pain hit me without warning; my fingers clenched the thick leather of his jacket.

Kat only smiled wider, walking up to him and throwing her arms around his neck.

I barely had time to back away.

I slid to the rear of the long seat, not looking at them or at the line of seers watching as he returned Kat's kiss. I felt pain waft off him as he fell into it, saw Kat press her body into his, her hand between his legs. Once I saw that much, I turned, staring at the brick of the alley wall until they finished. It seemed to take a long time.

Finally, Kat walked away, but not before she grinned over her shoulder at me.

"See you, cub. Thanks for the loan."

I bit my lip. I felt Revik watching me, his light cautious.

When he didn't look away, I faced him directly.

"Don't worry, *Revi',*" I said. "I'm sure they have plenty of whores in Canada, too."

That time, there was no question as to whether he had heard. Something rose in his eyes, a kind of furious disbelief. It disappeared as soon I saw it.

By the time I thought about it enough to regret speaking, he'd already shoved a second helmet over his head and locked the strap.

Revving the motor a last time, he took his feet off the ground, forcing me to make a grab at his jacket to stay on the bike as he accelerated out of the alley.

I CLUNG TO HIS WAIST, FEELING LIKE MY SKULL MIGHT VIBRATE OUT OF MY skin.

Resting my bulky head on his back, I watched the sun begin its descent into the water through a bug-speckled visor, feeling another rush of gratitude towards Ullysa for forcing the down jacket and scarf on me, in addition to the gloves.

Revik only stopped the bike once.

As angry as he might have been at me, I suspect he stopped for my benefit.

After using the cement-block restroom and washing my face, I'd stood in the picnic area swinging my arms while he walked a wide circle on the grass, ignoring me studiously.

Normally, the ride to Vancouver took only three or so hours from Seattle.

Because we took backroads for a border-crossing further east, it would take us closer to seven.

I raised my head as the bike slowed.

He came to a stop, placing his feet on the ground at the end of one of several lines of vehicles. Cars, RVs, trucks, trailers, and motorcycles started and stopped in irregular bursts before a widened section of road bridged with glass booths.

Seeing the Canadian flag snapping overhead, I felt a jump in my stomach. Revik lifted his feet, hitting the gas to roll us forward when our line shifted another spot.

He glanced back at me for the first time since we'd left.

"If we encounter a problem," he said through the helmet. "It will be here."

I adjusted my arms around him. "How likely is that?"

"They won't be watching from the physical." He paused, thinking. "Well. It is unlikely. Canada is too obvious."

"And if it isn't too obvious?"

He continued to look at me.

I couldn't see any part of him through the tinted visor. He shrugged.

"So why can't you use the Barrier?" I asked.

"Because it is easy to watch multiple places in shifts from the Barrier," he said. "There are not enough seers to go everywhere in person. Not even for the Rooks. Also, it is wholly unnecessary. They will watch from the Barrier, circulate our pictures to the humans, and wait for me to resurface. They know I cannot stay out of the Barrier forever."

"Why not?"

"Because eventually I have to sleep," he said.

I fell silent, watching cars inch forward.

A little boy in a minivan gripped his hands into fists as he stared at me and Revik, turning them towards himself rhythmically, lips puckered as he made *Vroom, Vroom* noises.

"So how do you know they won't be waiting for us here?" I asked.

Revik sighed, staring up at the sky. "I don't," he said. "But there are advantages to Canada that made it worth the risk. Via my old employer, I am registered through their branch of Homeland Security. Theirs has few Rooks, and none at the higher levels. I should come up green in a regular scan, at least until they revoke my status. Ullysa assured me they had not."

I frowned. "That doesn't make sense. They know you are with me."

Revik shrugged. "I am wearing blood patches. I won't come up as the same person up here. I'm hoping SCARB is not aware of all of my operational aliases. Ullysa seemed to think my employer gave them the bare minimum on that front."

Thinking about that, I frowned. "So what about me? The prosthetics only deal with the facial recognition software, right? My implant—"

"Has been altered. We told you this, Allie." Revik sighed. "We have people on the inside, too. The electronic security doesn't worry me. It is easy to tamper with, and by the time they found us that way, it would already be too late."

Nodding, I tried to incorporate this information into my more nameless fear. Before I could think of another question, it was our turn. Revik pulled the bike up to the booth.

A man wearing a black uniform stepped out from behind the glass.

He held out a hand.

"Passports."

Revik reached into his inner jacket pocket, handing them over wordlessly. The guard motioned towards Revik's face, and Revik unstrapped the helmet, tugging it off his head. I sat back, reaching up shakily to do the same. I kept my expression flat as I pulled mine off, aware at once of my sweat-damp hair as the Canadian-Washington wind blew at the back of my neck. I hoped my nerves didn't show, but knew from my previous inability to hold any kind of poker face that they probably did.

The guard sniffled in the cold, wiping his nose with one gloved hand.

He looked at me.

I got a whisper of familiarity as his eyes lingered on my face.

He stared at Revik next, scrutinizing him more closely. He was probably checking our implants through his headset as he stared, but his expression didn't waver.

"What is your purpose in Canada?" he asked.

"Tourist." The word was out of Revik's mouth before I'd heard the question.

"Any food with you? Fruits or vegetables?"

"No."

"Weapons?"

"No weapons. Only clothes."

"Why no headsets?" He pointed at Revik's ear. "No phones?"

Revik smiled, glancing at me. "We wanted to go without. Vacation. Is that a problem? Neither of us is registered as requiring one."

I swallowed. I actually *was* required to wear one, ever since that incident in the bar with the wine bottle and my ex-boyfriend.

The guard frowned again.

He stepped closer, looking at both photos, then back at mine. I felt more than saw Revik's fingers stray to his boot. The man's eyes were dark blue, kind, a little sad.

A rush of feeling hit me. I didn't want Revik to hurt him.

"We're visiting my friend," I blurted. "My best friend from school. She married a mountie, can you believe it? He's got a horse and everything. One of those hats! I couldn't make the wedding, but the pictures were hilarious, so..." My face warmed. "Well, not to you, I guess." I laughed, blushing deeper. "Well, I promised we'd visit, but my boss is a dick. You know how it is. I didn't want him to be able to track us to see if I'm *really* sick, so I talked Roy here into leaving our 'sets, and... hey, I hope that wasn't rude, that thing I said about mounties? They're just so cute in those red jackets. I didn't mean anything. Honestly."

The guard's eyes flickered in surprise.

Revik stiffened, his hand now on my thigh.

His fingers gripped me tighter, wanting me to be silent, but I kept my smile on the guard, seeing his blue eyes soften.

"No, ma'am. No offense taken."

"Do you ever ride a horse?" I asked ludicrously.

"When the mood takes me, sure." His smile relaxed, his eyes on mine, and now warm with a different kind of interest. He gave Revik a regretful look. "Well, be careful then." He tipped his hat. "You tell your friend congratulations for me."

"Thanks!" I beamed. "And you, get some hot chocolate or something. You look like you're catching a cold."

He chuckled again. "I'll see if I can't do that, ma'am."

"You'd better! Your girlfriend'll be pissed."

He laughed out loud.

Revik glanced at me.

I saw a smile on his lips just before he stuffed his dark head in the helmet, laying his hands on the bike's handlebars. The guard stepped closer, not looking at Revik at all now. I took the passports and zipped them up in my jacket pocket. I stuck my head in my own helmet. As we pulled away from the booth, I saw the guard looking after me. He raised a hand in salute and I waved back, then clutched at Revik in alarm when he gunned the accelerator.

"Don't push it!" he said loudly.

I laughed and, wonder of wonders, felt him smile.

He hit the gas harder and the bike leapt forward.

By then, the sun had dipped below the horizon. Fire-red clouds spread out over the ocean, and the sky behind them was dark indigo, almost the color of the Barrier.

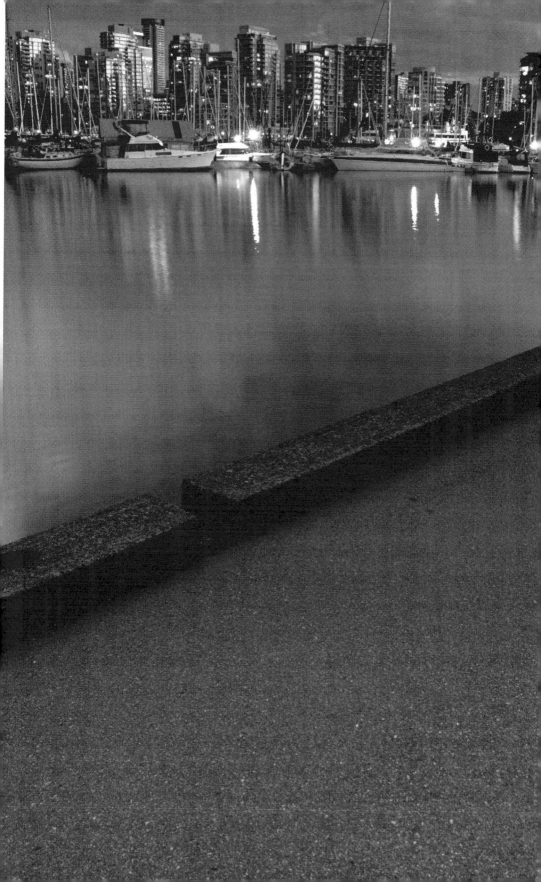

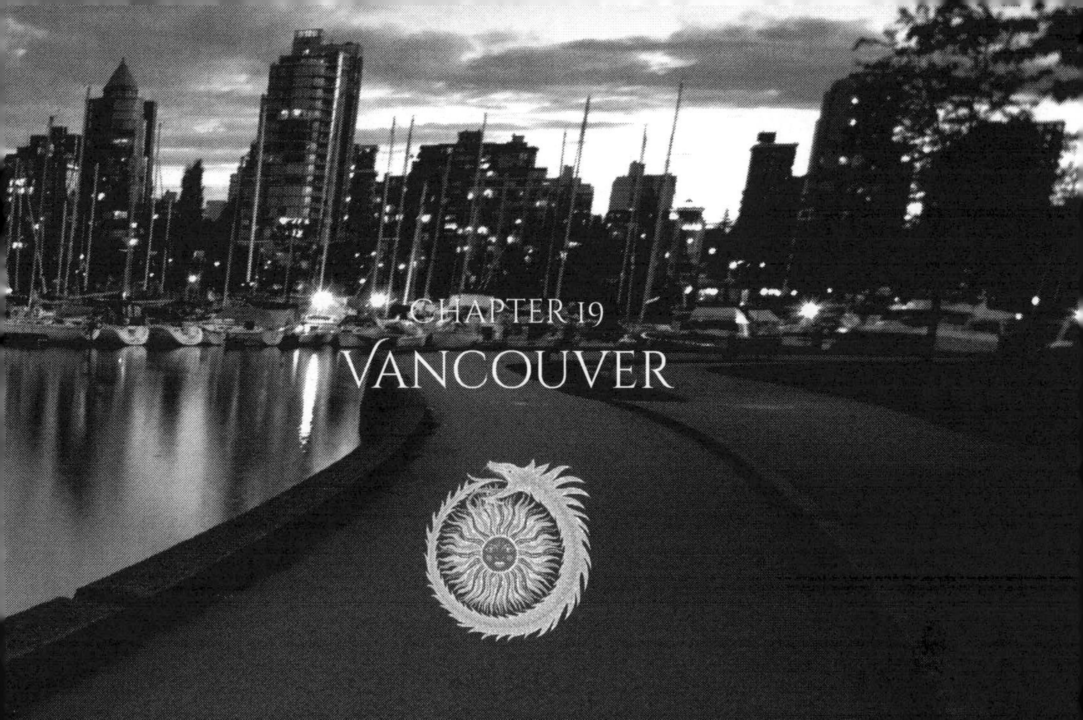

CHAPTER 19
VANCOUVER

He banked a few hours later, pulling us off a Vancouver city street and onto a small highway. Just before the fork to Lions Gate Bridge, he took us down another ramp.

I glimpsed a sign pointing to the forested dark of Stanley Park.

Exhausted, I now gripped him tightly around the waist, afraid I might accidentally loosen my hold and fall off if I didn't.

He bumped us over the grass to meet the bicycle and footpaths near the water.

He turned off the headlamp, so we were riding in the dark.

My eyes, stinging from fatigue, glimpsed dark trees to our left, a curve of bay and bobbing masts from the boat harbor on our right. Skyscrapers rose behind the docks, curved cylinders of glass that lit up the water like a wall of green-blue eyes.

We rounded the peninsula and a shock of cold air hit as wind gusted into the bike, forcing Revik to correct before he gunned it again.

Water flew by in a blur, the image vibrating.

As the bike's tires rose to meet the sloping footpath, I saw a small lighthouse with its light turned off. A swath of moving darkness lay behind it, broken by reflected glows from slow-moving ships.

Revik took us to the sea-facing side of the white and red lighthouse, parking below two sets of stone stairs.

Before I realized we were stopping, he'd already turned off the engine, leaving us in an eerie quiet with only wind and lapping waves. Unfastening the chin strap, he tugged off his helmet. Spikes of sweat-wet hair stuck up over his head.

Using a foot to dislodge the kickstand, he climbed off.

I watched him walk directly to the stone base of the lighthouse.

By the time I made out the square, metal panel, he was already kicking it in with his booted heel.

I took off my own helmet and climbed off.

Pain shot from my tailbone to my shoulders as soon as I landed on my feet. My arms hung like dead weight. I just stood there for a moment, clenching and unclenching my hands inside the leather gloves, trying to get the feeling back.

I watched Revik finish knocking in the panel.

Then he turned, his face shockingly pale after being behind a tinted visor all day. Behind him, a three-by-three hole gaped in the cement.

"I suppose a hotel is out of the question?" I joked.

Walking back to me and the bike, he opened the motorcycle's seat storage, pulling out a blue backpack and blankets, then a cheap, battery-powered lamp. Igniting the last, he set it down just inside the hole in the stone wall and crawled through, pushing the backpack and blankets in front of him.

Inhaling a last gulp of salty sea air, I crawled in after him.

Once inside, I turned around in the surprisingly large space, and leaned against a curved cement wall. I watched in disbelief as Revik crawled back out, leaving without a word. He lay the metal panel back over the opening, and I called out without thinking.

"Hey!" I said, close to a yell.

He bent his knees. He met my gaze, visibly startled.

"Where are you going?" I asked.

"To hide the motorcycle."

"Oh." I blinked, then exhaled, feeling stupid. "Of course. Okay."

He straightened, then disappeared.

I just sat there while he was gone, numb with fatigue. I was starting to nod off when he climbed back through the square opening.

After rearranging the panel door behind us, he sat on the opposite side of the lamp as me and began pulling off his leather gloves. In the yellow lamplight, dark circles shadowed his light eyes, which were glassy with fatigue.

I reached over his lap for a blanket.

The smell wasn't bad in there, but a faint reek of empty beer bottles and trash lingered. I eyed a used condom just past the circle of electric light and unzipped my jacket, running fingers through my matted hair.

He hooked the backpack with one hand and set it by my leg.

Feeling him waiting, I realized that had been a courtesy of sorts.

Jerking the bag closer, I unzipped the main compartment and groped inside, knocking my hand into water bottles before closing on something squishy in a plastic bag.

"Food," he said.

Holding up the plastic-wrapped, burrito-looking thing, I sniffed one end of it and grimaced involuntarily. "Jesus."

Leaning over the space between us, he took the backpack from me.

"You are used to human food," he said.

It wasn't a question.

I answered him anyway.

"Obviously," I said, sighing. "Will I ever get used to this stuff?"

"It is likely, yes." Pausing, he smiled faintly. "Seers live a long time."

I grunted in surprise, realizing that was a joke.

Smiling back at him, I shook my head.

Remembering he'd tolerated human food for me on a number of occasions, I unwrapped one end of the seaweed-looking burrito and took an experimental bite. I gagged, then forced myself to chew. Even as hungry as I was, it tasted like moldy dirt.

He watched with impassive eyes, then surprised me by smiling again.

"Good?" he said.

"No." I fought not to spit up what was in my mouth.

His smile became a suppressed laugh. "You're doing it wrong, Allie."

I grunted, lowering the burrito to quirk an eyebrow at him. "Want to enlighten me? Or are you having too much fun smirking?"

His smile evaporated.

"That was a joke," I said, feeling my face warm.

His eyes shifted away. "You should be able to feel your light without using the Barrier." He cleared his throat. "Try with me. It's easier with someone else."

He held out a hand towards me.

I stared at it, but didn't make any move to reach back.

"The sense of motion. Of light. Try to feel it." His voice remained casual, but a faint tension grew audible as he offered his hand again.

Realizing I was in danger of offending him, I clasped his fingers.

His were warmer than mine.

"Light has a component that is nearly physical," he explained. "It has dimension. It is subtle, but you should be attuned to me, so—"

"I think I get it." My skin was starting to warm. I wanted my hand back, but I still didn't want to offend him. It wasn't that I minded him touching me. I was more embarrassed he might feel me reacting to even this much contact between us.

"I feel different than you?" he said.

"Yes."

"Other than skin?"

"Yes." I gently dislodged my fingers. "I get it, Revik."

He released me with a shrug. "Then eat."

My hand continued to tingle after he let go.

I felt the part of me that wanted to reach for him again, or maybe put my hand on his leg. Clenching my jaw briefly, I lifted the wrap instead.

I tried to concentrate on that feeling of motion as I bit down, especially around my lips and tongue.

I was chewing for a few seconds before I could pay attention enough to notice it really did taste different. Well, not *taste* exactly, although a subtle array of textures lived under that bitter, damp smell. The real difference felt more like touch, but so infused with my other senses it blurred them together. Absorbing the plant's light was like inhaling gentle breaths of deliciously scented air.

The feeling was nearly… sensual.

"Don't go too far into it, Allie," he warned.

I watched him relax as he chewed, like someone getting a massage. His pale eyes flickered to mine, as if he'd heard me.

"I had to learn to eat blind when young," he explained. "To blend with humans. It is why human food doesn't bother me so much, compared to most seers." He swallowed what was in his mouth. "It is not uncommon for the Council to require service of seers born of certain castes. My parents were asked to give one of theirs. As an infiltrator."

He returned my blank look, coloring slightly.

"Given my blood type," he plowed on. "I was the logical choice. The food was of particular issue to me. I would fight them on it, which angered my father. He did not want me embarrassing him in front of the Council. I was already..."

He paused, then shrugged again.

"It is complicated. I was not his blood child, and moreover, he did not favor me. Raising me was his duty. He was adamant I do mine."

I took another bite of the plant burrito, if only to keep my face from showing a reaction.

"That sucks," I said.

I felt like I should say more, maybe confess something about myself.

Instead, we continued eating in silence.

Finishing the wrap, I rolled the plastic into a ball and stuffed it back in the backpack. I grabbed a bottle of water and twisted off the cap.

"There is more," he commented as I drank from the bottle. "If you are still hungry."

Nodding, I finished off the water and leaned back, sliding around to avoid sharp spots with my shoulder blades.

I closed my eyes.

He cleared his throat. "You cannot sleep," he said.

Realizing he was right, I felt my heart sink.

Sleep sounded heavenly, even on condom-strewn dirt.

"We may as well talk," he said.

Sighing, I sat up straighter.

I stuck my arms back into the sleeves of my jacket.

"Okay," I said, steeling myself a little. "What do you want to talk about?"

There was a silence. Then he exhaled, clicking under his breath. "Is there more you wish to know about the myths? About who you are?"

I scowled, involuntarily that time.

For a long-feeling few seconds, I didn't answer him. Then, resolving myself, I turned to face him. My face began to warm even before I'd opened my mouth.

"How about we talk about something real, for a change?" Pausing when his eyes narrowed, I firmed my jaw. "Are you ever going to tell me what happened between us that night? You know… the thing that everyone understands but me?"

There was a silence.

When it stretched, I exhaled in exasperation.

"Seriously, Revik. Can we cut the crap for once? Just tell me what I did."

He was already shaking his head. "No."

"No?" My jaw hardened more. "What do you mean, no? You're really not going to tell me what that was about?"

He turned, his voice as cold as his eyes. "What *what* was about?" he growled. "Which part, Alyson?"

I stared at him, taken aback.

When he didn't go on, my surprise turned to incredulity.

"Which part?" I said. "How about the part you told everyone else *not* to explain to me? How about the part where you got all of your hooker friends to keep me in the dark about whatever the hell it is I did to you?" When he flinched, his expression hardening, I raised my voice. "Jesus, Revik. Just tell me! What is it? What did I do to you that was so terrible? You must know by now I didn't do it on purpose!"

He shook his head again, clicking at me angrily.

"I'm too tired for this, Allie."

"You're too *tired* for it? But you want to lecture me about obscure seer texts all night? Maybe teach me a little more about how to eat seer food?"

His eyes grew cold as ice. "I am too tired for this, Alyson."

I just stared at him for a few seconds.

Then, realizing I was too tired for it, as well, I looked away.

Clenching my jaw, I just sat there for a few seconds, staring at the walls without seeing them. When I felt his hostility intensify from next to me, I slid further away from him on the dirt, sitting on the folded blanket.

Watching me, he ran fingers through his black hair, muttering in German.

I caught enough words that I flinched.

I saw him notice, and stare.

Not needing that all that much either, I drew up my knees, resting my face on my crossed arms. Suddenly I was more tired than I thought I could stand.

"I'm sorry," he said.

I glanced up, then wished I hadn't.

He was staring at me, his eyes holding guilt.

"I did not know you knew German," he said.

"I really don't." At his silence, I sighed. "I had a roommate from Stuttgart. I picked up a few words. 'Immature' and 'bitch' happen to be two of them." I saw him wince and pretended not to notice. "She argued with her girlfriend a lot."

His skin darkened.

Lacing his fingers, he nodded, staring at his feet.

"I apologize."

"Forget it."

"I did not mean—"

"Yes, you did. I said forget it." I rested my face on my folded arms. "I know you're trying. You suck at it, but you're trying."

Thinking for a few seconds more, I shrugged.

"I'm sorry, too. It was stupid to bring that up now." At his silence, I added, "It's just that I've been wondering about it for weeks. Mika said you made them promise not to tell me anything. She thought maybe you were trying to get me to ask you directly." Still thinking, I shrugged again. "So I asked. Directly."

The silence lengthened.

"Do you want to know more about who you are?" he asked.

Grimacing, I shook my head. "No. Please." I closed my eyes, then opened them again, remembering I really couldn't sleep.

"Allie." He waited until I turned my head. "It's not only to stay awake. I want us to talk. I want to… move past this somehow."

I nodded, dejected. "Okay."

His brows drew together. "You would rather fight?"

"No." I said. "I don't want to fight. But I don't see how it's much better, for us to talk about things I could read in a book. It feels the same as not talking at all."

At his silence, I bit my lip. Looking at his face, I sighed again.

"I'm sorry," I said. "I get that you're trying. I appreciate it. I'm just really tired. And that Bridge stuff gives me nightmares sometimes. I can't do it right now."

He frowned. "You have nightmares."

"Sometimes. Yeah."

When he didn't break the silence that time, I tried again.

"Look," I said. "That whole thing in Seattle." I felt him stiffen, but went on anyway. "I'm not going to make you talk about it, all right? I just want to say something. Is that okay? Can I just *say* something? About my end of things?"

When I glanced over, his light eyes were wary.

After a long-feeling pause, he nodded slowly, that wariness still in his eyes.

"Okay." I exhaled. "Here it is. I'm sorry about the Kat thing."

Feeling anger come off him in a harder wave, I clenched my jaw.

"Look," I said, sharper. "I'm not trying to trap you into some kind of discussion. I just want you to know, I didn't *give* you to her, okay? I had no idea she'd take it that way. I told her she could see you. As in, go to your room and *talk* to you. And yes, that was me avoiding you in the moment, and avoiding whatever the hell was going on with us. But I thought I'd be avoiding you for like an *hour* or so, while I pulled my brain off the floor. I wasn't thinking it was going to piss you off so badly that you'd avoid me for *weeks.*"

I felt my cheeks warm as I fumbled around the other thing, the real reason I'd stayed away from him.

I met his gaze.

"I didn't *offer* you to Kat. I need you to hear me on that." I hesitated, watching his eyes. "I mean, clearly, I fucked up. I said the wrong thing… I get that. It's also pretty clear I offended you. So I'm sorry. I'm really sorry, Revik. That wasn't my intention. At all."

There was another silence.

Seeing his expression grow slightly less hard, I added,

"We can talk about whatever you want now." Waiting another beat, I tried again. "Even the apocalypse stuff, if you're dead set on it. I don't need to worry about nightmares tonight, anyway, since we're not going to sleep."

He just looked at me.

Then he exhaled, clicking softly.

"Thank you," he said.

I bit my lip, then shrugged, feeling my face warm. "Sorry I didn't say it sooner."

He didn't answer.

I watched him stare straight ahead, his eyes showing him to be thinking.

After another pause, he looked at me, his mouth set in a faint frown.

"I want to tell you something, too," he said.

I nodded, tensing a little. "Okay."

He looked up the cement walls of the lighthouse.

I saw his eyes cloud, then focus, as if he were practicing more than one way of saying it.

Turning, he seemed to give up.

"I didn't fuck her," he said. "Not even that morning."

I winced. "Jesus, Revik."

"I wanted to," he said. "But I didn't."

"Great," I said, fighting anger. "Good for you."

He studied my face, then rubbed his own with a hand. His accent grew stronger. "There is no reason to be embarrassed. Seers are naturally possessive. I gave you cause. I didn't mean to." Thinking, he reconsidered. "Well. Yes. I did."

I stared at the floor as I sorted through his words.

Finally, I shook my head.

"Yep. Still not asking, Revik."

He stuffed the remains of the plant burrito he'd been eating into the backpack. He looked tired, and now, angry. I shouldn't care. Why did I care about this? Taking off my jacket, I bunched it up for a makeshift pillow, stuffing it under my head.

I felt him staring as I dragged half of the blanket over my body.

"Allie," he said. "You cannot sleep."

"I know."

"Tomorrow," he said. "Maybe."

I sank my head into the jacket. I was angry, too. I couldn't bring myself to shove it aside, even after I felt him notice, even when he continued to stare at me.

It didn't help that at least half of my rage came from confusion, an almost cloying inability to understand him. Why had he told me that stuff about his childhood? Why the chess? And why had he been so sure I'd want to know about him and Kat?

What had he even meant by it, anyway?

Did him saying he hadn't "fucked" her mean intercourse only? Because that left a pretty wide range of inbetweens my imagination was more than happy to supply with images. Especially since he hadn't minded getting a dick massage and shoving his tongue down her throat right in front of me.

And why in the hell did I care about this again?

I heard a snap and sigh of plastic and air, then the sound of him drinking.

The backpack rustled, followed by his leather-covered shoulders meeting the cement wall. I closed my eyes, opening them when I remembered I couldn't sleep.

"Can I go outside?" I asked.

He shook his head, clicking softly. "No."

"Then talk. Tell me something."

"What?"

"Anything," I said. "Who was your real father?"

He sighed, moving so that the leather crinkled again. "My biological parents were killed by humans when I was very young. I do not remember them."

I closed my eyes, cursing myself silently, then turned to look at him.

"Revik. I'm sorry—"

"I raised the subject," he said, waving me off. "It's fine, Allie."

I watched his face as his mind seemed to go somewhere else.

"Were you really a Nazi?" I asked.

His eyes turned slowly in my direction.

"Yes," he said. "Well. In the way you mean it, I was. In the strictest sense, meaning politically… no."

I wasn't sure how to follow on that.

"So," I said. "How did you end up leaving them? The Rooks, I mean. What made you—"

"I don't want to talk about that." Averting his eyes, he shrugged. "I don't remember most of that time, anyway."

"What do you mean, you don't remember?"

He sighed, clicking his tongue.

"It was a condition of my coming back. A portion of my memory was forfeit." At my silence, he shrugged. "I believe it was partly mechanical. I lost some simply by being separated from the network. Some was a bargain Vash made for my life. With Galaith, the Rooks' leader." His eyes remained on his laced fingers. "I imagine I knew things. Things the Rooks needed me to forget."

Realizing I was staring at him, I blinked, firming my lips.

"Forfeit?" I said. "How much is gone?"

His eyes grew a touch colder.

"I don't know. I can guess, by piecing together dates with what I remember." His face smoothed to neutral as he cleared his throat. "It is very strange that you saw any of that time. No one else ever has. Perhaps it has something to do with who you are." He glanced at me, his eyes and voice casual.

"May I ask… how much did you see?"

Great. I'd just walked into another potential minefield.

I'd assumed he knew everything I saw.

"Not much. You and your wife—"

He flinched visibly.

Swallowing, I backpedaled quickly.

"I saw you in jail, and that guy, Terian. I also saw you in Russia, I think. Something about tanks being stuck in the mud. You seemed unhappy about the way the war was going…" I trailed, figuring that last part was safe, at least. "You and some guy talked about who would lead that part of the front."

His eyes grew calm as he rested his chin on his hands.

"How old are you?" I asked, when he didn't break the silence. "You and that guy Terian. You both look exactly the same."

He laced his fingers together.

For a moment, I saw him thinking again, as if considering possible responses.

Finally, he shrugged.

"I am young for a seer," he said.

After a lengthier pause, he leaned his head against the wall.

It wasn't until another minute passed that I realized that was all the answer I was going to get.

CHAPTER 20
MURDER

The date was May 12th.

I recycled that piece of information from a dropped comment by Revik about our flights, when we would arrive in Tai Pei versus when we left the airport in Vancouver, BC.

I didn't really hear him when he said it.

The detail hit me right as I was about to push on the white, triangle-shaped skirt of the woman symbol on the bathroom door of the diner where we'd stopped to eat breakfast.

I stood there, frozen.

My eyes lit on a pay phone bolted inside a shadowed alcove to my right.

I blinked at it, nearly hallucinating with fatigue, then glanced behind me, watching Revik's back as he slumped into a red vinyl booth.

Completing the motion of my hand, I entered the restroom.

On my way out, minutes later, I spotted a black plastic tray covered in Canadian coins on an empty table. Scooping it up, I dumped the change into my palm and left the tray on the bar without breaking stride.

I slid into the creaking booth across from Revik.

"You got me coffee?" I asked.

He nodded.

Over breakfast, I drank coffee and he used his to warm his hands.

Our waitress came back, topped off both of our cups, then lingered, smiling at Revik.

"Want anything more to eat, honey?"

He frowned, looking up from the menu. "No. Go away."

The woman froze, her mouth open.

I stared at him too, equally surprised, but more amused than our waitress.

Snapping her mouth shut, she turned and walked away, taking her coffee pot with her. I watched her go, then noted Revik's eyes on mine.

I followed his gaze to my hands, which were methodically shredding a paper napkin.

I pushed the napkin away.

"They can't help it." He seemed to mean his words to be reassuring. "We'll both distract people for a while. Humans, too."

"Distract people?" I raised an eyebrow. "What do you mean?"

He shrugged, lifting his coffee mug to his lips. He took a sip of the dark brown fluid, then grimaced, lowering the mug back to the table.

I smiled. "Did you forget you don't like it?"

He fingered the mug's ceramic handle, frowning at me slightly.

Glancing back at the bar counter, I said, "Well, you'd better not order anything more now. They spit in the food sometimes, you know." When he didn't look over, I tried again. "How will we know Ullysa's people? At the airport?"

"They'll know me. I'll likely know some of them."

I nodded, reacting slightly to his words.

I didn't know what triggered my reaction at first.

Then my eyes followed a man outside, watching him stare at a woman in a skin-tight miniskirt standing across the street. She smiled at him, her mouth a dark red slash, and I found my thoughts drifting to Seattle.

"So we just get on the plane?" I said evenly.

"Yes." Watching my face, he added, softer, "There is nothing to worry about, Allie."

Hearing the second meaning under his words, I pretended I hadn't.

I fought to think instead about myself, about where I'd be in a few days.

During part of our night of not-sleeping, Revik told me a bit about where we'd land in Russia, and where he intended to take me in India. He made Russia sound interesting. According to him, that part of the country remained wild, practically untouched. We were likely to see wild animals as we traveled over land by train: bears, eagles, wolves, foxes. I thought about my mom's fascination with wolves and smiled… then frowned, glancing over my shoulder at the bathroom door.

"Okay." I looked at him. "I have to go again. I think it's the coffee."

I watched his eyes focus out the window, coming to rest on the same woman I'd been looking at seconds before.

His gaze sharpened and flickered down, appraising her.

"Okay," I repeated. I planted my hands on the table and stood. "I'll be back."

He didn't look over as I left.

When I glanced back, he was still looking out the window. He took another sip of lukewarm coffee as I watched, and grimaced.

I SLID ONTO THE WOODEN BENCH UNDER THE PAY PHONE AND LIFTED THE receiver, throwing all the coins I had into the slot. I found myself relieved they even *had* public phones in Canada; I couldn't remember the last time I'd seen one in SF, much less one that took hard currency.

I punched in the familiar number, shifting so my back faced the corridor.

The phone rang.

After a pause, it rang again.

"Come on," I murmured. "Pick up."

A click startled my ears. My heart lifted…

But only in the pause before my mother's antique answering machine switched on, playing a message so old I'd memorized it before high school.

"We're not at home right now." Mom's voice sang out the words like small bells. "So pleeease leave a message after the tone… BEEP!" She laughed. "Ha ha, just kidding! Here it comes!"

"Dork," I muttered, out of habit.

The message machine beeped.

Terian gazed in fascination at the metallic box on the tile counter.

He hadn't known such machines still existed.

It was like looking at an old linotype machine, or a working trebuchet and its pile of stones, waiting to be flung over a castle wall. The phone stopped its high-pitched trill and the recording device shuddered to life.

Silence wafted after the initial message, but from the static, Terian knew it hadn't finished.

"Ha ha, just kidding! Here it comes…"

The machine let out a loud, atonal beep.

Terian's new body, still unfamiliar in passing glimpses on reflective surfaces, watched the machine with a mixture of fascination and excitement.

After all, he knew who *wasn't* calling.

The background sound of children's voices rose, and he glanced at the television monitor. Small faces pressed close to the likely-illegal camera, laughing and screaming in delight as that cheerful tune began to sing-song out of bow-shaped lips smeared with white and blue frosting.

"Happy biiiiirthday to you! Happy biiiirthday to you! Happy biiiirth-day, dear Al—"

"Mom?" A voice emerged, panicked but low. "Mom, are you there? Pick up! Please pick up! I don't have much time!"

Terian blinked.

Voices came to him in this body sometimes.

They sang to him, like the children on the other side of that cracked wall monitor. This voice sounded real, however.

Could it be real?

A little girl ran into the room even as Terian thought it. This one was neither trapped behind glass nor a hallucination. Paint covered her small hands, matted her dark hair in clumps. Her bare feet poked out from under a tattered purple dress, scratched and stained from play. A stuffed white rabbit dangled from her sticky fingers.

Red had bled onto the velvet fur.

Terian waved at her to be silent as he pointed at the machine.

"Mom?" the voice from the machine said.

The girl froze, staring at the dead-metal box.

Excitement slid through Terian's skin, a liquid heat, shared between himself and the girl. He wasn't hallucinating the voice. She was right there, on the other side of the line.

He could simply lift the receiver, speak with her.

"Mom! Please… pick up!"

A symphony lived in that voice. Physical imprints could be so endlessly fascinating, like motes of dust, each containing a singular world. Terian winked at the little girl, who took another step towards the machine.

He held up a hand, warning her.

"Crap," the voice said dully. "Of all the times for you to actually be out of your cave." Another silence came and went. "Mom, listen. I can't tell you where I am. I'm not dead or in a ditch. And I'm not a freaking *terrorist,* okay? I'm with a friend. He's helping me figure things out…"

Terian's smile widened.

"…I'll be home as soon as I can. Tell Jon and Cass… well, tell them I'm okay. And I miss them. I love you, Mom. Tell them I love them, too."

Terian grinned, hearing the ups and downs in her voice as her moods shifted from reassurance to fear and back again. She'd called to reassure her mother, but she'd also hoped to reassure herself.

Terian chuckled again.

Dehgoies didn't know where she was.

He was sure of it.

Perhaps by now she'd learned more effective means of distracting him, too.

From the wall, a moan redirected both Terians' focus.

Red lines and small handprints snaked across sun-faded wallpaper, running in places, like rusting metal. Whenever two of Terian's bodies shared physical proximity, they tended to share traits. The doc had said this personality configuration would be creative, and she hadn't been wrong. At the foot of the same wall, another groan grew audible, meeting the voice still coming out of the answering machine.

"…and Mom?" The voice hesitated. "Don't let any strangers in the house, okay?"

The little girl giggled.

The stuffed white bunny bounced against her chest.

"There are some people after me, and… well, it would be better if you could just go to Grandma's for a while. Or Aunt Carol's. Please? Just do what I—"

There was a click.

The voice abruptly cut off.

Raising his eyebrows, Terian looked at the little girl.

Seeing the blank look in her eyes, he smiled.

"Are you finished?" he asked her kindly.

She held up her hands, pinning the bunny to her chest with one short arm. He understood her without words.

"No more paint?" he said sympathetically.

She shook her head, bouncing her dark curls.

Terian clucked his tongue, rising easily to his feet. Following her back into the other room, he lifted a paint brush from the edge of the television stand, using his fingers to wipe away stray hairs. He handed it to the little girl.

"Let's see what we can do about that," he murmured.

Squatting fluidly, he examined the woman. No sound came from the area by his feet, but a single eye stared up, almost childlike in its attentiveness. The woman whimpered as Terian touched her skin. The eye closed, leaving the face featureless under hair and paint.

He checked the belt he'd been using as a tourniquet.

He considered loosening it, then pulled a flip knife from his back pocket instead, scanning options on the marred skin. Both arms had tourniquets already, both legs. The obvious choices had been tapped; to overuse any one would bring an end within heartbeats. He clasped a handful of her hair, speaking to her softly.

She had already given so much.

The little girl fidgeted. "Paint!" she shrieked. "Paint!"

"Relax, dearest," he murmured.

The woman groaned when he sliced into her scalp. The eye flickered open and she fought to breathe as paint ran past her eyelashes, making her blink and gasp like a panicking child.

"Shhhh," he said. "Shhh…"

The little girl jumped up and down.

He straightened, watching as she pushed the metal brush into the fresh pool, using one chubby hand to balance on the woman's forehead and scraping the brush back and forth on the wall, leaving a sweep of broken red lines. Occasionally, she would look back at him, showing him one part of the drawing or another.

"Good," he said, approvingly. "Yes, very nice work... very nice. Looks just like your bunny... yes."

The little girl beamed at him, her eyes shining.

I CLUTCHED THE RECEIVER. SOMETHING WAS WRONG.

I couldn't breathe.

This pain wasn't like what I felt in Seattle.

This was something else.

Cold sweat broke out on my skin. A kind of liquid dread made it difficult to breathe. I felt sick, repulsed. It was like watching someone tread in circles over a rotting corpse.

"...and Mom?" I fought to swallow. "Don't let any strangers in the house, okay? There are some people after me, and... well, it would be better if you could go to Grandma's for awhile. Or Aunt Carol's. Please? Just do what I—"

A hand reached in front of my face, depressing the phone's silver tongue.

I glanced up and back, still holding the receiver.

Revik stood there. His face looked blank—until I saw his eyes.

He motioned with his hand for me to get up.

When I hesitated, he caught hold of my elbow, jerking me to my feet. He steered me down the corridor. The sick feeling in my stomach didn't go away; if anything, it got worse, until I no longer cared whether Revik was angry.

He took me through the glass front doors of the diner and to the street outside. The sun reflected coldly from the windows of high-rise buildings. It blinded me, making my sickness worse. I planted my feet when Revik stopped.

Still holding my arm, he pulled out a mobile phone, hit a single key.

His message to whoever picked up was brief.

"Yes," he said. "We'll need it."

He clicked the phone shut, extracted the battery and threw both things at a nearby garbage container, hard enough for the bin to vibrate. Jerking me closer by the arm, Revik turned to speak, then stopped, staring directly at my face.

The anger in his eyes faltered.

"What?" he said. "What is it?"

I tried to answer.

"What, Allie?" His voice sharpened, but he didn't sound angry at me anymore. "What is going on? What's wrong with you?"

My stomach lurched.

I turned away from him, throwing up coffee and most of my Danish in a thick sluice on the sidewalk. A family was walking past us, aiming for the diner, and one of the kids gave a sharp cry of disgust.

"Ewww! Mommy, that lady's barfing!"

I heaved again, bent in half.

I didn't think about moving, not even to aim for the potted tree in the cement walk. Revik stood impassively, holding my arm, his eyes sweeping the street. I heaved a third time, gasping. When it started to feel like it might be over, I wiped my lips with the back of a hand.

Revik cleared his throat. "Are you finished?"

"I think so."

Spitting to get the excess saliva out of my mouth, I plugged my nose with my knuckles when the stench of stomach acid and coffee reached it.

"You need the restroom," he said.

It wasn't a question. He exhaled.

"I'll wait. But not for long, Allie."

"I had to call her."

His voice became a snarl. "So you pick the stupidest way imaginable? You could have *asked* me!"

"I *did* ask you! You said no!"

"That was weeks ago! Why *here,* Allie? Why now?"

"My fucking dad died today, okay?"

He opened his mouth to answer—then his face went blank.

I looked away, pausing on a couple staring at us from where they'd just been about to enter the restaurant. Meeting my gaze, the woman hesitated, clutching her jacket to her throat. Great. Revik and I had just become drunk domestic-violence couple. I fought to give her a reassuring smile, lost in the woman's wide, concerned eyes.

When I looked back at Revik, he stared at me like I'd lost my mind.

"Allie, you realize that anyone could have picked up?"

"I wasn't in..." I remembered we were in public. "I wasn't in that other place."

"It doesn't matter! You could lead them straight to her. If they weren't there already!"

"With my *mom?*" I shrieked. "That's *great,* Revik! You told me you could keep her safe!"

"You think you are helping her?" He stepped closer, dropping his voice to a rough whisper. "I *listened* to you, Allie. You might as well have *told* them to use her to get to you."

He seemed about to say more, then bit it back, adding,

"...And you let your voice be recorded. Do you have any idea what that is, to have a recent recording on a target? For an infiltrator this is like... a present! At the very least, they could trace the call. Every branch of law enforcement has Rooks in it. SCARB more than any other."

"I wasn't on long enough for that."

He stared at me, openly disbelieving. He averted his eyes, forcing his gaze back to the diner. His jaw hardened.

"Should I go in with you?" he asked.

I shook my head. "No. I'll come back. Then you can yell at me all you want."

He released my arm so suddenly I lost my balance.

I pushed my way back through the double glass doors.

Our performance hadn't gone unnoticed inside the diner, either. Staff and customers gave me a wide berth as I staggered past the cashier's desk. I retreated into the restroom. My fingers grasped for the bumpy silver handles and twisted the cold water on full. Because of the prosthetics, I couldn't stick my face in the sink like I wanted.

I cupped water to my lips instead, washing out my mouth, then dabbing my forehead.

I checked my face in the mirror. It looked the same.

It still wasn't mine.

Revik was waiting when I came out, but on the other side of the door, away from my puke.

"Ready?" His voice remained cold.

"Yes."

"Are you going to tell me what happened?"

"You heard me. I said I was alive, and with a friend. Nothing they didn't already know."

He stared at the cement, hands on his hips.

When I didn't go on, he turned, walking in the direction of the harbor, passing the parked motorcycle without breaking stride. I followed him at a distance. Straight ahead, glass buildings blocked my view of the water, but I glimpsed a white complex adorned with sail-like tents.

At the next stoplight, I approached his side warily.

"Aren't we going to the airport?" I asked.

"No," he said. "We're not taking a plane anymore." He looked at me. His voice leaked frustration. "Will you not tell me? You say no one picked up. You weren't in the Barrier. So what is this?"

"I don't know."

"But you felt something?"

I hesitated, then nodded.

"What?" he said.

I started to answer, but the cold feeling rose, forcing me to take another breath.

"I don't know," I said. "I really don't."

When I didn't say anything more, he shoved his hands into his pockets, walking as soon as the light changed. I followed after he'd gone a few steps. Then the feeling surged back, so intensely it blinded me… and suddenly I knew.

I knew.

She was dead. My mom was dead.

Halfway across the street, everything around me grayed. I collapsed before I realized that the problem wasn't a sudden eclipse of the sun.

It was me.

CHAPTER 21
REVIK

When I opened my eyes, cars honked loudly, like alarm clocks going off around my head. I didn't know where I was.

Shadowy people stared down at me with blank faces. I didn't know any of them.

I heard a voice I knew—

"Allie! ALLIE!"

Revik's face appeared.

His eyes, wide with panic, startled me.

He tried pulling me to my feet, then slid his arms under my knees and shoulders. He held me against his chest, murmured in my ear.

"Stay awake… please, baby. Please. Don't fall asleep."

I thought I had to be hallucinating.

My voice seemed to come from far away.

"I'm here," I said. "I'm still here."

I burst into a sob.

He stared down at me, then around at the gathering crowd.

I still lay in the middle of the street, so he tightened his hold on me and stood. Pausing to adjust his grip, he began to walk, fast, with long strides. He had me across the street and halfway down the block before he spoke again.

"Can you walk?" he said. "We're conspicuous."

I nodded. He stopped to set me on my feet, reaching back to unlock my fingers from around his neck. Standing there, I wiped my face. My legs shook.

"We have to go under the complex," he said, his voice nearly a mutter. "Look for 'Llysa's people."

His eyes tracked faces.

Some paused to stare at me curiously until they saw Revik.

Whatever expression they saw on him made them look away.

"I wish you weren't so damned conspicuous to humans," he said, still muttering. "It's not just..." He glanced at me, coloring. "...Us." I flinched at the intensity in his voice. He was thinking aloud, filling space, but the emotion felt real. "Like blood on a white sheet. They notice you, then make up a reason why. Even that fucking customs officer. You didn't just flirt with him. You let him *see* you..."

He looked at me, his eyes hard.

"You have to stay out of sight on the ship! I mean it, Allie. Please. *Please* do as I say in this. I'm begging you."

I stared at him, hearing his accent come out stronger, confused at the expression I saw on his face. Then his actual words reached me.

"Ship," I repeated dully. "You said ship?"

"Yes." He watched me wipe my eyes, his accent still unusually strong. "We need the construct now. You have blown our cover. A plane is not big enough. You need mass for a construct. Weight. They take time to set up. Ullysa's people prepped one as backup."

I nodded.

He stood there a few seconds more, as if unsure what to do with me. Then he clasped my hand, half-dragging me down the sidewalk that led under the tented complex.

When we stopped at the end of the line for customs, his arm wound around my waist. I didn't feel any affection in the gesture. Instead, a kind of angry control seeped over from him into me as he held me tightly against him, like he was trying to contain me in some way, or maybe keep me invisible.

I probably should have minded.

Right then, I really didn't, though.

ONCE MORE, REVIK FOUND HIMSELF AT A LOSS.

They stood at the end of the security line that led into the customs kiosks, and he still didn't see any sign of Ullysa's people.

But that wasn't what threw him, not really.

His senses remained on high alert, his fingers conscious of the gun nestled in a side holster under his jacket. It was a Glock 18, illegal for civilian use even in the United States. Just carrying it risked jail time here, but he needed a full automatic for seers.

Her hand clutching his was in the way of him reaching it quickly, but for reasons even he didn't understand, he didn't let go of her.

Seeing the row of metal detectors, he resigned himself to the fact that he might have to dump the gun. That, or risk pushing security to get them past. He spotted a trash can in one elbow of the zig-zagging line and decided the former was safer.

He was reluctant to do so until he'd ID'd the security team and knew they wouldn't have to make a run for it. He didn't see any other garbage cans along the line, though, so he might not have any choice.

The crowd picked up, thickening as they crushed into the main line leading to security and then customs.

He glanced down at the Bridge.

She was staring up at the advertisement screens that hung over the lines of people.

A dim confusion lived in her eyes as she gazed at a row of pictures of wildlife in Alaska. Grief wavered below that, and it occurred to him again that he had to get her on board, find those guards before she recovered from her shock and lost control of her light for real.

He needed her inside a construct before that happened.

As he thought it, five beings emerged from around him on the causeway.

In different ways they each made him aware of their presence.

Despite their casual stances, each in some way also blocked him from the ropes leading into security. Revik felt their movements occur as one, a near-perfect synchronization that was not human.

He reached for the Glock, using his other hand, but the female closest to him shook her head minutely, and he found he knew her.

Relaxing his fingers, he opened his palm to sign his question.

Are we inside the construct?

She answered him with her mind.

Yes, brother. We have arranged for you to board another way.

She nodded towards his fingers, indicating his gun.

Revik found himself relieved they were letting him keep it. As he began to follow her away from the security line and down a side passage, he realized two of the Seven's Guard wore United States Homeland Security uniforms.

When Revik turned to look at the female hunter, Chandre, he caught her studying Allie's light, a thinly veiled curiosity shining from her own structures.

He felt his jaw harden.

He knew it was natural.

They would be interested in her.

Still, he would rather have a few minutes' breathing space before he had to handle more reactions to her light, whether human or seer.

He continued to watch Chandre warily when the infiltrator visibly started.

She looked between the two of them, her dark eyes widening as she confirmed what she'd seen above each of their heads.

Revik sent a ripple of irritation until the woman's red-tinted eyes shifted to his.

Manners, Chandre.

Sorry, brother… er, sir. They did not tell us.

Some discretion would be appreciated.

The woman bowed. *Of course, sir. And congratulations.*

Revik nodded, once. He glanced around at her unit. That time he saw two more, in addition to the original five who showed themselves to him on the causeway.

Won't seven be conspicuous? He'd expected four. Five at most. *How big is your whole contingent?*

Chandre quirked an eyebrow.

It's a large ship, sir. You won't even know we're here.

Hearing the subtext in her deliberate misunderstanding, he gave her a look that made it clear he wasn't amused.

He brought the Bridge with him as he walked past Chandre and another smiling seer, then glanced back to see if Allie had noticed the exchange. Her gaze took in the other guards before coming to rest on the dark-skinned Chandre.

Allie stepped closer to him as she stared, her eyes faintly glazed, still almost not-there as she crushed into his side as they walked.

From her face and light, he knew she was in shock.

It made sense that her light would draw to his, as the safest option there, but the ease with which his own light responded made him tense all over again.

In a way, he even understood her reaction to Chandre. The East Indian Sark looked exactly like what she was, a highly paid infiltrator. Despite their reddish tint, her eyes had a hint of cold to them, as if she assessed all objects from a distance.

She looked at Allie that way, too.

It occurred to him in the same breath that Chandre had already been briefed on the contingency.

Then it clicked.

They would no longer trust him to perform it himself.

He had been effectively removed from duty.

Staring around, another piece fell into place.

Having such a large Guard presence was part of that message; they needed enough seers to take him down if he got in the way.

Meeting Chandre's gaze, he realized she was putting the same thoughts together behind her dark red eyes.

His fingers tightened around Allie's as they reached a small desk, where a lone customs official examined their documents before waving them through.

Revik could tell from the man's eyes that he was human, and had been heavily pushed into believing some lie. So had the woman who smilingly directed them around the obligatory photo backdrop that the rest of the ship's passengers were being escorted through in an assembly line, getting their pictures snapped while two photographers danced around, trying to get smiles from the humans and pump up the cruise-goers for their vacations.

"Come on!" he heard one of the photographers half-shriek. "Let's see some party faces, y'all! There now! That's better!"

"If either of you need anything, sir," Chandre said politely, in English, as they neared the gangplank and the line of people boarding. "You need only say the word. We will of course expect you to restrict your movements around the ship."

Revik glanced at Allie, saw her listening to the infiltrator intently.

He hoped like hell Chandre wouldn't make some crack about—

"We have purchased an entire corridor," she continued, her voice still smoothly polite. "And made some modifications for your comfort. You will be briefed on the rules once we are underway. Clothing and food have already been sent to your cabin, as well as training materials for Alyson. You will not be expected to adhere to ship's routines."

"You mean I can't leave the room," Allie muttered.

Revik glanced at her again.

Chandre smiled at her faintly, quirking an eyebrow.

"That is correct, Esteemed Bridge… for you, anyway. Dehgoies may leave, provided he follows the rules of the construct, and checks in and out with one of our team." She smiled. "Vash seemed to feel he might be tempted to break rules if we restricted him too much. But perhaps he can smuggle in anything you need, Esteemed Bridge? Anything you do not wish to ask us for…?"

Revik gave Allie another brief look.

She was studying the infiltrator, her eyes faintly wary.

He saw a glimmer of that older look in them, and felt himself reacting to her again. She was such a fucking paradox; it frustrated the hell out of him. She'd nearly gotten them killed as often as she'd saved his life. He'd already noticed he reacted to that more intense part of her differently, even before Seattle.

Unfortunately, those reactions were all exponentially worse now.

Moreover, Vash warned him.

The aged seer said she'd do things differently, that she'd act in ways that appeared impulsive, counter-intuitive—even foolish. He said Revik would have to trust her, even when those things seemed irrational. Or dangerous.

Realizing he was still crushing her fingers, he loosened his hold, gesturing to Chandre that they understood.

He moved them away a beat later, aiming his feet up the ramp to the gangplank, where the velvet-roped corridor joined the line for the other passengers. He entered the crowd thickening before the portal before looking at Allie again.

Leaning down so he wouldn't be overheard, he squeezed her hand.

"Are you all right?" he asked.

"Who are they?" Her eyes continued to follow the seers who fanned out behind them. Each of the infiltrators let themselves be absorbed into the crowd, but Allie's eyes found Chandre among the faces. She tracked the hunter's movements through the crowd with an ease that unnerved him a little.

"Friends," he said. "Ullsya's people."

She looked up. Her eyes still shone with that faint light, greener even with the contacts. A whisper of pain went through his chest.

Fuck.

"You aren't acting like they're friends," she said.

He shrugged, forcing his eyes off hers. "They are curious about you." He hesitated. "Do not talk to them, Allie. Stay out of their way."

"You just said they were friends."

"I just mean… do not distract them from their job."

"Did she call you 'sir'?"

His face grew warm.

Her attention to detail was starting to unnerve him.

"Yes."

"Are we in the military now?"

"No." He stared down at her face, at a loss. "We'll talk about it later. After we sleep, Allie."

She nodded absently, clearly hearing the "sleep" part and not much else.

He hesitated, glancing over his shoulder at Chandre.

He needed to get them in contact with the infiltration team in San Francisco, as soon as possible. When he looked at the hunter, he saw her nod, just before she signed that they had someone on it already.

Apparently Chandre had done more than look at the structure in Allie's light that connected her to him.

We'll have news in under an hour, sir.

Revik gestured for her to give it to him alone.

He waited until Chandre gestured in assent. He didn't miss the appraising look she gave him at the request.

He glanced at Allie again. He suspected she already knew what had happened in San Francisco. Even so, he knew from experience that knowing and *knowing* were two different things. He didn't want her receiving verification of some loved one's death as an emotionless report from an infiltrator who viewed her family as nothing but human collaterals.

He continued to study the Bridge's face as she gazed up the ship's high walls. He tried not to care that the guards were watching him look at her, or that her proximity was having an effect on him again, an effect they could probably see in his light.

He had to remind himself that she'd only been awake a few weeks, that she still didn't understand how she was different. He had to remind himself also that she really had no idea what was going on with the two of them, either.

Perhaps it had been a mistake to not let Ullysa and the others explain it to her in Seattle.

He was still watching her face when she leaned on his arm, merging her light overtly into his. Sucking in a breath, he closed his light, glancing reflexively at the seers watching. He saw more than one of them smiling.

He turned his gaze up the white face of the ship.

Shuffling his feet forward with the rest of the crowd, he willed the line to go faster.

CHAPTER 22

GRIEF

A wolf runs across the tundra, tongue flicking over its black lips, body elongating in rhythmic waves. It extends to full stride and retracts, stretching paws so that none of its feet touch the ground. Insanity flickers behind its eyes, joy in its feet pounding the snow in steady bursts of powder. It runs at a tall, dark form marring the white plain.

I scream, my voice torn by wind.

The man doesn't turn. He is too far away.

He doesn't hear me.

Dawn colors the sky. A dark shape burns in the distance, filling the pale blue with a curl of smoke like ink expelled in the ocean. My chest feels as if someone's taken an ice pick to it, hitting it again and again, digging out the tender light at its core.

It is a feeling worse than death.

I JERKED AWAKE. FOR A LONG-FEELING FEW MOMENTS, I COULD ONLY LIE there, gasping. Behind my eyes, the wolf is tearing the man apart, eating his heart out of his chest.

My breath caught…

Then someone moved.

An arm tightened around my waist.

Warm weight pinned me to something soft.

I looked down, staring at the arm; it took another few blinks before I recognized the lean lines, the fine black hair, the long fingers. My eyes focused on the silver ring he wore around his smallest finger. I felt his chest press against my back, his fingers clench lightly on my shirt.

Then I remembered.

Grief came without warning, with a depth and intensity I had no way to evade.

Days had gone by and it still wouldn't let me forget, wouldn't let me push it from my mind for more than minutes, even seconds at a time.

Everything amplified, got harder to control.

Revik told me that was normal, part of the "awakening" I was experiencing from being a seer. Seers felt more, he said.

They were more irrational, more volatile with their emotions.

I'd been living among humans so long I'd learned to adjust, he explained, but my seer nature was waking up. I was changing.

Knowing that didn't help anything. Knowing it was normal—feeling like I was being punched repeatedly in the chest—didn't do anything to alleviate it.

I couldn't talk to my brother.

I couldn't go to her funeral.

She was just gone.

Even more than Dad, she'd just vanished totally out of my life. Forever.

And it was my fault. Adopting me had done this to her.

Revik heard me thinking that. He told me I was wrong.

He didn't elaborate, although a few of the other seers tried. One told me I had a greater purpose, that my mother's sacrifice was noble, that she was honored to be in my life.

I hit him in the face.

I probably would have hit him again, but Revik dragged me back, then took me to our cabin. I knew they meant well. But I fought a near-violent reaction towards all of the seers as I replayed his words again like a dead-sounding record.

Revik told me how it happened.

He didn't soft-pedal it. He didn't pull any punches at all.

He relayed all of it, word for word, watching my eyes as he spoke.

I remembered everything he'd said.

Found her in her house. She'd been dead several hours, Allie. Most of her blood was gone.

Behind me, his arm tightened, then slid upward, wrapping around me lengthwise. His fingers curled over my shoulder, drawing my back snugly against his chest.

His mental voice had been soft as he translated for the infiltration team in San Francisco, not leaving anything out, not embellishing. As he spoke, I'd seen and heard what they found as they picked their way through Mom's house like shadows among the SFPD.

Images accompanied his words.

My mother's eyes stared up from where she lay by the television below a section of wall painted in her blood. A child's handprint stood out, small and innocuous looking, like the outline of a Thanksgiving turkey drawing made in kindergarten.

Someone had eaten a sandwich.

They left the crusts on Jon's old Transformers plate on the low coffee table beside the body, along with a half-full glass of milk.

The bedroom showed signs of a struggle, sheets half on the floor, a lamp broken.

The cops took pictures of a dark stain on the carpet by the lamp.

They took pictures of another rust-colored handprint on the refrigerator door, that one adult-sized. They photographed the body from every possible angle, then zipped it up in a bag, like the garbage Mom always forgot to put on the curb.

I felt the weight of guilt on Revik as he relayed details ruthlessly.

I didn't blame him, though.

My mom's safety couldn't possibly have been his priority.

It should have been mine.

The news media agreed. Within an hour, the feeds began accusing me of matricide, saying I'd allied with seer terrorists against *homo sapiens.* They argued on talk-show feeds about whether other seers brainwashed me into going along, or if I'd masterminded the whole thing. The police claimed to have DNA proof that I'd done the actual killing, as well as evidence that a male seer, possibly more than one, had ejaculated in my mother's bed while Mom lay dying.

That last part, Revik said, was deliberately crafted to incite public outrage.

It didn't make it any easier to hear.

We sat on the couch in the small ship's cabin for hours that first night.

He led me there before he told me anything.

Sitting me down, he peeled the prosthetics off my face carefully, throwing them one by one into a small trashcan while I watched. He indicated for me to remove the contact lenses. Once I had, he threw those away as well.

He pulled me to him then, holding me against his chest as if to contain something that might otherwise explode outward, coating the cabin walls with their seashell-decorated wallpaper and bland paintings. After he'd gotten the initial reports back from Chandre—the small, muscular, female seer with black braids and frightening-looking reddish eyes who commanded the shipboard Guard—I still hadn't been able to cry.

I have no idea if he drugged me, or used his light to get my vigil to finally end, but eventually I fell asleep.

That had been days ago.

The cruise ship docked at least once during that time, letting human tourists off for shore excursions and kayaking, trips to see wooden totem poles carved as eagles and bear spirits, and authentic salmon bakes with real Native Americans.

Revik parked me in front of a media player with a remote, the room service menu, and a list of pay-per-view channels. I'd flipped through listlessly before settling on a bland comedy with a talking dog and two teenagers who were doing… something.

Now, it was dark outside again.

I heard the sound of water being pushed out of the way by the ship's prow, flowing outside past our cabin. The glass door to the balcony stood propped open, a single orange bulb glowing over its frame, illuminating spray-filled wind.

Revik disliked enclosed spaces, especially while he slept. Air always had to be flowing from somewhere, no matter how cold. He'd sat with me again that night, once he got back from one of his wanders outside the cabin.

After what felt like hours where we curled up together on the couch, he got up, stretched, and left me sitting on one end like a posable doll. He went through cabinets, searching drawers and in-built closets along the curved walls and even in the bathroom.

I had no idea what he was looking for, until he emerged with a bottle of vodka and a gun.

I'd laughed aloud.

He aimed a quizzical look in my direction until I motioned for him to pass over the vodka, which he'd done reluctantly. Taking the bottle back as I started to open it with my fingers, he poured me a glass, watched me down it in a single shot. He poured me one more, and while I drank it, the bottle promptly disappeared. I didn't see where he hid it, although I watched him, fighting a head rush from the alcohol, so tired I literally couldn't make myself stand, although I'd barely moved all day and badly needed the toilet.

Taking my arm, he'd pulled me to my feet.

Opening a series of drawers, he grabbed the tank top, underwear and sweats I now wore before steering me into the bathroom and laying the clothes on the sink.

Seeing him about to speak, possibly to say something more meaningful than I could handle right then, I pointed at the clothes.

"Are those mine?" I actually recognized the shirt.

He nodded. "Ullysa took care of it."

I felt a strange surge. "Oh."

He felt where my head was going. "Before, Allie. While your family was still being questioned by SCARB and the Feds." He hesitated. "Do you need help? You should take a shower."

After a pause that stretched longer than it should have, I shook my head.

Studying my eyes a few seconds longer, Revik let go of my arm and backed out of the room, shutting the door behind him. Fingering the clothes still on my body, I realized those were mine too. I wondered how long I'd worn them, and replayed Revik's comment about a shower.

That was probably his way of telling me I stank.

I felt broken; I couldn't believe how broken I felt.

I couldn't believe I was letting him be the one to pick up the pieces.

My mind tried to wrap around what that meant. I fought to snap out of it, to let him off the hook. I needed to pull my shit together. I needed to at least convince him I had, so he didn't feel like he had to hover over me night and day.

I thought about that the whole time I showered.

The room had filled with steam by the time I finally came out, but it felt like no time had passed at all.

It had, though.

He already lay on the bed, his pale legs sprawled on the coverlet beneath gray sweat shorts. His legs were muscular, I noticed, with a fine coating of dark hair.

He caught me staring.

"It'll be cold," I said. "With the door open."

He gestured me over, not speaking.

I followed the motion of his hands in something like resignation, despite everything I'd been thinking while I showered. Other than guilt, I didn't know what motivated him, but I couldn't make myself care enough to ask him to stop. I let him hold me, thinking I'd never sleep after sleeping all day, then—

Nothing. I must have passed out.

He'd been talking to me, even then.

I don't remember everything he'd said, but some of it painted pictures in my mind, things that pulled at my light, distracted me. He'd shown me light patterns in Barrier starlight, nebulas made of gold and green light, volcanos erupting.

Thinking about that now, I looked at the balcony door.

Outside, black sky beckoned.

Pulling his fingers off me gently, I slid out from under his arm, shivering at another curl of wind that gusted through the cracked door. I angled my legs off the bed, touching my feet to the carpeted floor, trying not to move the mattress as I regained my feet.

Seconds later, I slid through the gap in the glass sliding door, stepping out onto our room's balcony. My toes curled when they met the icy deck. Gripping the railing, I looked out over white and dark churning ocean before letting my gaze travel up.

Stars met the horizon in a cluster of pinpricks, creating a curved black bowl.

I traced the swath of the Milky Way as I listened to faint music from other decks. When I reached out lightly with my seer's sight, I saw the ship from the Barrier. From there I glimpsed bars, casinos, hot tubs, restaurants, a dance club. I saw maps inside the construct I swam through, what might have been tracers of the various seer guards moving through the ship, some of them on duty, some off.

They still felt like strangers to me.

My gaze drifted a few balconies over, to where a lithe form stood alone by a painted rail. I glimpsed the telltale cheekbones of Chandre framed by thin, black braids. She stood unnaturally still. It wasn't the stillness of a living being.

It was the stillness of a boulder, or a parked car.

Warm fingers touched my bare shoulder and I jumped violently.

I turned, relaxing when I saw his face.

I watched his gaze follow mine to the adjacent balcony. He stared at the other seer, and I wondered briefly if they were talking.

Then I remembered Kat and wondered something else.

His pale eyes flinched, shifting to mine.

After a pause, his hand grew warmer on my shoulder. His fingers ran lightly down my arm, then wound around mine.

"What are you doing?" he asked, quiet.

I shivered, staring at our joined hands.

Thinking about his question, I pointed up.

His gaze followed mine and I saw his expression grow less hard as he took in the wash of stars. He continued to stand there, not moving. When the wind rose, I felt him shift the angle of his body so that it shielded more of mine.

Something about having him near brought the emotions back without warning. I felt that kicking, punching thing at my heart begin again. It mixed with a silent photograph of a decomposing eye staring through matted, dark hair I used to like to tug on with my fingers.

He wrapped his arms around me.

"You need to cry," he said. "Why don't you cry?"

I didn't have an answer.

"Do you want someone else here? A female?"

I shook my head. "No. I want you here."

There was a silence.

I felt myself blush at my unthinking honesty; I also felt my words touch him in some way. I felt him try to suppress it, even as his hands on me tightened.

Still thinking, I sighed. "I want a favor, though. You can say no."

Looking up, I studied his face. Seeing the taut look there, I smiled humorlessly.

It didn't take much to arouse his paranoia.

"Tracking," I clarified. "Shielding. I can't stand being this helpless. And I need to *do* something. I'll lose my mind for real if I spend another day in bed."

I felt him think. Interest grew in his light. Real interest.

"Tomorrow?" he said.

Relieved, I nodded. I leaned into him again and felt him react.

I pretended not to notice, just like I always did when it happened. I knew I was taking advantage, letting things blur for both of us. I wondered if he'd even give me sex if I asked, if only to distract me from this.

I felt his breath pause.

"Is that what you want?" he asked, low.

His words vibrated his chest against my ear, but I heard every one.

I considered pretending I hadn't.

"No," I told him instead.

I did want it, though.

I was pretty sure he knew that.

I wasn't about to go that far in letting him try to fix me, though.

I felt him hesitate, as if hearing all of those things.

I felt conflict in him, indecision as he tried to decide if he should say more. But his relief was palpable. Palpable enough to make me feel worse.

I let my embarrassment be there, knowing he felt that, too.

There was nothing I could do about it, whatever I told myself. Pride became meaningless when someone could read your mind; you could either accept being pathetic in hundreds of unexpected, unacknowledged ways, or go crazy.

He withdrew slightly from our embrace, then slid his light into mine as if to compensate, merging into me until I couldn't move. I got lost there, like wandering into a vast space with no walls or corners. No sexuality lived behind it, nothing but warmth and light.

He relaxed more, willing me further in.

I started to react to him sexually again, but managed to dull it, aided by the fact that I didn't feel anything from him other than calm as he leaned into me.

Later, I would remember clouds. Giant clouds of light.

There is a valley between high mountains, a red and gold crevasse. It opens out to an ocean of gold, a perpetual dawn that covers the rolling waves with diamonds.

In this place, I am never alone.

My friends surround me, and the water caresses every worry from my mind. My mother swims in that light-filled ocean, open in a way I barely remember. She laughs like she did when my father was alive, splashing me with her hands. Her dark eyes shine with a soft calm, in a way they never did when—

I jerked, dropped back to my body.

The sound of the ship's prow pushing through water greeted me, along with the motion of his breath under my cheek from where he held me tightly against his chest.

He was breathing harder; I felt him fight to control it.

Pretending not to notice, I turned my head to gaze at the ocean.

Here, the water stretches out into black nothingness and cold.

Then, out of nowhere, he speaks.

"Allie." His voice is a low rumble against my ear. "Allie, I lied to you. I remember my parents. I remember when they died."

It is a clumsy thing to say.

I feel his awkwardness as he looks for a way to re-express it, to give it meaning to me. Tears well in my eyes. He holds me tighter, and I feel his relief as some part of myself finally lets go.

I won't see my mother again, except in nightmares.

In those dreams, as in life, I am always too late.

CHAPTER 23
SCHOOL

Revik stood before me, his height outlined in stars.

The night sky around us was virtual, reconstructed in exacting miniature.

I extended a hand to one of the fist-sized flames, feeling its warmth, wondering at the detail in the illusion. I knew from previous experiments that I could actually burn myself, if I grasped one of the tiny suns in my hand.

"Where do you get these toys?" I asked wonderingly. "Jon would love this."

Seer tech, he sent. "Are you ready?"

I nodded, gripping his shirt because it somehow helped with the illusion of flying.

Do not leave me, he warned. *Not even a little, Allie.*

I smiled, tugging on his shirt. "We're just looking this time, right? A little psychic tom-peepery?" Feeling him hesitate, I shooed him with my free hand. "I won't leave you." I crossed my heart. I watched his eyes follow my fingers. "Promise."

"In Prexci, Allie."

Thinking briefly, I switched languages. "I vow it!"

He continued to look doubtful.

I had asked for this.

We'd been eating breakfast the morning after that night on the balcony. We were halfway through plates of eggs, toast, and sausage when I reminded him of what he'd agreed to the night before. Instead of hesitating, or seeming reluctant in any way, he'd nodded at once, as if he'd been thinking about it already.

He asked me what I wanted to learn.

"Everything," I said, taking a bite of toast.

He smiled. "I'm not sure I can accommodate that—"

"Tracking," I said. "Can you teach me that?"

A light sparked in his eyes. "Yes." He leaned closer to me. "Where do you want to start?"

"Who ordered the hit on my mom?"

His pale eyes immediately flattened. They returned to the dull cold of an infiltrator's eyes. He leaned back in his chair.

I got up when he didn't speak.

I found a pen in the drawer of the inbuilt cabinet under the wall screen, and grabbed a sheet of the ship's stationary. Plopping the paper down on the table in front of him, I bent over where he sat, sketching an outline of the Pyramid from memory. I took a few minutes, delineating the nodes that I'd seen change places, marking tiers I'd seen.

Revik watched me draw, shifting slightly in his seat, his arms crossed.

I circled the man sitting on top.

"Him. He's the guy, right? Who is that? Is it that 'Galaith' you told me about?"

Revik met my gaze from less than a foot away.

I could tell he was grudgingly impressed, but I wasn't sure by what. He's the one who told me my pyramid paintings were accurate.

He must have heard me. Grunting a little, he wiped his mouth with a cloth napkin, fingering the glass of juice by his plate. He gave a short laugh.

"*D'gaos,* Alyson." His pale eyes flickered up. "The best trackers in the Adhipan can't answer that question. If you want to learn how to track, start with something small, something you have a connection to. These things go in stages—"

"So you won't help me?"

His eyes narrowed. "Did you hear what I said?"

"I heard you. It's just that I really think—"

"Alyson!" He gave another outraged laugh. "No!"

"But how is it different from tracking anyone else?" I leaned my palms on the table, ignoring his uncomfortable look as his eyes flickered down my body. "Personal connection, right? Or a connection to something that's connected to the target? How hard can that be? I felt that guy, Terian. I could probably still get a flavor of his light. And you two were friends, right? And aren't there, like… a million Rooks? You must still be connected to a few of them."

He stared at me, his eyes horrified, bemused—even a little wary.

Pushing me gently aside with one arm, he stood and picked up his plate, placing it on the room service tray, stacking it on mine with the covers.

"I'll teach you tracking," he said after another pause. "But you're going to have to do it my way." He glanced over his shoulder, surprising me by smiling. "As far as the 'everything' request, I have some ideas. How open are you?"

Open, as it happened.

Partly to distract both of us, and partly because he had too much time on his hands—Revik was Type-A with a capital "A," I was learning—he made me his project.

He pushed me to learn not one, but several languages, mainly the seer tongue, Prexci, and Mandarin. He also wanted me to learn Russian, Hindi and Sanskrit, but apparently wasn't enough of a masochist to start me on those until I made some headway with the other two.

He lectured me on seer history, politics, culture, mythology, biology, law—especially law, he was big on law.

He obtained recordings for when he might be absent or asleep, covering subjects like the entire Sark Codes, a sort of bible for his people.

He outlined the evolution of legal controls on seers following the death of Syrimne, and let's just say, Revik's version differed substantially from what I'd learned in school. He explained how the Human Protection Act evolved to include mandatory registration, travel, employment and residency restrictions, forced implantation, sight slavery, collaring, and the evolution of Seer Containment, or SCARB, which initially grew out of a branch of the World Court.

He tested me, trying to gauge what I could do with my light.

He didn't pull any punches, either, pronouncing me worthless at blocking and not much better at reading, what he called "the basics." He said my concentration had to improve about a hundredfold before I could do anything in the Barrier alone.

To teach me blocking, he'd taken to hitting out at me with his light when I wasn't expecting it. A few times, he caught me off guard enough, and hit me hard enough, that I got a nosebleed, like he had in the car.

He also obtained permission to have Eliah, one of the Seven's Guard, teach me *mulei,* the seer martial art. When I asked Revik why he couldn't just teach me himself, he mumbled something about how he wasn't allowed. I heard the word "penance" muttered somewhere in that speech, but he didn't explain to me what it meant.

The Seven's Guard kept regular passengers and crew out of our part of the ship, which meant seers performed all housekeeping and food delivery.

They stripped one of the larger rooms of furniture to make an exercise arena where Eliah could train me in sparring.

The sparring itself was damned hard—seers had faster reflexes, better hearing and vision, more intolerance to pain because they could detach their light from their physical bodies, and they mixed sight skills in with their physical fighting. There were also totally different rules from the sparring I'd done with my brother, Jon, in his kung fu classes.

For one thing, seers fought dirty.

No matter how much I absorbed, I earned new bruises daily.

Revik taught me "normal" things, too.

Before I was fully awake that morning, he sat on the end of the bed, explaining semi-organic machines to me, and the basics on how they worked. Laying Barrier images over virtual, he also showed me the primary theoretical models or "breeds" of living machine.

He explained how they arose from Barrier experiments by seers during that brief period of integration with humans in the early twentieth century, and how seers were banned from scientific research in the forties partly because a handful of renegade seers took to "persuading" the more intelligent organics to turn on their human masters.

He said Syrimne basically invented the wires, too, while experimenting with ways to both enhance and control seer powers using organics and semi-organics.

I'd never heard that version of history before, either.

Some of what Revik taught me was blatantly illegal.

Like how to break keypads and access-locked computer networks, pulling passwords and bypassing firewalls with my sight. How to avoid racial tagging systems and blood monitors as well as closed-circuit cameras and other security surveillance. He taught me how and when to push humans into giving me things I needed, how to feel facial recognition software and other external scans with my *aleimi*, how to fool a DNA, fingerprint, or iris scanner into a false positive for human, or a false negative on an ID, if I was wanted by SCARB or Interpol.

Other things he taught me were relatively benign.

Like how to greet strange seers and the rules on asking other seers for help. Legal loopholes such as when and how to claim clan status to avoid certain searches and seizures. Etiquette in seer temples and homes. How to act towards older seers, especially family members or any other category of seer to whom respect or deference was owed.

Revik informed me I would get a new identity and a clan tattoo once we made it to Asia.

The Seven would likely reclassify a dead seer with my stats.

After that, Alyson May Taylor would cease to exist.

I wasn't sure how I felt about that.

Revik further explained how I could claim proportional citizenship if they set me up with a human sponsor. Meaning, if I gave up some rights of movement and association, including sexual rights, depending on the contract, I would get limited citizenship rights proportionally related to the contractual agreements with whomever I worked.

"Your world is terrifying," I told him.

"We didn't make it so," was his response.

He paused then, thinking.

"Well. Mostly."

He went on to explain that contractual citizenship was just one way humans pressured seers to work for the military and in other quasi-legal occupations. Civilian contracts could only grant rudimentary rights. Those rights generally didn't include travel or association beyond specified categories—"entertainment," including prostitution, being one of those most easily granted.

The military offered, among other things, nearly unlimited freedom of movement when not on the job, coupled with moderate rights of association without the need to sell sex.

Not surprisingly, a big market for seer contracts also existed in organized crime syndicates. But, Revik noted wryly, the life spans of those seers tended to be shorter, and Rooks dominated that market almost exclusively. Even the mafia didn't make a habit of killing seers indiscriminately, however; trained seers with high sight-ranks were far too valuable.

Seer mafias existed as well, according to Revik, mainly dealing in seer children and organic material, including blood.

I got flickers as he spoke, glimpses of Asian seers on donkeys, leading dirty, barefoot children with dark eyes across the snow, metal collars around their necks like those I'd seen on the prostitutes and other owned seers in San Francisco.

He'd also mentioned to me casually,

Even if you are able to legally change identity, you should know that seer females like you are not legally sentient to other seers, either. If your race were made public by the Council, I would officially be your owner. And if I forbid it, you cannot consent.

We'd been eating on the balcony, and he paused at this, taking a bite of apple as he waved his hand vaguely.

It can be good for us, for they cannot lie and say you have consented where duress was involved. Providing you trust me with this, of course.

I stared at that particular mouthful, not sure where to begin.

"Not sentient?" I said. "As in lacks sentience?"

He'd shrugged. "It is a legal fiction, to require ownership."

"But why *females,* exactly?"

"Not females," he said, looking at me. *You misunderstand. These laws are to control seers with telekinetic powers.*

That took me another few seconds to process.

Even so, I had to admit it made sense, given the Syrimne thing.

Finally, I shrugged. "So I'm a different race now?"

Revik startled me, gesturing in the affirmative.

"Well," he amended, glancing at my expression. "Not really. Your blood is somewhat different, but other seers have this genetic anomaly who are not telekinetic. You can reproduce with us. Well… as far as I know."

He hesitated, looking up at me where I stood by the balcony. He seemed to pick up on the fact that I knew he wasn't telling me something.

He added, *Telekinesis is believed to be at least partly genetic. So with females it could potentially be passed to offspring. This fact alone makes you extremely valuable, in a way that is more real to those who may not care about your significance as the Bridge. It is unclear to me how superstitious some of the higher-ranked Rooks are. Although it is believed Galaith himself is quite religious.*

At my continued stare, his colorless eyes grew impatient.

"You must have known they would have recorded what you did in the diner. You have no one to blame but yourself, Allie."

But I'd been remembering something else.

The bridge over Lake Washington—the way the guardrail seemed to fold into itself just before we hit. I had to assume at least some of the Rooks chasing us had seen me do that, too, if they'd been watching from the Barrier.

When I glanced at him next, Revik's stare had grown irritated once more.

More than that, I got a flavor of angry puzzlement underneath.

"Allie," he said. "You should not have done that. Not while they had access to your light. That was extremely foolish."

"Excuse me," I said, giving an outraged laugh. "I believe I saved your ass during that little screw up… *Dehgoies.*"

"Never do it again." Anger grew more prominent in his eyes. "Not for me or anyone else. I mean it, Allie."

Feeling my anger turn real, he clicked at me sharply.

Whatever story the human media gives, be sure that if the Rooks know you are telekinetic, then SCARB knows what you are, as well. Even if we change your identity to the humans, the seers will want assurances that you will remain docile. And some will want to breed you. Consensually, or not.

"Docile?" I said, barely containing my fury. "*Breed* me?"

Focusing back on his food, Revik shrugged. He arranged a cloth napkin on his lap as he looked out over the sunlit ocean.

"We'll deal with it when we have to. You have protection for now. Vash will do his best. As will I." He didn't look up from where he was cutting a piece of meat.

"I won't leave you in a bad position," he added, gruff. "And I'm sorry if I seem ungrateful. I'm not. I just don't understand how you can do these things, Allie. Or why you don't seem to understand how serious it is."

That had been a few days ago.

Now we stood in a cluster of virtual stars, and he'd promised to take me somewhere.

In Revik-world, this was probably the closest to a date I'd get.

"Where first?" I asked in Prexci.

"Balixe," he said. "It is a seer city."

Balixe means water in the seer tongue… my mind recited.

"Yes." Surprise wafted off him. *You know of it?*

"Only by name," I joked. At his flat look, I sighed, thinking loudly that I'd watched a history program on ancient seer culture. In that particular program, it said Balixe housed the ruins of the last Elaerian city.

Revik nodded. "That is correct."

"I know," I said. I tugged on his shirt. "Can we go?"

He caught hold of my wrist.

I barely had time to take a breath when—

CHAPTER 24

HISTORY

I'm not breathing.

A horizon forms as I watch, framed by distant mountains. I see currents, streams of swift-moving, velvet black light, a myriad of colors that all convey dark.

I love it here.

The sheer beauty of this place is staggering.

Dark clouds hang heavy in the distance, shot through with even more subtle frequencies of light. They make me long for a sunrise, for stronger beams of illumination in the churning aliveness of the night, just to see the colors.

Then I am looking at him, and I forget all the rest.

Geometrical patterns flow around Revik's hyper-detailed form, sparking out in small, colorful arcs. I reach out, touching one of the shapes, and from his reaction, it isn't dissimilar to poking him in the eye.

Cut it out, he says. *Look for the track, Allie.*

At my hesitation, he sighs, sending up more plumes of feeling.

You know the theory. His thoughts carry a thin veneer of patience. *If you don't know the thing you want to resonate with, find another way in.*

When my confusion doesn't lessen, he prods me again.

There are three ways seers track. The first is inprinting. That is what I am doing now, using an imprint given to me by Vash.

He flashes a multi-dimensional image, too quick for me to take in.

I could also use a personal object, audio or visual recording, blood, fingerprints, urine, hair, even a smell. All of these are imprints. Imprinting is the most common track, as imprints are everywhere. Imprinting is the reason for the image ban.

He gestures with one light-drawn hand.

The second method is a location track, he continues. *This is based on the principles of spatial intersection. In simple terms, if you know the location of something in the physical, you can track it in the Barrier. To do so, however, your knowledge must be very precise. It also does not work so well for time jumps, or Barrier echoes.*

I have no idea what these are.

The third way, he says, ignoring my implicit question. *Is a line track. It denotes having a personal connection with, or a "direct line" to the thing you are tracking. Or, in this case, having a direct line to something or someone that is resonating with the thing you are tracking. Which is me.*

He waits for me to follow this train of thought.

Use the opportunity to feel me under a track, Allie.

I am following his logic now. If I resonate with him, and he resonates with the target, I will resonate with the target, too. Simple.

I focus on a current of light I don't recognize in one of his hands.

The vibration immediately changes my own.

Resonance does not have a spatial or interconnectivity limit, he adds as I play with his light. *If you resonate with something that resonates with something that resonates with something… in theory, you can track any part of the chain. Distance can muddle the imprint, but it doesn't have to. The military, of necessity, depends mainly on secondary or tertiary links. Sometimes they are forced to use links of much greater distances from the target. Most of the work of infiltration is this. Uncovering lines or "taps," which can be complex, even tedious. Infiltrating the target's life, hunting them to get close to their light…*

I am fascinated, picking up images from him.

You still do this? Professionally?

Yes, he sends.

For who?

His light sparks in irritation. *Try to match my light… or go back and wait for me in the room, Allie.*

Touchy, touchy, I send softly.

But I am trying to do what he says.

When he notices, his thoughts grow slightly less grumpy.

When you track, it is better if the target does not feel you, he advises. He waits for me to adjust, based on his words. When I don't, his irritation returns. *This is not subtle, Allie. If I were a target, I would know I was being tapped.*

I heard you. Just let me get the hang of it, okay?

He gives in, letting me openly examine his light.

He is cranky today, though. I have no idea if it has anything to do with me, but I decide to try and do as he says. I keep being distracted by the mechanics of our lights' interaction, but I am trying to find the track, too.

My *aleimi* really wants to resonate with his. It is less a matter of trying, more a matter of letting it. So I relax, unfurling a fist that I hadn't known I clenched.

My vibration changes.

I feel Revik's approval.

Good, he sends.

He is closer to me now, and suddenly I am fighting the other thing.

The pulling-nausea-pain feeling I get around him is stronger without my body, carries more of an imperative. It occurs to me that pain is likely how my body translates that imperative, like converting electrical signals. Then it occurs to me that I'm embarrassed, trying to make it scientific.

Revik politely withdraws his light.

Are you ready? he asks.

I consider, for the hundredth or so time, asking him about that pull, then decide to leave it for when he's in a better mood.

I let him feel that I am.

Ready, that is.

He releases whatever he uses to keep us in place and we shoot across the night sky.

Sometimes there are tunnel-like vortices that take us from place to place, but not this time. This time, the movement from one location to the next happens fast, almost instantaneously, without a breath between states.

A city bursts out of the dark.

Its many windows reflect the morning rays of a bloated sun peeking over the horizon.

I recognize the skyline from my dreams.

I see jagged steel and glass squares sticking out of the ground, the dense layer of smog over honking cars and bicycles and auto-rickshaws on the street. People walk down the sidewalk in ragged patterns. They stand by coffee shops and older-looking buildings with red and gold facades. I see flickers of the city from all sides, from the ground to a vantage point somewhere in the clouds.

I am afraid, staring at the metal and glass squares looming out of the dust.

I am waiting for the air raid siren.

I'm waiting for the bombs.

The light brightens, sunlight pouring over the land, and then—

—I am hovering over a different square, filled with people.

The sky in this new place is the opposite of the one over apocalyptic Beijing.

The atmosphere looms so high and clear I think it must belong to a different planet. The sun shines hotter here, but gentler somehow. It hangs in the sky, a pale white that is nearly blue, so small and bright I can't look at it for long, even from inside the Barrier.

The city's buildings crouch around one another like small hills, yet have a kind of regal elegance, covered in greenery that makes them appear almost alive under the dense shadows of dark stone. Cut windows without glass overlook the center of town behind balconies covered in dripping sprays of purple and blue flowers.

A fountain marks the center of the square. Watery creatures decorate the basin, foaming more of that crystal blue water from mouths and fingers.

The streets radiating outward are paved with black volcanic tile. Statues mark the passage into arterial roads like spokes in a wheel.

Flags ripple in a light breeze like silken snakes.

A portly man who looks to be in his mid-sixties stands at a balcony, giving a speech to a packed crowd standing below. He wears dark red pajamas and a long, embroidered tunic that looks Asian yet is not.

The crowd listens raptly as he speaks.

I look over the crowd, fascinated by the beauty in so many faces, regardless of age or sex. Men and women both wear their hair long. The men's is wound in wooden clips studded with brightly colored stones, and the women's hangs loose down their backs, woven through with thin metals, feathers and silk. More jewelry adorns men's hands and ankles, compared to the women who wear stones at their throats and wrists.

I listen to the crowd murmur, although the language is new to me.

It is apparently new to Revik, too.

It is so different my mind's translations inside the Barrier aren't quite right.

"I do not present this... concept from... ego, for self-aggrandizement." Words go missing in the male's speech, words for which my mind cannot find context. "I merely wish for sight... the urgency behind... my plea. It can be peaceful," he adds, holding up a finger. "There is no wanting to... war. Or... living miseries."

The sixtyish man continues to speak.

I continue to get only bits and pieces.

He speaks of working through differences, of wars that have come before.

He exudes confidence, yet is unsure if they really hear him, if they truly understand what he is trying to express. I feel a lot about his mind. It is almost disconcerting, how well I understand how he thinks.

This is Balixe, Revik says.

I startle. I'd been so focused on the man giving the speech, on trying to understand his words, I forgot I wasn't alone.

I look around me as Revik's words sink in.

This is more than prehistory.

This is history most humans don't acknowledge having taken place at all. This is history before humans.

If Revik is affected by this, I cannot tell.

He continues to teach, even here.

This is our *history, Allie. It's not prehistory from a seer perspective, but early history, certainly. The Merensithly Address, prior to the First Displacement.*

The First Displacement? I say wonderingly. *So these are Elaerian? The first race?*

Revik acknowledges this silently, then adds, *Most cannot even see events of this kind. Vash is very generous to share it with us.*

He gestures towards the podium, and the sixty-something man.

This man, he is very famous to seers. History describes him as the final war's architect. It is unknown whether he was a Rook, as we think of Rooks today. He was definitely some kind of precursor to the dark forces that exist on Earth now.

His words cut me somehow.

Focusing back on the man in the red pajamas, I shake my head.

No, I tell him. *That's not right.*

I feel Revik's puzzlement, riding the edges of his bad mood.

He looks between me and the man speaking from the balcony.

It is right. He makes an effort to be conciliatory. *Do not be naïve about his words, Allie. He was a politician. A rich man who only claimed to be a humble scientist. He used his studies to further his social and political agendas.*

It's not his words, I say, pointing. *It's his light. Look at it!*

Revik barely glances at the man before frowning back at me.

Light can be disguised in many ways, Revik warns me. *Do not be naïve about that, either. It is the oldest game in the Barrier, to impersonate light frequencies of one kind or another. I have done it, as an infiltrator. To pretend to resonate with someone or something safe or familiar to your target is often the easiest way to get them to lower their guard. As a Rook, I did this all the time. I would adopt the light connections of relatives or loved ones, simply to get the person to open to me. I impersonated gods, angels.*

I try to take this all in, shielding myself slightly from Revik's emotions. But I cannot just go along, letting his words stand, when they feel so wrong to me.

No, I say. *You're wrong about him. You've been misinformed.*

I feel Revik's stare.

Allie, he says, and I feel him fighting the bad mood, the anger I feel under it. *These scenes have been studied extensively by the clan elders. I'm not defending my own sight, but that of the greatest seers in the clans.* He adds, sharper, *I do not say this to cause offense, but you are a beginner, Allie.*

Before I can think how to answer, the scene around us shifts.

It is difficult at first to tell where we are.

A stone platform has been erected in the middle of a ripped-up town square.

Looking at the broken pieces of estuary and volcanic glass, the piles of burning bodies and the mountains looming up above the remnants of the ancient city, feeling fills me without warning. The emotion that rises shocks me with its intensity.

Revik grabs my light arm.

Calm, he murmurs. *Yes, it is the same square.*

It affects him too.

I feel his grief, but mostly I feel anger in him, unconnected to this place.

Before us stands the same man from before. He is older now, and thinner. His eyes look haunted. Someone has tied him to a pole at the center of the platform. Bruised and cut, his gaunt face hangs over a dark-colored robe spotted with blood. His feet are bare and look like they've been beaten with sticks. Blood drops down on them from a long gash on one leg.

A man on the young side of middle age stands next to him.

He has a thick beard, large eyes, a handsome, riveting face under dark, curly hair. There is something about him that is hard to look away from.

He pulls eyes. He pulls light.

Feeling explodes in me at the sight of him.

That feeling is unfocused, irrational.

Love, regret, grief, horror, betrayal—they tangle my light.

I can't tell if those are my memories, or something from the imprint Vash shared with us. Whatever they are, they hit me in a wave, too strong to fight.

The man with the beard raises his hands to silence the crowd.

They look up at him, and I recognize that look.

They love him.

They positively adore him.

Haldren, I murmur.

I feel Revik's light focus on mine.

The bearded man's voice rises, whipping in the wind.

"Kardek will die!" He speaks with passion, raising his hands as he shouts. "Yes! He will die! His death will not save us. There is no *redemption* here! It is too late… the sickness will take many more. We will starve. We are almost out of water. Our enemies will kill us!"

Moans rise from the crowd, cries of pain.

I flinch from that pain, feeling a part of me smashed into pieces like the volcanic rock. I feel the older man's crushing grief, his sense of responsibility. Not responsibility in the way that Revik said—but there is more sadness in him than I've ever felt in my life.

His grief is overwhelming.

It is failure. It is crushing, unequivocal defeat—the pain of defeat's results.

I have let all of them down.

I have failed them all.

"...And for those of us left behind," Haldren called out. "There is no justice! He cannot bring back our joy!"

Haldren's dark eyes fill with emotion.

"But I promise you this! He will harm you no more!"

Shouts rise from the crowd, screams.

Fists raise into the air.

I make myself look at them, at their faces.

I look at their city, which had once been so beautiful. Flowers no longer bloom from balconies. The stones are broken like jagged teeth. Rags are crammed in cracks to keep out diseased air and icy wind. Blankets covered in ash and blood flap in smoke-filled wind, warning passersby away from what lay inside.

The crowd wavers on its feet. They are sick, thin, dirty, desperate, clothed in rags. Many have volcanic shard knives and spears strapped to their backs. I see a few who look more like soldiers carrying branch-like devices that feel like weapons.

The stone skeleton of the city is all that remains.

"This man," the bearded man shouts. He points at Kardek. "He, who has called himself *the Bridge!* He stands before you, a traitor to our people! A heretic, and a liar!"

I feel Revik's shock ripple through my light.

His whole attention is on me now.

I cannot look at him, though.

I cannot even care about his reaction.

I am being slowly crushed under the weight of this city's pain. Like the rest of them, I focus on Haldren. Haldren, who will redeem the old man, cleanse him through fire.

It feels right. Just, even.

Moans rise with his voice, emotion-laden screams.

People throw things at the old man, hitting him with pieces of ripped up cobblestones. I wince as the lines cross, but feel nothing, in my body or my mind.

The man with the beard finally holds up a hand.

He speaks quietly, for the old man alone.

"You should have listened to me, Liego." His voice breaks. "How could you do it? You will die the greatest mass murderer the world will ever know..."

With these words, it hits me.

More than that.

It annihilates me.

I scream into that blue sky.

NO NO NO! Get me out of here! NOW! NOW!

Allie! It's okay! Revik is beside me, alarmed. No, afraid. *It's all right*—

I shake my head, half-crushed by grief. I see bombs behind my eyes, the plume of mushroom clouds over Beijing. That feeling worsens, fear and dread slamming into my chest, cutting my breath.

NO! Get me out of here! NOW!

He surrounds me, and then—

I am back in that quiet place.

It is the place he took me when my mom died.

We float over a valley of sunset red. Towers of light billow like gold silk before an ocean with gentle waves. Normally, I think of it as his place, as Revik's, or maybe ours.

This time, it feels like mine.

Friends surround me, try to comfort me.

So much relief exists in being there with them, in knowing it is finally finished, that it is finally over. I don't have to go back until...

Revik is there, too.

He is a different Revik, just as I observe a different me standing with him in waist-high water. We cling to one another, standing in that golden current. My friends are around us, and I'm so relieved to be here, to be finished.

That other Revik talks to me in a low voice.

He holds me tighter, caressing my face, and we are alone. He is still talking; he has perhaps been talking for some time.

It feels as if parts of us never stopped whispering together in the dark.

I feel myself grow calm.

His light coils deeper into mine.

That pain of separation is alive now, a living force.

It grows fucking unbearable.

There is familiarity there, beyond what I've felt from anyone—beyond what I've felt from him. We know each other here. We are more than friends. It is his comfort I seek, above all others. I know he understands. He understands in a way that none of the others can, in a way they never will, no matter how hard they try.

He is like me. He is so much like me.

Yet he is different, too.

We are as we always have been, crucial pieces of the same mosaic. He succumbs to that pull, without reservation, and wishes—

STOP! STOP IT!

Panic fills my light. This time, it's not mine.

STOP THIS, ALLIE! Please, stop…!

I have not come to this paradise alone.

The other Revik's light flashes out.

The arc blows us apart like dead leaves, until—

I TOOK A BREATH. I TOOK ANOTHER.

Air shocked my lungs. I choked on it, fighting to work the rhythms of my physical body.

I was lying on the floor.

Virtual stars met my eyes, flooding the ship's stateroom. Flat-seeming now, those stars shone palely as they ran down the cabin's walls.

I felt him move next to me.

When I glanced over, he raised a hand, covering his face.

I saw his jaw harden under his fingers. I stared at him, bewildered, not sure what I was seeing, or why my heart hammered in my chest, as much in fear as confusion. I only realized I clutched his shirt in my hand when he pushed my fingers off roughly, forcing me to let go.

Some emotional kickback made it hard for me to look at him, but also hard to look away. I watched him sit up, trying to wrap my head around him again, around his familiarity, even through the shield he wore like a metal wall.

I couldn't reconcile the impression of complete impenetrability I got off him with the sense that I knew him behind it, somehow.

I tried to push both feelings away.

I tried to pull my mind back into one piece, but could only breathe, watching him as he fought to do the same. I don't remember moving, but somehow, I was sitting up, too, still watching his face. I couldn't seem to unclench my hand.

He looked at me.

His eyes held the same expression they had that morning in Seattle.

Even as I thought it, he shook his head.

"I can't do this anymore," he said.

His voice was hollow, lost-sounding.

Whispers of that other place remained, pulling at his light and mine.

I felt him wrestle with it, forcing it out of his light only to be compelled to look at it again. Pain wafted off him, for the first time in weeks, and he didn't seem to be trying to hide it from me. Without thinking beyond a vague desire to reassure him, I reached for him, touching his face, pausing to finger his long black hair.

He jerked from the caress, but afterwards he stared at me.

His eyes flickered to my mouth, lingered there.

For an instant, just an instant, he hesitated.

Then I saw his eyes change.

They grew openly angry—just before the light in them died.

"I can't do this anymore," he said again. His voice roughened. "I want to sever us. Do you understand me, Alyson?"

I didn't understand, not really.

But he waited for an answer.

"I think so," I said. "I mean, I—"

"Will you agree to it?"

"I don't really know what..." I trailed, seeing his eyes harden to glass. I cleared my throat. "Of course. Whatever you want, Revik."

"Good." He nodded, once. "Thank you."

Without waiting, he regained his feet.

For a moment he only stood there, over me, as if catching his breath. Then he moved, stepping around me to reach the stateroom door.

He opened it without a backwards glance.

I saw him murmur something to the guard, too low for me to hear.

The guard stared at him, as though he couldn't believe what he'd heard, then he looked at me, his expression openly bewildered. The guard continued to stare at me, his eyes a near question, when Revik's voice sharpened, bringing his eyes back to him. Revik didn't speak Prexci, but something else, one of the languages he hadn't taught me.

Eventually, the guard stammered a reply, bowing to him.

I watched Revik slip around the guard.

After a last, piercing look from the guard himself, the door closed.

I heard the lock glide into the wall with a soft click.

Through all of it, the stares and Revik's anger, it slowly sank in that something had just happened—something decidedly more than one of our bantering back and forth bickering matches, or even the fight around Kat in Seattle.

Even knowing this, I found I couldn't move, or think really.

I could only sit there, fighting to control whatever rose in me at his absence.

But I knew. Maybe I'd known for weeks now.

I was in love with him. Like, *really* goddamned in love with him.

Clearly, that wasn't going to work for him, either.

CHAPTER 25
CONSTRUCT

Terian studies the construct, mesmerized.

Like all constructs, the images that obfuscate the border contain some flicker of truth.

Like now—they show a monolithic parade of living stills that coalesce around certain themes, despite how quickly they morph and change.

In this construct, water figures in abundance of course.

Given their mode of transport, that is hardly surprising.

The construct flashes with waterfalls, waves, cracking ice in metal trays, rivers and streams gushing over dark stone, puddles on city streets, saliva, sweat, tide pools, rain.

Terian recognizes some of these images from providing light to Dehgoies in the past.

Others must belong to Alyson, or one of the Seven's Guard.

Terian has studied the construct for days.

It takes that long to notice differences in the ripples of light.

Now he knows the rhythms of its normal state, the range of its oscillations.

Therefore, when a change occurs, even a relatively small one, he cannot help but taste the new flavor, a faint whisper of something that wasn't there before. The change is subtle, but distinct enough, Terian picks it out before it can be reabsorbed.

A flicker of warmth greets him, a fleeting image of limbs entwined, clouding breath and glowing eyes, gone as soon as he catches the scent.

He has felt masturbation before this, of course.

There are over twelve seers inhabiting this particular construct. Only a few of those seers are female, including the Bridge. Even fewer of them are currently having sex.

Terian even swears he's felt Dehgoies masturbate, although he can't be certain of something that specific, not from outside the construct's walls.

This feels different.

The images stabilize, enfolded by whoever is currently tasked with monitoring the construct walls. Terian knows that whoever that person is, it is not Dehgoies.

An old steam engine floats by, whispers of blood and illness, and then back to water and night, ice and mountains, eagles winging silently over cold waves, tastes of Asia and even flickers of Germany and the war, South America and the United States, Russia and Ukraine.

Withdrawing more of his consciousness from the Barrier, Terian pinpoints the new flavor again, rolling it over his tongue, so to speak. His living light acquaints him with the difference, making sure he understands what it means.

Once he *is* sure, he snaps out entirely…

…and his blue eyes focused on polished wood.

Alone in the fireplace-heated room, he laughed aloud.

The raw flavor of sex was a new development, certainly.

It could be one of the other seers.

Given the impact it had on the construct, however, Terian doubted that very much. No, it had to be the Bridge—or Dehgoies himself.

Probably both of them.

Which meant Dehgoies had been uncharacteristically restrained with her.

Terian had a few guesses as to why. In any case, it was almost a pity he would have to interrupt them so early in their little courtship ritual. If Terian had more information from behind those construct walls, he might choose not to, given the option.

After all, nothing was more vulnerable than a seer in the first stages of a mating ritual. As it was, Terian strongly suspected they had not yet consummated, likely because Dehgoies did not wish to be that vulnerable, either.

Still, Terian suspected there was more to it.

Terian had flown several of his bodies to this base in Alaska, to be on the waiting end of their slow excursion through the inside passage. Most cruises took a week to make the journey north to Anchorage. Dehgoies and the Bridge followed a route that spent nearly a month on the coasts of the United States and Canada before entering the open seas for Russia.

They'd likely done that on purpose, to throw them off.

Terian had examined the route carefully, of course, as soon as he knew which ship they would take. Once the ship left the shores of Alaska and entered the open ocean, Terian's people would move on the Seven's Guard.

Despite his careful planning, however, Terian was growing impatient.

He also feared Galaith might have other plans, given all the movement in the Pyramid of late. Knowing the big boss, he might be angling another of his squadrons into place to make the collar on the Bridge.

Terian knew how things worked.

One minute your team led a key op.

The next, it was relegated to clean up duty.

A security mechanism in part, the changes often had a mechanical component, built into the fabric of the Pyramid itself. The rotating tiers formed the primary defense that secured Galaith's position as Head, by keeping all the tiers below him in constant flux, and thus all of Galaith's potential successors in flux, too.

Despite the mechanical aspect of the rotating hierarchy, however, Terian knew Galaith had discretionary control at the top.

Terian could only be pulled if Galaith allowed it to happen.

Terian had been getting the feeling for a while now, that the boss wanted to put some distance between him and Dehgoies—maybe between himself and the Bridge, too.

He'd been unhappy with Terian's decision to kill the adoptive human mother, so that was part of it. He thought it unnecessary, overly gruesome, and a likely impediment to easy recruitment of the Bridge later. He lectured Terian about giving the Bridge reasons to distrust the Org, to view them as anything other than her friends.

Galaith also claimed the issue was closed after their discussion, but Terian could feel it was not.

Galaith had grown secretive again. He'd been stalling for weeks now on providing details of their final approach and extraction.

Terian knew he would never be told outright if he'd been sidelined.

All he could do was run his own secondary op, ignore the edicts from above if they seemed to pull him from the center of action.

Still, that such maneuverings were necessary struck Terian as tiresome.

He wasn't just *any* second-tier aspirant.

He'd been with Galaith since the beginning.

He'd been there before Dehgoies.

Frankly, Terian was pretty sick of being second-tier altogether.

They would have grabbed Dehgoies years ago if Terian was in charge, not left him in the Seven's caves to rot. Terian would have done for his friend what he hoped Dehgoies would once have done for him—help him see reason. Help him realize the depth of his mistake, that it wasn't too late to make things right.

Dehgoies was family.

He was certainly the closest Terian had ever had.

A pulse sounded from the implant he had grafted to his spine at the base of his neck.

A voice rose. "Sir? Are you there?"

Terian adjusted his focus. "Yes, Varlan. I see you."

"Has something changed, sir? Shall we continue to hold?"

Galaith had been unambiguous.

He wanted Terian to hold back on a direct assault, wait until their forces could gather in Russia. Terian read additional motives in Galaith's desire to wait; he wanted to be in a part of the world where there'd be a minimum of human witnesses.

He also wanted to give Dehgoies time to grow more attached to his new charge.

This last thought was laughable, of course—but Terian hadn't told Galaith everything he knew about *that* particular situation yet, either.

He glanced at the little girl curled up on a stuffed chair, her face slackened in sleep.

He knew what that part of him would say.

It meant insubordination.

And yet, Terian had a good feeling.

Rarely had his good feelings steered him wrong.

"No," Terian said to the seer on the line. "No more holding. It is time. Engage silent mode from the hierarchy proper. Report only to me, and wait for an opening. I strongly suspect we will see one, soon enough."

The seer on the other end acquiesced.

Then, his presence faded.

CHAPTER 26
BETRAYAL

Cold water. It was exactly what Revik needed.

Unfortunately, the pool water didn't look at all cold.

Steam rose over shallows filled with splashing kids wearing cartoon-covered flotation devices. Revik stood at one side of the arch leading to the covered, lagoon-shaped pool with its glowing, underwater lights. So far he hadn't done anything but walk.

He'd contemplated a drink, but couldn't bring himself to act, not yet.

"Fuck," he muttered.

Hearing him, a woman glanced up as she walked towards the pool, wearing only a bikini and a towel. He didn't return her look directly, but his body responded to her stare, enough that he tensed.

Feeling his mood worsen, he realized he'd already made his decision.

He only had to decide where.

His mind ticked through options.

He automatically rejected the atrium or any of the casinos. There was a neon affair with a dance floor and a padded leather bar crammed with drunk tourists, a poolside bar on the other side of the ship, a few scattered piano bars… and a smaller, faux-colonial British pub, replete with high-backed chairs, bamboo tables, potted palms and a real tiger skin on the wall over a fireplace.

Poor taste, touring the remnants of what had been some of the world's most stunning glaciers, now a meager, patchy white only in the dead of winter, with the skin of an extinct animal nailed to the wall.

Snorting in a dark kind of humor, Revik decided it was perfect.

He walked in that direction, passing the entrance to the salon and gym.

He located the pub the next floor down, and after a quick scan, found an empty barstool that placed him with his back to the wall in the far corner.

He hesitated only another breath before extracting a copper-colored clip from his pocket and hooking it to the collar of his shirt.

He hadn't been careful.

The bartender frowned.

Pretending not to notice, Revik waved for a drink, pointing at one of the taps.

Reluctantly, the human took a glass off the back shelf, and filled it.

"You got a permit?" he grunted, setting down the pint in front of Revik.

Revik ignored the man's hostility, nodding.

"The management wanted it discreet. Clips only. No wires." He lifted the beer, and the thread of the man's mind.

...we'll just see about that, ice-blood. Can't hurt for me to check with "the management," after all...

The human's thick fingers were already reaching for his earpiece when Revik brushed the thought from his mind.

Instantly, the large hand dropped.

The bartender stood by the computerized cash register, puzzled.

By the time he'd moved a few steps away, he forgot Revik entirely.

Sighing, Revik moved his stool further into shadow and settled himself in to wait. On a ship of this kind, most wouldn't even recognize the clip. If he relied on that alone, he might have a long wait before he got approached.

Still, it felt cleaner this way.

If he got no interest after a few more drinks, he'd reassess.

He let his eyes go to the monitor over the bar, which displayed the day's news. He got through a few beers watching brightly-colored avatars argue about terrorism and China's inadequate response to the threat of renegade seers on their own soil.

An hour later, he'd switched to bourbon.

He contemplated a walk to the neon bar to try his luck, when he felt eyes on him and turned. A slender woman in tan slacks and a form-fitting ivory sweater stood a few paces behind him, probably in her early forties.

He'd seen her walk in, but dismissed her when she pulled out a book and settled in a corner to read, an appletini parked on the round cocktail table in front of her. She had money, but looked the type who wouldn't go near a seer bar if her life depended on it. The kind whose human husbands tended to be Ullysa and Kat's most regular customers.

He saw her study the clip on his collar, then glance down the length of his torso and legs.

Seeing his eyes on her, she hesitated only a second longer.

Clutching a small black purse in one hand and the martini glass in the other, she walked briskly up to the bar, her lips pursed.

Approaching him directly, she leaned against the wood.

He didn't move his leg when she pressed into his thigh. She glanced up at him cautiously, a disarming mix of nerves, daring and curiosity in her eyes.

"Are you what I think you are?" she asked, soft.

He nodded, still watching her face.

"Yes."

She studied his eyes, looking from one to the other as if trying to see past them. It was almost a seer's stare. He found he was already reacting to her, and kept his mind carefully away from hers. As if she'd heard him, she asked,

"Are you reading me now?"

"No," he said, smiling.

"Do you want to?"

"Yes," he said truthfully.

When she didn't move away, he slid down further in his seat, glancing for the bartender. The woman looked down at him, reacting to his mind's nudge, and reddened. Giving a nervous laugh, she brought her martini glass to her lips.

"I see. How much?" She hesitated. "You charge, right?"

"Yes." He thought fast. "Five hundred."

"Five hundred? Are you worth that?"

He dipped lightly into her mind. She waited, as if she knew what he was doing. He pulled out a moment later, shifting slightly on the stool.

"For you, yeah," he said.

She smiled wanly. "I bet you say that to all the girls."

He smiled politely.

"This is crazy," she muttered, taking another swallow of her drink. "I've never even talked to one of you before." She switched her purse to her other hand, looking down the bar to buy herself time.

Revik didn't answer.

He'd learned more than he wanted in his brief tour.

She was lonely. Her husband was on the cruise, too, but with someone else, likely someone he'd arranged to have come on the ship so he could slip away from his wife every chance he got.

This woman knew, obviously, but for some reason wasn't ready to leave him.

Human sexual relationships depressed the hell out of him.

He was about to tell her to forget it, when she nodded decisively.

"Okay." She downed the rest of the appletini, her eyes bright. "What the hell. Do you have a place, or—"

He shook his head. "Not yet."

She pursed her lips. "Really? Then when?"

Revik hesitated. He hadn't thought this through. Now that he had an actual person to react to, he realized he wasn't worth anything close to the price he'd quoted. He needed an appetizer first, even if it was just his hand.

He nodded towards the fireplace.

"In an hour? There's something I have to do first."

She looked doubtful, and he shook his head.

"Not that," he assured her.

She nodded, but clearly didn't believe him.

Hesitating another beat, he got up from the barstool, realized he still had an erection and paused, willing it to subside. When it wouldn't, he felt his face warm. Instead of walking away, she lingered by him, shielding him from the rest of the room.

His pain worsened briefly.

"Thanks," he said after a moment.

She glanced down, a faint smile on her lips.

"So the rumors are true, then? Is your kind always this... enthusiastic?" She waited for his answer, then added, "It's good to know I don't repel you, at least."

Bitterness colored the last of her words.

Impulsively, he touched her hand that held the glass, letting his fingers linger on her skin. She shivered as it turned into a caress, and for another instant, he hesitated. He would lose her if he left now, he realized. He made up his mind as he felt her blush under his stare.

He circled her wrist with his fingers.

"Forget the money," he said. "And the hour."

She blinked at him, and for the first time, he noticed her eyes were green.

His cock hardened painfully again, even as nausea slid through his chest, making it difficult to breathe.

"We're not always like this," he said, watching her look at him. "It won't be as good."

She studied his eyes. "It'll be good enough."

"Now," he said, to be clear. "Are you ready?"

"Yeah," she said. "Okay." She balanced her martini glass on the edge of the bar, following the insistent tug of his fingers. He unhooked the clip from his collar, shoving it in his pocket as he led her out of the room.

CHAPTER 27
REVELATIONS

Slowly, the view around me changes.

Clouds hang bright and sharp, still against liquid black.

I'm not supposed to be here.

Even without Revik's warnings, my gut tells me so.

The construct should keep me safe, or so I tell myself.

I'm in a big fishbowl of protected space, cut off from the Barrier proper. But even I know the construct's not foolproof. I also suspect that what I'm doing right now might actually put some part of me outside of the construct's protective shield.

That whisper of nerves isn't enough to stop me.

Not now, and not the countless times I've done it before, when Revik wandered out of the room late at night or in the early morning. He thought I didn't know he roamed the halls while I slept, but I did. I'd wait for him to leave, and I'd sit like this.

I'd even snuck in a few jumps after he passed out on the bed.

Those were a lot riskier.

He was a light sleeper.

I no longer need to pause at the edge of those dark, light-filled clouds. I'd eliminated a lot of preliminaries, and even some of the intermediary steps. I'd learned to make these jumps economical, due to the time constraints.

Even though I have time now, I do the same.

I don't screw around, or waste time looking at the scenery.

I aim directly at the spot at the top of the Pyramid.

Images hit me at once. Most center on the keys I turned to get this far. The faceless man is elusive, hiding behind a confusing multitude of different doors.

Sometimes I use Terian to try and get close to him.

This time, I have something closer than Terian.

I have Haldren.

I don't know how I know this Haldren, but I do.

I also know what he is.

Haldren is the faceless man. He is the man who approached Revik in that prison during World War II, offering him a job with the Rooks. He is the man who sits on top of the Pyramid now. He is the apex of that Pyramid. He is its mind.

He is its Head.

In some sense, Haldren *is* the Rooks.

Somehow.

I don't understand the exact mechanics of this.

I also don't care.

Haldren whispers over an old man's battered body.

Liego… Liego… why did you do it?

Just like Revik, Haldren tries to blame Kardek for the war that killed the Elaerian.

I know better. I know Liego Kardek better, too.

Liego and Haldren go way back, sharing a timeline of lives I don't understand, but that I'm forced to accept on some level.

I can at least accept it enough to *use* that information.

I see Liego with Haldren when Haldren is a child.

Haldren is a squalling, sickly child, wearing rags, alone and abandoned. Liego rocks him to sleep, sings songs when the orphanage comes late to pick him up from the school where Liego teaches. Liego pities the boy.

Eventually, that compassion becomes a deeper love.

The boy moves in with him and a man named Massani after no one claims him from the first set of wars. I watch Liego feed the four-year-old. I see him talk to an angry, confused adolescent, hold him as he cries at some disappointment or rejection.

I see Liego teach him in his private laboratory. He readies the boy for exams, introduces him to a society that accepts him because of who Liego is.

Hatred wells up in me, mixed with a love that hurts more.

It is not my life, not my problem, but I take it personally.

I take *him* personally.

I crash through wall after wall, following the thread of that gaunt, crying child.

He still exists. Somewhere.

He may be Galaith now, but he is Haldren, too.

A recklessness lives in me.

I decide I'm tired of the slow way, the seer game of hide and seek, step by step, mapping and remapping of lines, all the cloak and dagger bullshit I've tried my best to follow as Revik taught me. I don't need to understand all the threads that tie me to this place and time.

I am looking for the monster who killed my mother.

I don't care that he was once a child in some ancient version of Earth.

Except that it might help me find him now.

Dropping the pretense, I envision the child in front of me.

I call to him.

I call his name through the faceless shadows of a distant Pyramid, but most of the beings tied to that prison do not hear me.

I think it is futile, that I am wasting my time, when…

I am with him.

Abruptly, I am there, at the top of those chafing lines.

I float over the apex of the Pyramid.

Shocked by my success, I see him. He sits alone, in a structured room. Lines of silver and hard metallic white stick to his head and heart.

The child is one of a thousand whispering masks.

The Pyramid has disappeared.

It disappeared because I am inside it. Haldren doesn't move, doesn't seem to see me at all. He rests inside a dream. A flat, pleasant emptiness. He looks just like a machine, devoid of pain, devoid of light.

Watching him exist in this state, I find I almost understand.

He is safe here.

He is protected, in a way the old man couldn't protect anything. Haldren is protected from feeling, from vulnerability, from caring about anything that might hurt him. He can sit in this empty space, untouchable, because the silver light ensures that he doesn't have to feel any of it. He can give orders, and tell himself he is the cause of none of it.

He can be king of the ghosts, the already dead.

He can kill my mom.

Or he can simply let it happen.

Anger flares my light.

A white arc leaves me, utterly different from the seething strands eclipsing Haldren on his metal throne. The flame sparks as it comes in contact with the Pyramid's trembling strands.

It finds one of the connecting points.

There is a strange silence.

Then a tangled, silver ball explodes.

I hear the crack below that single pearl of flame.

Something totters, begins to fall.

Voices scream, awakened from their collective dream. I watch that piece of the Pyramid tumble into a void-like abyss. Everything disappears below the connecting point I have broken. Lights disappear, erased from the network mind like branches cut from a dying plant.

Haldren vanishes.

I fall. I fall for a long, long time.

Until I see only one face, one being.

A narrow, wasted mask looks at me, its eyes like poisoned urine.

The being smiles.

It hits me… I'm not looking at a person anymore.

I am looking at one of the Rooks.

I see you, Bridge, it whispers.

I see where you are.

…I SAT UP, GASPING, BATTING AT MY HEAD WITH MY HANDS.

Just like that afternoon, I found myself lying on my back on the carpet, but instead of virtual stars, I see the low, white-painted ceiling of the stateroom.

My head hurts. A sharp pain throbs my skull, but also a feeling of despair.

I realize I'm still partway in the Barrier. I dig my nails into my arm, trying to force myself the rest of the way out.

My eyes clicked back into focus.

The silver light still clung to my head in some undefinable way, so I sparked outwards with my *aleimi,* trying to get it off me.

All I felt was amusement, laughter as the being left.

I was still sitting there, gasping, when a sharp knock rattled the cabin door.

I turned to stare at it, fighting to breathe.

Revik wouldn't knock.

"Allie?"

I recognized the Irish accent.

Eliah. My *mulei* teacher.

"What the hell's on in there, love? What're you doin'?"

Only minutes had passed. Seconds, maybe.

White hands on green mirrors. Blood with water.

He was thirsty. So fucking thirsty. Everything hurt, and…

Pain blinded me. I held my head, biting my tongue as hard as I could.

"Yeah," I managed. "Okay. What do you want?"

I don't remember saying he could come in, but the door opened.

Eliah crossed the threshold into the room and stopped, looking around as if startled by a strange smell. Closing the door behind him, he studied me, head cocked.

"What've you been doin' in here, love?"

I pulled myself shakily to my feet.

I couldn't help but wince at the bruises from our earlier fight in the ring.

"Feeling sorry for myself, for sucking so hard at *mulei,*" I said, forcing a smile. I clenched my hands to keep them from shaking. "Why? Do you want to kick my ass again?"

He smiled. His sharp eyes didn't leave my face.

"You all right, love?"

"I'm fine. What's up?"

There was the barest pause.

"Orders." He hesitated, then glanced at the bed, as if involuntarily. "To hear tell it, your other half will be out for a while. I'm supposed to keep you company until he gets back." Trailing, he watched me rub my temples. "Allie-bird? Seriously. You don't look so hot."

I flinched at the nickname.

My mother had called me that.

Revik said a lot of our thoughts and memories would float around the construct, though, that it was part of sharing a construct with other seers. I knew it didn't mean anything. I'd been thinking about my mom a lot, so yeah, it made sense.

It still made me feel sick.

Casting around for something to keep me focused on the room, I dug my nails into my palm as Eliah sat on the bed. I watched him look out through the balcony doors.

When the pause went on too long, I cleared my throat.

I'd never seen him in street clothes before, apart from glimpses through the door when he guarded our stateroom. He had two different-colored eyes, one nearly black, the other blue, yet with his hair combed back and the blue sweater he wore, the combination worked well with his square jaw and salt-and-pepper hair.

Sitting casually on the end of the bed, hands clasped between the knees of his dark-brown slacks, he looked like a cologne ad, or maybe a feed advertisement for high-end coffee.

What was it with these seers, that all of them were so damned good-looking?

The men all looked like male models.

Eliah had the air of a man who'd never bother with a midlife crisis. He'd be too busy scuba diving the Norwegian fjords or tackling K2.

He smiled. "Cheers, love. Although the 'midlife' crack stings a bit."

Watching him look at me, I decided the normal thing to do would be to sit. I let my weight sink into the plush armchair across from him.

"So what now?" I said. "You're on babysitting duty, is that it?"

"I suppose so, yes." He continued to study my eyes. "That all right with you, love?"

I shrugged, voice casual. "Sure. Whatever. Not sure why it's necessary, but knock yourself out. It's not like this is the first time Revik's gone on walkabout."

Eliah flushed.

I couldn't help but see him glance at the bed again.

"Yeah, well." He gestured vaguely. "I guess Chan was worried you might overreact this time. She doesn't want anything happening. Not with a ship full of human witnesses."

"Overreact?" I frowned. "Overreact about what?"

He gave me a shrewder look.

"You know where he went this time, don't you, love?"

I hesitated, wanting to ask.

Then I shook my head, once.

"No. And I really don't see how it's any of my business. Or yours." I cleared my throat, rearranging myself on the chair. "Since you're stuck here, though, do you mind helping me work on shielding? I need a shower, but then we could practice. I could stand to eat, too. Have you had any dinner?"

"I want to ask you something, first," he said.

My fingers tightened on the chair. "Okay."

He smiled. "Don't say yes too quick, love. It might offend you."

Thinking about his words, I nodded, my expression unmoving. "Go ahead. Ask. It seems to be my day for that kind of thing."

He laughed.

When I didn't say anything more, he made a vague gesture towards my body.

"All right," he said. "You and the walking corpse. What's going on?"

I raised an eyebrow. "Excuse me?"

"I hear his first wife strayed. Is he feeling bitter? Testing you, perhaps?"

There was a silence.

I fought with how I might laugh off his words, sidestep the question altogether, or smack it down, like I had the first time he'd baited me.

But the silence had stretched too long.

Regaining my feet, I made my way to the bathroom.

Eliah got up to follow.

"Allie… wait."

"It's fine. I just really need a shower," I said. "If you want to order food, go for it. Or you can leave, honestly. Unless Chan says you really have to stay."

"Allie..."

I shut the door on him, not quite in his face, but close enough that I felt him flinch. I knew it was probably too much to hope for, that he might take the real hint and leave.

He wouldn't even leave the door.

As I tugged the stretchy tee I wore over my head, bending over the tub, I heard him lean against the metal panel.

"Didn't want to ask it, love," he said, his words slightly muffled. "But I've been hearing things. You know. Small ship. Even smaller construct."

The echo of water splashing against the fiberglass tub drowned out his voice as I turned up the faucet. He spoke louder, but I missed a few words.

"...Most of our females won't touch him, truth be told. There's rumors about what he did when working for those Rooks, some of it to women..."

"Eliah," I called out. "I can't hear you. Can it wait?"

He raised his voice. "I could see it, if you just wanted a roll. Hell, he sells it, so he's got to be competent at least..."

Wishing I hadn't heard that part, I bit my lip.

His voice rose again above the water.

"...But gods almighty beyond the Barrier, Alyson. How in the realms of hell did he talk you into *marrying* him? Was there coercion involved? Because, love, if so, you have grounds for severance. Even apart from what he's done since."

I'd been about to flip on the shower nozzle. Now I froze, hearing his words even as they replayed in my mind. I stood there for a few seconds, half bent over, wearing only my underwear. I watched water flow out of the silver tap.

"Allie?" He paused. "You know he's got no social status to speak of, right? Hell, I think he's officially still in penance. You've basically elevated him about ten ranks, just by agreeing to the bastard. And I really don't see anything in it for you. Then he treats you like this..."

The linoleum blurred.

My mind pieced together words, fragments of conversations, references.

I remembered the look on Ivy and Ullysa's faces in the kitchen when I wouldn't go to him that morning, his half-assed apology about Kat, the constant, oblique references to whatever happened between us that first night we spent in Seattle.

"You know it's illegal for seers, right?" Eliah said.

"Illegal?" I repeated numbly.

"Infidelity. You need permission. I'm assuming you didn't give him that?"

I stood there, unable to answer. Thinking about Jaden, my parole, the look on Kat's face when she thought I'd offered her Revik…

Tugging my shirt back over my head, I turned off the water.

After standing by the door a second more, I opened it, and found myself meeting the serious eyes of Eliah, one blue and the other nearly black. He started a bit, to find himself facing me so suddenly. For a moment we just looked at each other.

Then my jaw hardened.

"Okay," I said. "Order food. I have questions."

Eliah grinned, looking about to speak.

Before he could, I shut the bathroom door in his face.

I CURLED UP IN ONE OF THE ROUND-BACKED CHAIRS THAT PASSED FOR comfortable, a half-eaten plate of oysters on the counter next to me. I wasn't hungry anymore, but food and alcohol seemed to be the way to get Eliah to talk, just like it was with most humans.

My hair was still wet from the shower.

I wasn't cold, though.

Unlike Revik, Eliah liked the doors closed, the heat cranked up. He sprawled on a chair to my left, drinking a beer as both of us faced the glass doors out to the sea.

He grinned at me, eyes glassy from alcohol.

"So then I just picked myself up," he said, his accent stronger with the beer. "…Dusted m'self off. Then I pretended I'd *meant* to stick my hand in that letter box." He returned my smile, shaking his head. "Those poor worms."

I stiffened and he added apologetically,

"...Humans. We end up acting fairly idiotic around them sometimes, just to avoid the hassle of an exposure threat. It's a real bitch to get your license back once it's been yanked." Grunting, he downed another swallow of beer. "It's one thing to move undetected by humans. When you've got SCARB on your arse, it's a whole 'nother story."

He gestured around us, pointing to the television and the stocked bar.

"But hell. This is my home. Living in caves, chanting... not the life for me. I don't much fancy being sold at auction to some rich dickhead, either. Clan tattoos can get burned off. Happens all th' time." He motioned at the race-cat tattoo on his arm. "Overambitious Sweeps who want a bit o' extra dosh get bought off by traders. O' course, being in the Guard protects me from most o' that. Even SCARB won't mess with the Seven much.

"...Thank Christ," he added, leaning over the arm of the chair and swigging more beer. "But there's the flip side o' that, too. If I don't make th' effort to act a bit human-ish, the Sweeps would have me living out in the middle of Mongolia somewhere, milking oxen. Not much of an improvement, really."

"The Sweeps?" I said, puzzled. "But they're human, right?"

"No." He shook his head. *"I'thir li'dare...* that bastard Dags doesn't tell you anything, does he? No. The Sweeps is part of the World Court, yeah. But they're culled from the clans. They're the police. Couldn't rightly be human, could they?"

"You have your own police," I repeated, a little dumbfounded.

In the human media, the Sweeps were always portrayed as a kind of global Homeland Security. They worked under SCARB, sure, or maybe adjacent to SCARB, tracking renegade seers, but it never occurred to me they weren't human.

He flicked his fingers to the right and up, a gesture I recognized as "yes."

"The Rooks have a heavy presence on SCARB as a whole, of course," Eliah added. "They're sort of a competing nation with the Seven, you could say. But it's more a philosophical difference, really. The other nations tolerate 'em because whatever else they may be, the Rooks're good at concealment. Ironic really, as they were the first to advocate dominance over isolationism."

He leaned on his elbows.

"Containment's a real controversial issue with seers these days, love," he explained. "Before, humans were seen more as animals…" He gave me an apologetic look. "Most of us didn't even *want* to interact with them, truth be told. The world was bigger back then, and it was easy to talk about non-interference, live and let live, will o' the gods an' all that. Now humans fly everywhere, go everywhere, want to see everything. Even our most isolated clans are stuck having to deal with 'em in one form or t'other… and there's sex and mixed marriage and all kinds of nonsense on our side, too."

He winked at me. "We've got nasty libidos, we seers."

I rolled my eyes, but grinned slightly.

"Damn, that's cute." He leaned back over the arm of the chair. "Fuck. How can he keep his hands off you? Between that ass and those eyes, I'd never leave the goddamned room."

Feeling myself stiffen, I brushed it off.

I cushioned my jaw on my palm, resting my elbow on the rounded chair back.

"Okay," I said. "I'm just going to ask. Do you really believe all this Bridge stuff? About me killing everyone? Ending the world?"

He broke into a laugh, spilling his beer.

"Trust Dags to put a positive spin on it. What a morose bastard."

"Eliah," I said, sighing. "What do you think? Honestly. If it's true, I think it must have something to do with the Rooks. I've been studying their network, but until today, I never really—"

"You've been *what?*"

Eliah raised his head, staring at me.

The sharpness of his voice took me aback.

"Studying their network," I repeated. "I'm interested in how it works. The way the whole top part seems to shift—"

"The succession order?"

It was my turn to stare.

When I glimpsed images in his mind however, watching the different pieces of the Pyramid move up and down, trading places under the top spot at the apex of the Pyramid, I found myself nodding. It was oddly reassuring that the thing I'd been looking at had a name.

"That's right," I said. "The succession order."

"Why on earth would you be interested in that?"

His voice remained sharp under his disbelief, and I saw what might have been wariness under that. For the first time in our conversation, I remembered he was an infiltrator, like Revik.

"We've never been able to see that, love," he warned. "Why would you even *look* there? What do you expect to find, exactly?"

I smiled humorlessly.

Even so, I had to fight to keep the anger out of my voice.

"I know," I said. "It's practically Revik's mantra. It's way over my head. I'm just a beginner… I get it. You don't need to go there, Eli."

"That's not exactly what I meant, love."

"So you really don't understand why I might be interested in the people who killed my mother?" At his silence, I bit my lip. "So what do you think, Eli? Really. About the Bridge stuff, I mean."

The harder look faded from his eyes.

"Love, I know you're worried about reincarnation an' all that," he said, sighing. "But I don't think that's the point, really."

"Then what *is* the point?"

"It's about roles, see. Some are too important, and affect too many people to leave to chance. The Bridge is like that. There needs to be someone overseeing things, when something as heavy as a Displacement goes down."

For a moment, I could only look at him, replaying what he'd said.

"You really believe all that stuff?"

He grinned, resting his head on the chair's back. "You sound surprised."

"For a seer, you're almost… normal. I had my hopes."

Leaning forward, he rested his free hand, the one not gripping his beer, on my thigh. He massaged the muscle there sensually.

"Does that mean you're warming to me, love?"

Smiling, I rolled my eyes. Taking his hand, I moved his fingers off my thigh and back to his chair. "There's a serious shortage of female seers on this ship, am I right?"

"Brutally small," he agreed cheerfully. "And Chandre's as likely to try for you as I am. But you'd be a peach anywhere, love. And that pain coming off you is simply… maddening. I don't know how he can fucking stand it…"

I felt my jaw harden.

Thinking about his words, I folded my arms.

"Revik said that seer relationships were 'complicated'… and largely biological. He said I shouldn't take it personally. Is that true, too?"

Eliah snorted. "Bloody romantic."

"Is it true, Eliah?"

He shrugged. "It'd be true in a way, I suppose. We're a bit more biologically wired for monogamy than humans. But that's not exactly the same thing, if you don't mind my saying… and doesn't have anything at all to do with who we choose as mates. In fact, you could say the reverse is true."

At my puzzled look, he shrugged with one hand, seer-fashion.

"The biological symptoms could be unsettling, I suppose. Especially if you didn't know what was happening. Someone like you, who thought they were human, it's got to be that much harder…" He frowned, studying my face. Leaning forward, he looked at my eyes. "Gods. You're not in love with him, are you, Alyson?"

I shook my head, but felt my chest clench a little anyway.

"I barely know him."

"That's not what I asked." Still studying my eyes, he added more cautiously, "The rest of us, we assumed you chose him for protection. Or, frankly, because he was the first male seer you met, and bad luck on you for that."

He hesitated, laying a hand on my arm.

"But if you *are* in love with him, well… that changes things. Won't be so easy to pull out of this thing with him then, pet. And I'm sorry for that." He gripped my arm. "I truly am."

I focused on his eyes.

They seemed to brighten strangely in the dim light of the cabin.

Ambient noises grew deafening: the sound of the ocean through the closed door, the wind whistling past the glass, the ticking of the old-fashioned clock.

I heard an odd hitch in Eliah's breath as he watched my face, his heart beating through his rib cage, slowing as he listened for my answer.

I got the chance to think the timing was ironic.

Then everything in the room dimmed.

I should have known I'd feel it when it happened.

From everything Eliah told me, everything that happened with Jaden in San Francisco… even from what little Revik himself had said… I really should have known.

I should have known a lot of things.

But they still always managed to surprise me.

CHAPTER 28

BREAKDOWN

I stand on a rock bluff, above a valley riddled with spider-web cracks. Wind tunnels between chasms. Everything is gone.

I'm alone.

But not really. Not really alone.

...He raises himself up on his arms, sweating, reading her, watching her eyes as he brings her to the edge. I see the tattooed writing on his arm, sweat sticking black hair to his neck and forehead as he moves over her, arms tense as he adjusts the angle of his body.

He holds her still, fingers clenched in blond hair.

I feel him holding back.

I feel the pain there… there is so much.

Enough that he can barely control himself.

He arches deeper, deep enough to pause when she cries out. Yet even now, he holds some part of himself back.

He goes in with his mind so he can feel it when…

She climaxes, gripping his arms. It's not the first time. Pain ripples off him as he watches.

Then it worsens.

Red sunlight shines behind my lids, but that pale, bird-less sky fades.

I feel him fighting. With himself, with me. He loses control and then he groans aloud, asking me, winding some part of himself deeper into my light.

He pulls me inside of him, even with her lying between us.

Gaos. Why did you leave. Why did you leave me that morning?

My own pain worsens at his words.

He tries to stop himself, fights to pull away.

Come here. His voice yanks on me, harder, more violently in that space. It is demanding, harsh, but lost, out of control. *Come here… gaos, come here. Let me in. Let me do this…*

…and he's inside both of us now.

I feel his pain skyrocket.

Gaos… fuck… Alyson…

I feel his relief mixed with frustration, a kind of horror at what he's doing even as he arches into her harder, trying to read me as he feels her cunt.

He wants me. I feel it, that want, although he won't tell me, even now.

He wants me more than I can stand, more than I can let myself feel.

It hurts, that want, but I'm lost inside the conflict on him, too. Fear hovers behind desire, masked in anger at me for forcing him to revisit that place, to remember.

I would turn him back. I would make him over into that thing he hates.

He is sure of it. He feels it with every atom of his being.

Above, the Pyramid rotates. There is more to see.

For now, alone… further back, below.

He would remember.

"HEY." THE WOMAN FOUGHT TO SLOW HER BREATHING. SHE REALIZED SHE'D never gotten his name. "Hey… are you okay?"

His pale skin wore the same sheen that matted her blond hair to her neck and shoulders, stuck the cotton sheet to her legs.

She clutched at him, unable to help it.

Her whole body still vibrated from what he'd done to her, seemingly again and again and again.

He'd been unnervingly focused as he brought her to orgasm, but by the end, he'd surprised her by being verbal, too—a lot more verbal than she would have guessed from their brief conversation in the bar.

He'd warned her it would be fast, and yet, there'd been something vulnerable about him once he let himself go. That vulnerability edged into a near-violence at times, but he hadn't hurt her. He'd removed her clothes before they were all the way in the room, and she could tell he'd been holding back even then, using his mouth to buy them time, pushing her to talk to him.

Once he'd really started, she doubted he'd been aware of her at all.

When he finally came, he'd been nearly begging her.

Or begging someone, to do… something.

Now he just lay there, like a dead person.

She wondered how she'd let him talk her into coming here.

Her husband got them separate cabins—his idea, of course, to give them "more space" and because he claimed he couldn't sleep with her snoring. But he had no compunction about stopping by when the mood struck him, or if he and the dance instructor had one of their spats. She cringed at the thought that she might have to explain a naked, male seer in her bed.

Although, really, it would serve him right.

"Hey." She laid a hand on his chest. His skin felt cold. She kept her voice light, trying to smile. "Who's Allie?"

She saw his expression change, just before he closed his eyes.

She couldn't help wondering, though.

A girlfriend? Did they even date?

Looking away, he shifted his weight on the mattress.

She caressed his hair. "Are you sick?"

He raised a hand, pushing hers off. She watched in disbelief as he wiped his face, doubting what she'd seen. Then his breathing changed, and she couldn't deny what she heard. He was crying. He wiped his eyes with the heel of his hand.

"Hey," she said, a little alarmed. "What's going on?"

When he spoke, his voice made her jump.

She'd forgotten the accent.

"I'm married," he said.

A surprised laugh caught in her throat.

She tried to keep it out of her voice.

"So am I," she said. "I thought that was the point."

He looked at her. His pale eyes reflected light shining from under the door, like a cat's eyes. Again, she remembered he wasn't human.

He stared back as if she were just as alien to him.

Then he sat up. She watched him feel around on the floor for his pants, pulling them up over his legs and looping then hooking his belt. Standing, he found his shirt and drew it over his head, and now she felt emotion waver off him, clear as a scent. It was self-loathing.

She pulled the damp sheet tighter around herself. "I'm sorry," she said.

He shook his head. "It's not your fault."

"Do you want money?" She recoiled in spite of herself, afraid of him once she saw the look in his eyes.

"No," he said flatly. He didn't look at her again.

Before she could think what to say next, he bent down, picking up the shoulder harness that had shocked her so much when she'd first seen it.

He donned it like a vest, velcroing it tight, checking the gun in obvious rote before shouldering his jacket on over it. She was still staring when he turned his back to her, aiming his feet for the door.

The light blinded her as he opened it onto the corridor.

It wasn't open long.

Following the click of the latch, she lay back on the bed with a sigh. All she could feel was relief that he was gone, that she'd likely never see him again.

WHEN ELIAH FINISHED SPEAKING, CHANDRE REMAINED SILENT.

Eliah shared the construct with her, so he knew she was thinking to herself how ridiculous this was.

Further, that it went beyond her job description as infiltrator to the Seven's Guard to babysit two full-grown seers who, in her mind, should be alone in a cabin somewhere, getting acquainted in the carnal sense for at least a month before they were allowed to talk about their relationship in anything but monosyllables.

That was the traditional way it was done.

The old forms existed for a reason.

Eliah kept the smile out of his light with an effort.

These two-hundred-year-old seers always groused about the past.

Is she all right? Chandre sent finally.

Well enough, yeah. He let her feel his frown. *Threw up when she came to, and she won't talk about it. Physically she's fine. She's out on the balcony—*

Get her back inside. Now.

Pardon my saying, sir, but no. She wants to look at the water, let her bloody well look at the water. It's dark. No one'll see her. He paused. *Has he checked in?*

No. She exhaled a Barrier sigh. *Vash said it's up to us to determine what's needed to keep the situation under control. You said she won't press charges. Do we discipline him for breaking vow? She could be waiting for him to come back. To stab him, try to hurt him, whatever.*

Eliah gave a humorless laugh.

I don't think so. She still thinks too much like a human to let herself go into plotting that kind of thing.

Feeling Chandre's skepticism, he added,

...And if by disciplining him, you mean shooting him in the head, I'm all for it. His thoughts leaked anger. *He didn't shield it from her at all. If I had to guess, I'd say he pulled her into it deliberately.*

Recommendation, Eliah? Chandre sent dryly. *Beyond the firing squad for Dehgoies for the crime of wanting his wife?*

Separate them, he returned promptly. *Keep him away from her. When she's up to it, I'll ask her what she thinks.*

Fine. I leave them to you. She clicked to herself in irritation, folding her light arms. *Watch her, Eliah. And no taking advantage of the situation to try and talk her into your bed. We still don't know why he did it.*

He grunted. *Why he did it? Are you serious?*

You're damned right I'm serious. Her red eyes flashed brighter in the Barrier space. *Something strange is going on with the two of them, and you know it. Half the males on this ship are looking at the Bridge, and you're going to tell me her own mate isn't? Yet he won't touch her, and now he's openly strayed. Don't tell me you know why he did this.*

I'd say it's more'n half. Eliah gave her a wolfish smile. *And it ain't only us that's been looking, either, chief. I've seen you staring at her ass on more than one occasion.*

Chan gritted her teeth. *My point is, don't go there. Tell the others, too. You get Dehgoies coming up here in a jealous rage and we're going to have ourselves a real problem. That is one piece of bullshit I don't intend to deal with tonight.*

Understood, he sent.

You'd better. Or so help me I'll let *him shoot you.*

Eliah was still laughing a little as he clicked out of the Barrier, feeling his legs against the hard padding of a stateroom chair.

He waited for his eyes to clear, then faced the window out to the balcony where he'd last seen her. The instant he could focus, he flinched, frowning.

Then he jumped to his feet.

The balcony—the entire cabin in fact—was empty.

CHAPTER 29
EXIT

The elevator car came to rest on the higher of two main floors, dumping me and seven other passengers into a wide foyer carpeted in red and gold.

The foyer was full of people.

From the sheer number of human minds milling around mine, I surmised I'd arrived during the latter of the two dinner meals served for general passengers, a stroke of luck in that it provided visual cover at least.

I hadn't had much time while Eliah was in the Barrier, talking to Chan.

As soon as I saw him shift out of his body, I ran for the wardrobe.

In seconds, I'd yanked on jeans and a tight-fitting tee from a band I'd seen years ago in Oakland. I donned my boots and a sweatshirt to deal with the cold, throwing the hood up to cover my head and putting in the brown contacts I'd fished out of the trash and washed. I projected some of my consciousness out on the balcony while I dressed behind the wardrobe door, just in case Eliah looked for me at any point in his conversation with Chandre.

That was another trick Revik taught me.

Grabbing a pair of mirrored sunglasses I found in one of the drawers, I stuffed them in my pocket and headed out the door.

I'd come up with a whole story for the guards at the end of the row of staterooms.

It turned out, I didn't need to use it, because, well…

The guards weren't there.

Not wanting to look a gift horse in the mouth, I walked to the elevators as fast as I could, donning the sunglasses clumsily as I hit the call button.

That had been at least fifteen minutes ago.

I got off on a few random floors, ran into several different groups of humans before I decided to head for the lobby and look for a place where I might hide out in public. I figured my best chance of getting even an hour out from under the Guard would be to find a place where no one would be looking at me.

Of course, the Guard might be looking for me already.

It crossed my mind that I also might run into Revik.

Maybe he'd see me when he went out trolling again, going for round two.

When my light reacted to my own bleak attempt at humor, I suppressed it, but not before the image of me collapsing on the atrium floor flickered through my thoughts, along with a taste of what it felt like the first time.

Maybe coming out here was stupid.

I wasn't even sure what the hell I wanted.

Just to push back, I guess. To not be sitting in that room, waiting for Revik to return. The thought of waiting there under armed guard, just to play normal when Revik strolled back through that door—the whole thing made me physically sick.

Clearly, he wanted me to take his divorce request seriously.

I got the memo.

I still had zero illusions he'd really talk to me about it when he returned.

In the meantime, I needed space. From all of them.

I knew my little jailbreak wouldn't last long. Hell, I'd go back on my own eventually, assuming the Guard didn't find me first and drag me back to the room by my hair. But I couldn't just fucking *sit* in there for the next however-many hours, waiting for Revik to come back.

I couldn't fucking do it.

Truthfully, more than anything, I'd probably really left because I knew it would make Revik completely nuts when he found out.

And yeah, okay, I was pretty buzzed.

I definitely drank too much with Eliah.

Keeping my mind carefully blank, I focused on my surroundings.

The décor hovered somewhere between Vegas, which I'd visited once with Jaden, and a suburban shopping mall. Except here, only about half the signs and VR projections spoke English. Most switched languages as they scanned room keys, following customers with higher credit limits and adjusting products until the person waved them off or stopped to listen to the pitch. Corridors twisted off in all directions, making it hard to track which side of the ship I was on until I stood still long enough to feel the whole thing moving.

Even then, it was easy to get turned around.

After the silence of the past few weeks, both here and in Seattle, hearing voices echo up and down the five stories both comforted me, and felt like a psychic attack.

A feeling of paralyzing aloneness tried to creep around me, as well.

The groups of laughing, shopping and even bickering humans somehow reminded me just how completely alone I really was.

All I'd had was Revik.

Now I didn't have him.

For the same reason, I needed to be around other people. Even if I couldn't talk to any of them. Even if all I could do was watch them be normal from a distance.

I had my doubts the humans on board would be on the lookout for a seer terrorist in their midst, even if they weren't on vacation. Half the people around me were drunk, or focused solely on free food and gambling in the ship's casino. Anyway, I looked pretty different from the photos of me plastered all over the feeds.

My hair had changed color and length.

My face had thinned. My eyes were a different color.

And I just looked... different.

I couldn't really pinpoint in what way, but I could see it, whenever I looked in the mirror.

From wall maps, I got the basic layout of the ship.

I located the main casino, two dining areas and five bars on the lobby floor alone, along with a full-sized theater and an indoor swimming pool. Thinking about the last of these, I seriously contemplated going for a swim.

I didn't have credits to buy a suit, or even a room key.

I wondered if I could push a clerk to give me one anyway.

Thinking about this, I abandoned the idea. I'd save pushes for if I really needed them. Anyway, I had to figure the construct would find me the second I went into the Barrier.

Photography stands flashed virtual backdrops of Alaskan coastlines next to people dressed in VR-paneled costumes. Those costumes used computer-generated images to make the wearers look like everything from bald eagles to caribou to penguins.

A piano bar stood next to the long lines of people waiting to be seated for a five course, sit-down dinner. It was flanked on both sides by gilded waterfall balconies. Lining the guardrail above the sunken bar stood kiosks that sold everything from jewelry to shore excursions, pedicures and massages, dance classes and raffle tickets, tax-free wires, *hiri* and tobacco cigarettes, perfume, alcohol, handbags.

I saw a woman holding a brochure on seer services that could be purchased in Anchorage, including a trip to what Revik referred to as an "unwilling" bar, and what every human I knew called a whorehouse.

Another surge of sickness hit.

That time it was bad enough to make me stop.

I took a breath, leaning a palm against the wall in a shadowed observation area outside the piano bar. Only a few tables stood there, populated by couples sipping drinks and looking through large windows to the ocean.

Jesus. Whatever the hell was wrong with me, I had to get it under control.

I was sweating too much.

I could see in the reflective glass that I was deathly pale.

Maybe I should just go back.

Allie?

I stopped breathing, mid-exhale.

Scanning faces to my left, I paused on the bay windows overlooking the ocean.

Allie? Will you answer me?

I swallowed, my eyes on the rolling waves.

The sky was dark, but a rim of reddish-purple remained by the water. My eyes returned to the dim lounge with its few tables. I didn't recognize anyone, didn't feel him nearby.

He wasn't there, I realized.

I'd been thinking about him, and he'd heard me.

Allie. Please… I need to see you.

I stood motionless by a men's bathroom.

I didn't move, not even when a man smiled at me as he left the swinging doors.

Allie, I'm sorry. I'm really—

I don't want to talk about this.

At his silence, I forced my thoughts back to neutral.

I breathed in and out, forcing myself to be logical about this.

Revik, I thought at him. I took another breath, and my mind leveled more. *Revik… you really don't need to explain anything.*

Allie, I do. I do need to—

No, I sent. *You don't. I understand. You can have a divorce or whatever you want—*

Not like this, he broke in. *I don't want to talk to you like this. I want to actually sit down and talk to you. Please.*

I felt him trying to think how to persuade me.

Please, Allie…

He reached for me with his light and I jerked back, pulling away from him without thought. When he came close to me again, I threw up a wall.

He ran into it… then withdrew all at once.

It happened so fast, I barely understood what I'd done.

The silence went longer.

I could tell it shocked him, my forcing him away. I felt pain on him, cloying, hard to keep out of my light. He was still hiding something from me, but I was trying to hide how I felt, too. It never seemed to end with us.

Revik, I sent. *Really, I'm not just saying it. You don't need to do this. I'm cool with us being friends. You maybe didn't have to go to such extremes to make your point, but—*

Allie… no. It wasn't like that—

Eliah told me, I sent, cutting him off. *So I get it now. I get what happened in Seattle. I get why you think I was pushing you. I didn't mean to, but—*

Eliah? His thoughts grew still. *What did he tell you, Allie?*

Revik. I'm trying to say I'm sorry. Can't we just—

No, he sent. Pain wafted off his light. *Please... gods. Don't make me talk to you like this... please, Allie...*

I felt the vulnerability on his light, and couldn't answer.

His thoughts grew quiet, almost a murmur.

Please, Allie. Please let me see you... please gaos let me talk to you.

I stared out at the night sky, watching the horizon dip gently up and down.

Okay, I sent, reluctant. *But jesus, Revik. We don't have to do this—*

You're in the room? Is Eliah with you?

No. I hesitated long enough to find it odd he'd mentioned Eliah again. *...no to both, actually. I'm on the other side of the ship. Near that big piano, with all the shops. We could meet out here, or—*

What? His light changed. *How did you get there?*

I walked. His pain worsened and I gripped my chest, trying my damnedest not to feel anything more from his light. *Revik... I'm being careful. Eliah was all pissed off. I didn't see anyone in the corridor, so—*

Allie! Gods, baby, what are you doing? His pain worsened, along with a guilt I winced away from, clenching my jaw. *Wait right where you are. Wait there. I'll be there. I'll find you—*

"Sister?"

I jumped, turning at the new voice.

I was distracted, sick from being so close to his light, distracted by what he'd just called me, unsure if I'd even heard him correctly. As for whoever spoke, I expected it to be one of the guards, Eliah or Chandre or someone else they'd sent to find me.

Revik's presence faded, but I didn't feel him pull away.

Instead it felt like I walked into a dense wall and the wall entangled me, pushing him out.

Beacon-like eyes met mine, glowing in the VR projections from the nearest kiosk.

"Are you lost, sister?"

I blinked. A woman held my arm.

I watched her long fingers tighten on my skin. They looked blue in the light of the VR images. I struggled to focus on her face, couldn't.

I will help you, she sent softly. *You look very fatigued, sister.*

Relief washed over me.

I *was* tired.

I couldn't believe how tired I was.

The woman with the opaque eyes purred a lulling sound…

…and I fell into a complicated strand of light.

The world phased.

Everything grew breathtakingly clear around me. The interaction of minds, the way they formed building blocks into more and more complex reasoning, more and more fascinating skills—all of it grew visible.

I watch atoms dance on the beams of the causeway ceiling.

Light showers down in fractal rainbows as the lit strands cross and merge.

I gaze into the eyes of the seer female holding me.

She is beautiful.

We will show you, the blue-skinned woman purrs. *We will show you such wondrous things, Bridge Alyson. The world will never be so small to you again as it is in this moment.*

I can see what she offers me.

I can practically taste it.

In her world, I would have a purpose.

In her world, my life would mean something.

In her world, war doesn't need to come at all.

It's such a relief. I can just let all of that go.

The sickness and pain I felt just minutes before is already gone.

The woman is right.

Nothing could ever be the same again.

CHAPTER 30
FREED

ALLIE! Revik screamed her name into the Barrier. *ALLIE!*

He shoved at the space where she'd been, trying to force his way through.

He tried again, fighting a rising panic.

He knew what had her. He recognized the flavor of the metallic strands that forced him away from her light, taking her away from him. He didn't understand how yet, or who had her specifically, but the specifics didn't really matter.

They had her.

He slammed against that wall, using all of his light.

The wall started to give.

Then something rose up.

A sharp pain hit him over his right eye. He fought back, tightening his shields, when something bigger lashed out at him. The dark shape threw him sideways, knocking him out of the smaller construct—knocking him out of his body totally.

For a few seconds, he lost any ability to concentrate or see.

When his vision cleared, he'd come to a stop in the corridor, fingers splayed on one of the wallpapered walls.

He wiped his nose, stared at the blood on his fingers.

He didn't let himself think. He began to run.

Dread pooled in his stomach as he pushed his legs to move him faster down the hall. He fought to build momentum, putting most of his consciousness in his body to cross the distance between himself and her as quickly as he could. He still managed to throw a part of his mind ahead, and back into the construct.

It would take him at least ten minutes to get to the atrium, even at top speed.

Too long.

He scanned options.

He tried their cabin. It was empty; he got the equivalent of Barrier static.

No Chandre. No Eliah. No guard.

How the hell had she gotten out of the room, much less out the secured corridors on the seventh deck? Someone must have noticed she was gone by now.

And who *the fuck* had her? Did someone board at the last dock? A unit of the Rooks? Did they have someone in ship's security? Or was it just bad luck—a lone infiltrator in their extended network who happened to be working this route?

He tried a general channel, Guard security.

Nothing. He slid more of himself back into his body, running towards the bow of the ship, fighting to think.

His head hurt. Something dark clung to it, and to his right arm.

The hole over his eye was the most serious.

He attended to that first, reweaving his light, but the something there fought to hold on, hiding in parts of him he didn't access as often. He'd lost where she was. He continued to search, but his shields were up now, in hunting mode, which slowed him down. Still, if they broke too much of his structure, he'd be useless to her.

How in the gods' names had she gotten to this side of the ship?

His adrenaline spiked as his mind put the pieces together.

This was coordinated. They were under attack.

He was being hunted, and it had to be by the same people who had her. He felt them searching for weaknesses in his shields openly, trying to penetrate his mind even as they distracted him from making his way towards her.

They must have already been in place.

They saw their chance, with him and Allie separated.

Likely they coordinated her escape from the seventh deck.

At the very least, they left the door open, knowing she'd be more willing to leave, given what Revik himself had just—

He forced that out of his mind.

Blaming himself wouldn't help her.

Whoever they were, there were a lot of them. They'd likely been in place for some time, which meant they'd definitely been on the ship, waiting for an opening.

He'd given them one.

He recalled one of his reference memories, a detailed map of the ship's layout. Using that, he found an aberration in the Barrier that matched what he'd last felt from her. Hitting another shield around where he expected her to be, he searched for openings, making his light resonate with hers.

He remembered how she'd felt when she finally agreed to meet him—how his light had responded. His throat clutched and he shoved it off angrily. He had to concentrate. He was fucking losing it—

"Dehgoies Revik."

He landed the rest of the way into his body, coming to a dead stop.

Four men stood a dozen yards ahead, dressed in long coats.

Revik scanned in reflex. Seers. Well-shielded. He didn't recognize any of them, so they probably operated mainly out of Asia. Handguns, infrared, tissue extractors, some kind of propulsion device, grenades, flares, a shotgun—

Something stung his throat.

He reached up, jerked a sharp point from the side of his neck.

He stared at the thumbnail vial for a beat of his heart, scanning the clear liquid. His chest clenched. The dart trembled from his fingers even as he felt one of the seers lock on him with an extractor. He leapt for the opposite wall.

It all happened within seconds of his first scan.

He was still too slow.

The glass tube slammed him midair.

Knocked sideways, Revik missed his mark and crashed into the wall short of the alcove he'd been aiming for. He landed in a heap and pulled in his limbs. He fought to drag himself back to his feet when the cord pulled, making him lose his balance.

They still had him.

The cord left a hole in his jacket on the right side.

He grabbed the braided metal with his bare hands, scanning the glass vial embedded at least a thumb-length into his flesh, right through his jacket. The cord went taut. The teeth closed. Before he could let go, the vial slid out of him in one quick pull, the braided metal ripping skin off his hands as it went.

Revik screamed, clutching his abdomen. Blood poured out between his fingers, soaking his pants and jacket. He mashed his hand over the hole. Fighting shock, he picked himself up, stumbled backwards.

That time, he practically *dove* into the Barrier.

Everything grew crystal clear.

Ripping the Glock out of its holster, he fired, blindly, running in the opposite direction. The first shot cut a dark hole in the wall, but did what he intended, forcing them behind cover. He switched to his mind, knowing it would be overheard, no longer caring.

He sent up a high, sharp blast of alarm.

His warning cry slammed against something before it reached the main construct walls. He watched it dissipate, useless. Looking around in the physical, his eyes lit on a pull mechanism for a fire alarm. He caught it in the hand holding the gun and yanked it down.

Immediately, a shrieking bell went off.

Doors opened on several sides.

Dehgoies? Eliah's thoughts rose, as if coming through smoky glass. *Where are you? Can you hear me?*

Eli... have you got her? Revik blinked back pain, clutching his side. His mind shifted sideways. It threw off his balance, forced him into the forward part of his consciousness.

Gods, the drug. He'd forgotten about the dart.

Eliah... someone's trying to leave with her. The truth hit him again. It ignited a full-blown panic. *Look for boats, anything big enough to land a helicopter. They'll want her off the ship as soon as possible—*

Brother, calm yourself! Where are you?

Find her, goddamn it! Start with the atrium. Last I saw, they had her there.

Where are you? I'll send someone.

No. I'll come to you. He stared at the blood soaking his jacket, realized the truth. *Eli. Please... I can't get to her. You have to do this. Please. Please...*

Deghoies—

He kicked the other seer out of his mind.

The hunters were regrouping.

Limping backwards in a half-jog, he held up the Glock, mashing his other hand into his side. He scanned behind him, looking for open doors. He had to stop the bleeding, or he'd be even more useless. If it meant draining humans from the Barrier like a fucking *ridvak,* he would get the light he needed to do it.

He thought about Allie again and it got him moving, propelling his legs faster.

He'd asked her for a divorce.

He'd asked her for a divorce, then let her see him with someone else.

If he had to kill everything between here and the outside decks, he wouldn't let that be the last thing he'd said to her.

I AM BLOWN AWAY BY HOW LITTLE OF THE BARRIER I SAW BEFORE, EVEN WHEN I used Revik's eyes.

Now, for the first time, I really see its power.

I feel it all around me.

Even so, I can tell I'm only at the edges of it. Glimpsing just this much still manages to overwhelm me with sheer possibility. It makes the construct-shields and tracking simulations I've been working on seem like child's play.

The art alone I could create with this—gods.

Yet art itself seems trivial here.

I rise above the crowded causeway.

They are so lost. The people I see, they blunder around and into one another, blaming each other for the endless collisions. There is no direction, no purpose, no understanding of what drives them. Anything can fill that vacuum.

Anything.

The other seer's mind purrs inside mine. *You begin to see the problem. Can you guess the solution, Esteemed Bridge?*

Meeting her wise, sharp eyes, I lean my hands on a painted guardrail.

I bring my consciousness higher in the complicated light.

It's like having access to a hundred different minds all at once.

Not a hundred minds, the female next to me purrs. *Thousands, Esteemed Bridge. Hundreds of thousands. When you are with us, you have access to every aleimic body in our network. Every ability, every scrap of knowledge and skillset held by every seer who has chosen to align with us. All of it is yours. That is the power of the Pyramid.*

I log this information, appreciating its clarity.

Irrationally, I want to free all people, everywhere, even though I can see that they would simply use that freedom to destroy themselves. I am still thinking about this, watching them, when I am distracted by something going on in another part of the Barrier.

I feel fear. Violence.

I focus there.

Yes, the woman purrs. *You know this being. You know him well by now, yes?*

I do know him.

I know who he is, even under all his shields. I touch his light through that wall of protection, and the recognition strengthens.

The woman's perfect lips curve in a smile.

The Seven went to a lot of trouble to hide him. Even from himself. But they cannot hide him from you. Not from you, *Esteemed Bridge.*

"Revik." Recognition overwhelms me, memory, time. Feeling him makes my heart hurt, makes that pain in my chest flood back.

I had been angry with him.

Something wrong happened between us.

But something else distracts me. Something more urgent.

Wait. What's wrong with him?

The seer answers me, her mind calm, serene. *He is under attack, Alyson. Those seers will kill him, if you do not help him.*

What? My alarm spikes. *Kill him? Why? Where is he?*

As soon as I ask the question, I see him.

I see him as if he was standing right in front of me.

My stomach drops.

Pain rises in my chest, hurting my heart.

He's been shot! I have to go to him. I have to find him—

You are the Bridge, Alyson. You can help him from here.

I struggle with fear, a fevered helplessness as I watch him run down a distant corridor, leaving footprints of blood. I believe her now. He is outnumbered, injured, bleeding from multiple wounds. He is losing light and structure.

They're killing him.

I look for how I can help, how I can save him.

His light is broken somehow, ensnared by a thousand crisscrossing strands, holding him in place with a hundred tiny walls. His attackers are not doing this to him. The walls I see are old. They strangle his light, cutting him off from whole parts of himself, leaving pieces of his *aleimi* dark from lack of use.

I see the imprint of the Seven on those walls.

A soft memory flickers, dies.

Who did this to him? My heart hurts more and more. *Vash? Did Vash do this?*

The female's bright eyes remain motionless.

Why? Tears sting my own. *Why would they do this?*

They fear him, she tells me. *That fear will kill him now, if you do not intervene. Help him, Bridge Alyson. Set him free. He is not one of the lost ones. He needs only to remember who he truly is.*

But I am already looking at the structure encasing him, using the myriad eyes of the Barrier seers who surround me. Focusing on where those dense walls meet, I touch him with my light, trying to soften the intersections that imprison him.

I feel Revik react. I feel his fear.

I send reassurance, and when he realizes who it is, he lets me in.

His relief is palpable, his warmth overwhelming as he floods my light.

Affection comes with his presence, longing, regret.

For a moment it is all I can see.

He wants to know where I am, how I am, but I am focused on keeping him alive, so I extract myself, looking for how I can help. I zero in on the part of the structure that holds all the rest in place.

...and crack it easily with my light.

The walls around him begin to dissolve.

Very good, Alyson.

I barely hear her.

I watch Revik's light shift.

Inexplicably, tears come, blurring everything I can see outside the Barrier.

Gods, he is beautiful. He is so fucking beautiful.

He rises as I watch, his light flooding structures I've never seen in him, twisting around his head, around his whole body, expanding in high, white flames. His whole being flares, shaking the Barrier, trembling the nonphysical space with a burst of light.

Without knowing I am doing it, I rise with him.

For a breath at the top, we are together, truly together.

I break free of the finely-woven silver light the woman has shared with me, and instantly I feel lighter. A pressure evaporates from around my heart.

From this height, the metallic strands that seemed so fascinating look fake. More than fake—they look clouded, dirty, filled with delusion and lies. I see the whole of the rotating Pyramid, the thousands of beings chained to its immovable lines.

Leeched of light, they dance like frail puppets made of wire.

I am still staring at it all when Revik falters.

Something jerks at him, hard, pulling him down, bringing me with him.

I fight back. I struggle to keep us above the smoke and silver clouds.

My own light recovers and I focus on catching his, grappling with him in the Barrier's waves. I can't hold him. His light curls sideways. As it does, a dark mass lights up around his head, turning that portion of his *aleimi* solid black.

He falls inside the Pyramid and disappears.

NO! I scream. *REVIK!*

Around me, humans mill in the casino. No one looks up at my screams. No one hears me as they hang over tables, drinking foul-looking cocktails with colored umbrellas and fruit dipped in formaldehyde. They look dead to me. They look dead.

I scream again, and the image ripples, turns to smoke.

REVIK! CAN YOU HEAR ME? REVIK! ANSWER ME!

I can't feel him anymore. I look for him, like a diver feeling blind through pitch dark water. My hands and light come up with nothing.

He is gone.

He will adjust.

I turn, sweating. I still grip something in my hands.

He will live now, Alyson. You have saved his life.

I feel the silvery light creep back around mine. I am still above it, but only just. From where I am, those metallic clouds look like filth. Mirrors and death, stolen power—it is a lie that coats the Barrier like an oil slick.

I focus on the woman's eyes. They no longer look wise.

They look dead to me. Cold.

My vision clicked all the way back.

...and I found myself staring at Ivy.

Ivy. The young seer in Seattle who bandaged Revik's shoulder, who laughed while she dyed my hair, who arranged for my passport and other IDs along with Yarli. But instead of the young, happy person I remembered, Ivy looked gaunt to me now, her skin too thin, her head and face too large. Her platinum-blond hair stuck up on her head, making her look more like a goblin than an elf. She also looked older.

She smiled at me, studying my face as she touched my arm.

Sister. Do not be afraid. Do not doubt that we are friends.

I looked around at the physical world.

The casino, the crowds, none of that had been real, either.

I stood on a deserted piece of the ship's top deck, buffeted by cutting wind. My hair whipped my cheeks as I looked up at a night sky.

Ivy and I were alone.

You work for him, I managed. *Terian.*

She smiled, and I didn't like that smile at all.

No, she said, shaking her head. *I work for someone far older than he. Far more knowledgeable than he.*

Galaith? I asked.

No. Her eyes don't move. *Not him, either.*

Who, then? I asked.

Your husband knows. He knows us quite well, Alyson.

Anger heated my chest.

Revik. This was about Revik. I could feel it now.

What the fuck do you want with him? Why won't you leave him alone?

That cold smile widens. I can feel she would like to tell me that, too.

She doesn't, though.

Clutching the handrail, I look down. The steep white hull stretches below to where a row of lifeboats hang over the water. Jumping is not an option.

A whisper-thin thread still holds me out of the Pyramid, but I feel Ivy chipping at it, trying to distract me from it, to convince me it lives somewhere else, inside the silver waves. A part of me has already started looking at the patterns, finding them fascinating again.

It's too late. Revik is gone.

Just like Mom. Just like Dad.

Allie, a voice whispers. *No.*

It sounds so much like him it stops my heart. It also snaps me out of that place of no hope. I haven't used up all my options. I still have one left.

I force my mind out of the Barrier…

…and pivoted my body in a fast, hard arc.

My hips snapped with my shoulder.

My fist hit Ivy in the sternum with a satisfying jar, exactly as Jon and then Eliah had taught me. I followed through on the punch, using my whole body.

Ivy slammed into the guardrail—then recovered faster than I would have imagined possible.

Grabbing the top rail with both hands, she aimed a kick at my head.

I avoided it, barely, but it was misdirection; she caught me with a lower, sharper heel to the knee, knocking me into the opposite guardrail by a circular vent.

Pain bloomed sharply up to my groin.

Gasping, I grabbed hold of slats in the round opening of the vent, staying on my feet. I managed to regain my balance right before the Rook's fist came down on the small of my back, half-crumpling me to the deck.

The second shock of pain brought a sharp, white moment of clarity.

I'd reconnected Revik to the Rooks.

I'd just fed him to them.

Pain rose in me, a crushing grief mixed with darker rage.

A scream ripped out of my throat.

Ivy hissed like an animal as I turned, back-fisting her face. I broke something. Without stopping, I kicked down, hard, aiming for her femur. A satisfying crunch brought my other fist around. That blow hit the Sark in the temple, driving her to the deck.

A sharp stab of pain lit up around my face and neck.

She was going after my light.

I threw myself at her as she tried to crawl away, putting all my momentum and weight into a kick to the face.

The seer's nose exploded in a spray of blood.

I grabbed her hair as her light faltered, slamming the back of her skull into the guardrail. Her eyes rolled up and the pain around my face and head receded. Before she could recover, I grabbed hold of her long jacket.

Regaining my balance against the railing, I hoisted her up to the top rail.

For an instant I felt the Sark's light, beyond that of the Rooks.

Looking into the eyes of the girl who'd sent me a pulse of warmth that night in Seattle, I saw a flicker of fear, a deeper understanding.

A half-beat of hesitation made me pause.

Then Revik's face swam before mine.

My heart clenched into a hard fist in my chest.

I threw Ivy over the railing, nearly going over with her.

She snatched at and grabbed my arm, screaming a terrible sound, like a giant bird.

Silver light exploded around my head. I felt those other beings, beyond the Pyramid itself, something larger, more frightening, made of massive clouds of metallic light. I felt them screaming at me, threatening me, pounding at my light. Agony ripped apart my mind as they beat against my *aleimi,* fighting for her… or maybe through her.

They told me I'd be dead.

They told me they'd kill me.

They told me they'd kill everyone I loved.

But they'd already done that.

Panting, bleeding on her hands, I wedged my legs against the guardrail. I fought my way free of her attempts to save herself, disentangling her slippery fingers.

A half-second later, the hands were gone.

I watched her fall.

Ivy receded into darkness as the ship slid forward on the water. I saw her body hit the edge of a lifeboat on its way down. No screams echoed up as she broke the surface foam. Darkness swallowed the splash and I fell to a crouch by the guardrail, gasping.

The whisper and pound of the ship's wake was deafening.

They were coming for me.

I could feel it now.

I grasped for him, blind.

Darkness spread over the ship, breathed into my skin. I look up as the Pyramid descends, blotting out the sky. Wire-like strands snake out from all sides. I call to him…

…and find myself alone, in a green, glass-tile room.

It is silent. My clothes are gone. A flat metal collar rings my neck. Against the back wall, three metal cages stand.

The image shimmers, breaks apart.

Red water runs on green glass, pools in dimples by the drains, dries in spots and smears on the ceiling. Hooks have instruments attached to them as wires spark close to the wet floor.

I scream, and I can't stop screaming.

Barrier winds shriek and tear. I clamp my hands over my ears, but it's not enough.

7, 10, 9, 33, 1099, 20, 41, 9883, 231, 87, 284, 2, 23, 66, 66, 994, 1, 1, 1…

I scream at the sky, feeling Revik and the man with no face.

The faceless man smiles, and I…

…opened my eyes.

My body hunched in a ball on the wet top deck, freezing in a raw, cutting wind. I wore a spray-wet hoodie, dark jeans, combat boots. I could feel them all around me. I could feel them closing in on both of us.

Fear exploded in my chest.

It wasn't for myself.

The realization got me to my feet, got me stumbling, then running for the stairwell.

REVIK RIPPED A LIGHT FIXTURE OFF THE WALL WITH HIS FINGERS. HE LAID HIS palm on the bare bulb, biting back a scream as hot glass seared his flesh. Mashing the hand against his side, he cooled it reflexively in his own blood.

The trick worked, briefly. His mind cleared.

Sliding up the wall on his good side, he regained his feet.

They'd trapped him in a floor of staterooms.

He could no longer remember which floor. He'd counted twelve more infiltrators in the Barrier, plus the four he'd seen, but they could be obscuring their numbers in either direction to confuse him, and to make him hesitate.

He hadn't seen any humans since that first volley of shots. He may have inadvertently helped them, clearing this section of the ship by pulling the fire alarm.

Something had happened.

Whatever it was, it blew out the overhead lights.

It almost felt like *he'd* done it—but he couldn't remember how or even why. The dart made it difficult to think in straight lines, to put the pieces together.

He'd felt Allie.

For a moment, the briefest instant, she'd freed him.

She carried him high on wings of light. He'd been alone with her, out of this nightmare.

She'd forgiven him.

Then she was gone, and all of his attempts to find her since only made him sick. He couldn't feel Chandre, Eliah, or even Vash, who always seemed to have a thread to him, no matter where he was.

He walked faster, holding the wall.

Images flashed. They turned the blackened tunnel to a stone cave with rough walls. Silver lights dripped from moss-covered boulders. His neck was swollen, heavy with chains. He could smell death. All around him, death. He rotted there, alone.

It was like being buried alive.

Depression tried to blank out his mind. He couldn't breathe. The space closed, thick and heavy. A man's voice whispers in his mind.

Uncle.

Wasted hands, holding a red-tipped dart.

This is your enemy, Nenzi. Not the guns, this.

Merenje stands over him, mashing the gun to his temple, an old revolver from the early colonials. The human clicks through chambers, telling him to disarm, yelling at him to disarm.

You little fuck. You think he'll let you live if you don't? What about your girlfriend? How many of us do you think it would take to break her?

A sob came to Revik's throat, a sick, dying feeling.

He is there again, trapped.

Faces swam past, fear washing through his skin like a tangible force. He remembers getting so hungry he ate dirt, hands locked to his feet so he stank of his own urine. He woke to insects and animals crawling on him. He woke screaming at first, but eventually got so hungry he tried to trap them.

This is what humans do. What I teach you can save you.

The gun clicks by his ear, louder with each turn.

Disarm, you fuck! Disarm or I'll blow your head off…!

A bright light flared behind him.

He remembered Allie and a part of him fought back. The Rooks were fucking with him, trying to break his mind.

He'd fix it. Allie would help him. Allie would find a way.

Irrational, the thought repeated.

He felt an opening in the corridor ahead, and a faint hope reached him.

They weren't desperate enough to gun him down in a crowd of human tourists. No matter how many they pushed, they couldn't be that desperate to bring him down. Besides, if they wanted him dead, they could have done it by now.

They were trying to bring him in.

He would have put the gun in his mouth already if it wasn't for his wife.

The thought echoes, paralyzing him.

He feels another sting, this one on his chest. He yanks at the source and stares at the dart, half-blind with pain as he understands.

He'd been wrong. They did want him dead.

They were going to kill him quietly, where the tourists wouldn't see him collapse. Then they could explain it any way they liked. Blood-drenched seer with a gun, terrorism threat averted, SCARB coming to the rescue…

The helicopter that takes off in the night, holding Allie. Taking her.

They didn't want him.

They'd find her another mate.

The world tilts into darkness as he fights to focus his eyes. Once more, he finds himself in the cave, alone. Silver clouds mass overhead, metallic wardens to his prison in the dark. They watch, biding their time.

They left him there. They left him to die.

Sound jerks him out.

It slams him briefly back into his own body, into another darkened corridor that moves lightly beneath his feet. He feels them behind him, stalking him.

But it is the rumbling sound that gets his feet moving.

When a flash lights up the pastel walls, Revik breaks into a run.

CHAPTER 31
COMPROMISED

I aimed for the seer segment of the ship.

I couldn't reach Chandre, Revik, or Eliah through the private channels they drilled me on.

I considered a public kiosk, but a fire alarm had gone off on deck five and I heard disjointed thoughts about gunshots in the crew.

Given that no announcements had gone out, damage control on one or both sides must already be in play. For the same reason, a public kiosk would be useless.

I considered heading for the fire alarm.

But even if Revik was there, I wasn't sure what I could do. I was alone and unarmed. I couldn't control the telekinesis, not even well enough to scare them.

My other option was to find someone in the Seven on foot.

That, or go to the humans for help.

Since the latter would probably get me tranked and stowed in the brig, I chose the former. The Rooks were likely controlling the human crew by now, anyway.

I rounded a corner on a family of humans.

They looked unreal to me in their tennis shoes and baseball hats, holding shopping bags and soft drinks. Glitter speckled the hair of one of the little boys. His father brushed it off absently, still talking to the woman, who laughed at something he said.

Then I saw them.

Five men whose faces fit together like differently shaped puzzle pieces were coming up fast behind the family. The men all looked young, late twenties to early thirties, yet their expressions were older, their eyes sharper.

One saw me.

Within a heartbeat, all five were staring.

Turning so fast I wrenched my back, I bolted down the hall, back the way I'd come.

I hit a fork and turned. I turned again. And again.

I began trying doors. They all needed card keys. I pounded on one.

When I turned, I found myself face to face with two humans.

The man blinked at me with watery blue eyes, clutching a woman's hand tight enough that her skin dimpled around his tan fingers. In his other hand, he held a card key.

"What are you doing?" he sputtered. "That's *our* room!"

His wife gaped at me. From her expression, she expected me to launch into a speech from one of the reality show feeds about cheating husbands.

My mind flickered, phased. I felt a whisper of the seers hunting me. I couldn't tell where they were exactly, but I felt them looking for me. They were close.

I raised my hand to a gun-like position.

The woman's eyes bugged out further. The man grew very still and pale, his eyes on what he saw as a black muzzle.

I showed him an image of Ivy's Baby Eagle.

"Open the door," I said, motioning towards the door.

Both pairs of eyes went blank.

"I'm not here," I said. "Open the door."

The man's face calmed.

He smiled at his wife, waggling his eyebrows at her suggestively. She laughed, squeezing his hand. They kissed, then he slid the key card into the lock to the right of the door handle.

It opened with a click.

I followed them inside, walking to the middle of the cabin while they shut the stateroom door. I pushed the man to flip the dead bolt lock. Stepping around the woman as the man trundled over to turn on the wall monitor, I walked to the balcony, drawing back the curtains with a sharp yank as the woman disappeared into the bathroom. I glanced back as the man straightened his crotch, adjusting his seat in the round-backed chair.

Another ripple of warning touched my light.

They were coming.

Pushing my way through the opening in the glass door, I ran to the balcony railing, peering around the etched-glass partitions on either side. A line of flat, lit windows greeted me on one side as I looked out past the wind barrier.

No balcony.

I turned my head. On the other side, a twenty-foot span separated me from the next set of cabins with balconies.

Damn. I'd assumed it would be like our section of staterooms on the eighth deck, where all the balconies were attached.

I felt my breath start to come in short pants.

They must know where I was. After my stunt with those humans in the corridor, they would have tracked me here easily.

Now it turned out I'd picked the wrong couple to hijack.

Gripping the railing, I swung myself up on top of it.

I squinted down at the white balconies stretched below me in a long row, separated by those glass dividing walls. The nearest one was ten or twelve feet down. If I hung from this one, the railing itself would only be about six or seven more feet to my toes—but there was no way to jump and not kill myself when I tried to land.

I would have to swing inward enough to land on the balcony itself.

Something pushed at my light.

It sparked a fresh shot of adrenaline.

Realizing the heavy sweatshirt restricted my movement, I ripped it off my arms and threw it over the rail. It flew sideways with the motion of the ship and got stuck on one of the lifeboats. It remained there, flapping in the wind.

Fuck.

Nothing I could do about that now.

Not letting myself think, I climbed down to the lower balcony rail and dropped my weight so I was hanging from my hands.

Almost immediately, this felt like a mistake.

My hand slipped, barely holding on. The other throbbed, bruised and bloodied from the fight with Ivy. I stared down between my combat boots at the railing below. If I let go now, I'd probably hit my head and end up in the water. I would have to get some momentum before I jumped—and try to remember to tuck my head.

This was starting to feel like a really stupid plan.

Unfortunately, I'd already negated all my other options.

Pushing off from the wall with the toes of my boots, I started to swing, lightly at first, then more vigorously, using my legs as a pendulum. In a few seconds, I was getting as much height as the range of motion allowed. Reaching the bottom of the arc, I let go, using my arms to propel me down and back towards the ship.

It happened fast.

I remembered to tuck my head—but not my arms.

My elbows smacked the railing hard, throwing my upper body forward. My arms wouldn't rise to shield my head.

Something dark approached.

My face slammed into what felt like rock.

I lay there, unable to move. My mind repeated, like a skipped record.

You can't sleep. He told you a hundred times you can't sleep…

Even so, I lost some time.

However much it was, as soon as it was over, I jerked where I lay, my nerves jacked up so high I felt dosed on amphetamines.

I opened my eyes. My legs were splayed. One arm lay bent under my chest, throbbing. When I raised my head, it seemed to unstick from the deck.

I stared at the dark stain where my cheek had been, then raised a hand to touch my face. I bit my lip to stifle a cry as I tried to move my legs.

My right knee screamed, enveloped in a fire-like pain.

I could only lay there at first, feeling like a broken toy.

Creeping in like a bad smell, that urgency came at me again.

I moved my limbs gingerly, testing as I went. My cheek had already started to swell. From what I could tell, I'd been lying there closer to a minute than an hour, maybe only seconds before my consciousness switch flipped back to on. My left arm felt like ligaments had been ripped out of the elbow and shoulder joints with pliers.

I forced myself to a sitting position.

Gripping the glass door, I sucked in a breath and lurched to my feet. I stood there, back pressed to the door, trying to focus my eyes, when I heard voices on the balcony above.

I froze.

"Here?"

Silence. I didn't move, didn't breathe.

"Could she jump that far?"

I heard a faint clicking sound, carried by wind.

"She was in and out too fast to pinpoint." The male voice paused, grunting. "Whatever she did, she hurt herself."

"Check the deck. I don't see evidence of a fall."

There was another silence.

I stood there, not breathing, focusing on my body like Revik taught me so I wouldn't inadvertently fall into the Barrier. He said it was normal for a seer to go to the Barrier when threatened. He said sometimes the hardest thing to do was to stay out, to remain in your body.

I pressed my back to the glass door.

I hoped like hell I was out of their line of sight.

The second Rook cursed.

I heard the crackle of a radio.

"She jumped. Confirm, she jumped. Looks like she hit the lifeboat on the way down. But she might have landed there, too. Bring the boat around, have them check the water on the port side. And if anyone's close, have them check deck…" He must have been counting. "…Four. If she made it onto the lifeboat, she would have tried to get back in there."

A longer pause.

"No, there's no blood. She might have bounced right into the water."

Seconds later, the balcony door above me closed.

I was still standing there, fighting to keep from passing out, when the light came on in the room behind me. I turned my head, terrified out of my mind.

A little old lady stared at me.

Her wrinkled mouth hung ajar as she gaped at a face I could barely see reflected in the glass. She clutched a pearl handbag, still holding the drapery cord she must have pulled to get a view of the night sky out her west-facing balcony. I had what looked like two blackening eyes, a swollen cheek, cut and bleeding lips. I touched my forehead, forgetting her briefly as I focused on my reflection. My hairline was bleeding, too.

I contemplated a story to get her to let me in, then simply turned, limping for the opposite balcony wall. Gripping the glass divider, I climbed, fighting not to cry out as I put part of my weight on my swollen knee to boost myself up.

Gripping the glass divider, I slid around it with one leg.

I eased down until my butt rested on the railing of the next balcony over. Once I had my second leg over, I placed my feet on the terrace floor and staggered to the glass door.

After trying the handle and finding it locked, I walked the length of that balcony and did the same on the other side.

I repeated this again seven more times.

Finally, I had to rest.

I leaned on a glass door leading into a darkened stateroom. I was a little worried I could pass out from the pain in my knee if the adrenaline wore off.

As soon as I'd regained my breath, I yanked myself up, teeth gritted, shielding my light more thoroughly than I could ever remember doing.

I hadn't tried the door. I gave it a tug.

The glass slid smoothly on its track, letting out a blast of warm air.

My brief elation flattened as I thought through my options once I was back inside. I had no way to get off the ship. I had no idea where Revik was. The Seven might be neutralized by now, or even compromised.

Whether I left the cabin or stayed, I ran the risk of being caught by roving bands of infiltrators, or humans whose minds had been taken over by Rooks.

I eased through the gap in the balcony door.

The room was empty.

For a moment I just stared around at the dim space, fighting to catch my breath. Even if there was a way to do it safely, I couldn't leave the ship.

I needed to find Chan, or Eliah. I needed help.

I needed someone to help me go after Revik.

Turning this over, I realized I had to go back to our section of the ship. I needed weapons, infiltrators—something. I had to find Chandre.

I'd take the stairs.

If they already had Revik—

But I couldn't think about that yet.

CHAPTER 32
SURPRISE

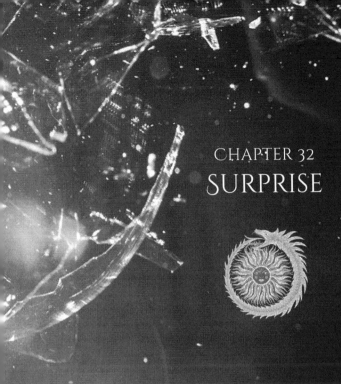

Terian stared at the VR shadow of the squad leader.

"I am confused," he said. "Please explain, 'we lost her.' I am not following."

The squad leader's avatar grew visibly nervous.

"Sir, we made visual contact and she rabbited. We tracked her to a stateroom—" He cut himself off, sensing the other's impatience. "We'll find her, sir. We're doing thermal scans of the wake now, in the event she jumped or fell—"

"Fell. As in, fell *off* the ship."

Terian's lips twisted in puzzlement, replicated in painstaking accuracy by his avatar.

"Really?" he said. "So that's a possibility? The planet's only living telekinetic seer may have accidentally *fallen off* a moving vessel into freezing cold salt water? Presumably to be chopped into small pieces for the seals to eat? We are exploring that option, yes?"

"Sir, I—"

"Do you have any idea what I will do to you, if that scenario eventuates?"

The infiltrator's shadow fell silent.

Terian smiled. "Yes. Good. Now, I would like you to explore options other than the 'falling off' one you seem so fond of."

"Yes, sir. Of course. We—"

Terian terminated the link.

His physical vision cleared.

He found himself in a damaged segment of corridor on the fifth deck, illuminated only by the sickly glow of an organic *yisso* torch.

It looked like what it was: the scene of a prolonged gunfight in a relatively tight space. They'd locked him down in one segment of corridor, but it took more than an hour to subdue him from there. The pastel and gold ship's interior was barely recognizable.

As the torch panned, the swath of light illuminated holes in plaster walls. One still smoked, but they had finally gotten the last of the guns away from him, too.

Terian's extraction team now stood in an uneven half circle, staring down at a being that was finally on the ground, if still not fully unconscious.

Two med techs hunched over him, trying to assess the damage to his nervous system, if any, from the third dart they'd finally hit him with.

"He wasn't to be killed," Terian muttered. He looked to the leader of the extraction team. "He wasn't to be killed, Varlan. I said two darts. No more."

"He was threatening to kill himself, sir," Varlan replied. "It was a calculated risk."

"He threatened to *kill* himself?" Terian stared at his lead infiltrator, fighting to incorporate the new piece of information. "Why? Why would he do that?"

Varlan didn't answer.

Turning, he focused his eyes back on the downed seer.

Terian watched as Dehgoies raised his head, groping for a med tech, eyes glassy from the drug. The young seer blanched, backing off. All of them had been unnerved by Dehgoies's apparent imperviousness to the darts.

Terian was a little more familiar with his friend's biological quirks.

Impatient, he pushed his way forward, kneeling by the dark head. He listened briefly to the male's muttered words, then clicked his fingers at one of the seers in the back.

"You… Legress. You are from Asia, yes? What language is this?"

A different voice answered, from closer.

"*Magadhi Prakrit*, sir."

Terian's gaze swiveled. The male tech knelt behind the two working on Dehgoies's abdomen. They lay a patch on his bare skin, trying to stop the bleeding.

"Is that a human language?" Terian asked.

"Yes, sir. Old, though. Very old."

"From where?"

"Nepal." The Sark paused, seeing all eyes on him. "I recognize it from the camps, sir. They used some of the older languages as codes." He smiled wryly. "That one was a particular favorite with the kneelers."

Seeing Terian's gaze sharpen, the tech let his smile fade.

"It was supposedly the language the Buddha spoke. When he was alive. He must have learned it while he was imprisoned there. He's about the right age."

Terian raised an eyebrow. "Imprisoned? Why not a slaver, like yourself?"

The tech caught the edge in Terian's words.

Losing the smirk, he met Terian's gaze.

He glanced around, noted the flavor of hostility from the seers around him.

"Smugglers don't use the language, sir," he answered carefully. "The prisoners did, so we couldn't understand them. We learned enough to prevent them from organizing, but it was never in common use in the barracks."

Terian motioned him forward. "What is he saying now?"

The Sark crouched by the floor, lowering his head as Terian indicated.

After a pause, he spoke.

"He's apologizing to someone, sir. Saying he'll do better. Something about wanting to serve, that he's ready to serve now." The man lowered his ear to another broken stream of words. "No cave. He doesn't want to go to the cave. A name… Merenj? Merenged? And something about wanting light, to touch light. I don't fully understand that phrase, sir. *Iltere ak selen'te dur*… that's old Prexci. I think something about the old God."

The man leaned closer, straining to hear.

"He's mixing languages. *Arendelan ti' a rigalem*… destiny is harder… *isthre ag tem degri*… to lead is… I think the word is sacrifice. It's some kind of scripture." Giving Terian an apologetic look, he added, "I've heard things like this before, from more arcane versions of the myths. I wouldn't swear by the translation, though. It's likely something local."

"And you say Magadhi Prakrit is a human language?"

"Yes, sir. Human. The other is a bastardization of old Prexci. I don't think they spoke that at the camps. He must have gotten it somewhere else."

Terian focused back on Dehgoies.

Slave camp. That didn't fit anywhere in the biography of Dehgoies Revik he'd read, and Terian had read them all. Nor did he really believe his friend would have worked in one, either. Whatever Dehgoies's ability to adjust ethical systems when it suited him, he never would have aligned with the worms to that extent.

Not for any amount of money.

Terian studied the angular face, noting its pallor.

The blood on his hands shone a dark red, almost black in the light of the *yisso*. He'd lost so much his skin looked gray.

He likely wouldn't last the night, no matter what the techs did.

Still, caution seemed warranted.

Reaching into a pouch under his cloak, Terian pulled out a thick, organic, sight-restraint collar he'd commissioned specially for the purpose. Catching hold of Dehgoies's hair, he lifted his head, sliding the collar around his neck. He clicked the ends together at the base of his skull, then bent down, opening a thumbnail latch to access a retinal scanner. He let the device scan his eyes, which it did, turning the skin of his friend's neck briefly red.

When it clicked off, Terian tugged at the collar briefly, checking that the lock activated.

Feeling the stares, Terian looked up.

The lead tech looked affronted.

"Sir, he's hardly in a position to—"

"Continue to listen," Terian told the other, ignoring the tech. "I want a record of everything he says. Translated and original. Every word. Understood?"

The Sark gestured affirmative.

Terian started to rise when Dehgoies caught hold of his wrist.

The long fingers clenched, ghostly white with streaks of blood.

"Terry." He swallowed thickly. "Don't hurt her."

Terian could only stare, his jaw slack.

"Please, Terry. Don't hurt her."

Terian grinned. He couldn't help it. He patted the other seer's arm.

"Now, now, brother Revik. No need to beg this early in the game. We're all friends here. I won't hurt your best girl."

The colorless eyes met his.

His voice half-filled with liquid, a near whisper.

"I'll kill you. Turn if I have to. Rip you apart. Feed you to yourself…"

Terian flinched.

"I'll remember," the pale-eyed seer breathed. "All of it. I'll find Feigran. You were afraid of me once…"

But Terian had heard enough.

Using his headset, he activated the pulse.

Two, needle-like prongs slid out of the collar around Dehgoies's neck, sinking wetly into the flesh at the base of his skull. The sensor lit up, the metal vibrating against white skin. Dehgoies blinked rapidly, wincing in pain as the prongs dug deeper into his neck. He tried to move his jaw.

Then he cried out.

The irises of his eyes ignited, like a spark to a pool of gasoline.

The faint glow brightened rapidly to a shocking hue, turning a sharp, pale green that flickered like candle flames in the dim hall.

Cries sounded in the corridor as the other infiltrators reacted.

Terian heard yelled instructions, movement as guns were raised, but he couldn't take his eyes off the glowing eyes of his downed friend.

Just when it occurred to him that the collar might not hold…

Dehgoies collapsed, as if all the muscles in his arms and shoulders unclenched in the same instant.

The silence grew deafening.

Terian glanced up. White faces stared at him from against the corridor walls. Several hunters stood with guns raised, fingers frozen near triggers.

"His eyes," one said. "Did you see his eyes?"

"He blew out the lights—"

"He's mate to the Bridge—"

"He can't be Sark, not with eyes like that—"

Mutters erupted from the group. Terian saw a few gestures warding off evil. He snapped his fingers at the techs.

"Stabilize his vitals."

When none of them moved, he raised his voice.

"Now," he said.

Movement erupted around him as his words sank in.

Terian rose to his feet, glaring around at the group until guns lowered, murmurs receding as they went back to work. The seer medical techs hunched over the unconscious Dehgoies, fighting to keep him alive.

Terian watched as Varlan approached where he stood.

An older seer, Varlan had a wide, Asian-seer face that sported a long, jagged scar in a diagonal line from his chin to his eyes. He was one of the old ones, an infiltrator since before the time of humans. It was even rumored Varlan was once trained by the Adhipan.

"General Advisor, sir." Varlan eyed Dehgoies's crumpled form. "You must be aware. Galaith has a particular interest—"

"Tell him he's dead."

Varlan didn't blink. "And if he survives?"

Terian gazed out over the group of infiltrators clustered by the far wall. His eyes came to rest on a tall Sark who stood at the back among the rest of the extraction team. Squinting up at the seer's body proportions, he motioned him forward.

"What is your height, Endre?"

"Six-foot-five, sir."

"You have a clan tattoo?"

"Yes, sir."

Terian plucked Varlan's Mossberg casually from his fingers. Pointing it at the tall, black-haired seer, he shot him in the chest.

The hollow bullet blew out the back of his spine, spattering the wall with blood and bone, right before the seer crumpled, falling to his back.

One of the techs cried out in shock.

A few others stifled cries of their own, earning hard looks from their Rook leader. The others moved quickly out of the way.

They left Endre's body in a cleared space of floor.

Terian handed the rifle back to Varlan.

"You have your answer," he said. "I will take care of the labs. Just make sure you destroy his face. Remove his teeth, if you can… and his hands."

Terian saw Endre's fingers convulse for his weapon.

Stepping forward, he kicked away the gun, motioning to one of the other seers, who raised his own weapon, shooting Endre in the head.

The seer's arm stopped moving.

"Make sure he's got the clan mark," Terian added, glancing over his shoulder at Varlan. "That's documented somewhere… and the sun and sword, too."

Varlan bowed, his eyes expressionless. "Yes, sir."

Terian looked down at Dehgoies, frowning at the blood, the pallor of his skin.

He faced the others.

"Get him ready to be moved." His eyes darkened as he stared around at faces. "I've decided my friend will survive this ordeal. You will make certain that he does." His voice grew cold as ice. "Do not disappoint me."

CHAPTER 33
WOLF

I limped down a darkened aisle, head low. I'd picked the movie theater because it was dark, and close to where the crew stairwell let out on the first floor deck.

The elevators were all down.

The stairwells were all blocked, too.

The excuse was fire, a terrorist attack.

The deck being used by the Seven was entirely inaccessible.

So was deck five, where the fire was first reported.

I'd felt some glimmer of Chandre down here, in the area of the main hold, so I came on the off-chance I could find her. Now that I was here, I wondered if I'd made a mistake. Maybe the Rooks led me down here, too. Maybe they wanted me out of the way, away from Revik, away from where they were taking him off the ship.

The thought brought a wave of pain so intense, I could barely think through it.

I needed to get the fuck out of here.

I needed to find a way to deck five.

I reached a side exit and grasped the door handle, giving a bare glance at the romantic comedy playing on the big screen. I opened the door, wincing when it struck me that the light on the other side would make my outline visible to every person sitting in the theater.

I needn't have worried. The attack didn't come from behind.

Strong hands grabbed me, yanking me roughly through the opening before my eyes could adjust. They swung me around, slamming my back against the wall. I heard the door close behind me with a sharp bang.

The seer turned me around, pressed my chest to the wall.

I felt amusement on him, a flicker of reaction to my pain.

His cock pressed against me from behind as he started to bind my wrists.

Writhing a hand free, I jerked my elbow back, slamming him in the cheekbone. I felt a flash of pain off him, anger. I missed his face a second time when he moved liquidly out of the way. He gripped my hair, smacking my face against the wall, stunning me.

I kicked backwards and caught him in the knee, forcing him to step back. I got him in the inner thigh the second time, narrowly missing his groin.

He grabbed my leg and deliberately bent my hurt knee the wrong direction.

I screamed.

He clamped a hand over my mouth, shoving me to the floor.

I fell hard to the deck, sucking air.

All of it happened so fast I couldn't move at first.

Standing over me, he reached over his shoulder, pulled out a black metal rod. An arc of current sparked from one end.

Staring up at it, I choked out a single word.

"Jesus."

Gripping the floor with my fingers, I tried to crawl away. He kicked me in the stomach. I crumpled, gasping for air, and he lowered the prod.

Before he could jab it into my back—

Shots echoed in the small corridor.

Two volleys followed, one after the other, barely a breath between them.

I flattened myself to the deck, flinching as bullets pushed air over me. The guy who'd been on the verge of hitting me with a cattle prod sprawled on his back next to me.

Turning my head carefully, I glanced at his face.

One eye stared sightlessly up at the ceiling. Part of his head was missing, and he wasn't breathing. I could practically feel the light leaving him.

He was definitely dead.

Down the hall, another seer lay on the floor, one I hadn't seen, though he must have stood there, watching as I failed to fight off the first guy. He lay on the floor too, holding his chest, making choking sounds. I stared at his blood-covered hands.

Then I turned.

Briefly, my heart lifted. I wanted so badly for it to be him.

But the man who lowered the gun had two different colored eyes.

His full lips curled into a frown as he released the empty magazine from the still-smoking Berreta, replacing it with a fresh one. Locking it into place, he motioned for me to get up, holding out a hand.

"Come on, love," Eliah said. "No time to get teary."

I tried to comply, but my knee wouldn't cooperate.

I got halfway up before it crumpled.

I gasped, blinded by pain.

Walking closer, Eliah slid a shoulder under my arm, still holding the gun. He brought me to my feet, then through a side door marked "Crew Only."

I stumbled onto a metal, mesh deck that started just past the door.

"Where's Revik?" I asked.

Eliah gazed down a fork in the corridor, surrounded by exposed pipes. He paused only long enough to glance at me.

"Sorry, love. He's gone."

I felt the world start to gray, like it had in Vancouver.

I forced it back, biting my tongue until the lines sharpened.

"Gone?" I bit my tongue harder. "What does that mean?"

"Hush now, love." His voice fell to a murmur. "I'll tell you everything. But I have to get you out of here first."

He waited for me to acknowledge him, shaking me until I nodded.

Moving fast, he brought me through the narrower of the two passages and down several flights of mesh stairs. I let him support most of my weight as we passed through a few more sets of doors to emerge in the main cargo area of the ship's stern.

Still holding me up, he led me through a long, towering row of boxes and covered crates, between one-seater forklifts and bolted-down luxury vehicles.

He stopped at a ramp that ended in a massive roll door.

Leaving me by the pulleys on one side, he jogged to the bottom of the ramp and hit a red button. I gripped a segment of wall in my hands and watched as the roll door opened, gears grinding in salt water, rattling rusted chains.

Churning ocean roared through the gap.

The opening sat low enough in the water that curls of spray shot up the sides of the ship, wetting the deck and me along with it. Wind and spray plastered my shirt to my skin. Pale light framed the clouds, illuminating edges.

Unbelievably, it was nearing dawn.

Eliah looked at his watch.

He held one of the chains by the roll door, swaying slightly in the motion of the ship. He caught my eye, smiled reassuringly.

"You all right there, love? That knee looks like it smarts some."

"Where's Revik?"

I spoke loud enough to be heard over the wind.

He hesitated. Letting go of the chain, he walked over to me, digging a hand into the front pocket of his dark pants. Once he had whatever it was, he held out a hand, motioning for me to take what he held.

"Go on." He motioned again.

I stretched out my hand, palm up, under his.

Something cold fell into it.

I focused on the silver ring.

He didn't have to tell me where he'd gotten it.

"I'm sorry, love," he said again.

I stared at the ring, unable to make my mind react.

"He was ambushed," Eliah explained. "Five of them, at least. It looked like they tried to save his life after they shot him down. They probably wanted to bring him in alive. But he was dead when me and Chan finally broke through."

When I didn't speak, Eliah caught hold of my arms, his eyes serious.

"Allie. Love. I know this is a shock. I know it. But I need you to focus right now. Put him out of your mind. Just for now, okay?" When I still didn't answer, he gave me a rough shake, forcing my eyes up to his. "If it gets down to the wire, you and me, we might have to jump. Now I know you're wounded, but you're a seer, so that's not as bad as it sounds. You'll live, easy. But it'll hurt. And that cold'll be something you remember to your grave."

I stumbled when he released me, catching hold of one of the hanging chains.

The wind tore at his words.

"There, now, love. I'm sorry. I truly am. But we can't fall apart, yeah? Or we'll end up like him. Then his sacrifice would be for naught. You can hold it together for him, can't you? Just a few minutes more? Then we'll be in the clear."

I stared out over the edge of the opening.

The water churned, white foam and dark blue beneath an overcast sky.

It looked like liquid ice.

Eliah blew on his hands, checked his watch again.

"We can't wait much longer, love," he said. "Why don't you—"

The rhythmic *thud-thud-thud-thud* of helicopter blades erupted low over the water.

I heard Eliah curse as one set of propellers joined another, then another, until a fleet of dark gray Apaches passed overhead, riding the light of first dawn. The sight was so surreal, all I could do was stare. Eliah grabbed my arm as the helicopters got closer, pulling me into shadow behind the lip of the square opening…

…And I find myself with him, inside his mind.

Flashes fill the Barrier sky.

Lightning cracks downward from overhead clouds.

All over the ship, bursts of staccato charges fall, plummeting around military helicopters as they fly past in formation. The bursts don't come from the helicopters, but from the metallic cloud ceiling above, falling like bombs.

I'm still staring upwards as a light-bomb falls from directly overhead.

Eliah grabs me with hands of light, pulls me away to narrowly miss being hit by a second bomb I hadn't seen.

A net, he tells me. *They are looking for you, Bridge. And for me.*

Looking for you, I repeat numbly.

I wince from a sudden, sharp pain at the back of my neck.

Eliah stares at my hand clutching that pain, my fingers rubbing my own neck in reflex.

Unexpectedly, he grins, his eyes shining with moonstone light.

Well, he says. *That's good news, at least.*

I am gripping the silver ring so tightly it digs into the skin of my palm. Through the Barrier, I gaze down the length of the ship, no longer caring who sees me. I am looking for him, trying to see his body. I need to see it. I need to know it's real.

I let myself fall deeper—then deeper still.

Without warning, he is there.

Revik lies broken on a patterned carpet, his neck at an odd angle. A metal collar circles it, and the skin there twitches, dancing under a coarse electric charge.

He is covered in blood. His chest isn't moving.

We're losing him! A doctor kneels beside him. *Goddamn it! He really will kill us. Did you see his face when those eyes lit up—?*

Eliah grabs my arm.

Turning me towards him, he punches me right in the face.

I GASPED, CLUTCHING A HANGING ROLL DOOR CHAIN IN ONE HAND, A SILVER ring in the other.

My jaw hurt where he hit me. My skin felt flushed, almost feverish. I faced Eliah, who held my wrist to keep me from going over the side.

He gave me an apologetic look—but I knew.

That hadn't been the past.

Which meant everything he'd just told me was a lie.

"You did this." I gripped the ring tighter. "You're him. Terian."

Surprise flickered in those mismatched eyes.

He broke into a slow smile. At the end of that smile, he let out a low chuckle.

"Alyson, my love." The Irish accent evaporated. "I must say—I am endlessly impressed by you. So many delightful little surprises."

When I tried to wrench away from him, his grip only tightened. When I struggled again, he slammed my back into the edge of the roll door, a warning in those mismatched eyes. He held up a finger, unholstering his gun. I watched him aim that gun at my midsection.

"Hush now, little Bridge. The fighting part is over." A lazy smirk formed at his lips, the same one I remembered from the diner. "Anyway, you should be thanking me. You have no idea how much more *fun* you will have, playing for our team."

The man who'd killed my mother smiled.

He gripped my bicep, his thumb absently caressing my skin.

"I suppose it is fortunate I met you before you were fully trained," he remarked. "How on *earth* did you find Galaith?" Clicking his tongue in amazement, he shook his head. "I really am just so *very* impressed. How I wish I could have seen what you and Revi' might have become. Together, I mean. In your *full bloom,* as it were."

I tried to yank my arm away, but his fingers gripped like talons, pulling me closer. Without warning, he forced me back into the metal wall a second time, ramming my spine into a sharp protrusion on one of the beams.

I gasped, fighting against the pain.

"You've put me in a bit of a bind, dear heart," he added drily. "I had hoped to be out of here before *der Fuhrer* showed up. He was quite fond of your mate." Terian gazed out over the water. "I suppose I'm in for a bit of a spanking. I'm afraid your sweet Dehgoies isn't long for this world. And I really *had* hoped I'd get the package deal."

I threw myself at him.

I grabbed for the gun, trying to force the barrel towards his face. I don't know if I thought I could do it without being shot, or if I just didn't care.

There was a loud sound in my ears.

Eliah jerked backwards, as if sharply pushed.

The gun he'd held in his fingers dropped, clattering to the deck. I watched a patch of red expand over his blue sweater, and realized he'd been shot.

I turned my head, looking for the source.

I knew it hadn't been me.

I focused on a high pile of wooden storage crates right as Chandre stepped from behind them, raising a gun towards my face.

"Move away from him! Allie, step back!"

Eliah burst into a laugh.

"Move away!" Chandre repeated, louder.

When neither of us moved, Chandre fired a shot past our heads. The bullet clanged loudly when it impacted the metal hull.

I don't think I even flinched.

Eliah ducked his head, then grinned at Chandre.

Chan aimed the gun at my face.

"Move away from him, Alyson," she warned. "Right now."

"Kill him." Tears ran down my face, but I barely felt them. "Please. Kill him."

"What are you doing with him?" she demanded. "Why did you leave the cabin?"

I didn't answer.

Chandre fired off another warning shot. I felt it whiz by my head. I continued to look at her, but my mind felt far away.

I didn't care if I died.

But I cared if he did.

"Shoot him, Chan. Please."

"Do not mistake me for him!" Chandre warned me. Her voice rose, coming out emotional now, angry. "Do not mistake me for your husband the *Rook,* Alyson! I don't kill simply because you tell me to! I demand an answer! What are you *doing* with him?"

"I do believe I've made her angry, Chan." Smiling, Eliah pointed from where he held his hands above his head, indicating my face. "Look at her! If I didn't know better, I'd think—"

"Shut up!" The hunter aimed the gun back at Eliah. "Get away from her, you piece of shit! We know what you did."

"He's not Eliah." My voice sounded strangely calm. "He took his body. He's not real, Chan. Whoever Eliah was before, that person is gone."

Chandre rounded the gun back on me.

"Do not push me, cub. I would just as soon shoot you with him. For all I know, you were in on it. For all I know, this is you starting your *fucking* war."

Eliah laughed louder. "Are you crying over Dehgoies, too, my sweet, sweet, Chandre? I would never have guessed!"

Chandre aimed the gun back at him.

"Eight of my people are *dead!* Three of them had mates. Families. Dehgoies at least carried the karma of such a death. That, and a hundred times over. What did my people do to deserve such a fate?"

I watched her draw nearer, feeling her grief, her rage.

I wondered at her ability to feel so much.

My own body felt like stone.

I couldn't see through the light in my eyes but the woman's outline shone there anyway, a shadow with two hands gripping a Desert Eagle I recognized the gun from a different set of long, white fingers. Chandre took another threatening step in our direction, stopping when I didn't react, or change expression.

After a pause, she exhaled, pointing the gun at Eliah without taking her eyes off mine.

"Gods," she said to me. "You're even starting to look like him."

Under my feet, the deck trembled.

A hollow booming filled the cargo bay, shaking the metal walls.

Eliah lost his balance on the edge of the open doorway.

I saw my chance.

Without thinking, I lunged towards him, helping gravity and the shaking metal under our feet.

It didn't take much.

He'd been standing too close to the rim.

GRIPPING ELIAH, I PLUMMETED THROUGH FREEZING WIND AND SPRAY.

I was sure I would die in those few seconds it took to fall.

I was less sure I cared.

I hit the dark surface and it was like being thrown onto a thousand, razor-sharp blades.

Tossed downwards, Eliah and I were ripped apart.

I felt his hands clench then leave my skin. A curl of wake threw me upwards and I surfaced, gasping.

Not far from me, another body slammed into the water. Then another.

I fought to keep my head above the white foam.

My leg hurt so badly I could scarcely force myself to breathe.

Next to me, a dark head surfaced, and I backed away, using my arms. I recognized Chandre, braids plastered to her head. Another dark form breached next to her. I made out the features of another of the Seven's Guard that I recognized.

I tried to paddle backwards, but I could barely stay afloat.

My legs wouldn't cooperate.

I looked for Eliah.

My eyes scanned the water, following the ship all the way back to the churning wake. In the curling waves of ice-blue water, I saw what looked like another person, their face white above dark swells. I watched the body struggle against the current.

The churning foam sucked him downwards, pulling him inexorably towards the lower stern and the propellers.

It was Eliah.

Seconds later, he disappeared.

"You're fucking crazy, Bridge!" Chandre yelled.

I tried to work my arms, to get away from her, but Chandre swam after me, groping for my limbs. "Bridge! It's okay! It's okay, Bridge!" Once she had ahold of me, her eyes followed mine down the length of the ship's wake.

"He's gone!" she shouted above the spray. "You killed him!"

"Are you going to kill me?" I asked.

"No," she said, spitting water. Unbelievably, she smiled. "No, Bridge. Not today. I wouldn't kill the mate of the man who exacted the only revenge anyone on my team got against these bastards." Her red irises sharpened. "Besides. If you'd been working for him, I don't think you would have wanted him dead so badly."

Hearing her words, I looked up the steep sides of the ship. My throat closed. I looked down at my hand. Somehow, I still clutched Revik's ring.

...15, 2, 1, 111, 99, 3326, 1, 42, 47, 15, 15, 12, 996, 651, 222, 231, 244, 4, 4, 4, 4, 6, 27, 13, 15, 15, 21, 66, 24, 89, 97...

At that exact moment, the sky caught on fire.

CHAPTER 34
FIRE

The explosion flared out of the darkness.

It blew back the nearest of the helicopters, causing it to careen into the one flying alongside it. The propeller clipped the vehicle's hull, splintered like dry kindling.

Galaith watched as the bird in front of him fell in a nearly straight line, breaking apart as it slammed the surface of the dark water.

The booming from the ship continued.

Shock waves from the second explosion reached the part of sky where Galaith's larger transport helicopter maintained a safe distance. The concussion shook the metal walls, forcing the pilot to compensate.

A third explosion rattled the glass.

Galaith heard the pilot curse through his microphone, forgetting himself momentarily as he leaned on the cyclic, moving them sideways below the cloud deck.

Frowning in disapproval, Galaith decided to let it pass.

The long, white cruise ship had come to a halt on the dark water.

Plumes of fire reached up to the low deck of clouds, staining them red and gold.

Galaith watched the flames mix with the dawn light, reflecting against lightly falling rain. Another blast lit the nearby land mass, illuminating dark, featureless hills. Scrub evergreens and broken boulders grew sharply visible in the sudden brightness.

People the size of ants jumped off the tall sides of the ship as he watched.

Even under the steady pulse of the helicopter's blades, Galaith heard screams.

He heard impact sounds as they hit the surface of the water.

Feeling the other occupants of the helicopter looking at him, Galaith made the sign of the cross.

Fixing his brow and mouth in the proper display of anger and grief, he signaled to the pilot with a hand, pointing towards the shore.

It wouldn't do to be caught gawking at the scene.

Anyway, his work here was done.

Alyson's last known location was the starboard end of the stern, where his team set and detonated the first set of explosives. Galaith would have his seers look for her in the aftermath, and retrieve her body if at all possible, but it was over.

It had not been an easy decision to make.

Still, he was convinced it was the right one.

Better to send her back to those beyond-the-Barrier shores of which she was so fond. Better that, than let her go alive to Terian, and whatever dark scheme his broken brother's mind had concocted. Galaith knew of Terian's ambitions. He knew exactly why Terian would want a newly-awakened Bridge to take her place at Terian's side.

It was an alliance Galaith could never permit.

Even apart from protecting his own position, Galaith had the rest of the world to consider. Given her reincarnation status, he could not help but think that such a combination would bring the Displacement crashing over them as surely as drought brought fire.

It was good he thought to install a second team, to watch Terian.

Even so, he'd almost reacted too slowly.

Whatever bizarre sequence of events was set in motion on the ship a few hours previous, it appeared to have been less a plan by Terian than a reaction to an unexpected opening. Perhaps Terian even imagined it would be so. It was the only way he could have moved fast enough to avoid any ripples of warning inside the Pyramid.

Ironically, though, it was *she* who called him here.

She found him, somehow.

She showed him where to go.

It was a genuine pity he'd arrived too late to reason with her.

As for Terian and whatever he'd been up to—

"I'll be back for you, my old friend," he murmured.

He didn't let himself think too closely about the loss of Dehgoies.

That would have to be contemplated another day.

"Sir?" the pilot shouted.

Galaith met his questioning look, wiping his face with one hand.

Luckily, the gesture fit the moment, and played all the more convincingly for its sincerity. One of his secretaries, Martha, touched his arm in sympathy, and he clasped her fingers, letting his face show a flicker of gratitude.

He raised his voice to the pilot. "Take me to the airport, Gene. We'll coordinate the rescue teams from there."

"Aye, sir." The man saluted, grinning with obvious pleasure that Galaith had used his first name. Popping the wad of gum jammed into one corner of his mouth, he let out a half-shout above the rotary blades. "Wow! What a day!"

Seeing Galaith's dark look, his smile faded.

"Of course it's terrible, sir. Terrible. All those people. No one deserves that."

Galaith did not give him a reassuring smile.

Still, he found the man's comments amusing in their blatant insincerity.

Pity there was no way he could let any of them live.

Above me, rosettes bloomed in a pale gray sky.

Clouds shone red and gold in billowing tongues of reflected flame.

I was still pretty sure I was dead.

Then a wave rolled up, filling my mouth with salt water.

I choked, only to be fully submerged.

Physical pain brought my world sharply into relief as my head and mouth broke the surface. Salt burned the cuts on my skin. My knee felt pulverized. I forced my limbs forward through the blue liquid ice.

I gazed at the fire and a dense wave of pain hit me, not all of it physical.

Water filled my mouth and I spit it out.

Somewhere in that lull, it hit me. It really hit me.

For a moment, I disappeared.

Shouts overhead and nearer screams snapped me out. Another wave submerged my head as I groped around for something to hold on to, something to support me. I grabbed at something as it floated by. It turned out to be a life jacket.

I let it go, paddling like a one-legged dog.

Trying to follow the others, I glimpsed the burning white hulk behind me as I pumped my arms harder. The ship continued to belch smoke, but it no longer produced a churning wake. Instead it sat lower in the water, like a child squatting in a stream.

I had to find Jon.

The thought repeated, irrational.

Rain had begun to fall, along with soot, white ash, pieces of fabric and paper. I heard screams all around me. I closed my eyes, still trying to get my limbs all working in the same direction, when someone grabbed my arm.

Chandre's reddish eyes met mine.

She looked afraid.

I gazed up at black-tinted clouds, a white tower rising from the middle of the ship, where a blue, tail-like fin rose to meet the sky. A burning figure stood on the fourth deck, fighting to climb the railing. The wind flared the fire on his body.

Chandre yanked harder on my arm. "Come. This will get ugly, fast! The Rooks are exterminating witnesses."

She began to drag me through the water.

I let her.

A plane skimmed overhead, lights ablaze. No one paid any attention to us.

Revik's face rose in my mind. My sight flared, bringing even more pain.

More death rose in that glimpse of darkness. Images of falling bodies ripped apart by ice-cold water. Mom's face. Dad's. I missed Jon so badly it hurt. I needed him. I really fucking needed him now. I floated, fighting to push past it, dragged through the current.

Chandre didn't stop pulling on my arm.

It felt like she'd pull it out of the socket.

"There's some chance," I managed. "I saw him, Chan. I saw him. Alive. Terian had doctors there. He could still have him. They could've saved him."

Chandre looked at me.

Like me, she struggled words out between breaths as she stroked hard with her free arm, pulling me with her.

"No," she said. "Different light signature. We tracked it. Saw him die."

I shook my head, trying to free my arm.

She only pulled harder.

"You must feel it." She looked at me. "Separation sickness. It's all over you. This will only get worse. You have to stay out of the Barrier, Esteemed Bridge. Do whatever you have to. Or he will have died for nothing."

I didn't answer, remembering Eliah saying the same thing.

When I didn't speak after a few seconds, her expression softened.

"I am sorry, Bridge," she said.

We were still a few hundred yards from shore when a sudden, sharp boom jerked our eyes back towards the ship.

Like something from a dream in the rising light, yellow and orange plumes billowed upward. The ship sank fast after that. I saw glass blow out as windows exploded, pouring water, flames—more smoke. The wind changed, bringing us screams, the smell of charred flesh and burning plastic.

Chandre resumed swimming.

Between strokes I heard her speak through clenched teeth.

"Hopefully they will believe we are dead, as well."

A wolf runs on the tundra, tongue lolling past its blood-stained grin—

When I came to, I was aware of hands on me, people pulling me out of the water.

Rough gravel and dirt met my bare skin. My legs dragged like dead weight. I couldn't move my knee. My thigh felt numb, weightless, like it wasn't there. Someone wrapped a coarse blanket around my back, talking over my shoulder to Chandre.

I felt grief on the man holding me and realized I didn't know him, or the woman standing next to him, watching me with pity in her dark eyes.

Only Chandre's voice remained.

The rest stood silent, emotional despite their weapons and training, unable to tally what they'd lost.

...the wolf runs, his feet sending up puffs of white snow.

I want to tell them it's all right.

I want to tell them they are safe.

The wolf is no longer looking at us.

He runs at a single dark form marring the white plain. Again it is dawn, and a black shape burns in the distance on the horizon.

My chest feels as if someone has taken an ice pick to it, hitting it again and again, digging out a delicate, pale light at its core.

It is a feeling worse than death.

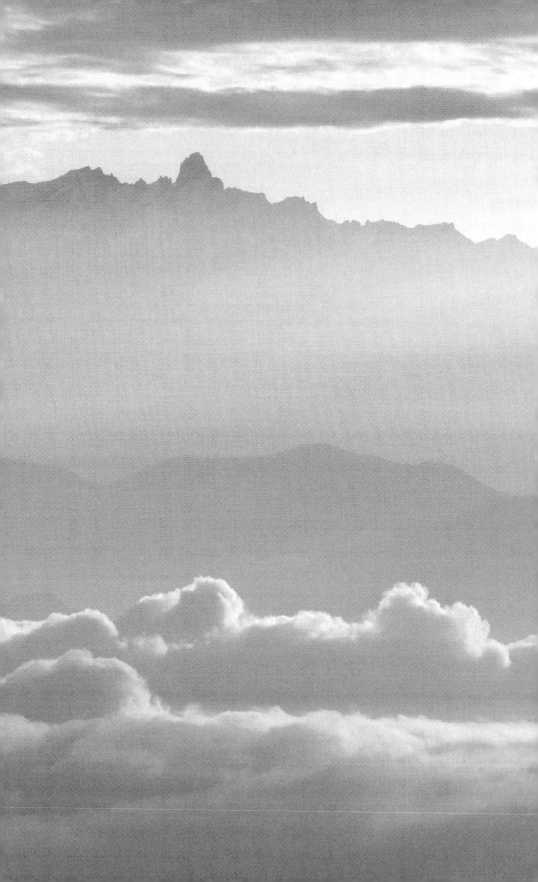

CHAPTER 35
INDIA

News feeds ran nonstop in the background.

I tried not to look at their fast-moving images, or hear anything the avatars said. Still, fragments reached me, no matter how hard I tried to block them out.

"...dead now tallied at four hundred and sixty-two... over a hundred still missing, also believed to be dead..."

"...President Caine lays responsibility for the cruise ship bombing on terrorist Alyson May Taylor. He calls for international cooperation in bringing her and her terrorist cell to justice, meeting with SCARB branches in Russia and China, as well as in Europe and Africa. Initially thought to have been killed in the attack, it is now believed Taylor escaped and is still at large, following..."

"...last seen in Europe, at a café in Spain where she..."

"...eluded authorities outside a train station in Munich, now believed to be headed east as she reunites with the larger terrorist cells that placed her as a sleeper agent in San Francisco all those years ago..."

"...every member of her adoptive human family now dead or missing..."

I heard my name, over and over. I saw my face.

I saw pictures of people I loved, heard strangers argue about how many of my family and friends were dead versus accomplices fleeing the authorities. I listened even though I didn't want to listen, until my brain fogged over. I crouched in hotel bathrooms to get away from feeds blaring in the adjoining rooms, hands over my ears, counting tiles while infiltrators pounded on the door, trying to get me to let them in.

I traveled everywhere in a faceless cloud of seers.

They bought me wigs, wrapped scarves around my head, gave me earpieces to wear, make-up, different configurations of prosthetics, contact lenses. They forced me to eat, drugged me when I wouldn't sleep in the constructs we hopped in and out of, shoved me into vans, cars, trains, scolded me when I drank too much or stood next to windows.

We moved every few days, always in a zig-zagging line east.

I stared at the skylines of different cities across land masses I didn't recognize through the windows of whatever vehicle they happened to put me in. We went for days where I couldn't sleep, could barely remember who I was.

They treated me differently now.

All but Chandre.

Despite their attempts to keep me alive, most of the seers seemed afraid of me. It was a reverential kind of fear, like they saw the end of the world reflected on my face.

Whatever caused it, none of them got too close.

I got through it by sleeping every chance I got, and, let's face it… a hell of a lot of alcohol.

Through it all, the feeds ran.

Some cult started worshipping me.

The cult's followers petitioned for space on the US feed network and got denied because of my terrorist status, causing a wave of sensationalist headlines both for and against. Protests erupted in the United States, Asia, and Europe, including at least three actual riots. The biggest took place in Los Angeles, started by Christians and human Third Mythers.

It got ugly by the end.

I saw surveillance recordings of a young female seer being beaten with tasers and pipes. The newscasters on the feeds clucked about it in regret, but no one put down their cameras long enough to stop the men doing it—men who would never be able to afford a seer like her, even for a few hours.

Rumors spread about me being the Bridge.

Black market feeds had whole sites devoted to me and Revik.

Human women loved Revik, especially after it got out that we'd been married.

It didn't seem to matter that he was dead.

World governments were already negotiating over rights to my telekinetic "powers." The United States and China dominated those discussions, but Russia, Germany, England, and Japan vied to be allowed at the bargaining table, hiding behind the veneer of scientific curiosity. Speculation erupted that I might have been impregnated by Revik before he died. Telekinetic rumors and rumors of sightings spread, more so after I was officially blamed by the World Court for the sinking of Royal Faire cruise ship, *The Explorer.*

People who lost loved ones posted bounties, wanting me dead.

The feeds fed on the hysteria, fanned it.

More people went missing.

One was my brother, Jon.

Another was Cass, who I'd known almost as long.

With the last two people in my family gone, I didn't much care what the world thought of me.

Weeks passed. Longer.

I waited for sleep. I craved it, but it didn't help when it came.

I can't reach him, no matter how often he asks. The asking hurts, more than the other pain ever did, and I feel him in pieces now—love, grief, sadness, hope, despair. The layers of him are infinite. Yet in some ways, they are simple, too.

Still, he doesn't feel alive.

I have to face that he isn't alive.

My mind grapples with that knowledge, argues with it.

The numbers won't leave me alone.

They are separate from him, but somehow connected. I dream of my father, the engineer. He jokes that numbers are our secret language, so we can speak to one another in code. They are a cryptic mantra, a broken song I can't get out of my head.

...17, 10, 42, 12, 1, 57, 12, 20, 332, 178, 12, 102, 9, 13, 15, 2, 2, 2...

I AM SOMEWHERE ELSE.

I've never been here before, but it feels familiar.

After the clean, picturesque towns, the chateaus and expensive hotels where we'd spent the last few weeks in Europe, the grittiness of this new place is strangely welcome.

We traveled through farmland for months.

We stopped in seer safe houses to sleep.

Churches, warehouses, hotels, mosques, a winery in the hills, a bombed out Jewish temple. I told myself I didn't know what was worse: the nights where I wasn't able to sleep, or having to suffer through the dreams and pain when I could.

But that was a lie, too.

I missed him by the time we hit the next construct, by the time I could dream again.

I missed him, looked for him, and when I found him, we would—

Here it was dirty, loud, colorful, hot, poor, crowded.

I walked up a dusty street where a mound of brightly-colored trash covered an open sewer grate, stinking already at seven o'clock in the morning. A shrine draped in winking Christmas lights and gold foil stood in a crack between buildings; on it, a monkey god cavorted among flowers and stick fruit covered in buzzing flies. A caramel-colored cow stood chewing over a pile of rotting greens, egg cartons, and chicken bones.

When I paused to pat its backside, it didn't look up.

Most of my face was wrapped in gauzy cream cloth, but I nodded anyway to a monk in red robes on his way up the street, wearing sunglasses and carrying an espresso in his hand. I felt oddly content with the horrible smells of human sweat, rotting melon, and maggot-covered meat. Even with the stench slowly heating in the morning sun, for some reason I felt like I could breathe here.

I chuckled at the next shrine, which held a picture of me covered in pink flower petals surrounded by white, paraffin candles.

It was an old picture, that time.

My high school end-of-year picture.

My hair had a streak of lime green in it—me and Cass's idea of rebellion, which infuriated my mother at the time, since she'd already purchased a photo package to give pictures to all our relatives. Because of the ban, real-time photos were expensive as hell, and needed special permission. Mom still had a job back then, working for the post office, and she made me pay for the photos out of my meager tip money from an earlier crap job I had.

Paying her back took months.

It was probably the last time we really screamed at each other, since my father—

I made my way up the hill, using the cane.

Mountains loomed over us, breathtakingly tall, draped in snow and wisps of low-lying, fog-like clouds. Colorful prayer flags flapped in the breeze, hanging from wires sagging between buildings painted in bright greens and blues.

Most windows had no glass, just wooden shutters and tarps covering square openings. A black paw emerged from one of these as I watched, a second story window in a hotel with tables and chairs on a roof where people sat and drank hot chai, speaking Hindi and Tibetan and seer pidgin. Following the paw came the rest of a squat, tan-colored monkey. Its pink face remained etched in a frown despite the sticky piece of mango clutched in one paw.

Gripping wooden slats with its free hand and feet, it climbed nimbly up to the roof.

When it reached the railing a yell pierced the early morning quiet, and a white-haired Indian woman swung at the monkey with a long-handled broom.

The monkey screeched and held his ground, still clutching the mango… and I laughed, watching the grumpy thing vault to the roof of a shack that housed the steaming chai pot from which a girl of maybe twelve ladled tea.

"You're awfully chipper," said a voice. "I'd have thought you'd be hung over after the quantities of bourbon you drank last night."

The seer's dry tone snapped me out of my view of the mountains behind the fat, ill-tempered monkey and the people on plastic chairs.

I turned to see the same red-brown irises I'd been looking at for weeks.

"Yeah," I said. "Guess I've got good genes for drinking until I black out."

The female seer with the dark braids sniffed, but seemed content to have received an answer.

She folded her muscular arms, gazing around us with distaste.

"Didn't Dehgoies explain how alcohol affects your light?" she said, for possibly the three hundredth time. "It's a wonder the Rooks didn't find us, with the flares you send out. Between that and..."

The lecture continued, but I heard little of the rest.

The pain slid forward as soon as she mentioned his name.

When I allowed myself to go there, briefly, to look for him, a migraine sharpened behind my eyes, forcing me to stop and lean heavily on the cane I'd been using to help out my knee. I waited for the pain to pass, breathing in garbage and incense from a nearby storefront.

Chandre didn't notice the change in me at first.

She stopped when I stopped, still complaining to me about me as she glanced around at the wooden buildings. Another cow, this one a chocolate brown, wandered past, grinding its long jaw sideways. It lowed plaintively, twitching its tail.

"Welcome to Seertown of Himachal Pradesh, Bridge," Chandre said after she'd finished her catalogue of my wrongdoings and ignorant, human ways. "...Sewer of the Himalayas."

Suddenly noticing me leaning against the cane, breathing unevenly, she snatched my fingers off my neck.

"Stop it. The humans are staring!"

I laughed. I saw a man in a doorway looking at me, holding a straw broom that looked handmade and wearing a sweat-stained fedora. His upper body was wrapped in a colorful woolen shawl. He shook his head at me ruefully, clucking his tongue.

"They think I'm high," I said. "I'm a bad Buddhist. A decadent white woman. Who cares?"

Chandre's mouth hardened. "I am sorry for your family, Bridge. But you cannot continue to dwell on the loss of them, nor of your mate. You must focus on the task at hand."

"Which is what, exactly? Avoiding ringworm?"

I gazed down to the street below, where a nun in dark red robes herded a cluster of kids in black and white uniforms across the cracked blacktop. Numbers rotated over the nun's shaved head like a disjointed countdown, floating in and out of the lights of the children.

6, 6, 120, 123, 2, 8, 88, 99, 40, 4, 2, 4, 6, 29, 29, 32, 4, 2…

I forced myself to speak, although I didn't look away from the nun.

"How far is it?"

"You tell me," Chandre retorted. "Use your light for something useful for once."

I frowned, glancing at her. "My light? The town is a construct?"

Chandre rolled her eyes. "No Rook comes here, Bridge. It is by treaty that they stay away. We are safe here. I told you that."

I gave her a skeptical look, but kept quiet.

Hearing voices raised nearby, I turned, saw a cluster of men dressed in Muslim garb talking excitedly to an Indian man on a bicycle who shook his head, making broad negative gestures with his hands. It took me a second to realize the Indian-looking male was a seer, and owned. The metal collar around his neck was so filthy I almost hadn't seen it under his stained shirt. While I watched, a man in a police uniform came up, waving what looked like a homemade nightstick. The seer cowered, holding up his hands.

Watching him pedal away on his bicycle, I frowned.

"Well?" Chandre said. "Will you lead us, or not?"

I looked at her, startled, then realized what she meant and laughed.

Limping away from her stare, I maneuvered the cane up the hill.

The number of storefronts diminished as we climbed higher, and the mud-brick apartment buildings and houses grew piled one on top of the other, colorful and strangely cave-like against the hills. Prayer flags waved beside shrines for gods with aura-like headdresses.

I saw more pictures of me, even a graffiti drawing of my profile with words drawn in the art-like, slanting characters from the seer language, Prexci.

Paths wound up into the forest as we climbed higher into the Himalayan foothills. The street deteriorated from crumbling asphalt to packed dirt, and the trees grew closer together.

The flavor of the town began to change as well.

Seer religious graffiti grew more dominant, along with a greater number of plastic bottles, used condoms and broken glass. I saw groups of girls in clusters on wooden stoops, drinking beer and wearing torn silk dresses next to men with greasy hair and jeans stiff with dirt. Most of the men wore plaid, long-sleeved shirts and scarves around their heads.

It took a few minutes of looking before I noticed the metal collars.

They laughed, passing bottles as the occasional Indian or Tibetan tromped up the wooden steps, leading one of the females inside, or sometimes one of the males.

As we passed, those left on the stairs noticed me and Chandre and stared.

We were nearly all the way past the building when a handsome man who looked to be in his twenties spoke up.

"Freedom is good, yes?" He spoke loudly, in heavily-accented English. "Tell your friend Vash that, eh?" He thumbed his collar towards me. "See what his peace love shit has gotten us." He raised his voice as Chandre and I walked further up the hill. "Tell him to bring the Bridge here, yes? Tell him we need some of her justice in India!"

The others laughed. One woman made a violent hand-gesture in my direction, then slapped the man next to her on the back of his head for staring at my body through the dark pants and scarves I wore.

The man sitting next to the couple laughed harder, spilling his beer.

A few seers in our contingent walked over to them, speaking that pidgin seer tongue and offering them cigarettes and vodka. I knew it was partly to distract them from me, but I couldn't stop myself looking back over my shoulder at those seers sitting there, on the dilapidated stoop. I got a sudden flash of Revik lounging on those steps, a younger Revik maybe, with a rounder face and eyes that hadn't yet developed the same faraway look.

Chandre clicked at me to stop me staring.

"Vash feeds them," she said. "He does what he can."

I nodded, glancing back a last time as I trudged up the hill.

Chandre added, "Fighting the humans overtly would only worsen their situation. It would bring death and pain to all of us, Bridge."

"Sure," I said, not wanting to argue.

"You don't know anything," she informed me. "You are a child. Raised by worms. What could you know of this? You have not *seen* war yet."

I didn't bother to answer.

When we reached the top of the rise, I stopped before a storefront with cracked windows and wooden steps with peeling, sky-blue paint. I stared through the dusty glass, knowing only that I felt compelled to stop there.

Moving to stand beside me, Chandre folded her arms.

She gave me a grudging nod.

"Good. Your tracking has finally improved."

My eyes fixed on a picture of a guru-type old man in sand-colored robes with hands at prayer position at his chest. A handwritten sign said in English: *Hot Meals 20 Rupee! Free meditation and yoga!*

Under the sign stood a three-foot Ganesha statue with a garland of pink and white flowers. More petals stuck to statues of Indian gods, only a handful of which I recognized or could name. Wooden prayer beads draped the back wall of the display case beside a painting of a blue and gold sun intersected by a white sword.

I saw a Buddha sitting towards the back, too, and smiled.

Part of it belonged to the mish-mash that is India, but the absurdity of mixing a godless religion with a multi-theistic one struck me as a uniquely seer mistake.

It occurred to me to wonder if seers believed in gods, or a God.

Revik had said "gods" or *"d'gaos"* like someone might say "shit," which didn't tell me much about his religious beliefs.

My eyes went back to the photo of the old man in sand-colored robes.

His dark eyes shone from an aged yet somehow unlined face.

"Vash," I muttered. "Jesus."

"Not quite." Chandre's quip had an edge. "Do not let his face to the humans deceive you. The rent must be paid. Even in Seertown."

She yanked open the wooden screen door.

Without answering, I followed her into a larger and cleaner foyer than I'd expected.

Tiled in black stone, the room stretched out over the side of the mountain.

Wooden baseboards and paneling accented white walls with deep-toned hardwood, water damaged in parts but gleaming from a recent polish. An old-fashioned fan stuttered in a window next to a mural of the Tibetan Potala in Lhasa, done in painstaking detail and with another of those gold and blue suns.

Directly inside the door stood a low desk, crafted of the same dark wood.

Behind it, a young Caucasian man with a shaved head and orange robes sat on a folding chair. The way his eyes lit up in wide-eyed eagerness told me he was probably human.

"Can I help you, sisters?" He looked at me first. Spotting Chandre next, he did a double-take, and grinned. "Cousin Chandre! India has missed you, my friend!"

I raised an eyebrow in Chandre's direction, fighting a smile.

Ignoring me, she bowed to the human, her hands at prayer position.

"Hello, James, and peace. We have an audience with the Teacher."

James beamed. "Lucky you! Shall I call ahead?"

"That won't be necessary," she said. "But thank you."

I stared at her, mouth open in disbelief.

Chandre called humans "worms" most of the time, when she wasn't ordering them around like robots programmed to do her bidding. She gave me a cold look, motioning for me to follow her up the stairs.

Once we'd climbed a few, she spoke to me under her breath through gritted teeth.

"We are in a construct now. I would appreciate if you kept your thoughts civil."

"Sure," I said agreeably.

I felt her irritation through the construct and smiled.

At the top of the stairs stood an opening in the wall covered with a tapestry of yet another sprawling blue and gold sun, bisected by a white sword. Grasping one edge of the heavy cloth, Chandre slipped through the opening she created and vanished.

After a bare hesitation, I followed.

I straightened inside a low-ceilinged room covered in bamboo mats.

Open windows revealed a dramatic view of the Himalayas and a tree-filled valley housing the rest of Seertown, covered over in prayer flags like a roosting flock of brightly colored birds. Against the wall, a handful of collar-less seers wore Western clothes, talking silently amongst themselves and gesturing with their hands.

Closer to me and the door, another group of seers stood in a loose ring, wearing sand-colored robes. The man from the framed picture stood in the middle.

He turned as I dropped the tapestry behind me.

His eyes met mine, a piercing black.

They carried so much light I found it difficult to hold his gaze.

Without waiting, he crossed the ten or twelve feet to the door.

I took in his angular, unlined face, a little taken aback by his height.

I didn't move as he pulled me into his arms, lifting me off the floor. Squeezing me tightly and then letting go, he laughed aloud at my strangled sound, his teeth straight and white, his eyes bright with tears as he drank in my face.

"You are here at last!" he said in perfect English, patting my shoulder in an awkward overflow of emotion. "I am very, very pleased! Very pleased!"

I could only nod, stunned by his tears.

"You are welcome here," he said. "Most welcome!"

I felt my face warm. I fumbled with something to say—

And heard a derisive snort.

I turned my head towards the sound.

Amongst the seers wearing Western clothing and sitting by the wall, a muscular male in a black T-shirt watched me with Vash, his full mouth curved in a cynical smile. I felt his light on mine and flinched.

My cheeks flushed at what lived in that single, darting probe.

Feeling my reaction, that same male gave me a sideways smile, glancing at the two seers sitting beside him, who stopped staring at me long enough to smile with him.

The first one's light stayed by me, though.

I felt him explore, felt a flicker of surprise in him at what he found, but I couldn't tell what surprised him exactly. When I met his gaze the second time, his chocolate-brown eyes shifted away. He nodded to Chandre in passing as she sat amongst them.

I glanced up at Vash, saw a hint of a smile in his black eyes.

"You must be very tired," he said kindly.

"You have no idea," I said.

THAT NIGHT I CURLED UP ON A FOAM MATTRESS ON THE FLOOR.

A sheet lay over me, covered in sheep and cow skins, soft and warm and smelling comfortingly of animal. Through the wooden slats of the windows over where I lay, I could see mountains framed by starlight and endless black sky, the outline of peaks just visible where the stars disappeared. Monkeys called to one another in the trees; they screeched and scuffled over roofs, their black paws scoring the slate tiles.

Mostly, though, it was quiet.

Lying there in the dark, feeling crippled me, more than I'd had to contend with in what felt like months. Maybe it was being in the home of a bunch of monks, or the warmth of Vash's greeting, or simply being stationary at last—and sober for a change. Maybe I should have expected things to come crashing down on me once we got here.

Regardless, I couldn't help feeling like I'd been stripped naked and left to feel every breeze and drop of sweat over my open wounds.

The construct exuded a simple warmth that worsened the feeling.

Even the Himalayas amplified it, until something inside me started to unclench, so quickly and effortlessly that I couldn't pull back the threads.

By the time the monkeys' footsteps receded, the middle of my chest throbbed as it had on those cold shores in Alaska.

I couldn't breathe, but my mind remained dead silent.

The moon rose, and I was still awake, despite being exhausted.

I lay there and watched as the valley filled with a soft, penetrating light.

Somewhere in that silence, I started to cry.

Once I started, it was difficult to stop.

YET, SOMEHOW I AM ASLEEP.

I find him easier this time.

He seems almost to be waiting for me.

He is alone here, as he always is. Just like every time before, I feel him, but I can't quite reach where he is. He floats like a corpse surrounded by gray curtains, and we touch one another through the morphing fabric, fighting to get closer, but we can't.

Before I understand where we are, we are kissing, like we are most of these nights.

I feel him more once we start, but it's not enough.

Gods. It's never enough.

Our mouths are careful, hands and fingers deliberate through the thin fabric. When I slide into his light this time it is fast, a slow groan before he opens, letting me nearer than usual, until I almost feel him, until he seems almost real.

He is pulling on me then, asking me, but I can't…

I can't give him what he wants.

A kind of desperation grips me.

He wants to give me things, too. He tries, in his own way.

Images and sensations weave into his light, his legs between mine, his weight on me, until it feels like he's inside me, like we are…

But it will only make things worse when he leaves.

I'm tired of this. Tired of fighting and losing him. Tired of looking and never being sought. He left me. He left me before he left.

He enters me now like a thief, because I'm all he has.

He pauses, raising his head.

…and the man with the chocolate-brown eyes stares back, only now he isn't smiling.

Lowering his head, he kisses me without hesitation, picking up where Revik left off. It feels different, and not only because I don't know him. The curtain evaporates, revealing warm light, a different body, less-cautious hands, unambiguous intent.

His arms and chest are larger, his hands smaller, his lips fuller, his tongue thicker. He's not as tall. The way he kisses is different. He doesn't wait for me to ask, barely waits for my answer. His hand slides into the crook of my knee, fingers caressing my thigh as he pulls my leg up around his waist. He is inside me, and I hear him groan.

He kisses me again.

I feel him breathing hard in the dark, in another room, naked under rough skins, and I know suddenly that it's not all a dream.

Somewhere, Revik watches.

I know it's not real, that he's not here anymore.

He's dead. I know that.

Yet somehow, it still feels like a betrayal.

CHAPTER 36
CHALLENGE

I got up before dawn.

When I left my sleeping quarters and wandered outside into new light, the man with the chocolate-colored eyes was the first person I saw. He sat on a wooden step, smoking a *hiri*, one of the seer cigarettes. A cup of chai rested by his thigh.

I'd spent the night in a sort of cottage, one of many rimming a wide courtyard just below Vash's house and the wider complex it formed a part of. The courtyard itself consisted of a large clearing that started at the edge of those street-facing buildings.

A white-painted stone cairn stood exactly in the center of it.

Paths dotted with smaller shrines and shade trees radiated outwards.

Even in the dawn chill, seers wandered through those trees, talking in a mixture of languages and hand gestures.

I wondered why they bothered to speak aloud at all, and why there were so many more men than women… then noticed the man with the brown eyes staring at me.

Watching those eyes linger on my bare feet, I made up my mind.

I approached him deliberately, walking to where he sat on the wooden stoop. He didn't stand when I reached him, and I didn't sit, but we eyed one another silently.

Unwillings, a voice said in my mind.

I jumped. "What?"

You wondered why there are no women. They are sold faster. A bigger market for unwillings. You should know that, Esteemed Bridge.

He took a drag of the seer cigarette, blowing out a perfect smoke ring as he waited for me to catch up. His smile turned wry.

And we speak for the same reason all beings speak, Esteemed Bridge. To be heard.

"Do you speak English?" I asked. "Aloud, I mean."

He quirked an eyebrow.

"Yes."

He had an accent, but I couldn't place it beyond Asian.

He studied my face, right before his brown eyes flickered down over the thin cotton pants I wore, pausing again on my bare feet.

"Did you…" His smile widened. "…Sleep well, Esteemed Bridge?"

I folded my arms. With one hand, I motioned towards his sidearm, visible under his jacket. "I take it you're not a complete pacifist?"

"Does this offend you, Esteemed Bridge?"

"You know how to fight? *Mulei?*"

He smiled again, nodding once. "Yes."

"Could you teach me?"

I glanced over my shoulder at the other seers in the courtyard.

It hadn't escaped my notice that a number of them stood closer to us than they had a few minutes earlier. They continued to inch closer, to watch and listen to me and the brown-eyed seer talk. Feeling my jaw tighten, I looked back at the smoking seer, shifting my weight on my feet.

"…I need lessons," I explained.

Curiosity flared in his eyes, just visible beneath the amusement.

"Why me?" he asked finally.

I sighed, then answered honestly. "You seem like you'd like to hit me. I figured I'd try harder."

The male seer stared at me.

Then he burst into a genuine laugh.

He stood up, and while he wasn't as tall as Revik, I stepped back in alarm.

His smile widened more. "Yes," he said. "I would like to hit you, Bridge. But I need to know if you are worth teaching, first." He flipped the jacket off his muscular shoulders, exposing a worn gray shirt that stretched over his chest.

When he caught my stare, his smile grew into a grin.

"What do I get, if I put you down?" His eyes flickered down my body. He gestured towards it vaguely. "Will you let me take care of that thing of yours? The problem your Rook husband left you?"

I didn't ask what he meant.

"No," I said. Thinking, I added, "You've got two minutes. If I'm still standing, you'll teach me. You'll also stay the hell out of my head at night. If I'm not standing, well..." I shrugged. "...I guess the mind stuff is fair game. And you got to hit the Esteemed Bridge. Consequence-free. That should be reward enough."

He chuckled, shaking his head in amusement.

Watching his face, I hesitated, then figured what the hell.

"...Everything else has to be negotiated separately. Clear?"

His eyes lit up at my words, but he only nodded. He stubbed out the *hiri* with the toe of one threadbare yellow sneaker.

"Okay." He stepped towards me, bouncing a bit on his heels. "I accept."

"What's your name?" I asked, when he began to circle me.

"Maygar." He glanced up from where he'd been looking at my body again. "Oh, and I should tell you, Bridge. I was assigned a new job today."

"What job was that, Maygar?"

He darted forward, moving so fast I didn't see anything but a shadowed blur before my vision went red, then abruptly white. I reeled back, fighting to recover from a solid left cross to my right cheek. I ducked when he went for me again, then kicked out, catching him in the stomach hard enough to push him back with the ball of my foot.

He laughed, but gave me the ground.

When he got closer again, I looked for an opening, any opening.

"...I'm your new bodyguard," he said, winking.

"MORE TEA?" VASH ASKED, RAISING THE DENTED POT.

I sat cross-legged on the floor beside him.

My face hurt. My arms, hands, and legs were bruised, too, and even my tailbone where it perched on a bamboo mat.

Two seers had brought in a platter covered with tea, cream, honey, and a plateful of small sandwiches. A second tray held two teacups and saucers. They laid everything out on a dark red cloth spread between me and the ancient seer.

I fought the impulse to touch my face in places I could feel the flesh rising.

I wanted ice, but hadn't asked for that, either.

Looking out at the rain falling lightly over the mountains, I glanced reluctantly at the seers sitting around us in a symmetrical ring.

Against the far wall sat Maygar and his friends. Amusement showed on more than one face. I felt their lights flicker around mine like curious moths, woven through with faint flavors of sexuality. When I caught Maygar's gaze unintentionally, he winked at me, kissing the air before tapping his temple with a forefinger.

Tonight, he whispered in my mind.

Taking a mouthful of cucumber sandwich, I chewed, gripping a teacup in my other hand.

More than anything, I wished it held coffee.

Vash laughed, startling me.

"Of course! You are American now."

He glanced at another seer, who rose at once and disappeared through a cloth-covered doorway.

"Is this Indian breakfast?" I asked.

His lips twitched in humor. "Elevenses, perhaps."

Fans rotated overhead with round, leaf-like blades, pushing cool, rain-smelling air through the room.

Vash patted my knee. "How do you like India, dear friend?"

"I like the cows. And the mountains." I looked around at the smooth-faced seers, avoiding Maygar's corner. "Am I a prisoner here?"

Vash swept his smile away. "Not at all." His voice grew troubled. "Do you wish to leave?" Leaning closer, he asked in barely a whisper, "...Or perhaps you would like some ice?"

I glanced around at the expressionless seers.

"I want to find my brother," I said, feeling my face warm. Somehow, the words felt overly personal here, with all of these strangers staring at me. I plowed on anyway. "And my friend, Cass. They're missing."

"Are you so certain they are not dead?"

He didn't say it to hurt me, or even to throw doubt on whether they were alive. The question felt sincere, and completely guileless. Even so, my jaw seemed to stick in my sandwich. Setting my teacup down on the tray, I forced myself to swallow what was left in my mouth.

I cleared my throat, looking directly into Vash's eyes.

"No," I said. "I need to know for certain, though. Maybe that's delusional, but—"

"Ah." Vash's dark eyes grew thoughtful. "I was not implying that." He paused. "Do they have meaning, these numbers? The ones I see around you now?"

I glanced away from Maygar, looking up at Vash.

Watching his nearly black eyes stare intently over my head, I felt my chest constrict, even though I saw nothing but curiosity in his gaze.

"No," I began. Thinking, I adjusted my words. "Well… honestly, I don't know." I tried to be more honest still. "They *feel* like they mean something, but I have no idea what. It started on the ship. Right around the time when everything bad was going down."

"Ah," Vash said.

He smiled at me. His long, white face erupted in fine wrinkles. "Your husband mentioned to me that your prescience often expresses itself in your art." He paused, waiting. "Is that true, Esteemed Bridge?"

"My…" I repeated numbly.

"…Husband, yes. Dehgoies Revik."

He smiled as I fumbled for a facial expression.

I couldn't help but wonder if he'd misunderstood me on purpose.

His eyes grew kind.

"Of necessity, we spoke often of your latent abilities," he said, patting my knee affectionately. "Truthfully, we often argued about this, too. He had difficulty understanding why you were not pulled for training sooner." Noting my bewilderment, he smiled wider. "Ah. This surprises you. Yes. Revik was not always the most forthcoming man."

Before I could answer, the seer with the bare feet reentered the room, holding a steaming cup that smelled deliciously of dark roast coffee. He set it down by my bent knee, bowing to me with one raised palm, like a salute.

"Thanks," I said to him, meaning it.

Taking another sniff of the coffee, I raised the paper cup and sipped carefully. "I draw pyramids," I said, looking at Vash. "Both Chandre and Revik said they are pretty accurate depictions of the Rooks' network. Do you want me to get them?"

Vash continued to study my eyes. "Perhaps later."

For a long moment, we just listened to the rain. I sipped more coffee.

Eventually, I cleared my throat.

"So, this Pyramid," I said. "Can you explain that? Revik, he..." I cleared my throat. "Dehgoies, I mean. He told me some. He said you would tell me more."

Vash seemed almost to have been waiting for the question.

"A pyramid," he said at once. "Being a three-dimensional shape, can be only a symbol, of course. The actual network is of the Barrier and contains a form of shifting dimensionality that marries properties of both partial and non-dimensionality."

My fingers clasped my hurt knee.

"Ah," I said. "Sure."

Vash smiled in understanding. "The Rooks' seers live inside a construct, Alyson. They live in it all the time. Unlike the constructs you've seen my people use, theirs is not anchored in the physical world. It lives with a race of beings who aid them from the Barrier."

"Yeah," I muttered, understanding that part, at least.

He looked at me inquiringly.

"I met one," I explained, setting down the coffee. "On the ship." I twitched my fingers on my knee in a shrug. "It was my own fault. I was trying to get a look at the Head of the network. The one Revik called Galaith."

Murmuring broke out in the circle of seers.

I ignored it, focusing on Vash.

He watched me without changing expression.

"Indeed?" he said, his voice inquisitive.

"Not that it did much good," I muttered. "But maybe I got closer that time. Those beings showed up and tried to scare me." At Vash's questioning eyebrow, I held up my hands with hooked fingers, like a movie monster. "Booga-booga... you know. They threatened me. Told me they were coming for me. Etc."

"Indeed?" Vash chuckled. "Fascinating."

He smiled as if I'd just told him I'd solved a Rubik's cube on my first try.

"We call these beings the *Dreng*, Alyson," he said. "They are, in truth, the real Rooks. It would be more accurate to call the seers down here slaves of the Rooks. Or, more generously, their followers. Of course, they call themselves 'The Brotherhood,' 'The Organization,' or 'Org,' for short. They title missions 'Operation Blackout,' 'Operation Great Hope,' and so on. The Dreng encourage these fantasies. They often frame their goals in terms of the greater good."

I listened to this, nodding.

"So, they're brainwashed, then?"

Vash took a sip of tea, his eyes thoughtful.

"In a way, yes. It is a symbiotic relationship, Alyson. In return for the power they provide through the Pyramid construct, the Dreng collect light from the seers in their employ. Those seers in turn parasitize other seers and humans, to supply the Dreng with light. It is the Dreng's primary motive and function down here, to steal the light of living beings, as they cannot generate their own. The Pyramid collects this light in large feeding pools for use by the construct. But their primary customer is still the Dreng themselves."

I frowned, picking up images from the old seer as he spoke.

Vash added, "In short-term, everyday usage, the Pyramid provides individual seers with an almost limitless supply of light. Especially those at the top. The shape of the Pyramid symbolizes the hierarchical nature of the macro version of the living resonant construct. It is known by us that the alpha tier shifts at irregular intervals, but—"

"Okay, wait." I held up a hand. "Time out. I need you to translate that part."

Vash smiled. "We are unable to see the workings of the structure from outside of it," he clarified. "We know it is made up of beings..."

A Pyramid made of silvery-white light appeared in the space above where we sat.

I looked up at it in wonder, realized Vash must be doing it.

He illuminated dots making up the Pyramid's walls, floors, ceilings and corners, then connected them with silk threads.

"These beings are represented by nodes," he explained. "We know the leadership changes, but not how. Or why. We can speculate on the latter. But we cannot be certain our theories are correct."

"Those dots are people?" I said to Vash. "Seers?"

"Yes." Vash nodded vigorously. "Incidentally, your husband was quite obsessed with determining the identity of those seers at the top, too." Vash highlighted the top spot, the one I'd circled for Revik in my untidy sketch on ship's stationary.

"He thought he might know the leader of the Rooks on Earth," Vash added. "But he could not remember. It was a function and condition of leaving the Pyramid that he lost much of his memory of the time he spent in it. But it demonstrates how high up he must have been, Alyson, while he lived inside the Rooks' network. Very few Rooks know the true identity of the Head."

I frowned, staring up at the Pyramid. "How few?"

"We do not know for certain."

Remembering Terian's words on the ship, I nodded, still thinking.

"So that's why they erased Revik. Because he was close to Galaith?"

"In part." Vash took another sip of tea. "Truthfully, that was a judgment call not only by the Rooks, but by us, as well. In fact, you may be operating under a misconception—one I feel I should clarify. It wasn't only the Rooks who erased your husband's mind. It was me."

Pausing, he added,

"Of course, some of what he lost was purely a result of leaving the Pyramid. Also, the Rooks had some say in how the erasure was performed. But it was a joint agreement, and their end of it was conducted entirely from the Barrier."

Vash waved a hand around at the bamboo mats.

"It happened in this very room. After he defected from their network, we could not exactly return him to them. They would have killed him at once. Or, more likely, forcibly re-assimilated him." Taking another sip of the tea, Vash added, "We are told Galaith was quite fond of your mate—that he thought of him almost like a son. He would not have let him go willingly."

Remembering what I'd felt on the ship, all the walls around Revik's light, I frowned.

"If you were able to keep him safe from the Rooks, why not leave his mind alone? Why erase him at all?"

Vash's voice turned matter-of-fact.

"There are several reasons. Some are complicated, and related to his light, as well as long-standing treaties with the Rooks. Others related to his emotional well-being. Had we not erased him, he likely would never have survived, Alyson. As it was, he was quite suicidal. For years, he struggled with those feelings."

"Suicidal?" I didn't hide my surprise. "Revik?"

"Yes." Vash set down his tea, his expression serious. "Quite a normal response, if you think about it. As you may have gathered from my description, living inside the Pyramid carries some very specific advantages. Servants of the Rooks are in a kind of trance. What they do in that trance makes perfect sense to them as long as they remain inside. But, break that spell, and suddenly they are able to see what they have done in quite a different light."

Thinking aloud, I said, "So when he was a Rook, what he did seemed normal. Moral even. And when he left—"

"It seemed less so, yes." Vash placed his palms on robed knees. "Further, upon leaving the Pyramid, one experiences a severe loss of power. The Pyramid culls skills and raw talent from all of its members, creating a sort of 'library' by which any of the beings inside can access the skills of all the others. Losing access to those shared pools of light and skill can be quite difficult… even painful. It is another reason seers don't often leave. The Pyramid acts as a great amplifier. It is also a distributor according to moment, status and need… of light and its structures, or *aleimi*, as we call it."

"So," I said, fighting to keep up. "Inside the Pyramid, you can access the ability of any seer inside it? Even if you never had that ability before?"

Vash nodded, taking another sip of tea.

"Wouldn't that make them all, like… super-seers?"

"In a way… yes." Vash set his cup on its china saucer, clearly amused by this idea. "There are limits, of course. One must know how to access particular skills in the first place. Therefore, knowledge is required, especially for more complex abilities. We believe skill sets are further stratified by the hierarchy itself, with some being reserved for use only by those at the top.

"Your husband was a strong seer in his own right," Vash added. "But he was much, much more powerful when he had access to the light and abilities of tens of thousands of other seers." Patting my knee, Vash smiled. "You can see now, also, why a telekinetic seer might appeal to them?"

I nodded. "So why did he leave?"

Vash sighed. "Do you really need to ask me that?"

"Well, yeah. If he was brainwashed, then—"

Vash waved a hand. "Suffice it to say, it is possible to experience moments of clarity no matter where you are."

At my silence, he shrugged.

"The Rooks have been quite shrewd in recruiting seers who fill out those skill sets they lack. Like any beings, we each have our own gifts and aptitudes, and they vary. Imagine if you could paint like DaVinci, have the mind of a Marie Curie or an Einstein, the oratory skills of a Martin Luther King. For seers, it is much the same. It is a tremendous loss to give this up."

He added, "It can also debilitate the minds of lesser seers to realize that what they had come to think of as their own was indeed never really theirs at all."

I nodded. "Got it. So as Rooks, they're crazy strong. And if they leave—"

Vash laughed. "Alyson! You misunderstand. I was trying to tell you that this power of theirs is, in the main, illusory. It comes from the symbiotic nature of the Pyramid itself. It does not belong to the individual seers, who are themselves quite ordinary."

Vash gave a graceful shrug, his dark eyes holding a glimmer of sadness.

"I also wished you to understand something of your husband, and the kind of man he would need to be to leave them, after he had been living inside that structure for over thirty years."

I felt anger from Maygar's corner and ignored it.

Outside the open windows, rain pattered on bamboo and slate tile roofs. A golden-colored eagle wheeled past one window, dark against the sky. When I looked at Vash, he was watching me with compassion in his eyes.

I cleared my throat. "If he were reconnected with them. To the Pyramid. Could he be, well… stuck?" I clenched my jaw when the old man's gaze didn't waver. "Could he get stuck there, somehow. Even if he died?"

Vash looked up at the ceiling, eyes thoughtful. "It is a good question." He leaned back in his seat, holding his knees. "What do you think?"

My throat closed. "I don't know. It feels like he is."

Vash studied my face. "I see. Well, it would not be ideal to leave him there, would it?"

I shook my head, my jaw hard. "No."

After another beat, he laid a hand on my leg.

"Alyson," he said. "You found the Head of the Rooks' network." He paused, his silence questioning. "Chandre told us this as well. You did not simply get close. You found him. This is very significant to us."

The room grew utterly silent.

Glancing around, I saw skepticism, fear, even wonder, in the eyes of the seers sitting around us. Even Maygar stared at my face, his expression showing a kind of dumbfounded shock.

"Yeah," I said, looking back at my coffee. "I don't know who he is on the outside, though. Outside the Barrier, I mean."

"Could you show us?" Vash asked.

I looked at Maygar. I saw the skepticism had returned to his eyes.

"Yeah," I said, watching him stare at me. "No problem."

CHAPTER 37
BROTHER

Less than an hour later, I lay on a beat-up recliner in the same building, staring up at a water-damaged ceiling.

Beside me paced Maygar. Another seer attached electrodes to my face and arms. I winced as he pressed down on bruised parts of my skin.

"Tell me something," I said. "This war—"

"It is only the most likely of outcomes," Maygar said, giving a dismissive wave.

"So not inevitable?"

"No." He gave me another look, slightly less hard. "I don't think so. Although I might have said differently before."

He ran a thumb lightly over his bicep. I noticed a tattoo there. His knuckles were bruised too, probably from connecting with my face.

He cleared his throat. I looked up.

He was focused on my mouth, not hiding the meaning behind his stare.

When I rolled my eyes, he only smiled.

"There's even some who say Death comes," he added. "*Syrimne d' Gaos*. 'Sword of the Gods.' It's where that other seer got his name, the one during World War I. It's also the meaning of the sword and sun you see drawn on the temple door. And on me."

He lifted his shirt's sleeve, showing me the full tattoo of the bisected sun.

"This is a terrorist's mark, Bridge. A real one."

He grinned at my unimpressed look.

"The real Death," he added. "The real *Syrimne*... he's supposed to be a creature like you." He gestured with one thick hand. "A brother, as it were."

My hands tightened on the chair.

Maygar shrugged again, his voice bored.

"I've also read interpretations that perhaps *he's* the one as causes the shift. But Bridge, the end of every cycle is a mystery. There are too many variables. Even humans have free will."

He glanced to where James, the robed human from reception, stood talking to Chandre by the door, smiling at her with obvious adoration.

"In theory, at least," Maygar muttered.

I frowned, glancing at James, too. "So what are you doing to fight the Rooks? Your people. The badass terrorists."

Maygar snorted a laugh. "You wouldn't understand, Bridge."

"Try me."

When he raised an eyebrow, skepticism in his eyes, I exhaled in irritation.

I shook my head, sinking back into the recliner.

"Forget it. You're probably right."

"Why do you even care, Bridge?" His voice held a tinge of real curiosity. "You were raised human. You are untrained, so you do not yet see all of these things we see. Is it all just revenge to you? For your family? Your mate?"

He spat out the last word.

"Is it some hero complex? Boredom? What?"

I frowned. I stared at the ceiling, thinking about his words.

"People feel it, too," I said after a pause. "Humans, I mean. They don't know what it is, but they feel it. They feel that things are wrong. They feel their world dying." Turning my head, I met his gaze. "I want a break in the clouds. A real one. If we took down the Rooks, maybe we would get that. Maybe we wouldn't need a war."

He just looked at me, then gave another grunting laugh.

"A break in the clouds. I like that, Bridge." His face opened a bit more, his expression almost friendly. "You asked what we are doing? Right now, we are trying to crack their hierarchy. The one Vash described to you. We look for 'the break in the clouds,' too." He smiled. "There are rumors that an order exists behind the rotating top tiers. That the succession order is mapped. Not random. Do you understand this?"

I shook my head. "No."

Maygar's eyes grew sharper.

I recognized that look from Revik; it was a hunter's look.

It also meant he didn't believe me.

Realizing I'd been holding out on him, I shrugged.

"Eliah may have mentioned it. When he found out I was screwing around with the Rooks' network, he seemed convinced that's what I was after."

Seeing Maygar's eyebrow go up, I rolled my eyes.

"I still don't know what it is, Maygar."

He gave me another skeptical smile, shrugging with one hand.

"It is exactly what it sounds like, Bridge. It is a map of the succession order for the Rooks' hierarchy. A map of the succession order would detail when and how each individual Rook ascends in that hierarchy to the spot above. Like when your American president dies. There is a list of who takes his place, correct?"

"Okay," I said. "That makes sense."

Maygar smiled wider. "This thing you were pursuing in your 'spare time,' Esteemed Bridge… it is what every Rook in the network would pay all of their fortune to obtain. Hell, any in the Seven would."

"Why?" I frowned. "I mean, I get it, you could assassinate people at the higher levels, but what's to stop them from being replaced?"

Maygar rolled his eyes.

Unfolding his muscular arms, he used his light to draw an image of the Pyramid in my mind. Thrusting it forward invasively, he highlighted the node at its apex.

"The Head, understand?" When I nodded, he pointed at it. "This man at the top, he is the only one who connects directly to the Dreng. The *only* link between the Dreng and Earth."

I nodded again, to show him I was following.

"He connects the rest to the Dreng," Maygar said. "He also distributes the light, the skill sets, everything. To randomize the succession order, it is his protection, right? Without that, what's to stop one of the other Rooks from stealing this top spot from him?"

I waited, figuring it was a rhetorical question.

Maygar smiled again, maybe because he heard me.

"The top of the Pyramid, it has a rotating hierarchy." Using his light, Maygar highlighted the top tiers. They began a jerky dance.

I recognized that, too.

"You see how at any moment," Maygar added. "A different seer falls into the position directly below the Head?"

I nodded again.

"This is to prevent assassination, Bridge. If you are big number two Rook, and you kill the Head but don't take his place, you can bet whoever *does* take his place is going to take you out. But…" He lit up the top tier. "…If you know the succession order, you can *coup* the big honcho right when you are about to take his place. Or make a deal with the one who does."

He smiled, clicking again softly.

"But Bridge," he said. "We could do the same. There is a gap after the Head dies, when the Dreng are not connected to our world. The Pyramid is vulnerable then."

"How long?" I asked.

"Two… maybe three minutes to connect the new Head."

At his meaningful stare, I sighed.

"Two minutes isn't very long," I pointed out.

Maygar laughed. "It was long enough for me to smack you down this morning!" When my face warmed, he smiled. "Of course, for any of that to be feasible, we would need to know who the current Head is. That is his other protection, Bridge. Anonymity."

He pointed at me, his lips curling in a frown.

"This is where you come in. Providing you can deliver on what you say. Your Rook husband never could. Despite all his bullshit."

My jaw hardened. "I already said I don't know who he is in outside."

"Well, you should, if you found him in the Barrier."

I grunted. "Should I? None of you jackasses could find him at all. And I'm untrained, human-raised worm-girl. How is it *I'm* the one who should be embarrassed?"

Maygar stared, his dark eyes holding disbelief.

Vash's voice rose in my mind, clear as a loudspeaker.

We are ready. You are on point, Maygar.

Maygar leaned closer to me.

His voice grew soft.

"A little touchy about the husband, aren't you, Bridge?" he whispered.

Alyson? Vash sent. *Are you ready?*

Maygar straightened back to his full height, a grin tugging at his lips. His eyes met mine, a dark eyebrow quirking in a silent question.

"Yeah," I said, swallowing my anger. "I'm ready."

CHAPTER 38
HUNT

Slowly, there are stars.

Earth appears, a pale blue dot.

It zooms closer, until it dominates my view.

It is beautiful, especially here, but I scarcely look at it. Urgency powers me, beyond what I've promised Vash. I feel the Rooks everywhere now. I feel them around Revik, whatever remains of him in this place. I feel them in the shadow they lay over the Earth.

Metallic threads cross and intersect over land masses in thick, silver piles.

The Pyramid moves like a mechanical toy at the top. Rigid. Dark. I watch the nodes dance as the pieces change hands. I hear a faint whisper of—

Well?

I turn, startled. I forgot I'm not alone.

Maygar floats beside me. *We are waiting, Bridge.*

I focus on him, but I'm confused.

It happened differently before. This is new. Before, when I focused on Haldren, I was just there. In the Pyramid with him. I'm wondering if having all of you here is changing the frequency somehow.

His tone turns acidic. *Is this your first jump?*

His question throws me. *No.*

Then you should know nothing happens the same way twice in the Barrier. His thoughts carry the distinct flavor of contempt. *For that to be, all other creatures would need to be static. And yes, of course—having us here will change things. You must compensate. You must do as we do. Follow the thread, Bridge. Hunt.*

I've heard this song and dance before. From Revik. From Chandre.

Variations of the same speech. All saying roughly the same thing.

It doesn't bother me anymore.

I have done this without Revik. I've done it without Chandre or Vash. I've definitely done it without this asshole, Maygar, who wants sex with me and to beat on me only because he has some kind of monster grudge against Revik.

Maygar hears me, and his amusement returns.

Not only for that, Bridge, he says.

Pushing his mind aside, I focus on why we're here.

For the second time in this jump, I concentrate on Haldren.

I focus on his face—the clear, confident voice that rises above the crowd. In my mind I see his darkly burning eyes, hear his laugh, feel his hand on my shoulder.

I remember other things, too.

Things no one else saw.

I remember waking in the middle of the night, hearing his shuddering sobs from the guest bedroom after we first let him stay with us. I remember him acting out, testing us, to see if we'd let him stay. I remember his crush on my lab partner, Massani. I remember his fear of the other children after we persuade him to attend school.

I remember his need to control them.

I remember watching his discovery that he could.

I remember smaller things.

The way he snorts when he laughs, cracks his knuckles when he's nervous. I remember that he likes to read poetry, and take baths.

I remember so much. I know too much.

I've learned to let that go, though. Not all questions need answers.

Not all answers really tell us anything we need to know.

Slowly, the Earth begins to rotate beneath my feet.

It rotates backwards, in the wrong direction.

The sun and planets revolve backwards as well, west to east, in well-oiled precision. I half-expect to hear beautiful music, like when my father and I viewed a miniature version of Earth's constellations sliding in rich ovals on smooth brass rails. In my mind's eye, my father laughs there still, delighted by the beauty of the kinetic sculpture.

"Music of the spheres, Allie!" he says, patting my back with his large hand. "Music of the spheres! Isn't it wonderful?"

Light grows brighter over the Earth.

The wires of the Pyramid grow less around our little blue and white world.

The dark threads unwind like a ball of yarn teased by a cat, and I can breathe again, in a way I don't remember breathing before.

Abruptly, the motion stops.

Earth begins revolving forward once more, like gears grinding back into their natural position. It is slow, inexorable. Regular time, which passes changing everything, so that we lose ourselves, so that we don't recognize one another.

Instead of the Pyramid, a gray cloud masses over Europe.

There, I say to Maygar, pointing with my mind.

I feel him acknowledge me.

Something shifts.

When it is done, Maygar and I stand on that earlier version of Earth.

Our light feet rest on a grassy, leaf-strewn hill dotted with aspens.

Below us, a circle of black mud runs before a row of whitewashed buildings. The mud is thick, grooved with wheel ruts. In the distance I see more buildings, what look like barracks, and below that, men in gray-green uniforms and cloth caps march in formation. Their boots and pants are covered in mud too. Most are carrying guns.

I recognize the uniforms in a vague kind of way, not well enough to—

SS, Maygar sends my way. Contempt drips from his light. *Didn't your husband teach you? They are Schutzstaffel, Frau Dehgoies.*

I don't answer.

This is all very interesting, Maygar adds. *But what is it?*

Looking around, I fight embarrassment. Not so much because of Maygar, per se, but all the older seers I can feel watching.

Maybe I can't do this with all of you along, I admit.

Patience, Vash breaths into me, soft. *It is stronger with us here, not weaker. Do not leave yet, Bridge Alyson. You are doing quite well.*

Apparently Maygar does not hear him.

He looks around, a scowl on his light face, light hands on his light hips.

Perhaps you miss your Nazi husband? he sends with mock politeness. *You thought of him, and it brought you here?*

I feel a sharp pain in my chest. I look at him, about to speak, when I stop, staring through the trees.

Three men stand there.

They are not light beings, like Maygar and me.

They are really here, in this time.

When I first see them, they are a few dozen yards away. Within a few blinks, Maygar and I are close, on the same muddy hill.

I can see their faces now.

One, I recognize as Terian.

The second, I know only because he has no face. Like when I saw him the first time, in that Nazi prison bloc, he is well-dressed, in a formal, dark suit, and tall.

He is not as tall as the third man, however… who is Revik.

I blink somewhere in my mind.

He is still there when I return.

I can't take my eyes off him, even knowing Maygar is watching—even feeling his disgust once he notices my stare.

Revik wears what likely passed for casual wear in the time period.

Dark brown pants, a white shirt with sleeves rolled up to his elbows, suspenders, boots. His clothes look well-made, and he is clean-shaven, still on the thin side but significantly healthier than when I saw him wasting away in a Berlin jail.

The bruises have faded from his jaw and face, although I still see scars on his neck, one in the shape of a question mark, another on his forearm that I recognize. He wears the silver ring on his smallest finger, just like he did when I met him in San Francisco.

My light hand moves reflexively to my light throat.

I wonder again if the ring is from his wife, Elise.

He combs fingers through his black hair, clearing his throat.

"What are we doing here?" he asks in German.

The shock of seeing him alive paralyzes me.

"...I thought we were done with this," Revik prompts again. "Why are we here?"

Terian laughs. He is pleased with his new friend.

That pleasure sparks clearly in his light.

"You see, sir?" he says. "He's barely here a minute, and already we are wasting his time."

"Manners, Terian." The faceless man claps Revik on the shoulder. "I would like to challenge you, Rolf, to think about this war differently. Until now, you have approached your role in this conflict as a slave does. I would like to persuade you to change that vantage point."

Revik folds his arms, shifting his weight in obvious irritation.

"I adhere to the Seven's doctrine of non-interference, if that's what you mean by 'slave.' Humans as a species must be allowed to mature undisturbed. The rules are quite clear about—"

"Spoken like a true believer," Terian mutters.

Revik turns, raising an eyebrow.

"Are these schoolyard tactics meant to persuade me to abandon Code?" He glances at Galaith. "Because I find them a bit tired... sir."

"We do not mean to insult you, Revik. Far from it." Galaith gives Terian a wan smile. "But I do wonder when is the last time you really thought about those words you just recited?"

Revik frowns, looking between them.

"I have had plenty of time to think about it," he says, his real emotion coming out now. "This is not the first war of theirs I've fought. I understand well the argument for interference, but it does not make it any less wrong."

I see that his pride is pricked, especially at the silence after his words.

"I curbed their excesses where I could—"

"You did nothing," Galaith says calmly.

Revik stiffens. "I disagree."

"You were a *Nazi,* 'Rolf,'" Terian laughs. "They were gassing your people and you watched disapprovingly from a distance, at best. Cleared the way for them with your panzers at worst!"

"Don't be offended, Revik." Galaith raises a hand to silence Terian. "It is not you that is the problem. The Seven certainly mean well, but they are judging my race as if it were their own. But humans are not seers, Revik. Humans—the ordinary mob of humanity—do not need more freedom. They do not even want it. What they want, more than anything, is for the world to make sense. They want to be a part of something greater than themselves."

The faceless man gazes out over the muddy exercise yard.

"They want someone to provide that for them, Rolf," he says, quieter. "They don't want a committee of their peers. They don't want the truth to shift with the sands of opinion, or time, or progress, or perspective. They want an *absolute* reality. One that makes sense to them day after day, year after year. Whether they control this or not is irrelevant to them. They wish the *illusion* of control—without any of the responsibility."

I glance at Revik's face. I watch him think about this.

I can tell he doesn't exactly disagree.

Hell, I'm not even sure I do.

Galaith watches Revik, too. After a pause, he smiles.

"Rolf, my dear, dear friend. Humans are, quite simply, made to be dominated. If not by seers, then by more powerful humans. In truth, they prefer it."

He gestures broadly over the rows of uniformed men.

"This war is a case in point. Is it the honest leader to whom the masses flock? The one who gives them greater freedoms? More responsibility over their own lives?" He smiles, shaking his head. "No. It is the one who gives them purpose, Rolf. The one who gives them an enemy. A beautiful dream that tells them their problems can be solved. Do they care that this dream is borne of countless lies? No. They do not. No modern human leader has ever been loved as the Germans love Hitler, Rolf. Not Churchill. Not Roosevelt. Not since the last of his kind was a leader so loved: Napoleon, Caesar, the Emperors of old Asia."

Revik stands there, blank-faced.

Then he laughs.

"You yourself are human!" he says.

"Yes." Galaith smiles. "I am. But I am also one who sees the truth. Moreover, I accept it. Would you condemn me for this? Call me a race traitor to choose reality?"

Revik pauses, looking at him.

"No," he says.

Revik is in pain. I feel it on him. I feel it *through* him, even though it makes no sense that I should. I realize the pain is for Elise and something crushes the small bones in my chest, making it hard to breathe, hard to remain where I am.

The craziness behind this feeling doesn't escape me.

I am jealous.

I am beyond jealous, and of two dead people.

I follow his eyes to the muddy tracks below. Men in gray-green uniforms roll a tank of gas onto a wagon drawn by a mule. The soldiers cluck at the mule, pulling at its bridle until the mule, the wagon, and the tank stand in the center of a circular drive.

Two more tanks are positioned nearby, pulled by another mule and a horse.

The animals halt where men line up in formation.

I count over a hundred people.

"Why are we here?" Revik asks again.

This time I hear an uneasiness in his voice.

"I want to cure you, Rolf. Of obedience. Of being a slave."

I feel my stomach roil. I know suddenly, what I'm going to see.

I don't want to see it.

I turn to Maygar.

Let's go. You were right. This is a dead end.

But Maygar is focused on Galaith.

He does not see what I see, or if he does, he does not care.

My separation pain worsens, mixes with a grief too thick to think through. The resonance is too strong; I can't change my vibration enough to pull myself out. I am locked here, tied with steel cords to this past Revik and his grief for his dead wife.

That is him? Maygar says of Galaith. *He is* human, *Bridge!*

A silver channel opens above the three of them.

It feeds metallic light into the faceless man's form.

It is the Rooks, I realize, although their structure is less here.

The Dreng, I think, remembering Vash's explanation.

Terian's light body shines in resonance as Galaith's begins to glow. Even here, Terian is already covered in wire-like threads, but many fewer than when I glimpsed that side of him in the diner in San Francisco.

That same channel opens to Revik.

Sharp, silver light ignites through his *aleimi* like molten sparks.

The sickness I feel worsens as I watch his light change. The silver overtakes the softer gold-white, seeming to strengthen it, but I see it as a covering over, a slow eclipse of something I realize I still love, that I can't seem to stop loving, no matter how hard I try.

Seconds later, the auras around Terian and Revik gleam bright with metallic, silver light, emitting lightning-like flashes. An even brighter aura pulses off Galaith.

I hear Maygar mutter beside me.

Impossible…

Terian winks at Revik. "You see, my cantankerous, *Heer* friend," he says with a smirk. "Galaith is like a great, big mirror. Anything that lives in the network, lives also in him. Which means, if any of us has a present for the network, he is the first to unwrap it."

Terian's eyes turn slightly colder and, for the barest instant, more predatory. I see the covetousness in him, even back then.

He turns it into a smile.

"…We only get tastes. Right, Mr. G.?" he jokes. "Scraps and bites?"

Galaith doesn't respond. He watches Revik carefully.

"Are you all right?"

I feel Maygar's shock expanding, pulling on me.

What? I send, irritated at his pulling. I cannot take my eyes off Revik.

Did you not hear me? Maygar hisses. *That man… he is a human being! He is not seer at all. It is impossible that he can do these things!*

Galaith's outline keeps getting brighter.

Revik steps back warily as the human's light body flashes out in a hard arc.

Galaith raises a hand towards the field, and I see a Nazi soldier's eyes flash silver, just before he bends to light a torch on one of the loaded wagons.

Galaith turns to Revik.

"This war can be over in months," he says. "Already, two million have died in the camps. Should we wait until it is four million? Ten million?"

Revik hesitates, staring out over the field.

"Hitler needs to die," Terian adds. "If the humans want a leader, we'll give them one. We'll give them all the dreams and laws and bullshit racial policies they desire. But why should *seers* die for the madness of humanity? Why? When we can bring peace so easily?"

Revik stares down the hill.

I remember Russia, the frozen bodies, the smell of burning flesh, and realize Revik is remembering, too.

The first gas tank detonates.

An inexplicable grief expands in my light as fire blows back the line of soldiers. They are murderers, too, I think. But my thoughts and fears and rationalizations are all caught up in Revik's, the wanting to believe he can be a part of something, that he can make it better. That he can be more than simply a bystander, helpless as history unfolds.

Terian ducks as the fireball expands.

Then, he starts to laugh.

Screams fill the clearing, along with smoke and fast-moving shrapnel. Seconds later, meat comes crashing down. I realize it is from the mule that pulled the cart and feel another surge of nausea as legs and arms rain down, too, some of the feet still wearing boots.

"Revik?" Galaith watches him, waiting. "Are you ready?"

Revik hesitates. He almost looks afraid.

"How many seers did they kill?" Galaith asks. "How many burned in the gas chambers as you watched from the Barrier, cousin?"

Revik holds up his hand.

Seeing his fingers shake slightly, I will him to lower it. I know this is past, that it has already happened. I know I cannot change any of it now, that it's too late. I even hear the logic in Galaith's words. I want the same revenge Revik wants for all those who died, but I will him to hear me anyway, to not do this.

A blank-eyed soldier lowers a second torch.

When it explodes, I flinch along with Revik.

Shock rips holes in the turf, throwing wood and iron as shrapnel into standing lines of men. The SS don't move out of the way, even when burning metal embeds in their flesh, or catches their hair or clothes on fire, or splatters hot oil across their skin.

I see Revik's jaw harden. Without being asked by Galaith, he focuses down the hill again.

The third soldier lowers his torch.

There is another hollow boom.

Terian is laughing again, jumping up and down as black smoke plumes outward in a mushroom-shaped cloud. Revik stares at the torn-up field in angry shock as Terian hits him playfully on the chest, then starts down the hill to view the carnage up close.

He leaves Galaith and Revik to stand there alone.

"What are you?" Revik asks, looking at him.

I feel Maygar beside me, tensing for the answer.

Galaith smiles. "Perhaps you should ask yourself that question, Rolf." He smiles, squeezing Revik's shoulder. "I'm very, very proud of you, my son."

Revik stares down at the field below the hill.

His eyes still show a dim shock, but I recognize the predatory curiosity there as well. The intent focus accompanies a fire that powers a hotter engine beneath his controlled veneer.

Interesting choice for a mate, Maygar sends.

I turn on him, fighting the pain that throbs hotter as I fight to breathe.

Let it go, all right? Let it go! That pain in my chest worsens. *He reformed. He left them after this. You heard Vash. And you don't know anything about his life, why he would have chosen this—*

Maygar grunts, looking at Revik with utter loathing.

His self-righteousness infuriates me.

Whatever your trip is with him, it's infantile, I tell him. *He's dead!*

Real anger flashes in Maygar's light.

Infantile? He catches my light arm in his hand. *I saw it, Esteemed Bridge. I fucking* saw *it! I looked at all of the records from when Dehgoies Revik "reformed." I saw what happened when they brought him in. Half-dead, beaten to a pulp by his own and then our men. You should have heard the litany of garbage he spewed, as the Adhipan worked to detach him from that Pyramid filth! It took them days to get it off. Weeks. And all the while, the whole construct was treated to the lovely things your husband did while in the Rooks' employ...*

Maygar's eyes flash colder as he looks down the hill.

The things I saw as they unwound those structures made me physically ill, Bridge. I did not sleep. I could not want anything but his death for days. So do not tell me I am infantile. Do not tell me anything *about that man. Not until you've seen what he is for yourself!*

I stare at Maygar through the Barrier.

I can't think about what he's said. My mind is empty, blank.

Do not kid yourself, he says. *They recruited him for one reason. At his core, he was an evil fucking bastard. That's all he* ever *was, Esteemed Bridge.*

I look at Revik.

Revik from the past, but still the light I know.

He is looking at me, too, I realize.

I am standing there, watching his face, when roughly, Maygar uses his *aleimi* to change our frequency. As soon as he does, the past around me unravels.

The last thought I have as I lose him yet again is that I'm thirsty.

More thirsty than I've ever been in my life.

CHAPTER 39
SACRIFICE

He feels her. He feels her skin, the ends of her fingers as she caresses him.

She touches his face. She touches his arms, his chest… gaos, *his cock.*

He thinks of all the times he wanted her to touch him, that he fantasized about her touching him. He thinks about what he could have done differently, what he should have done differently—in Seattle, on the ship, even in the dirt that night in Vancouver.

They are kissing again. His tongue thickens, pain rising in his belly.

She reaches for him, and he opens at once.

But that something rears up again.

It fucks with him, twists his light, forcing him back.

His wanting turns to aggression, frustration, a bleak hopelessness when she returns. She opens to him. She tries to let him in, to let him feel her… but it's never enough.

It's never fucking enough.

Gods… she's screwing with him. She's teasing him, trying to make him insane. She knows he's in pain, that he can't go to her.

But something darker lingers there.

Someone else is with her.

She isn't alone.

HE GROANED, UNWILLINGLY AWAKE.

Lying on a wet tile floor, he couldn't move.

The pain sharpened as he lay there, worsening as the ache in his arms and neck returned. He was shivering, naked, freezing cold, so fucking thirsty he couldn't think about much else. The pain on his neck and back felt like fire.

Water still ran over his bare skin.

It occurred to him then. He hadn't been asleep. He'd passed out.

The other seer dropped the water spigot. Crouching down, he stared into Revik's face.

"Feeling better, Revi'?"

Revik threw out his light in reflex and the collar around his neck tripped, bringing another blinding jolt. His head snapped back. He groaned, unable to help it.

"Apparently so," Terian gazed down Revik's body. "Missing her again, are we?"

He fought to go unconscious again, willing it.

"Let's go over it again…"

Revik tried to remember the line of questioning they'd been on, couldn't.

"Who has the succession order, Revi'?"

The sickness worsened. "I don't know," he said.

"Really?" Terian walked around his inert form. "Shall we pull your friend out of her cage again? Maybe if I played with her a bit, that might jog your memory?"

Revik clutched the chain where it attached to the floor.

He avoided the female with his light, but he couldn't help looking for her with his eyes. Her naked body lay slumped in an iron box against the far wall, her eyes half-lidded, catatonic. The slack look on her face was more than he could bear, worse than the long cut that bisected her delicate features. He remembered the last time Terian brought her out here, felt his stomach lurch even as his eyes drifted to her feet bleeding through the dirty gauze he'd used to staunch the blood. He'd taken two of her toes that time, one from each foot.

"No," he said, hoarse.

"No?" Terian asked. "Say please, Revi'."

"Please." His eyes returned to the floor. "Please, I—"

"All right." Terian smiled, waving him off. "...Since you're being a good boy." His eyes narrowed. "The succession order, Revi'. The truth this time. I have it from very reliable sources that you were the only one who had it after Galaith."

Revik hesitated, trying to think.

Terian kicked him, hard, aiming at the muscled part of his thigh, and he gasped.

"I don't know," he said. "I swear it's the truth. You can read me... you know I'm not lying. If I ever had it, they wiped it when I left—"

Terian kicked him again.

Revik shifted half to his side, fighting to breathe.

Rocking on his heels, Terian touched his lips with a finger, gazing up at the ceiling.

"Yes," he said. "That memory loss is most irritating. But you know I don't fully believe you, don't you, Revi'? Your light is different, you see. Ever since that day on the ship, it is different than it was. I know you can't feel it with that restraining device around your neck, but take my word for it, brother. You. Are. Different."

He prodded Revik's back with his boot at each word.

"You feel much more like my old friend than you did in San Francisco. So much so, I have a hard time believing you when you say you don't remember."

Revik closed his eyes, breathing into the tile.

They'd been over this.

He'd lost track of answers he'd given, contradicted, lied about. He knew Terian likely no longer listened for details, anyway. By now he knew exactly what Revik did and didn't know. What he hadn't said aloud had been ripped from his mind—about Allie, every intimate detail. Work he'd done under Vash. His job in the Guard. How he'd spent his years in Russia. Work he'd done for the British government. Work he'd done for the Adhipan.

It wouldn't be enough.

This had become an endurance game, and he would lose.

Even as he thought it, the rod jabbed at muscles in his back, just enough that he reflexively tried to block it.

"What were you dreaming about, Revi'? Just now?"

Images swam forward. He saw Allie again, her hands on his chest, holding his arms. He felt her pulling on him and hardened painfully.

Now that he was powerless to block it, the separation was like a drug. It brought wanting, regret, memory in sharp relief, emotions he could barely comprehend, much less control. The sickness worsened. For a moment, he could only lie there, half-gasping.

The collar sparked.

Terian bent down, gripping his hair, pulling his head back.

"Every time. You know, Revi'... your eyes glow every time I mention her. You really are a mess, my friend." He relaxed his hold, adding casually, "It's not like I have a lot of telekinetic seers to study, to see the effects they have on their mates. But the glow eye thing of yours intrigues me. So do those lights you managed to shatter on the ship."

His eyes turned clinical, studying Revik's face.

"Incidentally, I was with your wife while you were fucking that human." A half-smile tugged at his lips as Revik looked away. "If your goal was to hear her beg, I think it was working, brother. Truly. I very seriously considered mounting her myself."

He gripped Revik's hair tighter, forcing him to look at him. He bent closer to his ear, his voice a murmur. "The images coming off her... gods. I could have called in the whole Guard. We could have taken turns. I don't think she would have minded a bit, Revi'. Not a bit."

Revik fought the image out of his light and the collar tripped, sending white fire down his spine. When Terian released him, he lay his face against the tile, breathed into the cold floor.

His eyes caught those of the other human in the room, who squatted in a cage next to the one where Cass lay broken against the wall. The man there looked even skinnier and paler than Revik, if that were possible. Seeing the sympathy there, Revik closed his eyes.

He felt Jon's light reach for his, a pale comfort.

Bright... so bright for a human.

Too bright.

The yellow eyes swiveled in Jon's direction.

"Interesting." Terian rose, starting towards the row of cages where

Jon was already moving, scurrying to put his back to the wall, as far away from the cage's door as possible.

Revik lifted his head, writhed to his stomach.

"Fucking dirt blood," he gasped.

Terian halted, halfway to where Jon hunched in the corner.

Revik fought for breath, pushing out words. "You'd give your cock to be me. That's the real reason you're doing this. Not to find Allie. Not for any fictitious 'succession order'… but to pretend you're stronger than me. That you *beat* me. It's pathetic, Terry."

Terian turned.

Behind him, Jon waved Revik off, his hazel eyes rounded in horror. Revik's gaze fixed on the human's bandaged hand. His jaw hardened.

"It speaks." Terian folded his arms, cocking his head with narrow eyes. "Wow, Revi'. Did you just… insult me?" His smile widened. "I confess, I didn't think you had it in you. Not after our last go-around."

Revik's throat was so dry he was hoarse. "You still can't *stand* the fact that Galaith made me second over you. He'd still take me back, Terry. In a fucking heartbeat. You know that, too."

Terian smiled, gesturing him forward. "Go on."

Revik saw the hardness beneath the smile.

He'd reached him.

But not enough.

"Feigran, right? Wasn't that your name?"

Terian's smile grew leaden.

"I remember." Revik's fingers tightened around the chains. "A shit-blood from Ukraine. Dugress, right? A town *I* destroyed… on accident, I admit. I don't remember." He barked a laugh. "I was drunk a lot back then, but there's no way I'd destroy a crap town of beet farmers on purpose. We were short on ammo as it was…"

Terian's full mouth thinned.

Behind him, Jon had gone rigid.

"I had to study files on all of my…" Revik barked another hoarse laugh. "*…subordinates.* It's coming back to me now. You're one of those inbred seers with an inferiority complex, is that it? Saw too many of your relatives go to the gas chambers? I guess that would hit at your self-esteem a little. Supposedly superior race, and you're exterminated like rats." He coughed, tasting blood. "Tell me, did your father really get so poor he sold his *wife?* Did he sell you, too, Feigran? Is that how the Rooks acquired you? For a few dead animals and—"

The rod came down hard, in the middle of his chest.

Revik stopped breathing, losing all sense of where he was.

Pain whited out his vision. He blocked it and the collar flared around his neck. Before he could go unconscious, Terian stepped forward and kicked him in the face. The shock yanked Revik out of his mind just as the mixer hit him lower with the rod.

That time, it was low enough to bring a scream.

For a long moment, Revik thought he was dead.

Terian lifted the pulse.

Groaning, nauseated, Revik tried to crawl away.

Terian stepped forward, kicking him in the stomach.

"You're damned lucky I want this body for myself, Revi'." The yellow eyes shone cold, lifeless, when Revik looked up. "I might find more creative things to do with it, if that were not the case. You should be thankful I have not yet run out of questions for your mind, too, because once I have, it will cease to exist."

Revik tried to clench his muscles when the Rook kicked him again.

He cowered, gasping, when Terian came closer, but that time, the other seer walked right up to his head. Crouching, he grabbed a fistful of his hair, yanking Revik's head back.

"Do you know what I'm going to do with this body of yours once it is mine, Revi'? Do you know the *very first thing* I will strive for? I'm going to find your darling Alyson, and I'm going to thank her properly for not coming for you. She won't walk right for weeks, I promise you."

Seeing the barely concealed look in the other's eyes, Terian grinned.

That time, it reached the rest of him.

"Ah, yes. You don't like that, do you? I bet you'd like to take an axe to *me* now... eh, Rolf?"

He let go of his hair, but didn't move away. He continued squatting there instead, watching him with narrow eyes.

"I don't know why you care so much all of a sudden, anyway," Terian said. "You were hardly the model husband, Revi'. Selling your cock to humans. Getting blow jobs from Seattle hookers while she slept alone. If she'd been raised seer, she would have stabbed you in your sleep by now, my friend. I wouldn't even be *able* to torture you."

Watching Revik avert his eyes, the Rook folded his hands between his bent knees.

He let his voice grow thoughtful.

"I can't help but wonder how long it took her to act on that separation pain, once she didn't have you around to screw with her head." Watching Revik's face, he clicked at him softly. "You could have popped that cherry, my friend. Can you imagine? Being the very *first* inside the Bridge. And as a mate, no less. And you call *me* pathetic."

Revik stared down at his hands. Blood dripped on them from his mouth. He remembered the presence he'd felt around her, and the sickness in his gut worsened. Terian's words replayed themselves in his mind, and he couldn't even disagree with them.

Terian laughed aloud, clapping him on the shoulder.

"Ah, that reassures me, Revi'. You know I am right!" The seer leaned closer. "Hey! Revi'!" A smile lit up the handsome features. "Do you think that's why she hasn't come looking for you?"

Reaching down, he massaged Revik's cock.

He smiled when the other man groaned.

"Maybe she doesn't even want this inside her anymore, eh Revi'? Or do you think she's the type to get off on mass-murderers? Tell me honestly. Are my chances with her better or worse, if she thinks I'm you?"

Revik writhed as far away as he could with his wrists bolted to the floor. He fought to contract his light, but the collar only flared again. Terian gave his testicles a brief, hard squeeze, laughing, then let go. Revik nearly blacked out.

Turning, Terian smiled at Jon, winking. "Want to help him out this time, sport-o?"

In the cage next to Jon, Cass rattled the bars. "Stop it!" she screamed. "Leave him alone!"

Revik raised his head. *Gaos.* Not now.

Cass couldn't get his attention now, not when Terian was—

"I think you have fans, Revi'." Terian glanced down at him. "Shall we reminisce about the old days? Or simply act them out? I'm sure they would love to hear about how we used to get our kicks, you and I. How much alike we once were."

"I hope he kills you!" Cass screamed louder.

"Oh-ho!" Terian laughed, squatting by Revik again. He tapped him on the head. "Remember that French girl in Bangladesh? The one Colonel Harding was so fond of? How long did you manage to keep her alive? Was it two weeks? Three?" He glanced at Cass. "You were a lot more fun back then. You had better taste in friends, too, as I recall."

His yellow-gold eyes went flat, studying Cass clinically.

Revik shook his head. "I don't remember."

Rocking his weight back to rest on his heels, Terian cocked his head. "You know, I can't even tell if I believe you. You so clearly want to believe yourself."

He rested his arms on his thighs, his voice serious.

"You know, don't you, Revi'? You know the truth about you and me. You know, deep down, that I have only the purest of motives in bringing you here. You are sick, you see. You have lost your way. I want my friend back. Back on the side of non-hypocrisy, of fun, of ideals with practical application. I want you to face reality. To remember who you are."

He smiled wider, glancing at Cass before he looked back at Revik.

"Barring that, I might have to peel your skin off in little strips like one of those ingenious devices we used in Prague… do you remember, Revi'? Just to deal with my disappointment, you see."

Revik swallowed, not looking up.

Terian grabbed his wet hair. "Are you telling me to flay the girl instead? Or maybe the pretty young boy-cousin?"

Revik's eyes found Cass and Jon without his willing it. The seer was pushing him to focus there, but he thought about them anyway.

Maybe he could make it quick.

If Terian tried to fulfill one of those fantasies, it would be the easiest thing in the world to break Cass's neck. The thought made the sickness worse, enough that he lowered his face back to the tile, fighting to breathe.

He wondered how much of it was his, and how much Allie's.

Laughing, Terian released him.

"Oh, Rolf. You are the clever one. I suppose I may have to wait on my fun, then. At least until you learn it's bad manners to break the nice toys I give you."

Still squatting beside him, he studied Revik's eyes.

"Tell me honestly," he said softly. "Tell me the truth, Revi', and I'll leave the girl alone. For today, at least… I won't touch her. Are my chances with your wife better or worse wearing this beat up body of yours?"

Revik closed his eyes, wiping his jaw with his hand.

He glanced up, feeling the sickness lodge somewhere in his chest.

"I don't know," he said.

Terian just looked at him for a moment. Then his smile hardened.

"You really don't." He clicked softly. "You may not believe this, Revi', but I find that sad." Straightening, he regarded the man lying at his feet. "The Dehgoies I knew wouldn't have played those games with someone he was courting, much less his *wife*. Your first wife seemed to think you were a good husband. When you weren't off gassing your own kind, that is."

Prodding him with a foot, he sighed, hands on his hips.

"Enough. Just looking at you is making me tired." He glanced around the green tile room, the splashes of bloody water on the walls and floor. "For your touching display of loyalty to Alyson's childhood friends, you have sustained a break."

Stepping back, he wiped his hands on his pants, grinning at him.

"I'd like to reward you, though. Your humans, too… once I've washed the shit smell off me from you. So expect another visit today, all right, brother?"

Without another word, he walked to the mirrored wall.

Touching a panel, he disappeared through the opening that formed in the organic metal.

Once the hole melted shut, Revik slumped to the floor.

He pressed his mouth to the wet tile, trying to inhale blood-tasting water, but the floor sloped in the wrong direction, leaving it slick but almost dry. The attempt only frustrated him, made his thirst desperate.

Jon's voice came at him jaggedly from the nearer cage.

"Revik." His English was hoarse. "Revik! Listen to me, goddamn it."

Revik turned, fighting his eyes clear, his voice. "What, Jon?"

"Keep pushing him like that and he's going to kill you. Stop it, alright? Just stop! I mean it, man… stop."

"Yeah." Cass's voice slurred. "Stop it."

Revik said, "It's okay. We're fine, Jon… Cass."

"Don't give me that shit!" Jon said. "You can't go suicidal on us, man! You can't! We need you. We fucking *need* you."

"We're okay," Revik repeated. "We're okay, Jon…"

He lay there, willing his mind blank, wishing more than anything he could go back to where Allie slept. She didn't always find him. There were gaps that went for days.

Eventually she'd stop looking.

Pain blinded him at the thought. He rolled over onto his stomach.

His eyes closed when Jon's voice jerked them open again.

"God." Jon stared at him, eyes hollow. He licked his lips, staring still, as if examining the damage. "Thanks… okay?" He clutched a bar with his mutilated hand, twisting on the metal. "Thanks. I mean it. Just take it easy. Don't provoke him anymore. Don't let him kill you. We need you, man. We need you…"

"We're okay…"

"Are you listening to me?"

Revik acknowledged the human's words with a nod, then let his head slump to the tile.

He promptly fell unconscious.

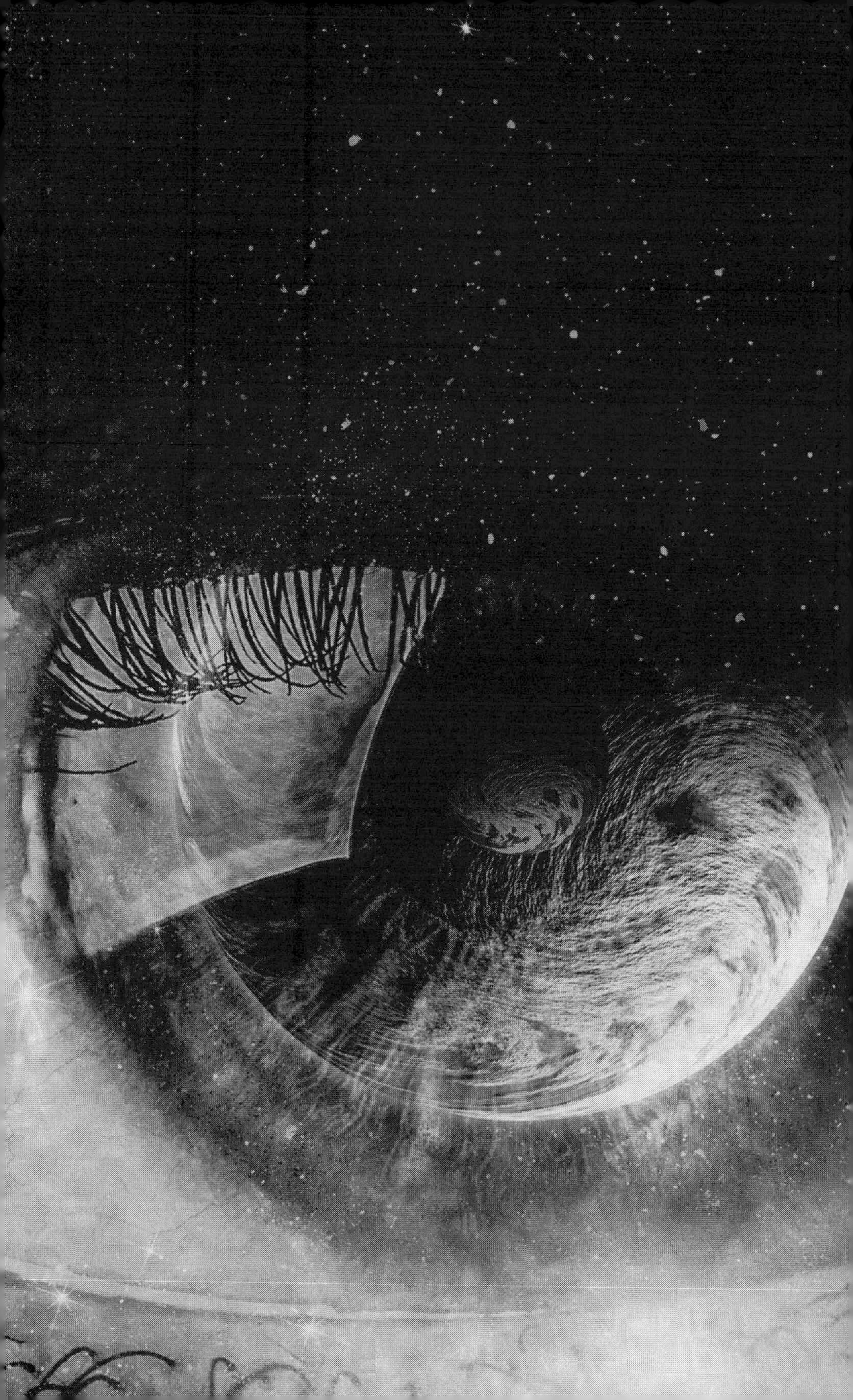

CHAPTER 40
WIRE

Revik! Wake up! Come back… come back to me!

He reached for her with his light. Fire shot into his neck, gritting his teeth.

"Dehgoies."

A different voice.

"Dehgoies Revik?"

He tried to lift his head. His tongue had dried into his mouth. He couldn't swallow. His temples pounded. He fought to clear his eyes, watching as a man placed a chair more than a body length from where Revik lied on the tile.

Middle-aged with dark skin.

Likely a seer from his physical appearance and the expression in his eyes.

His human-based ethnicity was closer to Indian than Eastern European or Chinese. He wore his wood-brown hair wound in a clip, and clothing reminiscent of Terian in the 1940s.

Revik focused on his own hands, feeling his pulse rise.

"What shall I call you?" the new body said.

Revik glanced at the far wall. The cages that normally housed Cass and Jon were empty.

Feeling his breath shorten, Revik tried not to let his panic show on his face.

The new body regained its feet, walking closer. Revik recoiled, but the seer only set something on the floor, within reach of his hands.

It was a glass of water.

The body returned to its chair, sat.

Revik stared at the water… but only for an instant.

Throwing his upper body forward, he reached for the glass, pulling the container closer with his fingers. He sniffed it… and ducked his head before he could come to anything conclusive, tilting the glass to his mouth as he sucked the liquid down greedily. When it was empty, he licked condensation off the sides.

He was still pressing the cold glass to his face when the body regained its feet and strolled closer, plucking the empty glass out of his hands. Revik watched in disbelief as the body carried the glass to the spigot on the wall, using the thin, high-pressure hose to fill it again. When the seer walked back, he placed the new glass on the same section of floor.

He stood there, watching Revik drink.

"You never answered me about the name," the seer said. "Is it Revik now? Rolf? What does your new wife call you?"

"Dehgoies." Revik tilted the glass for the last swallow, then pushed it carefully toward the other's feet. "Where are Jon and Cass?" His voice was thick, but he could speak again.

The seer smiled. "Would you like another?"

"Yes," Revik said. "Where's Jon? Cass?"

The body bent for the glass. He strolled casually back to the spigot.

"Cassandra required medical treatment." He refilled the glass and walked back, setting it on the floor. "And I wanted to talk to you alone, Dehgoies."

"You're Terian?" Revik brought the glass closer, lowering his mouth to the cool liquid.

He'd never tasted anything so good.

He drank with eyes closed, slower this time.

The body smiled. "Terian. Well, that's an interesting question, Dehgoies. Yes, I am Terian." He paused, watching Revik drink. He said, quieter, "Jon is right. You are pushing the other body too far, old friend. I can only control him so much."

Revik laughed. He didn't lose a drop of water.

Watching him, Terian clicked under his breath.

"Must I put you on suicide watch again?" He watched Revik gulp down more water. "Relax, my friend. Slow. I will not take it."

Revik tilted his head, finishing off the last of the water. He used his lips to take the condensation, cooling his face.

"You don't look very well yourself," Terian observed. "And yet, you still haven't met the worst of my personas, Dehgoies. Trust me when I tell you, the Terian I've been using to interrogate you is a petulant child compared to the ones I have for less... delicate exercises. I call him Terian-6. I am Terian-2." He spread his hands. "It simplifies things."

Revik made his face expressionless.

"Are you willing to talk to me?" Terian asked.

"Sure." Revik set down the glass. "Can I have more?"

The body made a line in the air with one finger, a seer's "no."

He added, "You obviously don't trust me to not kick it over or make you piss in it. So I will pace your consumption for you."

He folded his hands, tilting his head as he continued to examine Revik. His handsome face appeared greenish in the overhead light.

"You present us with an interesting puzzle, Dehgoies. You see, I do not wish for anyone to know you continue to exist on this plane. So I am unable to utilize the Barrier the way I would normally. Inducement wires would be tricky, at best..."

The seer ticked off the list with his fingers.

"...Drugs must be avoided for the same reason. I do not want to kill you. I would also prefer you with your limbs and organs intact. If I scan you outright, you will fight me, whether you mean to or not. If I scan deeply enough, there is a very good chance the telepathic restraint will kill you. Or destroy your mind, and I do not wish for that either. I obviously cannot deactivate the restraint."

Terian-2 spread his hands wider apart, smiling.

"Truly? I wish I had my friend Dehgoies to ask. He was always so very good at puzzles of this kind."

Revik kept the irritation off his face.

Terian-2 added, "You always had a bit of a dark twist in your methods, Revi'. I wonder now, was that from the wars, also? Did your creativity blossom questioning French prisoners? Or was it the Nazis themselves who sparked this in you?"

Revik stared at his hands clasped on the floor.

The bones in them pressed against taut skin.

He could feel something trying to get at him, a pale, silvery thread, hovering over his light. Paranoia bit at the edges of his mind, a vague memory of being lost. Worse than that, he felt the buttons the seer was trying to push, a flicker of pleasure that tried to insinuate itself, to flex into parts of him that lay dormant but unlocked. Memories tried to coalesce, to remind him of other things he'd been good at, once.

It occurred to him that his sight reflex ought to have kicked in.

The collar should have ignited when he flexed his light.

But his mind felt relaxed.

Too relaxed.

He stared at the empty glass.

"Yes. Well. I did say drugs should be *avoided,* Revi'," Terian-2 said apologetically. "But it is not practical to eliminate them altogether. They must be handled with care, of course. You always did have that odd tolerance."

Terian-2 studied him like an insect climbing wet tile.

"It may help you to remember. That would be good for you, yes? Less confusing?"

Revik's fingers tightened on the glass.

"You see, I have a theory," Terian-2 said, thoughtful. "I think you have been remembering for some time, Revi'. I am curious to see how much of you is awake ahead of your conscious mind." He watched Revik's eyes. "I also truly do believe you have the succession order, my friend. Or perhaps you did something with it, yes? Something you forgot?"

When Revik continued to stare at the glass, Terian sighed, clicking.

"I confess, I still find it very difficult to read you. Even now, when you are ostensibly under my power, I feel I know you less, not more." His dark lips thinned as he studied Revik's face. "Some of this is act, yes. But not all. You hide behind a veneer of obedience. Obedience to Galaith, to me, to the Seven. To your Ancestors. It does make me wonder what lies beneath."

Internally, Revik rolled his eyes.

Smiling, Terian lit an expensive-smelling *hiri* stick, exhaling a cloud of sweet-smelling smoke. Revik's hunger worsened.

"I suppose I understand," Terian said. "In part, at least. The way you were raised, you would have had plenty of practice in both lying and submission." He bit gently on the end of the *hiri,* sucking resin. "And yet, in all of these months, I find it astonishing that I have yet to see a response from you that did not feel amazingly well-scripted. I believe all of this actually bores you on some level, am I right?"

Revik stared at his hands.

When the silence stretched, he gave a sort of barking laugh.

Terian smiled, settling his weight back in his chair.

"If you do not wish to speak of the succession order, perhaps we can speak of other things. Tell me about Elise, Rolf." He ashed the *hiri.* "How did you come to marry a human? How did you come to be in Germany at all?"

Revik's mind remained lax.

Images seeped through cracks.

Her dead eyes grew into her living ones, smiling at him, laughing as she waded through tall grass, trailing dark hair. He caught her fingers, then the rest of her, and it was familiar, so familiar… but deadened somehow, far away. She was taking off his clothes before he'd caught his breath, asking him, and he lied with her. He could barely hold it once he was inside.

Time rushed forward.

He was older, bigger. She looked small to him now.

She blindfolded him, taking him into her studio. A wall of their house, painted with the sword and sun…

Everything went dark.

When he opened his eyes, he was on the cold tile, naked, shaking with pain.

Tears poured down his face. He didn't know where he was. He felt Terian with him briefly, his friend, laying an arm on his shoulder, laughing as he told another story about that hooker he'd loved in Paris…

Terian-2 clapped his hands. "Wake up, Revi'! Wake!"

He opened his eyes.

He heard her voice, but too far away this time; he couldn't make out her words. Walls dripped like liquid mercury around him. He was afraid he'd get some in his mouth, but he was so thirsty still, he almost didn't care.

Terian set down a new glass of water. He stood, watching Revik drink. Revik calculated the length of his arms, the range of motion provided by the chain.

He mapped out every centimeter, every millimeter.

"…like Alyson?"

Revik opened his eyes. He blinked. "What?"

"Elise, Revi'. Do you remember?"

"She slept with him," Revik managed. "Had his child."

The light evaporated. He dug frantically in the dark, his fingers broken and bleeding. He was starving to death slowly, so thirsty he couldn't swallow. Laughter came from outside the iron door, a shock of light after the lock screeched from the wall. Merenje stood there, drunk, stumbling at the top of the stairs. He had a woman with him, her eyes were green—

"Want to play with an ice-blood, girl? A real one?"

Revik yanked on the chain, growling. His wrists bled.

Terian slapped him, hard. "Who did you report to, Revi'? In those years?"

Revik saw a black swastika on a white circle, blood red behind. Bodies piled in pits, like bleached white dolls. Out of bullets. He was out of bullets. They wanted him to beat them to death now, hit them with gun stocks in the back of the head, rocks, run them over with panzers. Memories slithered forward. She ran through the field, trailing dark hair. Brown eyes laughing, teasing him to follow, to chase her.

Leaning down, Revik sank his teeth into his own wrist, holding the vein right where his canines would pop it.

He rolled his eyes up, fixed his stare on Terian.

The Sark chuckled. "You would not."

Revik bit down, hard.

Blood squirted into his mouth.

He was hungry, so fucking hungry. He drank his own blood, feeling sick, strangely relieved. It would be over now. Out of the corner of his eye he saw the seer rise, saw his mouth move just before everything started to gray.

HIS EYES OPENED.

Time passed, or not.

He couldn't move his head. He tried to lift it, then his arms. Terian squatted beside him, his yellow eyes calm.

"You will remember more now, Revi'," he said. "I can't say I envy you, when you do. But perhaps you will feel free again, yes?"

Revik saw a tube running down, dripping liquid, mingling with his blood.

Something squirmed on his neck and throat. Something alive.

He remembered Allie feeding him light, curled up in his arms when he first woke up in that bed in Seattle. Pain hit him, worsening as he wondered why he hadn't kept her there, why he let himself fall back asleep, why he hadn't followed her when she left the room. He remembered her fingers as she sketched, her jade green eyes concentrated... telling him she wanted to go after Galaith, the light in her eyes dying when he said he wouldn't help her.

He was right.

Gods, Terry was right.

Why hadn't he asked her? Why hadn't he fucking *asked* her, in all of that time?

A rusted metal building loomed over him, standing alone in the middle of a field.

He looked up, and saw windows smashing outwards, glass shattering, pulverized to the consistency of sand. He heard his own voice, laughing into the sky, laughing, imagining that fucker Stami's face if he saw him now...

Cass sat near him, chained to the wall. Giant insects crawled by her feet, touching her skin with softly probing antennae.

"Cass," Revik managed. "Don't move. Be careful..."

She grinned. *Hey, big guy. You want one?*

Raising her foot, she smashed the hard brown shell of a fist-sized beetle with her bare heel. She picked it up, stuffed the whole thing in her mouth, crunching noisily.

He watched her, feeling sick, faintly envious. Hunger tugged at the edges of his light, making his head sink lower, making it feel as heavy as iron.

"They gave me too much," Revik told her.

It's the wire, brother. The wire on your neck…

Cass laughed, her mouth full of jointed legs. She flattened another insect, popped that one in her mouth, too. Jon stood over her, making chopping motions in the air with his hands. He wore a robe like the monks wore back home.

Revik got dizzy, watching his flailing arms.

Stop screwing around, Jon told him. *Clock's ticking, man.*

"…Do not misunderstand me," Terian-2 was saying. "Over the years, I have found it patently not useful to judge the contradictory natures that arise within myself. Where they occur, I simply create a new vessel in which to house them." He leaned closer, clasping lizard-like hands. His tongue darted out, wetting his lips, and Revik recoiled. "You can see the symmetry behind this, can you not, my friend?" Terian's teeth lengthened. "All parts culminating in their most authentic expression? There is no need for repression, Nenzi. No need to hold back any desires housed in the darker corners of your attic…"

Revik swallowed, staring up at him. "I'm really fucking hungry. Can I have some food?"

Terian laughed. "Now that… *that* sounded like my friend! Is it possible I am reaching him at last? No, no… do not sleep. You have slept enough, Revi'…"

Revik glanced at Jon. "Do you believe this guy?"

Jon laughed. *Him? What about you, man? He's right, you know. You can't just spend the rest of your life asleep.*

"What choice do I have, Jon?"

You need to get laid, man. I mean bad. I hope Allie's been exercising.

"Gods." Pain clenched in his chest "Don't talk about her like that. She's my wife, Jon."

Blood darkened the water by his hands.

Someone slapped his face, disorienting him.

"Why were you in Germany, Rolf?"

Revik fought to see, couldn't.

His eyes were light, just light. He couldn't see past it.

Terian flicked his fingers impatiently. "Yes?" He tilted his head, as if listening. "You killed some humans? Really? Well, I ask you… *so what?* How many millions of seers have died at human hands, Revi'?" He leaned closer. "Tell me. Do you really care, even now? Or is this an act, too?"

Revik looked at Cass. "I care, Cass. I do care…"

I know you do, big guy. That's why you're talking to me. She grinned, making the crazy sign with a finger by her head. *Better than remembering* that *shit, right? Maybe you were right to wait with Allie. She's going to rip it open, you know. She can't help herself.*

Revik pressed his face to the floor. The cold tile felt good.

He was ravenous—so hungry he couldn't think straight, couldn't make himself want to. When he glanced up, Jon was throwing pieces of meat in the air, catching them in his teeth. He worried each one before he swallowed them, flecking the green walls with blood.

Revik felt himself getting hard, watching him. He stared at his fingers, broken and bleeding, digging in mud. He was almost there. He could see daylight.

Terian's eyes were dead, burnt glass. "You see, I am becoming increasingly certain it wasn't by accident that Galaith and I stumbled upon you in Germany, Rolf. Nor a coincidence that you *exactly fit* our most desired recruitment profile. Estranged from family. Few friends. No strong political beliefs. Willing to kill humans."

His amber eyes grew predatory.

"…Willing to follow questionable means for morally justified ends. You could have guessed we'd concentrate our initial recruitment efforts in the Reich."

Terian smiled, waggling a finger at him.

"You always were the clever one, Rolf. Were you Vash's man, all along? Were you, Nenz?"

"Why do you keep calling me that?" he managed.

"Do I need to bring her here for real? To get you to talk? I seem to recall you were at your most malleable when you thought I had your wife in custody, too…"

Revik saw her then. His heart clenched until he couldn't breathe. Allie watched him from where she lay twisted on the floor, her neck broken.

Her green eyes stared at his, dead-looking, a smoky gray.

He let out a groan, reaching for her. *"No. Gods… please."*

"So when did their plans go wrong, Rolf? Was it when we killed Elise?" Terian leaned closer, his amber eyes hard. "Did you blame the Seven for that? But that was *your* fault, wasn't it, Rolf? Dragging a vulnerable human into the middle of your very dangerous game? A bit arrogant, yes?"

Revik tried to concentrate on his words, couldn't.

"Give me food. Please."

"Will you talk to me, if I do?"

His sickness worsened. "Yes." He fought tears. "Just don't hurt her. Please."

Terian regained his feet. Revik clutched the empty water glass to his chest. When he was younger he could size someone's range and limbs in a single look. Back then, he'd always known what space his body possessed, what he could do in that space, limitations, strengths, possible weapons… in case anything bad happened, which it frequently did.

Terian reached down, leaning over him.

Revik waited until the seer started to tug the empty glass from his fingers.

…and caught his wrist.

He whipped his legs around, smashing them into the back of Terian's calves. Throwing his torso backwards as far as the chain allowed, he yanked him forcibly to the floor.

His other hand shattered the glass.

The seer fell on him.

Revik rolled, half-pinning the body under his chest. Working his fingers quickly into strands of his hair, he jerked the head back. The Sark's eyes showed white.

"Rolf, no! This won't help you—"

Revik ground the shard of glass into the seer's throat.

A thin spray of blood hit him in the face.

Sliding the glass in as far as he could, he gasped, crying out, seeing himself covered in blood and fresh wounds and scars, naked, bearded, in a hundred mirrors. He tore through muscle, veins and skin, then ripped the shard out. Blood sprayed upwards in a hot arc.

The white throat pulsed, pouring thick fluid.

Revik stared down, watching, feeling his mind clear as…

The seer's eyes gradually lost light.

The blood slowed, pumping erratically from the jagged hole.

Revik continued to stare down, but the seer felt dead. He smelled dead.

Realizing he wore more than a collar, that it wasn't only drugs affecting his mind, he ripped the inducement wire from around his own throat. He stared down at the twisting, organic coil once he had, then flung it to the ground, looking in the room's corners.

Gasping, he fought to clear his head, to think.

Jon wasn't there. Neither was Cass. All he saw was his own reflection, replicated over and over. This might be more inducement dream, too.

If not, he had minutes, maybe seconds.

Flipping to his side, he brought the back of his neck down to his hands, fumbled his fingers over the length of the organic-metal collar he wore. It took him a few tries to activate the thumbnail switch. By the time he got it open he felt light-headed.

He thought he heard a noise in the outside corridor and grabbed the dead seer's hair. He flipped to his side, turning on the slick tile, angling the body's face towards the back of his neck, trying to align it with the retinal scanner.

Nothing happened.

Revik craned over his shoulder, saw the corpse's eyelids half-open, smeared with blood. He picked up a smaller shard of glass, slicing his fingers as he fumbled with it. He used the edge to shave off the eyelids, careful to not puncture the eye, wiping blood off each iris. The lids kept slipping from his fingers but he got most of it, prayed it was enough.

Shifting to his side again, he struggled to grip the blood-soaked hair, to hold the eyes in position. Dread, adrenaline and fear nearly made him black out.

He wrenched the head back, then fought to concentrate, crying out when it tripped the collar's anti-sight mechanism enough to cause a jolt of pain. He nearly let the body drop.

He didn't, though. He positioned his neck over those staring eyes…

He felt the click as much as heard it.

The prongs retracted, receding from his neck in one smooth pull. Gasping, he raised his head. The old reflex kicked in and that time it felt so good he groaned aloud.

Without waiting, he focused on the chains. He already knew they were tied into the organics of the room. He looked for the right organic being… and he remembered doing this before, although he hadn't done it in years. Within seconds, the being had stopped listening to the artificial intelligence that normally directed it, and was listening to Revik instead.

He heard footsteps. They sounded real this time.

Regaining his thread with the organics, Revik tried to talk to the damned thing, to coax the living metal to open.

He was breathing in so much oxygen he nearly passed out.

His vision cleared as an opening morphed in the wall, revealing a man with long, auburn hair. Terian-6 paused, seemed to take in the entirety of the scene: Revik contorted and cuffed to the floor, the dead body lying in a pool of blood behind him.

"Oh, Revi'…"

Terian-6 held the edges of the opening, his liquid eyes shining.

"You have no idea how much fun I'm going to have with you." He finished entering the room and Revik jerked back, startled when his arms moved with the rest of him.

He looked down. The chains lay open on the floor.

Terian-6 halted. He stared at Revik's hands, his muscular body suddenly tense.

"Revi'…" he said warningly.

Revik threw himself at the seer, using the water on the tile floor to slide across the meters between them. He saw Terian fumble for a pocket, moving frantically so that he jerked his elbow into the wall. Their bodies collided just before they slammed into the green organic surface together.

There was a loud crack as they hit, but Revik didn't stop grappling for the seer's neck.

Grasping hold of his throat, he slammed Terian-6's head against the glass, then again.

He did it again… and again… until the light eyes glazed.

He didn't realize the glass shard remained clutched in his hand until blood seeped through his fingers from the seer's throat.

Revik reached for the pocket the seer had been groping for, ripped a serrated knife from the cloth jacket. Without a pause, he flipped it open, plunged it into the seer's chest to the hilt and cut downwards, sawing like he was dressing meat. Hitting bone, he pulled it out and stabbed him again, going deeper into the chest cavity.

He did it again. And again.

He felt the shift in the other seer's light.

Revik held the dead weight against the glass wall, staring at its face.

Hesitating, staring between the Sark's eyes, he flipped the knife in his hand, letting the body slide down the wall to the floor. He knelt over it again, taking steps to ensure it wouldn't come back.

It wasn't until he'd severed the head from the neck that he felt the urgency and adrenaline in his limbs begin to abate.

He looked at the mutilated body, feeling light-headed. Ripping the deactivated collar from his neck, he leaned on the glass wall.

He couldn't pass out… couldn't.

He felt light again, his and others. A flood of presence grew so near and warm it shocked him, brought tears to his eyes. For a long moment, he let it hold him, trying to pull himself out of the dark, to feel something different.

Slowly, he felt himself grow almost calm.

There would be more bodies.

Terian built redundancy after redundancy into every system he created.

There would be more. Maybe a lot more.

He remembered Jon and Cass then, and dragged himself up the wall to his feet.

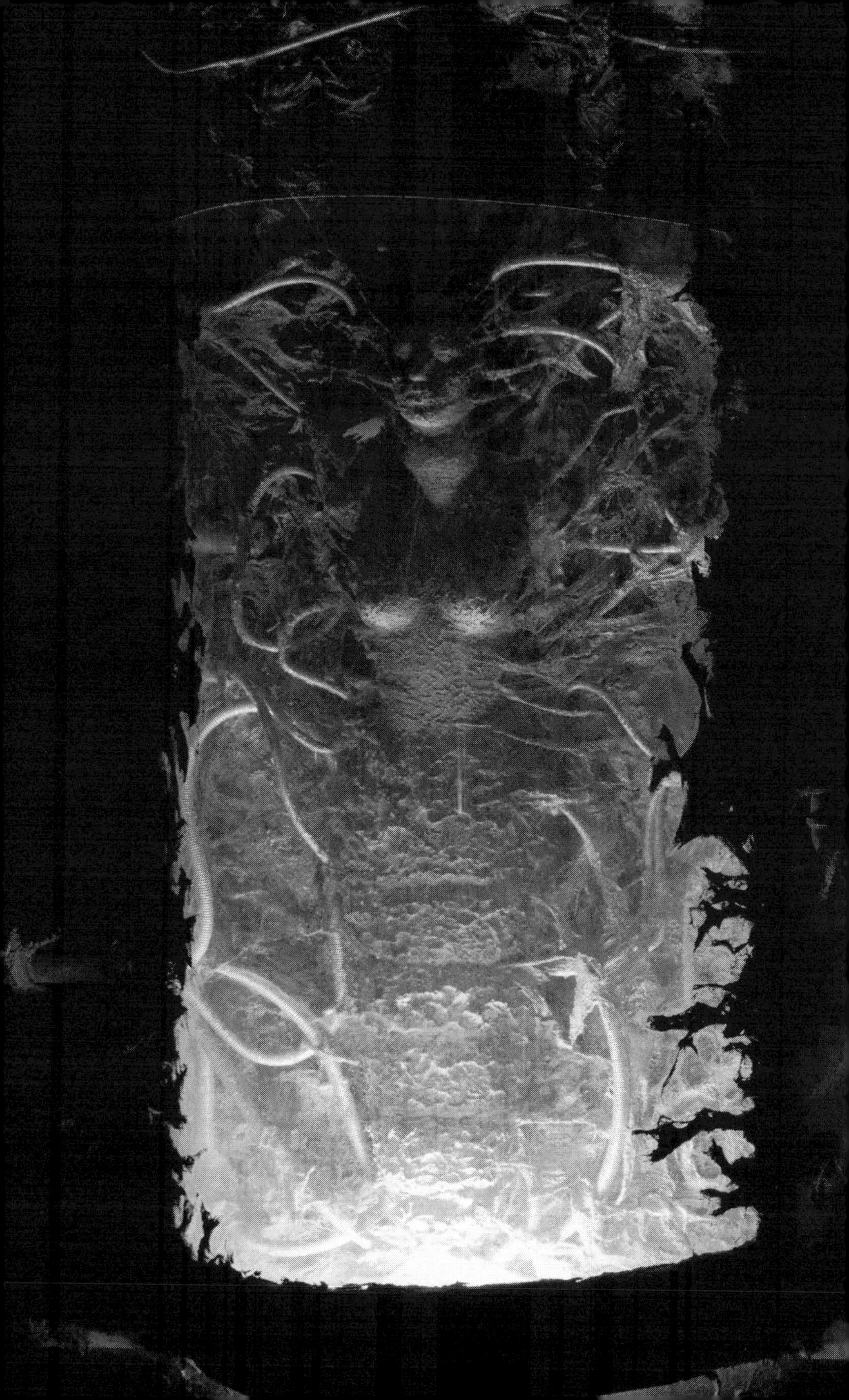

CHAPTER 41
RESPITE

Revik limped down a narrow, military-green corridor.

He felt a larger room up ahead.

Naked, he still had only the knife he'd gotten off Terian-6 and the body's belt wrapped around his knuckles. Hitting the panel to open the second set of doors, he slid behind the wall before peering out, using his sight to scope the room beyond.

His head felt clearer with the wire gone.

He was pretty sure he wasn't all right, though.

He could still feel something else, drugs probably, clouding his mind. Now, with the sight-restraint collar off his neck, and having left the green tile room that shielded his light, the drugs fought to take him out of his body, to make him too visible in the Barrier.

Taking a breath, he centered himself.

Stretching out his light, he located a weapons locker.

His periphery remained on high alert, looking obsessively in the background for other seers, for any ripple or touch from the Barrier. His light detected more bodies behind glass or maybe embedded in the organic wall.

Once fully using his seer's sight, he can tell it's blunted from the drug.

He feels strangely alone.

Even so, he knows his scan is only long subjectively.

He clicked out as the door to the next room finished opening, and found himself staring at what looked like an enormous fish tank hanging from steel and organic cables. Hookups for at least three living beings floated in the jelly-like liquid, but only one had an actual body attached. Revik focused on the floating male form.

He felt his heart stop as it occurred to him it might be Jon.

But it wasn't Jon.

He studied the man's features.

He didn't recognize him, but he was young, in good shape, handsome. It must be another Terian. He looked at the other three hookups. One seemed to be rigged for a body the size of a dwarf.

Or a child, perhaps.

The thought sickened him. It also felt right.

He didn't flinch until the remaining body moved in the tank, opening its eyes to stare at him. Gritting his teeth, Revik walked around the transparent window until he found the control panel. Using his sight to discern keystrokes, then to speak to the organics, he gained access to the main computer. He turned off all functions supporting life support.

When he looked back at the tank, the tubes leading into the suspended body were no longer pumping liquid.

It took a few seconds for the male in the tank to comprehend the change.

Then Revik watched him start to suffocate.

He banged on the transparent shield. His fists were sharp at first, a harsh demand. Then he thrashed in panic, screaming, beating against the curved tube. Revik felt sick. He wondered if he should break it open, snap the creature's neck.

He could feel more living beings here, somewhere. But no other seers.

Before he could confirm what he felt by looking physically, a voice nearly made him jump out of his skin. He slammed his back into the semi-organic tank, hard enough to hurt himself.

"Jon! Look! LOOK!"

Revik fell into a half-crouch.

He should have started with weapons.

Unable to comprehend at first what he was seeing, unable to get over the fact that they could have shot him in the back if they'd been armed, he didn't move at first, fighting to get his equilibrium back.

He found them then, with his sight.

Still, he couldn't make himself relax.

He crossed the room, knelt down in front of the low cages he hadn't seen buried in a military-gray wall. He peered inside, confirming with his eyes what he'd already felt with his sight.

"Revik! Holy shit!" Jon banged on the hard plastic of the kennel. "You got out! How'd you get out, man?"

Revik barely heard.

He jumped into the Barrier the second he verified their appearance.

...and now he is lost there, scanning their light. It is something he hasn't been able to do since he got here. He studies every structure in their *aleimi*, segment by segment. He risks going deep, needing to be sure. He checks it twice, then rechecks it.

After a few moments, he feels his shoulders begin to unclench for real.

He checks each of them again, just to be thorough.

No threads are leaving them into the Barrier, no sign or flavor of the Pyramid, the Dreng, or Terian lives in their light. Nothing lives in their light but themselves, their ties to him and each other, their ties to Allie and other friends and family. Everything is dampened by the overall fog of this place, but they are real.

He checks them again, going over every inch of their *aleimi* a last time.

Then, he lets himself smile.

Clicking out, he met Jon's hazel eyes.

"It is you," he said.

"Well, duh. Who'd you think it was?" Jon grinned at him, banging on the glass. "Come on, man! Get us out!"

Revik glanced at Cass. She clutched the transparent wall of her four-by-six box, staring up at him. Her splayed fingers reminded him of a tree frog in a glass aquarium, especially with her wide eyes and too-thin face. A mixture of fear, hope and another emotion he couldn't identify shone from her eyes.

Revik rose to his feet.

Crossing the room, he opened the weapons locker, where he found four custom Beretta M9s with organics, a Steyr TMP, and six SCAR-H fully automatic rifles. Stacks of magazines for all of the weapons filled metal shelves above and below the main locker, which had hooks on the back wall for the handguns and slots for the rifles.

Grabbing one of the heavier rifles off the wall, Revik looked for a box of shells, and loaded it. Once he'd filled the reservoir, he chambered a bullet, and walked back to the cages. He motioned Cass back first.

"More," he said, until her back was pressed to the wall. "Cover your face."

The mixture of relief and fear and... gratitude, he realized... returned to her gaunt face.

"Did you kill him?" Her voice was muffled, but raw.

He nodded, barely meeting her gaze.

Raising his arms, he aimed the gun at the lock, and fired.

LESS THAN AN HOUR LATER, REVIK SAT AT A DESK CHAIR OVER A FLAT computer console, chewing on a piece of canned meat with his back molars and thinking he'd never tasted anything so sharp, salty, tangy... just so damned *good* in his entire life.

He exchanged grins with the two people sitting across from him, who were chewing with equal enthusiasm from separate containers.

While Jon and Revik checked the structure for more bodies and weapons, Cass found them food—and clothing. Luckily, there'd been enough of both in the bunker's storage lockers for all three of them.

Extending a filthy arm in a designer wool shirt, Revik pointed at a juice carton sitting on the table next to Jon, making an unintelligible noise. Jon threw him the carton, laughing when Revik missed and it went spinning to the floor. Scooping it up, he ripped the paper open with his teeth and drank deeply, washing down the meat and belching.

"What is it you said?" he gasped. "Holy fucking God... that's good."

Cass laughed, shaking her long, black hair with the dyed, bright red ends. It was still thick with sweat, blood, water—gods knew what else. Both Jon and Revik had beards. Jon's red-blond hair fell past his shoulders, still streaked with black and white-blond at the ends.

"So why are we still *here,* man?" Jon propped up his bare feet, wearing pants from one of the Terian bodies. He was so thin they bunched up baggily around his waist, held there by an expensive-looking leather belt.

Revik took another long pull of the juice. He motioned at the console.

"We need to figure out where we are." He belched again. "...Find a shower, maybe. But not here."

Jon laughed, shaking his head. "What's wrong with my plan?"

"What's your plan?"

"Getting the hell out of here... now. Walking out. Now."

Revik motioned towards the metal ladder built into one wall, and the round, submarine-looking hatch that stuck out of the top.

"Be my guest," he said. "You might want a jacket, though."

Hearing this last, Cass frowned.

Before Jon could move, she dragged herself to her feet, and crossed the room to the green metal ladder and its circular cage. She climbed up it on bare feet, dwarfed in a dark sweatshirt and a pair of sweatpants that were comically large on her.

Revik watched her carefully. She'd barely spoken since he'd gotten her out of that cage, but she felt open to him still, strangely clear in her mind.

Clicking out, he was still watching when she reached the top of the ladder and twisted the locking mechanism counterclockwise to open it.

"Careful," Revik warned. "Hold on to the rungs."

She opened the door. Immediately, sound filled the metal chamber. Bits of white were blown in through the open portal. Wind echoed down, filling the small space, beating against the walls, penetrating Revik's clothes.

"Jesus." Jon stared up as Cass yanked the metal door shut, spinning the wheel to close it. "Where are we? The North Pole?"

"The North Pole is water, Jon," Revik reminded him.

"That's not what I—"

"My guess would be Russia." Revik sat up, stretching his arms. "Maybe the mountains in Norway... or Asia. Could even be Greenland, but that's a bit much, even for Terry." He grunted. "I don't think he'd risk the Himalayas, even in winter. But there are many places to hide on the southern border of China."

Jon looked at him. "You could feel that out there? The snow, I mean? You knew what it was like?"

Revik shrugged. He stuffed another piece of meat into his mouth, chewing.

Both humans were staring at him now.

"So what do we do?" Jon asked.

Revik hesitated. He'd thought about that, but he doubted the humans were going to like what he'd come up with. "We have to walk, Jon. But we'll need to gear up. And we might have to go the long way, in case Terry's sent for reinforcements already. Cass found us heavy jackets. And boots. You'll both need guns. At least two… and a rifle, if you can carry all that. We need to leave within the hour. Less, if you think the two of you can be ready."

Cass nodded in agreement, returning from where she'd finished descending the ladder.

She sat cross-legged on the floor and began to eat again, silent.

Revik checked her mind. He clicked out seconds later, exhaled.

"We'll need water," he added, turning to Jon. "As much as we can carry. And food, of course."

Cass looked up at them suddenly.

Her eyes widened, grew bright—as if a light had just gone off somewhere in her head. Revik didn't read her, but both men watched as she got to her feet and crossed the small space. She opened one of the lockers she'd explored earlier, began rifling through the back of it. Revik took another drink of juice, still watching her warily.

She turned then, jingling something in her hand.

When they only stared, she jangled the metal harder.

Revik's eyes snapped into focus. In her hand dangled a set of keys, clearly fitted for some kind of vehicle.

"Shotgun," Cass said, grinning.

It was the first time Revik had seen her smile since watching her and Allie together in that diner in San Francisco.

Meeting her gaze, Revik grinned back.

CHAPTER 42
CANDOR

Candor was a poor city, even smaller than its sister city of Mestia in Upper Svanetia, the higher half of the Svaneti region in the country of Stalin's birth.

Georgia is smaller than most people imagine, at the southernmost tip of what had been, once upon a time, the Soviet Union, and closer to Tehran than Moscow. In the winter, like now, the Caucasus Mountains were buried in snow and ice, more so since the climate started changing and increased the average snowfall across most of Asia, especially in the last decade.

Historically speaking, the town of Candor was also new.

It had grown up from the slave trade between Asia and Europe that erupted after the second world war.

Trade in young seers remained the town's only real industry.

Sight slavery was, of course, legal in Georgia.

Ironically, the dearth of visiting free seers made it easy to slip past racial checkpoints unnoticed, even in the heightened paranoia caused by rumors of a telekinetic seer terrorist.

No one expected a free seer to walk into Candor willingly.

At present, according to the few feeds they could access via the snow-cat's comm, Allie was said to be training seers in India, readying her nascent army to wage war on the United States and China. While no one in Candor was overly fond of the governments of either place, purges had occurred there as elsewhere, in reaction to the news of a telekinetic seer in their midst. Bids on her blood and any genetic "samples" were whispered on the sidelines, of course, but Sark settlements in places like this were work camps, or else holding pens.

They were also recruiting grounds for the Rooks.

Revik was able to think through this much just from his own knowledge of the area combined with what they'd heard on the English news feeds.

The snowcat was fitted with organics like their prison had been, in this case to give it satellite capability. Even so, the weather and the mountains interfered off and on as they wound their way into the valley, and he avoided any feeds with two-way capability, which meant most of the majors as they tended to cull demographics for ads.

Jon and Cass didn't look like seers, so that helped.

Revik's blood type would help them fly under the radar, as well.

No one stopped the snowcat at all as they approached the town.

At the registration checkpoint, the guards seemed bored.

Dirty, horny, and bored.

They only noticed Cass with any real interest.

They wanted to know race-cat, local contact, settlement preference—the usual for clan-based systems. Revik knew they'd bother him less if he was specific, so after giving them all the ID info they asked for, he told them he wanted the 4th, nearest Multe markets, hoping they hadn't burned down in any recent riots.

They hadn't. The human took their blood on the spot, and Revik waited, the snowcat's engine still on, while they ran it.

In the pause, he assessed his two charges.

They both still looked dazed and dirty, which luckily wasn't unusual up here. Their condition couldn't have been helped by staring at nothing but snow for two days straight. It occurred to him how thin all three of them really were. The same thing seemed to have occurred to Cass, who had wrapped her face and neck in a thick scarf just before Revik rolled down the window to speak to the guard.

Thinking about this, he smiled at her.

For a human, she wasn't stupid.

Neither was Jon, for that matter, who kept his hand by his gun the whole time the guards were gone, his hazel eyes alert even through their fatigue.

The guard returned. He motioned towards Revik's arm.

When Revik held it out, the man clamped a white wristband around his bony wrist. The guards continued to look bored, and now slightly drunk. Cass and Jon followed Revik's lead, sticking out their arms. Revik watched them look at the wristbands, dazed, and realized again it was probably the first time they'd ever seen anything like them before.

The guard motioned to Revik again, speaking in heavily accented Russian.

"...You know where to go?" He glanced at Cass.

Revik nodded, giving him a quick three-finger salute in thanks.

He pressed down the clutch, shifting down to first and hitting the gas before the man could ask him anything about Cass's status. Women got sold here, too, seer and human. He'd rather not make his companions any more paranoid than they already were. As they slid past the entrance to the mountainous town, Revik pointed up at the skyline.

"Mount Shkhara," he said. "Over 17,000 feet, I think."

Jon's eyes didn't leave the band on his wrist.

"You speak Russian?" He glanced up. "Any other languages?"

Revik shrugged. "A few."

Cass laughed.

When Revik looked over at her, she was smiling at him, but her eyes were clear. He returned the smile, shaking his head.

"Are you ready to sleep?" he asked.

"Can *you* sleep?" Cass countered.

"No." Revik glanced at her, again surprised.

He wondered just how much they'd picked up in their months with Terian.

"...I can't," he said. "Not yet. But you can. I thought we'd get cleaned up and you two could rest while I do some scouting. I'm hoping we can hire a small plane, head to T'bilisi in the morning. We can probably get an international flight from there."

Cass was staring at him. "Have you been here before?"

"Yes."

"When?"

Revik glanced over at them. Jon was looking at him too, waiting for an answer. Revik shifted slightly in the snowcat's bucket seat.

"A while ago," he said finally. "Seers have photographic memories. I'm not unusual in that."

"So what next?" Jon said. "After that place that sounds like a skin fungus, where do we go?"

Revik had been thinking about that, too.

He knew where he wanted to go, but he also knew he'd be a fool to risk it. He could think of only one other place with constructs close enough and safe enough that he could reach within a reasonable time-frame. Even with that location, there were complications.

"England," he said. "London."

"London?" Jon stared. "Didn't you say Allie was probably in Asia by now?"

"Yes." Revik glanced at the two of them, then sighed, clicking softly under his breath. "There are things I need in London." Seeing Jon's frown, he added, reluctant, "...and I don't want to go straight to Allie."

"You don't?" Cass's voice held genuine surprise. "I thought you'd want to go there first."

Revik nodded. "I do. It's just—"

"You think we'd be followed," Jon finished.

Revik glanced at him.

Again... not dumb.

He nodded, shrugging with one hand. "Yes."

Cass studied his face. "That's part of it." She hesitated. "Is it also because of the stuff Terian said? About you cheating on her or whatever?"

Revik sighed, but felt his body react regardless.

Waiting for the nausea to pass, he turned the wheel of the snowcat slowly, navigating around a stone fountain in the middle of the town square. Slowly, he shook his head.

"No," he said. "Not exactly."

"But that was true? You did cheat on her?"

Revik glanced at the human, flinching slightly at the look in her eyes. "Yes."

Shaking her head, Cass folded her arms. "Figures."

But Jon looked between them, his eyes holding a faint wonder.

"So you guys really are married?" he said. "That wasn't just Terian being a dick?"

Revik didn't answer at first. Feeling both of them looking at him again, he turned, blowing air out from his cheeks.

"Yes. We're really married." Hearing the silence this produced, he glanced over at the two of them. "Seers are different. It can happen like that."

"Like what?" Cass said, snorting a little. "Like... overnight?"

"Yes." He made a more or less gesture with his hand. "Well. What I meant was, before the rest of the mind catches up with it. Ours happened fast. A little too fast for us." He shrugged with one hand. "Well. For me, anyway."

She frowned. "Terian said you hadn't slept with her."

Revik hesitated, feeling himself tense. But there wasn't a lot of point in keeping secrets from the two of them. Not now.

"We haven't consummated, no." He glanced at her. "That's complicated, too, Cass. For seers, I mean."

She folded her arms, giving him an openly skeptical look.

"So you didn't want sex with her?" she asked. "With Allie?"

"I didn't say that," he said, giving her a warning look.

"...Because a lot of guys do," she said, her voice pointed. "A *lot* of guys."

His jaw tightened. He considered answering, then didn't.

"So what, then?" she asked. "You slept with someone else, so sex clearly isn't the problem." Her frown deepened. "Is marriage more of an arranged thing with seers? Some kind of social contract? Like a business thing?"

"No, it's not a... a business thing."

"So what's your issue with Allie?"

He looked at her. "There is no issue, Cass."

"Is she not your type? Isn't she pretty enough for you?"

He felt his jaw harden more. "You are getting too personal for me, Cass. I don't want to talk about this, all right?"

Anger touched her eyes. Then she exhaled, and he could feel her thinking. Folding her arms tighter, she frowned a little, but nodded.

"Okay. Sorry."

"It's fine."

Jon was looking at him too, his hazel eyes thoughtful. "You think Terian let us go. To find Allie for him."

Revik hesitated, then nodded. "Yes. I do."

Both of them fell silent.

Revik saw them exchange glances.

"So we can't go to her at all?" Cass asked.

"We can," Revik said. "First I need to go somewhere where I can jump safely. I want to see what's going on with the Rooks… the seers Terian worked for. It's pretty clear he and Galaith aren't working together as they used to. I want to know how many people might be looking for us. I also want to talk to the Seven…" He cleared his throat. "…the seers who have Allie. I can't do that here."

He squinted through snow on the windshield to see the sign for the hotel.

"England could be complicated. I was owned." He paused, letting that part sink in. "I don't know if my employers will have my place under surveillance or whether they would turn me in to SCARB. My guess is no." He glanced at Jon before the human could speak. "It's more likely my stuff has been destroyed, my space given to another seer."

There was a silence. Some of the sharpness left Cass's light.

"Oh," she said. "That sucks."

Revik smiled at her. "Not really."

"So what would we do then?" Jon said. "If that happened?"

Revik blew air out from between his lips. "I know people in London. People who'd let me use their places to jump. People who would help us."

"Other seers, you mean."

"Yes."

Jon nodded, leaning back in the seat and folding his arms.

"All right," he said. "London it is, then."

Jon closed his eyes. Watching him lean on Cass's shoulder, it occurred to Revik that Jon really thought he had a vote.

In the same moment, Revik wondered if maybe he did.

It took him another few breaths to realize what he felt for the humans was more than just responsibility for having indirectly gotten them into this. They felt like friends.

More than that. They felt like family.

Gazing up at the whitewashed sky, he forced the tense part of him to relax as he thought about the reasons that might be. He thought about Cass's questions about him and Allie, and realized he already knew why that was.

She was more seer now. He could feel it.

Pushing the thought from his mind, he downshifted in front of the wooden hotel sign hanging from the edge of a steep roof. Bringing the snowcat to a stop where it wouldn't hang out in the faint outline of road, he stepped on the foot brake, turning the wheel to wedge the tires into a line of rocks.

He turned off the engine. The silence once he had was strangely disorienting.

All he could hear was the wind through the thick glass, the faint squeak of the chain holding the sign from the roof.

"Hey, Revik." Cass watched him pull the keys out of the ignition.

"What, Cass?" he said, not looking over.

"I'm sorry about what I said."

He glanced at her.

She looked timid, lost inside the bundle of blanket and scarf. She touched his arm with her bony hand, and he flinched, feeling the emotion behind the gesture.

"I just don't get it, I guess. You seem like one of the good guys."

Looking at her, he felt his fingers grip the steering wheel, still holding the keys. He glanced at Jon and saw the male human looking at him, too.

Revik exhaled shortly, rubbing his face with a gloved hand.

"There is nothing to get, Cass." He met her gaze, jaw hard. "...And I'm not that good."

Jon spoke up, surprising him.

"Do you love her?" he asked.

Revik looked at him. Focusing back down on his hands, he watched the leather crinkle around his fingers. After another moment, he exhaled again.

"I love her." He nodded, half-surprised he'd said it. "Yes."

For a long moment, none of them spoke.

When he glanced up next, Cass smiled at him. Jon clapped him on the shoulder with his good hand, shaking him lightly in the same gesture. A faint smile tugged at his lips.

"All right." Jon smiled wider, tugging at his shoulder, to get Revik to look at him. "Come on, man. Let's find that shower."

Watching Cass fumble with the door handle, Revik nodded, wiping his face before he turned to do the same.

CHAPTER 43
LONDON

I aimed my body in a jagged line down a busy London street.

I scanned faces as I walked.

I took in buildings as well, and the occasional car as we strolled past yet another wooded park, a different park from the one we'd passed as we left the tube station.

I stopped at a newsstand and stared blankly at the morphing feed headlines.

"BABY" SYRIMNE KILLS 28 IN PAKISTAN BOMB BLAST!

ANTI-HUMAN TERRORIST PLOT LINKED TO CHINA!

RIOTS BURN DOWN WEST HOLLYWOOD SHOPPING CENTER!

EUROPE WARNS OF NEW AGE OF ALL-OUT RACE WAR!

Even after months of travel and India, I still commanded the front page.

I read details as they ran out under the headlines.

Apparently, I was believed dead again.

I wondered if that would make border-crossings any easier.

I was still reading when Maygar came up from behind me and took my arm none too gently in his thick fingers. He led me down a street lined with white houses that looked like they'd been torn from the pages of a London storybook.

Flags from different countries flapped over our heads. A limo slid by with tinted, bullet-proof glass and small square flags on the front of its hood. Another followed, flanked by military police on motorcycles.

It struck me as interesting that Maygar brought me here, where representatives from a dozen or so countries seemed to have taken up residence. Every one of the people inside those limousines would pay top dollar to see me collared and locked in a windowless room.

Still, it was pretty.

Flowers lined the spotless walkways, framed by well-manicured shrubs and graceful trees. Strolling men in suits wandered the park in the center, holding the arms and hands of women wearing hats and sundresses, giving it a somehow timeless feel, even with the designer headsets, armbands, and sunglasses.

I looked down at my hands, which were dyed darker than my normal skin tone. My normally stubby nails had been replaced with elegant fakes to go with my new ID, although now my clothes didn't match that ID so well, or the dark red nail polish I wore.

Touching the silver chain necklace I wore around my neck, I shoved my hands in my pockets.

For the plane ride over, the seers used everything but surgery to disguise my appearance.

They didn't let me leave through New Delhi, which was too close to Seertown.

I flew out of Kolkata instead, wearing facial prosthetics, skin dye, blood patches on all my fingers in the event of a random race screening, colored contact lenses, a wig, a hat, and several scarves over an expensive *salwar kameez,* a type of Indian clothing made up of a long tunic and baggy silk pants. My fingerprints and DNA matched my ident, which was that of an East Indian woman traveling for business with her merchant husband.

My current attempt to blend was significantly more West than East.

It consisted of men's mirrored sunglasses and a hoodie.

Pretty low-tech, as disguises go, but surprisingly effective against the street-level facial recognition software employed by cameras that dotted most London public areas.

I still wore the black wig and skin dye, blood patches and contact lenses under the dark shades, but the facial prosthetics had started to hurt, so I took about half of those off, after Maygar assured me half would still be enough to fool the software.

The Seven employed seers in London who could intercept a breach, as well.

According to Maygar, London was a very "Seven-friendly" city.

The Guard's contacts in Scotland Yard and the local branch of SCARB would pick up any flags well in advance of the human authorities. The main reason for our caution had more to do with the Rooks, who still had people here, as well.

Oversized and shapeless, the pants and long tee I wore, plus the lime green tennis shoes, made me look like a punk American tourist. Considering the multiple versions of my face now in circulation on the feeds, I figured it was as good of a disguise as any.

I gazed up at another gabled house with high windows.

Maygar thrust a carton of juice into my hand.

"Stop looking up," he grumbled. "And drink. We're not far."

"Have you been here before?"

"No, Bridge. Your husband and I were never on 'dinner guest' terms. Sadly."

I focused down another row of attached houses. Each one had a main story above the road that stretched up double the usual height, with white pillars and heavily curtained windows. I found myself thinking about seeing *Peter Pan* as a kid, in the theater.

"Maybe you got the area wrong," I said.

"And maybe I didn't. You know who he worked for, don't you?"

I focused on a bronze lion's head with a ring in its mouth. It guarded an entrance framed by more white pillars, and perfect, corkscrew shrubs. I saw cameras on both sides of the heavy oak door, but otherwise, I half-expected Mary Poppins to walk out, singing a song.

"No idea," I said.

Maygar clicked at me softly. "Bastard didn't tell you anything." He shoved his hands in his pockets. "Do you want me to tell you, Bridge?"

I had to think for a minute. "No."

He shrugged. I could tell he still wanted to tell me.

"Vash had to approve it," he said, trying to tantalize me instead. "Dehgoies was officially in penance, so the work he did remained under scrutiny." Stopping, he pointed up the street. "There. That's the one."

I swallowed when I saw where his finger pointed.

The corner building dominated half of one street block, also white, but taller than any of the others we'd passed. Given the height of the windows, at least one of the eight floors came equipped with twenty-foot ceilings.

Ionic columns of a similar height supported that floor, with smaller versions of the same on two of the others, each with ornate capitals in the shape of four-cornered scrolls. Flags rippled above the main entrance, displaying a distinctly British-looking coat of arms. Small trees decorated the upper balconies, cut in precise shapes.

"He lived here. Seriously?"

Maygar let out a quiet snort. "His 'employers' let him have it for security reasons, and because their main buildings are nearby. The penthouse flat was his. It takes up the entire top floor. The rest is leased out to rich humans and foreign dignitaries."

I focused on the doorman out front, who stood with clasped, gloved hands over a fitted jacket. He bent to open the rear door to a stretch limo that pulled up to the curb, taking a woman's hand to help her out. Watching as more doormen bustled around to remove packages from the limousine's trunk, I swallowed.

"Okay," I said. "You'd better tell me who he worked for."

Maygar smiled, his light exuding a flicker of triumph.

"This building, my dear Bridge, is owned by the British government. Around the corner, on that square we just walked through… which is the famous Belgrave Square, by the way… is the Royal College of Defense Studies. Your husband worked there as an instructor." He gave an odd kind of laugh, shaking his head. "Dehgoies taught worms how to fight seers."

I turned slowly, staring at him.

"You're not serious."

"I am serious," Maygar assured me. "From what I understand, his addition to the faculty upped the international student count considerably." Again he grinned. "He contracted for them on the side, as well, but a good seven months of the year he taught tactical inter-species warfare to rich military brats from all over the world."

By then we were approaching the high-rise building.

I stared up at it, gave a half-laugh.

"Then the big secret is... he was legit? He had a real job?"

"A *real job?"* Maygar's mouth hardened from its previous glee. "Bridge, do you have any idea how many seers would have actively tried to kill him if they knew he did this 'real job?' If there ever was a blood-traitor job, that was it."

Grabbing the juice from me, he took a long drink.

Once he'd lowered the carton, he gave me another look, humor once more teasing his full lips.

"The joke among those of us who knew was that Dags was a worm fucker." He grinned wider before clarifying, "...that he preferred worms to seers. Given he married one, and the Kraut daughter of a Nazi General, at that, I don't think it's such a stretch, do you?"

Tilting his head back to drink more of the juice, he swallowed as he lowered the carton.

"Come to think of it... he picked a human over you, didn't he, Bridge?"

"And a seer," I reminded him.

He grinned. "Yeah. That's right. But he fucked the human, yes?"

I felt this as a sucker punch to somewhere in the navel region.

I didn't look over.

"Yeah," I said. "Yeah, he did."

Maygar grinned again, clapping me on the shoulder.

"Don't be so sensitive, Bridge. He's dead."

By then we'd reached the front door.

The doorman opened it for us once Maygar showed his ID, but not before giving me a down-the-nose disapproving look for my attire. A security guard walked us to an old fashioned elevator and stepped inside after motioning us ahead.

Leaning down to the control panel, he inserted a key, twisted it sideways, then punched in an access code before pressing the top button labeled "Penthouse."

Watching all this, I felt a little sick.

"Maybe you were right," I muttered to Maygar.

"About what, this time?"

"I'm beginning to think this was a bad idea."

The security guard gave me a questioning look, but I barely registered it.

Did I really want to see where he'd lived? I was pretty sure I'd find out yet more things I didn't want to know. My stomach continued to hurt the higher we traveled, until I started to wonder what the hell was wrong with me.

Maygar apparently wondered the same thing.

He nudged me with an elbow.

"You look like you're going to throw up," he said out of the side of his mouth. "What is wrong?"

I shook my head, giving him an irritated look.

The elevator let out a soft ping, and the doors slid open.

The security guard used gloved fingers to point us down the hall. He smiled at me as we exited, giving me a wink as he hit the button to go back down.

He needn't have bothered with directions.

There was only one door.

It had no markings, no identifiers of any kind. A small eye of God stuck out of the ceiling, one of those cameras with a darkened bubble guarding the lens.

"Do we knock?" I whispered it for some reason.

Maygar held up a set of keys, jangling them. "Why?" he said. He bent to the lock, but the door suddenly opened, revealing a small, wiry man in his thirties with a wide face and thinning brown hair. Maygar and I both lurched back in alarm.

The man appeared startled, too.

Looking at him, I wondered if they'd rented out the apartment. The man stared between Maygar and me, then focused on me, almost like he knew me.

Hesitantly, I stepped forward.

"We're friends of Dehgoies Revik," I said. "He used to live here. We've only just now come around to pick up his things. If we're too late, maybe you could tell us where they've been moved to, or who might—"

"I know who you are," the man blurted.

I felt Maygar tense.

Taking a breath, I shook my head. "I don't think so, Mister…?"

"Eddard." He stepped out of the doorway, moving gracefully. "Please follow me." When I hesitated, Eddard said, more insistently, "Please, ma'am. Come with me."

I glanced at Maygar, who was shaking his head minutely, eyes adamant.

When I indicated with my head that we should follow, he shook his head again. When I stepped forward, however, he did the same, only pausing to hold up his hands as if to say, *Fine but this is a terrible idea.*

I knew Maygar was right.

Following a strange man into a government-owned building that used to be occupied by an alleged seer terrorist was pretty reckless. Neither of us could risk using our sight. The apartment was likely to be under surveillance no matter who this guy was. But, I figured, we could either risk going in now or bolt out and hope they let us leave.

With the former I at least had a chance of getting what we'd come for.

When the human got a few paces ahead, Maygar stepped closer, lowering his mouth to my ear.

"We're in a building owned by the British military," he murmured. "Following a man who says he knows who you are."

"It's going to be okay," I told him.

"Really? How reassuring."

"Just trust me. Please, Maygar."

He looked at me like I had brain damage, but shrugged when I didn't flinch.

I focused so intently on the man in front of us that I barely took in the house itself. Once we reached the first staircase, however, I found my eyes pulled off the human's back, and suddenly I was seeing the high, wood-paneled walls and ceilings, bronze sculptures, oil paintings, expensive rugs, and stone floors. Hanging tapestries the size of my apartment floor covered one of the walls of the main hallway.

Faded with age, they looked like they belonged in a museum.

Even the walls had been polished recently.

A blanket-sized *thankah* of the Buddha with the many heads drew my eyes as we passed to the left of the giant marble staircase. Staring at the *thankah,* then up to the landing below the second floor where I saw a massive Chinese-looking vase, I found myself thinking that maybe these were Revik's things after all, waiting for auction.

I let my eyes travel further up, taking in the domed cupola above the stairs. An oval window with ionic columns looked like the bell tower of a cathedral.

Eddard led us into a room with built-in, floor to ceiling walnut bookshelves. Worn but expensive-looking leather furniture sat in front of a marble fireplace. The walls were paneled like the others, but I saw an Asian-looking stand in one corner, a hand-painted Chinese cabinet, and several Japanese vases. Olive green drapes hung on either side of tall sash windows.

No paintings, I noticed. Nothing on the walls but books.

Even as I thought it, I paused, stopping on the fireplace mantle.

A small, normal-sized photograph sat on the marble shelf in a wooden frame.

As I walked towards it, I felt something constrict in my chest.

"Wait here, please," Eddard said.

"Hey," Maygar began. "Wait a minute—"

Eddard was already closing the double doors, blocking us off from the main hall. Folding his arms, Maygar turned on me.

"Great. This is brilliant, Bridge. He's probably calling his pals in the Sweeps."

My eyes remained on the photograph, tracing the lines of an image I knew so well I found it difficult to look at. In it, my father held me in his arms, smiling. He'd already lost weight from the M.S., but he looked happy, and strong.

My mother's face shone from the other side of the frame, so young it shocked me, and between them, I leaned against my dad's chest, grinning, one arm clamped around his neck as I played with my mom's hair.

The picture hit me like a punch in the face.

Maygar finally seemed to have noticed.

"What?" he asked. "What is the matter?" He looked at the mantle over the fireplace, where the picture stood. "What, Bridge?"

"I want to go."

"Did you feel something?" Wariness sharpened his voice.

"No." I forced my eyes off the photograph. "No. I just want to go."

The doors slammed open.

I turned, but couldn't see past the clouds in my eyes, couldn't take in the form running at me across the Persian rug. When she finally reached me, she threw herself into my arms, nearly knocking me over, then squeezed me so tightly I couldn't breathe.

But gods, she was so thin… like a ghost.

Even in my shock, I was afraid I might break her.

"Allie!" she shrieked. "Allie! Allie! Allie! Allie! ALLIE!"

I stood there, feeling like I'd been repeatedly hit in the face.

Cass snatched the sunglasses off my eyes, yanked the sweatshirt hood and wig off my head, then frowned and began peeling the prosthetics off my nose and cheeks. When I saw her without obstruction, my heart seized.

I saw Maygar jerk in our direction, unholstering his gun.

"Stop!" he said.

His tone shocked me. It jerked my eyes off of her, even as she was getting the last piece of modified latex off my chin.

"Take your hands off her!" Maygar growled. "Now!"

"No!" I held up a hand to him. "No! It's okay!"

Then I saw my brother in the doorway, and lost my voice.

I barely recognized him.

His black, red, and blond-dyed hair had grown out in a streaked tangle past his shoulders. His face was paler than I'd ever seen it, his eyes too large, his cheekbones too prominent. One of his hands wore a flesh-colored bandage, but he didn't look like Cass, who… I turned, staring at the scar that split her face, feeling sick for staring but unable to stop.

I wanted to touch it, to see if it was real.

She grinned, shaking my shoulders to get my eyes back to hers.

"Hideous, aren't I?" She grinned, but I saw a denser pool of sadness there. No, not sadness, a kind of brokenness that disappeared even as I glimpsed it. "Forget that! You're here! You're here!" She squeezed me, jumping up and down. "I'm so happy you're here!"

I hadn't managed to make my mind emit so much as a single coherent thought, but when she grinned at me, something in me seemed to break. I gripped her, pulling her against me. I held her as tightly as I dared, still afraid I would hurt her.

"How are you here?" I managed. "How did you get here? Cass!? How are you here?" I clutched her tighter, closing my eyes. "Cass."

"How are *we* here?" she demanded, shoving at me playfully. "We heard you were DEAD! That you blew up in a bomb? In Pakistan?"

By then, Jon reached me, too.

He pulled me away from Cass, crushing me in his thinner but still strong arms.

"Damn it, Al." He kissed my face. "I can't believe it. I'm so glad to see you." He choked, and when I saw him fighting not to cry, I felt myself do the same, although my mind still hadn't caught up with any of it.

I couldn't take my eyes off him.

I stared at his eyes, his face.

"Jon…" I managed. I clutched his shirt. "Where did you come from?"

"Where?" He gave a strange kind of laugh, wiping his eyes. "We finally caught a plane from Istanbul. Revik's going to freak, you know… like, lose it."

I froze in his arms.

Jon went on talking, not noticing.

"We had to dig ourselves out of some hole in Georgia… as in Stalin, not banjos." He let out another strangled laugh. "Since then, he's been moving us in circles for weeks, worried we would lead them to you, and now you come to us, like some kind of…"

Seeing my face, he trailed, as if confused by what he saw.

"Your picture's all over the news," he said. "We thought you were dead. They said you were *dead.* Revik's been talking to Vash since we got here, but no one's heard from you since they dropped you off in Kolkata." He wiped his eyes again. "They couldn't even tell us where you were going. Some security thing."

"Revik?" I managed. "Did you say—"

"Shit." Jon stared at my face. "I can't believe you're here. I'd given up. I really had."

"Revik?" I repeated.

"Yeah." Jon did a double-take on my face. "You don't know! He's with us, Al. Terian got me and Cass in San Francisco. They brought Revik in like a month later. He looked like hell…" Jon gave a humorless laugh. "Still does, if you want the truth. But he saved our lives. More than once. Of course, he nearly shot us dead, too, thinking we were more Terian bodies. Terian had him drugged, and we were all a little crazy by then."

He paused, thinking.

His eyes grew puzzled as he looked at me.

"Al," he said. "You're not here for us at all, are you?"

Cass laughed. "Who cares? She's here!" She yanked on my arm. I stared at her again, unable to take my eyes off the scar.

I looked at Jon's bandaged hand. It looked too small.

I reached for it, and he pulled it away, smiling at me wanly.

"Don't trip, sis. We're okay." His eyes remained on me, carrying an odd intensity I didn't recognize. "And what the heck happened to you?" He held out my arms, looking at me. "Even in that get-up, you look like you should be carrying an assault rifle. You actually look… taller. What have those crazy seers done to you?"

I couldn't force out words.

I stared between them, still lost in the reality that they were alive.

Just then, Maygar seemed to have come to the end of his rope.

"Bridge," he hissed through his teeth. "Who are these fucking humans? What is going on? If you don't tell me, I'm going to start shooting people… starting with myself!"

Cass and Jon's eyes swiveled, taking in the muscular seer who, I realized suddenly, still hovered over me, trying to decide if he should intervene.

Cass spoke first, looking Maygar up and down.

She nudged my elbow, giving me a wan smile.

"Who's the cutie?" she asked. "You two-timing, girl?" Lowering her voice, she murmured by my ear. "…I hope he has insurance."

I glanced at Maygar, baffled, not sure at first what she even meant.

But the look on Maygar's face brought me up short. His dark eyes were trained out through the study doors. As I watched, a deep scowl lined his features.

"I don't believe it," he said. "That son of a bitch has nine lives."

Without thinking, I followed his gaze, and my eyes connected solidly and without warning with Revik.

He stood several yards back from the doorway, wearing a dress shirt and black pants, arms folded tightly across his chest, talking to Eddard. From his face and profile he looked about forty pounds lighter than the last time I'd seen him. I felt him notice my stare, even as I realized he wasn't going to return it.

I watched his hand comb long fingers through his black hair. I noticed the absence of his ring, and suddenly the chain I wore felt heavy around my neck.

Averting my eyes, I clutched the back of the leather couch.

My hands actually shook.

I gripped the couch harder, but it didn't help.

Cass caught my arm, her voice excited again.

"You won't believe the crazy shit we've seen! We were in *Russia,* Allie! In this town of slave traders in the mountains! Some guy tried to *buy* me! It was freakin' psychotic. And Revik speaks Russian, so he basically told the guy—"

"Not now, Cass." Jon patted my shoulder when I didn't look up. Taking my hand, he rubbed my fingers with his. "You all right, little sis? Your brain's not going to explode, is it?" Once my eyes flickered up, he smiled. "Surprised to see us?"

I nodded.

"Did you think we were dead?" he asked.

I nodded again, feeling tears come to my eyes.

"And Revik?" Jon prompted. "You thought he was dead?"

Fighting the impulse to turn, to confirm what I'd seen standing in the hall… ignoring me, which should have been confirmation enough… I gave Jon another nod.

I wiped my cheek with the back of my hand, then sank to the leather couch. Cass and Jon sat on either side of me, each with an arm slung around my back. I don't know how long I sat there, but eventually, I took a hand from each of them. I cleared my throat.

"We haven't eaten," I said. "Maygar's probably—"

"Yeah." Cass's voice was quiet. "They're talking right now. Him and that other guy."

"Oh." I didn't look towards the door.

"So I guess Terian wasn't lying about you and Revik?" Jon smiled, punching my arm. "You've got a frickin' husband, Al? How did that happen?"

"He really did save our lives," Cass added. "He's a nice guy, honestly. If a little scary at times." Her voice grew tentative. "Is he still your husband though, Allie? He thinks you're really mad at him. It sounds like he deserved it. But, well… I like him, Al. A lot."

I stared at the pattern in the rug.

After a few seconds, I let out a short laugh.

It sounded like a seal's bark.

"I think she's in shock, Cass," Jon said.

"Well, where is he?" Cass said, sounding angry. "I thought he'd come in here at least. What's he doing out there?"

"Hiding." Jon laughed, poking me in the ribs with his fingers. "Turns out Rambo might be afraid of his wife. Are you going to talk to him, sis? Or let him stew out there?"

I raised my hands, using my fingers to comb the hair out of my face.

"Is there a bathroom?" I asked.

I felt them look at each other.

Then Jon's voice grew matter of fact. "Yeah, Al. Sure."

He stood me up, steering me gently towards the door of the study. He walked me right past Revik and Maygar, both of whom I felt looking at me now. I followed Jon to the base of the staircase without returning their stares, and he pointed up.

"Bathrooms are bigger up there. You can even take a bath if you want… in fact, I highly recommend it. There's clothes, too. Cass has bags of new stuff. Second door down, I think. He took us shopping a few days ago, and man does that guy have an expense account." Jon grinned when I glanced up, but the grin faded when he saw my face. "Al. Are you all right?"

I nodded. "Don't wait for me. I won't be long."

He pulled me into his arms.

I felt his heart, a warm flare in his chest.

"I'm so glad you're all right." His voice caught. "I've been so fucking worried about you, Allie. For months. I was beginning to think…"

Tears stuck in my throat. "Me too."

He let me go. After standing there awkwardly for a few more seconds, I turned and began to climb the stairs. When I glanced down from the half-floor landing, Jon still looked up at me, his eyes worried, his hands resting on his hips below too-thin arms decorated with tattoos. I noticed new scars, fading bruises, and looked away.

I need a bath, I thought.

Then I would feel normal again.

Then I would be all right.

CHAPTER 44
LUNCH

It took me longer than what I'd told Jon.

I didn't know whose bedroom I was in, didn't want to think about it too closely when I saw women's shampoo on the rack alongside men's.

Wrapped in a towel once I'd finished, I wandered into two different rooms before I found the shopping bags Jon mentioned. I was over two inches taller than Cass by then, with a chest about two sizes smaller, but I finally settled on low-hung silk pants and a stretchy tee. After scrutinizing my reflection in the mirror for far too long, contemplating make up, then abandoning the idea, I tied my hair in a loose knot at the base of my neck and made myself go downstairs.

Jon and Cass were alive. My best friends were alive.

By the time I reached the bottom of the stairs, that much had finally penetrated.

My smile as I entered the dining room even felt real.

I sat in the chair closest to the door without making eye contact with anyone other than Jon, who, seeing my smile, grinned back. I looked for Cass, found her sitting next to Revik in the opposite corner. He had an arm draped over the back of her chair, and she laughed as she told him something. He smiled, tugging the ends of her long hair.

I stared at his hand where he touched her, saw more affection in his eyes as he looked at her than he'd ever aimed at me.

I heard Maygar's mocking voice as we'd approached the building.

...prefers humans.

Revik's eyes swiveled to mine.

For the first time, he looked directly at me, and the look there was...

Christ. It was guilt.

I moved before my brain could process a complete thought.

"Allie." Revik's chair squealed on the hard wood. He stood almost as I did. "Allie." He held out a hand, what looked like a peace gesture, or something you might do to calm an animal. "Allie. Where are you going?"

Silence fell on the room.

I swallowed, looking around at faces.

Honestly, I hadn't fully realized I'd stood up until then.

Maygar leaned back in his chair, arms folded. He raised an eyebrow at me, but I flinched when I saw the pity in his eyes. Jon gave Revik a warning look I couldn't interpret, and Cass just looked confused.

I couldn't make myself look at Revik at all.

"I..." I cleared my throat. "Sorry." I waved vaguely at the spread on the table. "Go on, eat. I'll be right back."

Anger at myself made it hard to look at any of them.

I needed to regroup, to come back when I had my head on straight. I couldn't look at Cass like this. They'd obviously been through hell. I had no right to begrudge anyone anything that might have come of it, especially since I was—

"Allie!" Revik's voice was sharp.

When everyone looked at him, he cleared his throat.

"Can it wait? We need you here. Maygar didn't want to speak for you."

I looked at Maygar, who nodded, indicating for me to sit.

"We need a plan, Bridge. Your *husband...*" He said the word with open contempt, and I felt Revik's eyes shift to him. "...seems to believe they may have been followed. That they were allowed to escape in the hopes he would lead the Rooks to you." Maygar looked to Jon. "Did I get that right?"

"Yeah." Jon glanced between Maygar and Revik, wary. "Yeah. That's right."

I stood there, feeling trapped.

I looked at Cass, saw that Revik had moved his chair several feet from hers.

Feeling sick, I looked at Jon. His eyes openly asked me to stay. Noticing again how thin he was, I swallowed, nodding. I glanced at the scar on Cass's face, saw her looking at me with worry in her eyes, and hated myself more.

Gods, what the fuck was wrong with me?

"All right." I lowered my weight to the chair. "Sure."

I felt everyone around the table exhale.

Cass was the first to smile at me. "Maygar said you've been in India this whole time?"

I nodded. "Yeah. For the last few months, anyway. Learning. Training. You know."

"Why are you here?" Revik asked.

Before I could stop myself, I looked at him.

His face had fallen back into the infiltrator's mask, his eyes focused on the table. He really was thin. Thinner than Cass or Jon, although all three of them looked like concentration camp victims. When Cass shoved a plate at me, I tugged it closer with my fingers, picking at a pile of what looked like fried potatoes with a fork.

"I was looking for clues," I told him. "Imprints, I guess."

"Of what?" Revik didn't raise his eyes.

"I've been tracking Galaith. I got as far as you."

Cass shoved a forkful of salad in her mouth. "What's a Galaith?" she asked.

"The head of the Rooks' network," Revik told her. "Terian's old boss." His voice aimed back at me. "Why him?"

I shrugged, not answering.

I honestly didn't have a good answer. None I could say to all of them. I'd been tracking Galaith to find Revik, to get him out of the Rooks' network, where I thought he was stuck after he died. I couldn't say that to him, not now, so I shielded my mind.

I felt Revik react to my silence, a near flinch.

"What about the bomb?" Jon asked. "Pakistan. Was that you?"

I felt the illness worsen, realized Revik was actually scanning me with his light.

"No." I glanced at Jon, forced a smile. "No bombs lately."

There was another silence while everyone ate. I watched Revik cut up a piece of meat and stare at it. Jon and Cass ate like they were starving, like they might not eat again. I saw Cass nudge Revik to eat then, and looked away.

"Allie," Revik said, still not looking at me. "What do you want with Galaith? You know he'd only be replaced, if—"

"Yeah, I know, I..."

Realizing I'd cut him off, I stopped.

I felt my face warm, but kept my voice neutral, almost businesslike.

"The seers in India, they had a plan. It required knowing who Galaith is. In the real world, I mean. I've been able to help them some, with the tracking..."

I trailed, trying to decide if that was true.

"...Well, I had more of a direct line to him, anyway. For a number of reasons." I didn't look at Revik. "Their plan is kind of a long shot, but anything would have been. I couldn't just do nothing, and Vash asked for my help, so..."

Feeling them all staring at me again, I glanced at Maygar, maybe for help.

"Look, this isn't really the important thing now, is it?" I asked. "It sounds like they probably know I'm in London. Maybe we should split up. Head back to Asia separately. Revik can probably do whatever it is the Seven needed me for, now that he's back." I gave him a bare glance. "I only came here to try and tap his memories, anyway."

I felt a pulse of something, realized it came from Revik.

Whatever it was, it was intense enough to startle me.

I glanced over at his face, but his eyes were fixed on Maygar.

His voice flattened. "You should know... there's a factional struggle happening within the Rooks. Terian's making a play for the top spot. My guess is, he wants you to do it for him. Or to use you as leverage, maybe. Maybe even to do whatever it is you were planning to do with the Seven."

"I doubt that."

"Allie," he said. "All I meant is—"

"I know what you mean," I said, cutting him off again.

At his silence, I flushed, waving a hand over the table.

"I get it, Revik. You think he's playing me. That he maneuvered me into whatever I'm doing." I glanced at Maygar, who scowled, folding his arms. "Maybe you're right. I was just trying to help, like I said. Maybe you'll feel differently if you know it's not my plan. It's Vash's. I haven't known him that long, but he seems to have the confidence of the rest of the infiltrators."

Another silence fell after I said it.

I felt my face warm, but didn't look at anyone around the table.

Replaying my own words, I realized how they probably sounded.

I tried to decide how I could walk them back, or change the subject maybe.

Revik broke the silence.

"I didn't mean what I said as an insult, Allie," he said, his voice quiet. "He's good at that. Manipulating events. All I meant was—"

"I understand," I said. "It's all right, Revik. Really. Sorry for being so defensive. I don't know what I'm doing. Believe me, I get that. It's fine."

I felt my jaw harden when I realized I'd cut him off again.

Avoiding his eyes, I looked around the table, forcing myself to take in their physical condition, to really see it. I replayed Revik's words, looking at Jon's hand, the cut on Cass's face, whatever was wrong with Revik's neck. Suddenly, everything I'd been doing with the Seven struck me as borderline delusional.

"Maybe you're right," I said again, speaking into the silence. "You probably are right, Revik." I hesitated, looking around at them again. "I went after the wrong Rook."

I felt my face grow hot as I replayed my own words.

Shaking my head, I fought my voice.

"Look, I'm sorry. I really am. I'm not saying anything right. I guess I don't know how to say how terrible I feel about what happened to all of you."

"Allie," Cass said, softly.

I glanced at her. Seeing the brightness in her eyes, I looked at Jon. "The truth is, it's still not safe, being near me. It's not safe knowing me at all. You must realize that now. I wish that was different. I really do. But it's not. It might not ever be."

When no one said anything, I wiped my eyes.

"When we're done here, Maygar and I should probably go." I hesitated, glancing at Revik. He wouldn't return my gaze. Looking past him, to Cass, I added, "Revik can probably get you somewhere safe. I've got money now. Vash promised me funds. I could…" I glanced at Revik. "… Hire him, I mean. If that's all right."

Another silence fell.

I felt them staring at me, everyone except Revik.

Then Maygar grunted in amusement.

He glanced at Revik, tossing his napkin to the table.

"Hear that, Rook-boy?" he crowed. "You've been dismissed."

"Shut up, Maygar," I said.

"Oh, don't worry. I approve, Bridge. And you're right. He's probably screwing the hot Asian chick…"

"What?" Cass stared at him, then at me. "What did he say?"

I shook my head, giving Maygar a hard look. "He didn't say anything, Cass. Please, just forget it."

I saw her open her mouth, then look at Maygar. Her gaze narrowed, right before she seemed to make up her mind, folding her arms.

"Whatever."

I stood up, unable to look at any of them now.

"Look, this isn't me blowing you off. Maygar was assigned to me by the Council, so he's stuck. But none of you are." I looked at Jon. "I don't want to leave any of you. I love you. I hope you all know that. Revik knows how dangerous it is to be around me… he'll tell you."

There was a silence, this one longer.

Revik didn't move in his chair.

The human servant, Eddard, finally broke it by walking into the room.

He glanced around, one eyebrow arched in question at the silence.

Then he cleared his throat, looking directly at me.

"Ma'am?" He waited for me to turn.

For a moment I couldn't take my eyes off the others around the table. Jon was staring at Revik, as if willing him to say something. Cass was looking at me, her eyes holding a kind of disbelief, but I saw anger there, too. She glared at Maygar then, but he only smiled, winking at her before he kissed the air with his lips.

When I glanced at Revik, I found I couldn't look away. He was staring at the table, his face completely devoid of expression.

"Ma'am?"

I turned my head, finally realizing his words were aimed at me.

"What?" I said. "Eddard? What is it?"

"The military is outside."

"What?" Maygar leapt to his feet, shoving his chair back. "Which one?"

Eddard looked only at me. "I believe all of them, sir."

CHAPTER 45
DESCENT

I crouched in an alcove by a long row of chimneys.

Revik and Maygar pretty much took over once the military showed up. Within seconds they were using Revik's secure network, contacting people in the Seven's Guard, calling in a team to get us out through the roof.

Still, the silence was deafening.

I didn't know what the others thought.

I didn't want to read any of them, but I felt a fair bit of anger and hurt off Cass especially. I felt hurt on Jon, too, but more sadness than anger. I bit my lip, doing everything in my power not to point out that what was happening *right now* was exactly the kind of thing I was worried about dragging them into.

"I should have never come here," I muttered.

I'd been standing to the side of one of Revik's windows when I said it, looking down on the street. I felt a kind of futility wash over me when I saw the line of military cars clustered at the base of the building. Someone down there had a voice amplifier and was shouting instructions. I heard other languages besides English, so it was a good bet SCARB was down there, too.

Feed vans pulled up right as Maygar grabbed my arm, dragging me away from the window.

I let him lead me up the stairs along with the others, then to a smaller, hidden staircase behind a bureau in the master bedroom. Above that one, an even more narrow staircase lived, one that led up to a metal plated door and out onto the roof.

All six of us now squatted in a low line, gazing at the same expanse of gray sky.

Revik leaned on the wall beside me.

I hadn't really thought through the order in which we walked that last piece of stairs, but now he was clearly too close. Clutching the edge of one brick by my face, I managed to close off my light from his, but my eyes drifted to him again and again.

He didn't return my glances.

I focused on a fading welt that showed above his white collared shirt.

"I'll tell you, Allie," he said. "Anything you want to know. But not now."

My throat tightened. He'd felt me looking at him.

Of course he had. Even if he wasn't who he was, he still had a construct over this place. Given our connection, he could probably hear everything I thought when we were this close, whether I tried to shield my thoughts or not.

He gave me a bare glance, his jaw tight.

"No," he said. "I can't."

Maygar's voice rose behind me and I turned, saw him talking on a headset. He used the seer language mixed with what sounded like French.

"They're closing off the street," Revik said, translating.

"Didn't Maygar tell them we'd blow up the building?"

"Yes." Revik still wouldn't look at me. "They'd expect that." I saw him glance at Maygar again. His jaw tightened more.

Just then, Eddard shouted, "Sir! They're coming!"

I followed the human's pointing finger.

In the distance, black, insect-like shapes rose above the skyline. For months I had them burned into my brain as things that brought death and guns and capture, but this time, my heart lifted as I watched the black dots grow larger.

Maybe we really would get out of this.

I glanced at Eddard, studying his light inside Revik's construct.

Definitely human.

"Who is he?" I asked Revik.

Revik's eyes followed mine. "He works for me. He said he wouldn't tell the military unless I did something 'untoward.' He's clean," he added, preempting my next question. "And I'm paying him well."

I nodded, watching the approaching helicopters.

Seconds later, sound came pounding into the alcove where we crouched.

At first it came from the helicopters alone, then a whooshing noise ricocheted between buildings, soft at first then deafeningly loud. Revik tensed beside me. I barely recognized the flash of a pair of U.S. fighter jets, right before they fired.

The first missile hit the front helicopter and exploded.

I flinched back, unable to tear my eyes away, even through Revik's shielding arm. I watched as black smoke mushroomed up out of the tilting cockpit. Fire billowed out as the second one came to its end a breath later.

I watched uncomprehendingly as gravity began to take its toll only a few hundred feet from the roof where we perched.

Rising abruptly to his feet, Revik withdrew towards the small stairwell, motioning the others back towards the access door even as I heard the crash and grind of metal and glass. I still sat there, numb, as the two helicopters completed their falls, smashing down into whatever had the misfortune of lying on the street below.

I could feel the seers inside the cockpits, dying.

I was still standing there when someone grabbed my arm, dragging me towards the open metal door. I didn't realize until then that they'd all gone inside, that I was out there alone. When I glanced back at Maygar's face, he only yanked on my arm harder, his eyes and mouth exuding impatience.

With a last look at the sky, I retreated indoors with the rest of them, even as the jets flashed by in tandem overhead, leaving white contrails in their wake.

Inside the Barrier, winds whip, throwing to and fro the lit strands of millions of interconnected beings.

The Pyramid looms over London, casting a long shadow, bending and crushing living lights as members of the Org, the Brotherhood—the Rooks—dive in and out of buildings, through minds and connections, in and out of military and paramilitary and homeland security agents for three different nations.

On the ground, SCARB is running operations by now. They direct the actions of the military and local authorities, and even that of the Sweeps, their more bureaucratic counterpart that deals primarily with illegal seer incursions into human territory.

These days, SCARB employs far more seers than humans, although human authorities and the World Court do their best to keep that fact from civilians.

Above the mass of infiltrators, two light bodies stand alone, watching.

One directs no small part of the larger organism of the Pyramid.

He does this in the background, using pieces of his mind and light that no longer need to pull from the bulk of his waking consciousness.

The other being, the one standing next to him, is his oldest friend.

She's shielded, Xarethe comments. *Likely by Elan's boy, Maygar. Or those kneelers back in Asia. Maybe even Dehgoies himself, by now.*

You are sure that Dehgoies is here? Galaith asks.

Her only answer is a grim nod as she stares out over darting forms.

He is alive, then, Galaith breathes, unable to hide his relief. *Terian only took him from me. Likely to use him against me.* Still thinking, Galaith frowns. *Clearly, he wants the Bridge for those ends, too. Dehgoies could help him to obtain her.*

And to control her, Xarethe sends.

Galaith's frown deepens. *Yes. Of course.*

Both of them watch as the Org's infiltrators weave a dense Barrier structure over the white building, focusing primarily on the top floor. The net will push the Seven's infiltrators out. It will keep any out who might try to help the Bridge and her followers from the Barrier.

Following completion of the net, they will tackle Dehgoies's construct next.

Everything done by the Org is systematic, by the numbers.

Xarethe asks, *Isn't it more of a risk, to kill her now? Won't she simply return?* She studies Galaith's light through the Barrier's dark. *We could do as Terian is attempting, instead. Bring her in alive. Dehgoies, too. If we have her mate, she will have little choice but to cooperate with us. We could use her to bring the war when we're ready. On our own terms.*

Galaith smiles wryly. *You are assuming this war can be controlled. War can rarely be controlled my friend… a Displacement less than most.*

His light follows the swarm of infiltrators. *Anyway, the Bridge and Alyson are not precisely the same creature. She may not have any more control over this than we do. Beneath her surface personality there exists a drive—a pre-programming, if you will. It is very difficult to persuade such an influence. She is not the Bridge so much as possessed by it.*

Still. He shrugs, gazing back out over the cloak woven by his drones. *She has, and always will be, the very first choice to fulfill this role. That does mean something.*

Xarethe thinks about his words. *Can it be stopped? In your opinion, brother. Is this force able to be restrained?*

Galaith nods slowly, pensive. *Yes. I think so. With careful work.*

And Dehgoies?

Galaith chuckles. *Ah, Dehgoies. What will we do with him?* The smile turns affectionate. *He deserves partial credit for all of this.* He extends a hand over the cloud of infiltrators making up the network. *But Terian was wasting his time. It was not a temporary shield that we put on Dehgoies's mind when he left. We broke him entirely.*

He sighs, exuding pale light.

He is purely an invention of the Seven now. More dead than alive… at least in relation to what he once was. No. He shakes his head regretfully. *We have nothing to fear in him, old friend. Dehgoies is a ghost now. A shadow.*

Xarethe doesn't answer.

Peace, Galaith says. *It requires constant work, does it not?* His dark eyes burn like coals. *I want no more talk of Displacements, or prophesied wars.*

And Terian? she ventures. *He is one of The Four, is he not?*

Galaith's eyes flash as he turns. After a pause, he smiles enigmatically.

Does such a possibility surprise you, old friend?

Somewhat, yes, she admits. *Does he know?*

Galaith's light form exudes another cryptic smile. *I believe he is beginning to suspect.*

And what will you do with him? Xarethe persists. *Does it not worry you, that he might start this war, even without your Bridge? Or that you may damage history, by doing away with more than one of The Four?*

Galaith smiles wryly, clasping light hands at the base of his back.

He turns, meeting the other's gaze.

I promised my friend Xarethe that I would not exterminate all of her creations.

Galaith's smile grows harder, even as the black eyes turn sharp.

...But Terry, he says gently. *Your time is up. It is fortunate for me that you are as obvious as you are insane.*

The being calling itself Xarethe turns, its glowing eyes suddenly predatory.

Galaith adds, *I hope, at least, you got the explanations you were hoping for, old friend.*

A bolt of light strikes from overhead.

Terian sidesteps it, severing his connection to the Pyramid even as he leaves the false imprint of Xarethe behind.

The darkness disappears...

...AND TERIAN JERKED OPEN YELLOW-GOLD EYES.

He lay in a cream-colored seat on a private plane, a middle-aged woman with a tennis player's body. She was on her way to the Hamptons for the week, with husband number two and kids. When she blinked her eyes to clear them, a man appeared over her, holding a gun.

It was not her husband.

"Did you really think he wouldn't hear what you'd been doing, Terry?" the seer asked.

The woman held up a hand. A diamond wedding ring sparkled from her third finger. "We can talk about this, my brother—"

The infiltrator fired.

The skull of the slim woman in the thirty-thousand-dollar Chanel suit blew back from an entry point just at the inside of her right eye, decorating the seat's upholstery with a sickening thump. She slumped forward in the soft leather seat.

...just as a different man on another continent approached a girl patiently brushing a pony's dark mane. She looked maybe sixteen, but the expression in her eyes flashed older as the infiltrator fit a silencer to the end of his pistol. Her long hair caught in a gust of wind as she struggled to mount the small horse.

Before she could get her leg over, he fired.

Now they are all aware. All Terians, everywhere.

He is on the run, in all his various forms, but Galaith expected that, planned for it.

...A man in his mid-twenties bolted down an aisle lined with slot machines, eyes wide as he scanned for exits amid the flashing lights and sounds of the casino. He'd just about reached the cordoned entrance to the cocktail lounge when a security guard stepped directly behind him, stabbing him in the kidney multiple times with a straight-edged knife.

Before he could cry out, the same guard jammed a syringe into his neck.

He hit a button to depress the stopper.

A crowd gathered as the man convulsed on the carpet. Only the guard saw his eyes flash yellow before he expired.

...A businessman in Italy stepped out of his church, looking around frantically for his family's chauffeured car. He crossed the street with his coat collar raised, lifting a hand for a taxi when unknown persons gunned him down in front of ten witnesses, including the secretary he'd met an hour earlier at a nearby apartment building, and who he'd been banging behind his wife's back for over three months.

...even as, with a jerk and a gasp, the Vice President of the United States, Ethan Wellington, sat up in bed.

For a long moment, he didn't know what woke him.

He didn't know what was wrong.

Then, receiving a number of flashes from the Barrier construct he'd erected over the room, he felt in the bed beside him for the body of his wife, feeling a faint rush of panic when he couldn't find her. Seconds later, he remembered she was out, touring the Southern states on free school lunches, or one of the other social programs he'd asked her to support.

As parts of him whispered in the dark, he found himself thankful for her absence.

He threw back the covers, shoved his feet into plush slippers and reached for the drawer where he still kept a small gun, like in that apartment he and Helen shared when they lived together in graduate school.

The door to his bedroom opened.

Ethan tensed, blinking into the giant eye of a Maglite flashlight.

"Good," he said, exhaling as he recognized Wes, the lead of his security detail. "Have them bring my car around. There's been a family emergency, and—"

"Sir," the agent said. "That won't be necessary."

It occurred to Ethan that he'd made a mistake, even as his eyes adjusted enough to see the gun his security chief held beside the flashlight.

Ethan's mind toyed with regret—that this wasn't a seer's body, that he might have acted faster, that he hadn't remembered to call Helen that night, to tell her he loved her.

The agent emptied four chambers into his chest.

Ethan's brown eyes flashed yellow as he slid to the bedroom floor, bleeding on the new silk carpet his wife found for them in Dubai during their last trip with President Daniel Caine, Lisa Caine, and the twins.

The last thing Ethan heard was the elongated scream of a siren outside his window, and then everything went dark.

CHAPTER 46

CONTACT

I watched Revik check a security panel by the study doors.

Eddard hovered near him.

Jon and Cass stood out of sight of the tall sash windows, looking down onto the street where I could hear the activity ramping up even more. Maygar did the same by a third window, an assault rifle gripped in his hands.

While I watched, Jon shoved a gun in the back of his belt, holding another in his good hand, what looked like one of Revik's Glocks.

My brother the pacifist.

I glanced back as Revik passed by where I stood, aiming for the china closet. He moved aside a vase on a nearby accent table and slid a key off the wood with his fingers. I watched him unlock the double hutch doors, pressing a button concealed behind a faux wooden panel.

The panel slid back, pushing out a velvet-cushioned tray.

I could only stare as he pulled another handgun off the blue, velvet cloth, checking the magazine for how many bullets remained, then the chamber before handing it to Eddard. He picked up a second gun, then a third. He checked them all, shoving one in his belt before passing the other to Eddard, as well.

I saw him motion towards me, still muttering to Eddard in a voice too low for me to hear. Realizing he was talking about me, not to me, I looked away.

I held my stomach with one arm. I was having trouble breathing.

My brain seemed to have short-circuited somewhere between the conversation over lunch and the two helicopters exploding over a London street. Some kind of delayed reaction, maybe. To being fired on by military jets, prolonged stress, almost zero sleep in two days.

To finding out Revik, Cass, and Jon were still alive.

More than anything, I was still reeling from that.

Jon and Cass were alive.

Alive, but obviously hurt, traumatized, nearly starved to death, tortured for weeks, if not months. They both looked so different I barely recognized them, and not only physically. I was grieving and angry that I was getting them back only to put them in danger again… and even if we did all manage to get out of this alive, I'd only have to send them away.

All of it angered me.

The scar on Cass, Jon's missing fingers, how thin they were, the expression their eyes held—I looked at them and I wished I could do something. Anything.

But I couldn't.

I glanced at Revik. He didn't return my look.

I felt a push to move my limbs. I think I meant to walk to Jon and Cass, but my body must have had other ideas, because I only got as far as the china closet and the exposed tray of guns. Revik no longer stood there. He stood by another wall panel on the other side of the room. He was punching in keys, his eyes showing him to be in the Barrier.

"They changed all my codes," he muttered. "We'll have to take the stairs."

I stared at a gun on the tray I recognized.

It looked just like the one Revik held all those years ago in Germany. I picked it up, hefting the weight of the metal in my hand.

It was so small. It looked like a toy.

"We can't take the elevator," Revik said. I felt his attention on me, but I didn't turn around. "We have to get to the stairs. Now. There's some chance we can still make it to the basement."

"Revik." I shook my head. "No."

Everyone paused.

I thought they'd forgotten me in their panic, but when I turned around, the whole room was looking at me. Even Eddard stared, his expression a mixture of curiosity and pity. He probably thought I'd snapped. I didn't look at Revik, but felt his mind slide past my words, still thinking about how we would get out of the building.

He turned to Eddard. "Get the charges from my room. If I have more clips—"

"Revik. I said no. We won't get out that way."

He didn't look at me.

I watched him put a hand on the wall. He turned towards me, still without looking at me, his face closed.

"Allie. We don't have any choice."

"We can't go that way." I bit my lip. "We can't, Revik. We can't."

I saw his jaw harden. He still wouldn't look at me.

"Please trust me on this, Esteemed Bridge. I am not being disrespectful. I swear to you, I'm not. I simply know our options here. This is my home. Let me protect you in it."

I saw Jon and Cass stare at him, as if they didn't recognize him.

Then they both, seemingly at the same instant, looked at me.

"I do trust you," I said. "But I can't let you take us out that way."

"Allie!" Cass said.

I looked at her. My whole body was shaking. I stood there, in the middle of the room, barely able to stand upright from the pain in my chest.

"Allie, what are you doing?" Jon's asked. His voice sounded shocked.

Revik stared at me, his eyes flat now, wary.

I didn't realize at first I was pointing the gun at him. It wasn't until I looked at Jon, saw his mouth hanging open, his hazel eyes wide, that I realized something was wrong. I looked down at my hands. They gripped the gun, steady.

"Allie." Revik held out a hand. "Please. Give it to me—"

"No." I took a step back. "Please, Revik. You have to listen to me. He expects you to do this. He's counting on it." My voice lowered, growing angry, but not at him. My eyes blurred as they filled with tears, but I couldn't care about that either.

I knew I was right. I had no idea how I knew, but I did.

"Please," I said, my voice thick. "Please, Revik. *Please.* Just listen to me. This one time."

"I'm listening, Allie," he said. "Put the gun down."

I shook my head, gripping it tighter.

He wasn't listening to me. I could feel it.

I'd become a threat in his eyes, a dangerous animal.

"He wants to shoot at you," I said. "He knows I'll do something. Fold something, or break something. Or light something on fire. I can't control it. He must know that, too. It's gotten worse, Revik."

"Allie!" Jon's voice rose, pulling me to look at him. "Jesus, are you going to shoot *Revik?* He saved our lives!"

"Who, Allie?" Cass asked. Fear leaked into her voice. "Who wants us to do it? Do you mean Terian? Is Terian here?"

"No." Revik's voice sharpened. He held out a hand towards Cass. "We're all right, Cass." He looked at me, and now he felt angry. "Put the gun down, Allie!"

I heard all of this, and it affected some part of me, but I didn't take my eyes off his face.

"Please, Revik."

"Please, what?" he growled. "What do you want me to do?" He looked at Maygar, and the anger in his face worsened. "What do you want from me, Allie?"

"Did you give me those numbers?" I blurted. "On the ship. I thought you were dead. But you gave them to me, didn't you? You did it to keep them from Terian. That was you. It had to be you. No one else could have done that."

Revik's eyes drew a blank.

I saw Maygar turn, startled. He stared at Revik.

"It's important," I said. "It's really important, Revik."

"Allie, I don't know what the fuck you're talking about! I would tell you, I swear I would! But we have to go! Now!"

"You helped design it," I said. "The rotating hierarchy."

He blanched. Then his jaw hardened more.

"Even if I did. I don't remember."

"None of it came back with Terian?" I asked. "That's what he wanted from you, isn't it? The succession order? So he could go after Galaith?"

Jon and Cass's expressions grew openly startled, just before their eyes swiveled in unison to Revik's face. It was enough to confirm what I'd suspected.

Then Jon's voice rose, angry.

"Did Terian *help* him remember? You mean when he was beating him unconscious every day? Is that what you're asking, Al?"

I turned, staring at Jon.

I saw Revik look at Jon too, telling him to be silent with his eyes.

I focused on the bruises on Revik's neck, how his clothes hung on his long frame. I lowered the gun slowly, staring between them, then down at my hands.

"I don't want to hurt you." All the resolve and tension left my limbs. "I don't want to hurt anyone."

"Maybe not *shooting* us would be a first step," Jon snapped. "Jesus, Allie. Have you lost it completely?"

"Jon," Revik warned. "Stop."

I looked at Revik, startled. Then Maygar spoke up from where he leaned against the wall, out of sight of the high window.

"Yeah, Jon," he drawled. "Take it easy on little sis. We need to know what we're up against. Rook-boy here used to be evil. Or did he forget to mention that, in all of your touching inter-species bonding?" He nodded towards me, his voice openly approving. "About time someone went to the source for answers. I always *knew* this fucker remembered more than he was saying."

I felt Revik turn before I saw it, felt his anger flare into something closer to hatred as soon as it found a target. His voice nearly shook.

"You're right," Revik said. "She's not completely wrong. I do remember more now. *Maygar,* is it? Your mother, for instance. Does she still work for them?"

Maygar's expression turned hard as glass.

"Watch your forked tongue, Rook."

"I remember you," Revik said. "You were a little shit when they brought you in. A thief. Half-recruited yourself. Are you the reason my wife's got a *gun* on me now? Didn't I stay dead long enough for you?"

"As a matter of fact—"

"Just *stay the fuck away from her!"*

My eyes swiveled to Revik.

I stared at his face in shock, saw his jaw clenched, his hands in fists by his sides so that the long muscles in his arms stood out. I felt my breath stop when I saw his expression. I'd only seen it on his face once before, and that was before I'd been born.

Maygar burst into a laugh. "You *must* be joking!"

"I'm not. Don't push me, boy. I'll rip your dirtblood heart out."

"Revik!" Jon said.

"Boys!" Cass said, sharp. "We don't have time for this! Military outside, remember? Revik, calm down—"

"You broke vow," Maygar said to him. "You *have* no rights, you worm-fucking retard. I can court her if I want!"

"No. You can't." Revik clenched his hands. "You interfere with an attempt at reconciliation, and I'll press charges. If I don't kill you first."

I blanched, looking between them. *Court* me? I stared at Revik, unable to look away from the expression on his face.

"Reconciliation?" Maygar snorted. "You brought your human whore here!"

Revik's face drained of blood. He looked at me.

"Whore?" Cass broke in furiously. "Would that be *me?*" She turned on me. "Is that what the martyr crap at lunch was about? You really think I'd skank on your *husband,* Al? You're my best friend! And for your information, he hasn't been with *anyone* since you last saw him! We were with him the whole time. He didn't touch anyone for months, unless you count Terian and his—"

"Shut up!" Revik was breathing harder, staring at her. "Shut up, Cass! Right now!"

I looked between them, feeling sick. "I really don't—"

"No!" Maygar said, holding up a hand to me. "Do not accept *anything* from him, Bridge! You owe him nothing!"

Revik and Maygar were looking at each other again. Neither dropped their gaze, nor relaxed their stances.

I couldn't take my eyes off Revik's face. Some of it was the anger there, but more than that, I could feel him fighting to control himself, to remain standing where he was. Suddenly, my mind seemed to click back on. Lowering the gun the rest of the way, I placed it on the table. Giving Maygar a disbelieving look, I closed the distance to Revik.

I grabbed his arm, harder until he looked down.

"No." I shook my head. "Revik, look, he's protecting me, but not the way you think." I yanked on his arm again to get his eyes off Maygar. "Revik! Listen to me! There's nothing going on with me and Maygar!"

Revik turned. His eyes locked on mine.

"Are you with anyone?" Pain wafted off him.

I stared up at him, speechless.

"Allie." He gripped my arm, hard enough to hurt. "I would understand. I know I'm not acting like it, but I would. Tell me to back off, and—"

"No." I shook my head, still staring at him. "I'm not with anyone."

He didn't move. Realizing I still had him in a death grip, I let go of his arm.

After the barest instant, he released me, too.

We just stood there, staring at one another.

Then it occurred to me I'd walked up to him.

When I took a step back, started to move away, he caught hold of my wrists. His fingers tightened, pulling me closer to where he stood.

I watched his face contort, felt the emotion he was holding back. I felt it intensely enough that my breath caught. He seemed to be trying to speak.

He looked so damned thin. I watched his jaw harden, his eyes brighten as he looked at me, holding out my hands slightly, like Jon had done when he first saw me alive. He looked longest at my face, then down the rest of me. I felt his light on mine, cautiously at first. It grew stronger the longer we stood there.

I tried to decide if I should say anything, when an intensity rose to his eyes. He met my gaze again and I nearly flinched, but I didn't look away.

I'd seen that look on his face before, too, but never aimed at me.

I let him guide me up against him.

I followed his pull to wrap my arms around him once I stood close enough. He let go of my wrists once I had, curling an arm lengthwise across my back, gripping my shoulder in his hand and squeezing before he wrapped his fingers into my hair. I didn't move as he pulled it out of the soft knot, as he caressed the long strands away from my neck.

He slid his other arm around my waist, pulling me tight against his body. Before I could take a breath, he lowered his head, pressed his face against mine.

I didn't move, other than to relax against him.

I forgot all of it in those few seconds—my mother, all those months of believing he and Cass and Jon were dead, even the military outside. He held me tighter, tight enough that I could barely breathe. My throat closed as he pulled me deeper into the curve of his body.

Then he opened his light.

Gods. It nearly flattened me.

I felt him hold his breath as he wound it deeper into mine. I felt him asking me, willing me to open, asking me again. I held him tighter, unable to see as his hands clenched on my back. His light slid deeper, pulling on me. I think I made some kind of sound.

His mouth found mine.

It shocked me. It was there before I could wrap my mind around any of it.

The veil was gone. Warm skin met mine, real flesh. He kissed me, then breathed against my lips, kissing me again, opening his mouth, asking with his light for me to open mine. He pulled on me with an urgency I couldn't think past, couldn't comprehend.

When my lips parted, his tongue shocked me, hot against mine.

I felt him fighting to go slow, but he couldn't do that, either. He explored my mouth, his light flashing with a possessiveness that shocked me again, blanking out my mind.

Pain wound through me, so intensely I might have lost time.

God. Why now. Why here?

Pausing to take a breath, he let out a low groan, shocking my light again before he kissed me harder, his hand clenching into a fist in my hair.

Everything seemed to happen fast after that.

When I next blinked, Revik was massaging my thigh and ass, his other hand on my bare skin under the stretchy T-shirt, holding me flush against him. The possessiveness coming off him worsened. His light was open, telling me things that made me shiver and blush. I felt him react as my fingers explored him under the white dress shirt. My other hand clutched the back of his neck, holding him against me.

He was hard. I couldn't help but feel that, too.

I wanted to put my hand on him.

He groaned. He lowered his head to kiss me again—

When someone's arms grabbed me from behind.

He fought the hands around his shoulders and wrists as someone or several someones dragged him off me. A thick arm coiled around my waist from the other side, pulling me away from him. I glanced behind me, barely recognized Maygar.

"What, are you going to fuck her right here?" he snarled. He was staring at Revik, his eyes and voice furious. "What the hell are you *doing?* Are you trying to kill her?"

I felt Revik react to Maygar's hands on me.

I saw pain on his face, confusion as he looked at me, almost like he didn't know where he was. My own pain worsened as I stared back, and suddenly I couldn't bear being held away from him. I bit my tongue until it bled, fighting the impulse to punch Maygar in the face.

"It's okay." I held up a hand. "Revik. It's okay."

Then my light, everything about me that was me, was ripped away from my body.

CHAPTER 47

TAKEN

"*No!*" Cass dropped her gun, running for Allie as she collapsed in Maygar's arms. Revik got there before she did. Maygar tried to shove him back, but the taller seer grabbed the front of Maygar's shirt in his fist, and suddenly a gun was in his hand.

He pressed it to Maygar's face, his eyes cold.

"Let go of her," he growled. "I'll do it. I promise you."

Maygar released her, removing his hands. His voice shook.

"If she dies, so help me, I'll *skin* you—"

"Stop it!" Cass snapped. "Both of you!"

"What happened?" Jon crouched over Revik, but it was Maygar who answered in a snarl.

"Rook-boy apparently wants to get laid so badly, he doesn't mind killing his wife to do it. He just fed her to them."

Cass watched Revik pull Allie into his lap.

He stroked her long hair away from her face, caressing her cheek with his hand. His voice shocked her. It was quiet, but a near anguish trembled on the surface as he spoke.

"Allie… gods. Can you hear me? Allie!"

"*Hit* her!" Maygar snarled. "Do you think that's going to do anything but make it worse? Hit her, or let me try!"

But Revik's hands had gone still.

Maygar shoved Cass out of the way, grabbing Revik's shoulders.

When he turned the other seer around, looking him full in the face, he cursed, releasing him. Bending down, he slid his arms around Allie, pulling her roughly out of Revik's lap. Cass watched in disbelief as Revik made no move to stop him. She was still staring at Revik's unmoving form when a loud crack of flesh against flesh jerked her eyes back to Maygar.

She watched in disbelief as he backhanded Allie again.

A red mark flared on her friend's cheek, but Allie's eyes didn't flutter as her neck rolled with the blow.

Maygar wound up to hit her again when Jon held his own gun to Maygar's head.

"Do it again, and I'll shoot you, you piece of shit." Without turning, Jon aimed his next words at Cass. "What's wrong with Revik?"

"I don't know." She gripped his arm, kneeling beside him. His pupils remained pinpricks, his face a wax doll's. "He's just… gone."

Maygar pushed the barrel of Jon's gun out of his face angrily, as if it were a pointed stick.

"He's gone after her," he snapped.

Jon looked at Cass, then back at Maygar. He lowered the gun.

"Explain to me how that's *not* a good thing," Jon said.

"Stupid worm! The construct is gone! They're all around us. Everywhere, as we speak! Staying out of the Barrier was their only protection!" When Cass and Jon continued to stare at him blankly, Maygar raised his voice. "They're going to *die!* She was already dead when he pulled her in. Now he's gone to die with her!"

Seeing the anger and frustration on the seer's face, it occurred to Cass that maybe he wasn't the bad guy in this, after all.

A jet slammed by the windows, rattling the glass.

The roar of its engines followed, deafening in the narrow corridor between buildings.

Looking across the street, Cass saw tiny figures of men in black Kevlar climbing the building across from theirs, and a kind of despair reached her.

There was no possible way they could get out of this, not anymore.

NEAR TO EARTH, THE FAINT LINES OF THE PHYSICAL CAN BE SEEN FROM THE Barrier.

The penthouse library looks underwater, dark, yet illuminated by an otherworldly light. A swarm of beings hover over the library's three ghosting human forms. The Rooks know a third seer exists there, too, but they cannot see him as long as he remains outside the Barrier.

It doesn't matter. The hovering shadows are little more than sentries, left behind as the real work screams above.

I am the real work.

I streak through a star-filled sky, running for my life.

I try to make myself invisible but can't, so I jerk and jump, reappear and am hit, slammed, run over, caught only to writhe free. All lines leading to my physical body appear as snarled and confused, broken and dead ended. I can't follow them back to Revik's apartment. I can't follow them back to my physical body.

Prisons appear around me, mirages that look like fields full of flowers, warm lights, tropical beaches, even distant stars.

They pull at me, tempt me with inviting vibrations before I manage to twist away.

I'm not sure how I came to be here.

I remember Revik. I remember us kissing, his hands pulling me tighter against his body, the feel of his light, of his mouth on mine.

I remember him asking me—

But now everywhere I turn, silver eyes glow at me, chasing me through an endless-feeling night, leading me further and further away. They are looking for a way in, even as I look for a way out. I try desperately to get ahead of them, looking for any door or passage or tornado-like tunnel that might lead me out of this place. I try to feel Vash… Revik… even Maygar.

The more I call to them, the more silver bodies converge around me.

They are closing.

Eyes and hands appear and disappear. They belong to more beings than I can count. Precise, lifeless, they slam into me, knocking me further from myself.

I fight back. I try to change the vibration of my light.

I disappear. Reappear.

In the bare space of respite, I look for resonance with something beautiful, something not-them… but they have already found me. More and more join the hunt, called by the Pyramid above. I am losing myself.

I don't know where I am. I don't know how to get out—

ALLIE!

Relief floods my light. He comes at me so quickly it shocks me. His light collides, then coils into mine, and briefly, we are alone.

Allie!

I feel him, all around me.

Shield! Disappear!

He hands me imprints, keys to lead me out through this winding maze. I feel his desperation, his intention. I feel what he wants—

No! I twine my light deeper into his. *No! I'm not leaving you here!*

They don't know your light! You haven't spent enough time with them.

They know yours!

Allie, I have ways to evade them on my own. You need to listen—

No! My anger flares. *Don't leave me like you left Elise!*

Laughter echoes.

I hit a wall, one I did not see, and come to a painful stop.

Before I can reverse, I lose him. Revik is pulled from me so fast it is like mist evaporating from my fingers.

I am inside a blank room with four walls.

I can't feel Revik. Even so, I hear him, for one last—

Allie! Don't wait for me!

I throw myself in the direction of his voice, but something separates us. I crash into another wall, bathed in stinging threads. Silver eyes surround me, shimmering hands and torsos. Dozens of them hook into my light, but Galaith's is the only presence I feel.

Let him go! Please!

I know how futile my words sound, how meaningless.

Galaith's face appears, alone.

The silver bodies and eyes recede.

I focus on him as the grayish space around me grows brighter.

Galaith's features flicker like candlelight. His dark eyes meet mine, without precise color or form, yet I see hints of teeth, stretched lips and facial creases.

He is smiling.

Hello, Liego, he says.

CHAPTER 48
GALAITH

In the Barrier's shifting dark, Galaith doesn't look like a seer. He looks even less alike to the blurred, sheep-like lights I now associate with humans.

An odd sensation of familiarity lives in our stares back and forth. I know I am being influenced by the silver light, but it is different than when Ivy had me.

Here, the influence is comfortable instead of fascinating.

The normality of him, of being here, is almost cloying.

Calm seeps in, the desire to entwine with the silver strands—or, rather, the lack of desire to fight them. I know I am being influenced, but I can't seem to—

You worry yourself needlessly, he tells me.

He waves a fluid hand, breathing out that same soft indifference.

Every construct carries its own flavor, Liego.

I feel the part of me that slides down that path with him.

I try to come at it logically and fail.

What do you want, Haldren? I ask.

I feel his smile. I know what the smile means.

My pretense of knowing as much as he does is meaningless. I have no cards here. Inside his world, my mind is laid bare. He knows I don't really remember.

Ah, he says. *But I remember, Liego. I remember it all so well.*

His familiarity with me just irritates me now.

He stole my husband.

That's all I really care about.

His light body changes from pure *aleimi* to the illusion of matter.

In a heartbeat he stands at perfect ease, a faceless, tailored blue suit, elegant on a muscular form. I guess middle-aged, from the shape of his torso, but he's in very good shape. Dark hair grows sparsely on hands with manicured nails. He wears a gold and diamond ring bearing an iron cross.

He turns me into a solid person, too.

My hands are gloved in cream-colored satin at the end of bare upper arms. I wear an emerald ball gown with thin straps, similar to what Revik's wife wore at a party in Berlin, only dyed green to match my eyes. A wedding ring adorns one gloved finger. It affects me to see it, which I'm sure is his intention—or maybe a Rook's attempt at humor.

I look to one side and see myself in a wall-length mirror.

My hair is piled on top of my head in elaborate curls, studded with diamond pins and peacock feathers. The reflection shows a cavernous room behind me. High, carved ceilings rise over pillars that stretch off into the distance.

Only the swastikas are absent.

Hmm, I say. *Seems a bit overdone. Or did you bring me here to critique my wardrobe?*

Galaith laughs. Strangely, it sounds genuine.

I have missed you, Liego, he says fondly.

I look down the cavernous hall. Paved now in black volcanic glass, the corridor is draped in thick curtains of purple and green vines. Water drips down from a cracking ceiling above a rectangular reflecting pool. Ancient, cypress-like trees grow through one of the walls. I see a bird alight on a massive root. It sings a song that stirs something in my memory. At the nudge of Galaith's mind, I look up. A high, blue sky is visible through the crumbling stone.

He wants me to remember.

But I don't remember, not really.

I also don't really care.

What do you want? I ask again.

He shrugs with a manicured hand, seer-fashion. *I want to relieve you of the burden of your so-called destiny.* He smiles. *I am trying to stop a war, Liego. A war you seem as determined as ever to bring.*

My feeling of unreality worsens. *You think I want war?*

Galaith's eyes are serious through the shifting mosaic of his face.

I think you will bring it, regardless of whatever you think you want, he says. *I realize it likely would not be intentional, Liego. Probably more than anyone, I understand this. I know it tears you up, each and every time. I know you dread coming here.*

His eyes flicker in that blurred countenance.

I can help you, Liego. You can live life outside that singular role. You could be married. Really married. Without having to worry that your mate or children will be tortured or killed simply because of who you are…

My light seizes around a vision of Revik, one I realize Galaith is providing me, but one so recent I flinch at how real it appears. I see Revik's neck, the clothes hanging on his long frame, the slight limp as he crosses the library floor.

The image morphs.

I see my mother's graying, staring eye, lost in a face covered in blood.

I see the scar bisecting Cass's beautiful face.

I see Jon's bandaged hand.

My silk-clad arms fold tighter, cutting off air I don't even need in this place.

Do not worry about your mate, Galaith says. *He will not judge you for taking this stance. He has seen too many wars to welcome another.*

Now I am in a dim room.

A single hanging lamp sways above dirt floors. The room lives underground, smelling of decaying plant matter and blood. White-washed walls like pale skin bleed dark rivulets of mud. It is hot. Insects flicker over sweated flesh near a metal table.

The dead body of a young Asian man slumps in a chair.

I don't see him at first, but I am not surprised when he is there.

Revik's arms lay folded across a broader, more muscular chest. His black hair is longer, and he wears a Rolling Stones T-shirt and jeans with motorcycle boots.

Terian, the same Terian I know from San Francisco, is there with him. Hunched over the body of the dead Asian boy, he is trying to saw off one of his ears. Cursing, he tosses aside the knife, which is rusted and covered in blood.

"Damn it, Revi'. Hand me that razor, will you?"

The taller seer takes his weight off the wall.

Picking up a sling blade from a nearby table, he flips it open and hands it to Terian wordlessly. Revik doesn't move away but continues to watch Terian work, tugging a hand-rolled hiri out of his pocket and lighting it after a few tries with a silver lighter. Exhaling sweet-smelling smoke, he doesn't change expression as Terian saws determinedly through skin and cartilage to remove the dead man's ear.

Terian grumbles at him as he works.

"You could have let him live long enough to give me a turn," he says. "What, did he remind you of someone?"

Revik shrugs. "The maggot wanted to die."

Terian glances up, chuckles. "So this was a humanitarian gesture, then?" He turns his concentration back to the ear. "I hate to tell you, friend… but most humans who meet you tend to feel that way."

Terian straightens an instant later, a triumphant look on his face. He shows Revik the mutilated ear. Already the blood coagulates, barely a trickle from the stopped heart.

Revik's voice holds a thread of disgust.

"Why do you keep those?"

"Are you kidding? The press eats this shit up. 'Vietnam's own Jack the Ripper'… or hadn't you heard?" Reaching into a coat pocket, Terian pulls out a playing card, the Jack of Spades. Flipping it over in his fingers, he sticks it in the dead man's mouth.

"That's you?" Revik shakes his head. "Jesus, Terry."

At the grin on Terian's face, Revik snorts a half-laugh.

"We need to get you a pet."

"Yeah, speaking of that." Terian cocks an eyebrow at him. "Remember that jaguar you picked up for me in Brazil?"

Revik grunts another laugh. "I don't want to know."

"Anyway," Terian says, as he raises the ear to the light. "It's not only me. Galaith *wants* me to plant this stuff."

"Why?" Revik asks.

I hear only curiosity in his voice. His eyes rest empty, flat.

I barely recognize him. Yet, oddly, he carries a kind of easy male confidence that makes him look almost handsome, despite his angular features.

I tell myself I knew what he was.

He'd been a Nazi before this.

But even working for the Germans, feeling lived in his eyes, something with which I could relate, even sympathize. I'd been told by the rest of them—Maygar, Vash, Chandre, the seers training me in India—that what Revik had done under the Rooks was exponentially worse than anything he did as a Nazi.

Even so, it unnerves me beyond what my mind can articulate, seeing him this way.

It also occurs to me that I cannot un-see it.

Terian shrugs as he answers him.

"Why?" he asks with a flourish. "How should I know why? Why does Galaith want us to do anything? Recruitment? Fear? Shits and giggles?" Wrapping the ear in a clean, white handkerchief, Terian shoves the whole thing in a pocket and claps Revik on the shoulder. "Let's get a drink. I need a fuck before we do the next bunch, and I know you do."

The dark, blood-smelling room fades.

I find myself back in Revik's London study.

Galaith sits before me on the worn leather couch, drumming his fingers on a creased arm.

The picture of my parents still sits on the marble mantlepiece.

One of my sketches stands next to it, a charcoal drawing I did of Revik while he was still showing up at the diner every day in San Francisco. More of my drawings spill out of an open drawer in the nearby desk.

I see more images of Revik, my brother, Cass, the Pyramid.

I recognize all of them.

I was kind, Galaith says. *You must know I could have shown you far worse.*

Yeah, I say dryly. *Very kind. If you'd shown me anything too over the top, I could have dismissed it as pure insanity. Instead you show me a rational version, knowing I'll never forget it.*

Galaith chuckles in genuine pleasure, slapping the end of the couch. *Very good, Alyson! Perhaps you have some intelligence in this life, after all.*

But I know this is a negging little jab, too.

He knows I am aware of the gap between me and the other seers, especially between me and Revik. I know how slow I seem to all of them, how little I can do with my light. Gods, I know he could never see me as his equal. How could he? How could any of them?

I fight back the pain that wants to rise.

I fight to focus on Galaith.

I know he is fucking with me, even now.

I thought Terian was the one who liked to play games, I tell him. *Aren't you supposed to be the grown-up here, Haldren? The beloved and benevolent leader?*

Galaith makes a dismissive gesture with one hand.

These are not games, Liego. And you are wrong. I do not judge you for your newness. Nor do I confuse this for lack of ability or intelligence. Nor does your mate.

I don't argue with him. I don't fully believe him, either.

So where is Terian? I ask. *Out torturing more people in your name?*

Galaith's countenance darkens.

Terian is dead. An unfortunate necessity. He was out of control. Galaith's thoughts grow warning. *But there will be others like him, Liego. They will do the same and worse to get to you. I won't be able to reach them all in time.*

Drumming his fingers on Revik's couch, he lets out a long breath.

Do you honestly believe you owe allegiance to the Seven? Or to that seven-hundred-year-old seer, Vash? You barely know him, Liego. You barely know any of them. Their myths and superstitions mean nothing to you. Do not lie to me by pretending otherwise.

I feel the pull of silver light behind his words.

If you think Vash will keep you and yours safe, Liego, you should speak to your husband. He could tell you a few things about the Seven's willingness to sacrifice the loved ones of others for their precious Code.

The eyes inside that endlessly moving face meet mine.

Do you not ever wonder how he was able to work for the Nazis and also be a member of their nonviolent club? Hasn't this ever struck you as a bit hypocritical, Liego?

It has.

Galaith smiles, but I feel no humor there. *Well, then. Perhaps this will give you more reason to forgive your mate for what I showed you before.*

An image appears out of the dark.

In it, Vash and Revik sit cross-legged inside a high-ceilinged cave. They talk seriously, hunched together over food and drink, papers strewn about them on the stone. I cannot hear their words, but Revik wears a German infantry uniform, a swastika band around his arm. A third seer is with them, a middle-aged male with sharp, gray eyes, chestnut hair and chiseled features. He is handsome, almost startlingly so.

It was all planned, Galaith says. *Vash and the Adhipan deliberately planted Dehgoies in Germany. They encouraged him to work for the Nazis… to fight for them, even if it meant watching his own people be put to death.*

The mirage disappears, to be replaced by the image of a gothic church.

My light reacts, flinching as Revik appears in the doorway. He is wearing a tuxedo, smiling, holding the hand of Elise, who wears a wedding dress so stunning she looks like a living doll. Her hair is sleek and filled with what look like tiny diamonds.

They both look so happy it is difficult to look at their faces for long.

Revik raises a hand, waving at a crowd throwing flower petals.

He was placed there to be recruited by me, Galaith adds. *To infiltrate my burgeoning network. But then the Seven stood by while his wife was killed…*

The image of Revik and Elise fades.

…and your husband rethought his allegiances. And who could blame him? The Seven could have intervened. They did not, believing interference to be "immoral." Dehgoies could not forgive them for that. He could not. He felt betrayed.

I am fighting my own emotions, staring at Galaith's morphing face.

Briefly, I feel real sadness on him.

Something happened to make him want to return to them, he says. *I do not know what. I even considered sabotage by the Seven themselves. What I do know is this: by then, I thought of Dehgoies as a son. I was devastated when he left me.*

The image of Revik in that tux won't leave me.

I've never seen him happy like that, not in person. Not even in the Barrier.

Galaith pats my light arm.

He shakes his head in sympathy, clicking his tongue.

Vash and I made a pact. After we separated your mate from that part of his life, we each agreed to leave his mind alone. His mind sharpens. *You broke that promise, Liego. I don't know how you did it, but you managed to give him back some portion of what he lost.*

He pauses, his thoughts grim.

I sincerely hope you have not hurt him more than helped him in this, Liego.

Looking up, I glimpse the Barrier's dark clouds.

I feel lost in all this, buried in too many things I only partly understand. Revik was right. I would never be smart enough to beat these people.

But I cannot bring myself to give in.

I realize this, and it is almost a relief.

The light around me flickers, changes.

Then… out of nowhere…

I am somewhere else.

No great flash of insight or understanding greets me. Instead, it is ordinary, mundane memory. I stand before a leaky espresso machine. Wet coffee grounds decorate part of my waitress uniform as Revik watches me and Cass talk from a corner booth. He looks tired; I know him now, so I see it in him.

Still, he is watching me, and I see other things there, too.

He watches me minutely, I realize.

I make him nervous, fascinate him, but he feels he knows me. He contemplates how to approach. He wishes he could just tell me who he is. I still manage to embarrass him. Hearing me and Cass speak to one another, he feels foolish for watching me so openly. He thinks now it was a mistake, that it will only cause me to trust him less. He is embarrassed by how socially dysfunctional he seems to me, by the bet around learning his name.

Something in feeling him this way touches me deeper than I can express.

Over me, news feeds play on the monitor, the sound muted.

Suddenly, I know what I am supposed to see.

The diner, the espresso machine, my waitress uniform… it all melts away.

A stone holding cell morphs around me in its place.

Dark and dirty, it feels mundane to me now. Two men enter that dank-smelling space, pausing at the door to stare at the prisoner chained inside.

One of them has no face.

Revik raises his shackled hands, blinking against the shock of light.

As I watch, the blurred lines of the faceless man begin to clarify. Features appear. I see the outline of a handsome face, not completely young, but a young middle-age.

He studies Revik on the bench, smiles.

"Rolf Schenck?"

…and the three of them stand on a hill above scattered bodies of SS, as the third of three gasoline tanks explodes. The shock rips holes in the turf, throwing wood and iron as shrapnel. Terian smacks Revik playfully on the chest, then starts down the hill at a run.

"What are you?" Revik asks Galaith.

"Perhaps you should ask yourself that question, Rolf…"

I know who you are, I breathe.

…and again, I fight with an espresso maker.

A monitor displays news feeds over the bar, where the President of the United States smiles at a press conference. Young, handsome, charismatic, the whole world looks up to him. Cass hangs over the lunch counter, her butt in the air, and she looks so damned young, like an overgrown child compared to the woman I am jealous of in London.

"What's the pool up to now?" she asks.

…and I stand in Revik's study, pointing a gun at Revik.

My eyes glow a pale green, visible in the sunlight from the windows.

"Allie." Tension vibrates his words. "I would tell you, I swear I would—"

Revik! I insert myself between him and the version of me holding the gun. I remember that moment in Germany, where the younger Revik seemed to see me.

I had thought he was dead then, but he wasn't.

He's not dead now, either.

Revik, I'm here! I wave my arms, desperate. *REVIK! Look at me!*

"…Even if I did," he says to the other me. "I don't remember—"

REVIK! I scream. I slam into him with my light. *LOOK AT ME!*

He turns, staring at me.

The echo fades.

For an endless pause, he just stands there, looking at me with clear eyes. Those eyes shift between the past me and the present…

For the moment, Galaith is gone.

It is only us.

Revik... I'm here! I grasp hold of him with my light. When he tries to look at the past me again, the one holding the gun, I shake his arm. *No! This already happened! Where are you now? Can you show me?*

The London apartment melts.

I feel him slowly come back awake...

Then I see it. He hangs in a dark space, immobilized by silver strands. They feed on him. Eyes roll back in pleasure as they draw on his light. They are getting off on it, savoring it. They will drain him dry, and only feel cheated when there's nothing left to take.

In terror, he cries out...

...and in the study, Revik staggers.

I hold his arm, support him with my light. He looks back at the version of me frozen in time, the determination on my face as I grip the Lugar in one hand. Cass, Jon, Eddard, Maygar all stand frozen in various poses as they react to a scene that can no longer be played out.

Then Revik looks at me, and his eyes change.

This time, he sees me. He really sees me.

Allie? Where are we?

Revik. You're really here. Looking at him, my happiness fades. I feel the weakening of his light, the hunger of the beings behind him, devouring him slowly. He is dying. I grip him tighter. *Revik, listen to me. Can you get out, if I distract them?*

He shakes his head. *No... Allie, no. I won't leave you.*

I kiss his face. *You won't have to. The succession order. Do you remember how it works? How the pieces fit together?*

Confusion darkens his features.

Allie, I don't have it. I told you—

I have it. You gave it to me, remember? On the ship? But all I have are the numbers. I need you to make sense of it. Can you remember enough to do that?

His eyes shine with a faint light. Something is there, some glimmer of recognition.

I can only hope it is enough.

Yes, he says, still concentrating. *I think so.*

I kiss him again; I can't help it. As I do, I hear it, the whispering of the numbers. It's a sound I haven't stopped hearing for months.

Seeing the distance in Revik's eyes, I shake his arm. *Revik, listen to me. You were working for Vash. You were a Nazi for Vash. Do you remember? You let them recruit you. You've carried the succession order ever since. For Vash. For all of us.*

Doubt fills his face.

After a pause, he shakes his head. *No, Allie.*

Don't argue with me, Revik. I know this is true. Trust me, please. You're one of the good guys. Don't let yourself die. Please.

I slide my light into his; I feel him react as I show him the numbers. Even inside his confusion and pain, his light connects with them easily. I watch him unlock the sequence, rearrange it using structures high up in his *aleimi.*

It expands around us in clean, geometric shapes, rotating with a visual mathematical precision I cannot look away from. There is beauty in this thing, despite how it's been used. I see that beauty. Feel it. Awe steals over me as I realize he created it.

This is Revik's work I am seeing—Revik's mind.

I see it, I say. *Do you?*

When the numbers light up around us, a faint wonder touches his eyes.

Yes, he says.

They're ready, I tell him. *Vash and the others. I think I can get a signal to them. Wait for me.* I kiss him again. *I love you. Wait for me. Please.*

His eyes change. Before he speaks, his outline fades.

Terror reaches me, that feeling of being ripped in half.

I feel it fleetingly in my heart, that I may never see him again.

Then I am alone, in an endless chasm of dark.

But light lives in the tiniest of fragments, and I finally know exactly what it is I'm supposed to do.

Drawing the numbers, Revik's numbers, up and out of my light, I superimpose them over the model of the Pyramid itself…

…and imprint the succession order simultaneously onto every seer in the Rooks' network.

As I do, I know.

I've known all along who the Head is.

CHAPTER 49
REALIZATION

One seer watches quietly, from a remote corner of the Pyramid where he hides.

There are crevices here, even inside the group mind.

Places to hide. Places the others don't often go, where constructs live inside constructs and one can disappear for days.

The structure rotates inexorably in its prismatic dance.

He hides in that dance, still as death.

It's not easy, but the Pyramid is his home. It encompasses everything he knows, everything terrifying and magnificent all at once.

For the same reason, he feels it when she comes.

Her music is different than his. So different, he knows the precise instant when she enters his home. He feels the conflict, the chaos she evokes. He feels her with Galaith.

For a long time, he puzzles over what she is doing there.

Then, out of nowhere, he sees it.

The succession order spreads out neatly before him, a map of light connecting one Rook to the next, in perfect, beautiful lines. Like his brothers and sisters, he looks for the Head, tries to count how many steps he is from that highest, most coveted spot.

The Pyramid shakes.

Reflexively, Terian makes his light even more dim.

It takes him another moment to understand the cause of those tremors.

They are killing one another.

All around him, seers are attacking seers, hammering blows at one another, trying to destroy one another. Lower-level seers attack the lights they see above them, pausing only to defend against those seers who strike at them from below.

He sees lights flicker and snuff out.

He sees death around him, pain.

Ambition, fear, triumph, war—they break out on all sides of the silver threads. Resentments long held flare up in the dark, turn to life and death battles. He watches them feed on one another. He watches them kill. Silence and shadow show places where Rooks are dimming themselves as he has, trying to disappear.

Already, though, more than half have joined the fray.

Terian is lucky. Lucky he will not be missed.

He feels the structure tremble.

It shudders more seriously that time, more dangerously. He still cannot see the successor's chair, but he is getting closer, rising higher all the time as he seeks it, groping through metallic dark. He counts each place in the hierarchy, follows each piece as one fits into the next. He ignores the chaos in his single-mindedness, as he traces those lines all the way up to where his light hovers.

Until he can see no further.

It is quiet here. He is alone.

Eventually, the reason dawns on him.

Excitement flares his light, so that he makes himself briefly visible. He barely feels the ensuing blows, barely hears the cracking in several branches of his *aleimi*. They can't touch him. Not anymore. A smile lights up his entire being.

He occupies the successor's chair.

He. Terian alone.

As the realization hits, he is already giving the signal.

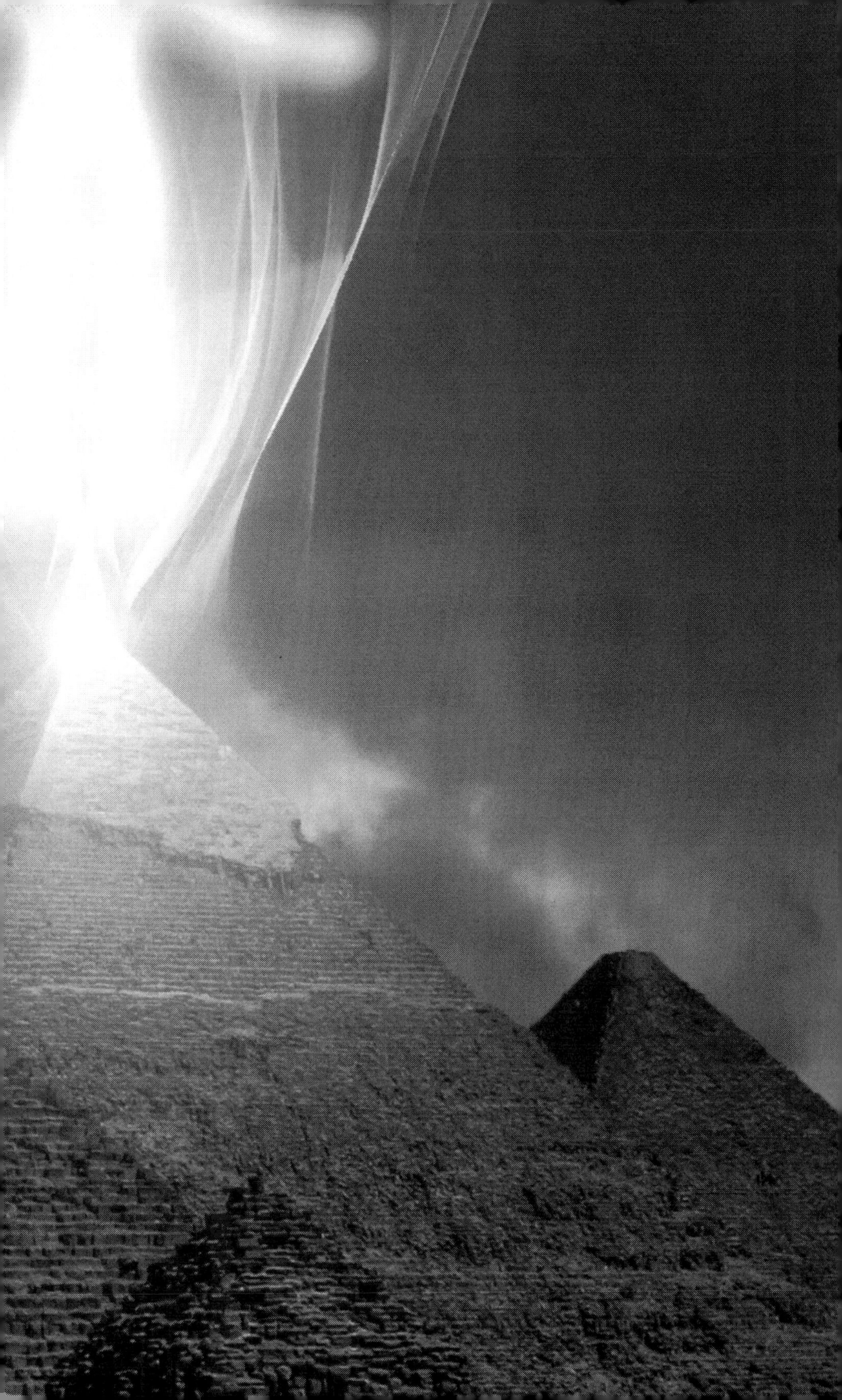

CHAPTER 50
PYRAMID

President Daniel Caine blinked to clear his vision.

Frowning, he stared around at the mostly older faces.

Something was wrong.

He could feel it, in every particle of his being. He needed someone else in the room who felt it, too. Someone besides Ethan, who, for obvious reasons, would not be joining them.

Caine barely noticed the silence.

That is, until the Secretary of State broke it.

"Sir?" As per usual, the man sounded as if he were about to go into cardiac arrest. "Sir," he repeated, as Caine knew he would until he turned and met the man's gaze.

Once he had, the Secretary resumed in the same, caught-breath voice.

"The terrorists have been isolated, sir," he said, flushing a darker red. "They no longer appear to be fighting back. The Prime Minister is asking whether you still recommend an air strike. They now estimate forty to fifty-five civilian casualties from that approach, sir, even with the evacuations. They also no longer feel it's necessary. Their Home Office Security is now recommending gassing the top floors, prior to any gunplay. I really think you should consider this approach, sir…"

Caine rose to his feet.

Normally he would smile here, even tell a joke.

His ability to play that role evaporated about thirty minutes earlier, however, when the network reported that his friend, Doctor Xarethe—the real one—could not be located.

He now had to assume that Terian, in one form or another, had killed her.

The prospect more than displeased him.

To call Xarethe irreplaceable was an understatement in the extreme.

Other unresolved questions tugged at his mind.

Alyson managed to evade him somehow within his own network, a feat that should have been impossible. That left the outstanding issue of what to do with Dehgoies if Caine found himself backed into a corner, forced to kill yet another of Revik's mates.

As much as Caine hated to admit it, Terian was right.

The entire cycle would be disrupted if he killed the Bridge now.

Before, when he'd thought Dehgoies dead, that prospect bothered him less.

Now, it struck him as borderline reckless.

The Four were already here.

Making up his mind, Caine walked to a telephone sitting on an antique wooden cabinet to the right of the couches and where most of his advisors sat. Without thinking, he picked up the old-fashioned receiver, held it to his ear and waited. Feeling eyes on him, Caine realized only then that he could have used his earpiece to make the call.

Or, more efficiently still, he could have used his newly implanted impulse-activated network, or IAN.

He ignored their collective stares.

Well, he did until it struck him that the old land line telephone might be purely decorative.

It was one problem with an abnormally long life.

Old habits had a tendency to return under stress.

Caine lowered the handset to hang it up, when a voice rose, sounding tinny and far away. He returned the receiver promptly to his ear.

"You needed something, sir?" the voice repeated.

"James?" Caine felt his shoulders unclench. "Where's Ethan?"

"Sir?" His security chief's puzzlement wafted through the line.

"Ethan. Our Vice President. Where is he?"

"The Vice President is still housed at his residence, sir," James said.

"You said not to disturb him. Not until we had a better idea of what the crisis entailed."

"Yes, well, I've changed my mind. I want him brought here. At once."

"To the bunker, sir?"

The bunker. It was what Caine's wife jokingly nicknamed the newly-renovated Oval Office when she first saw it with its bullet-proof window coverings and armored outer walls. The moniker stuck. She also called the Cabinet's main conference room The War Room, after that Peter Sellers movie mocking 1950s paranoia about the Russians hoarding telekinetic seers.

That name stuck, as well.

Like a faraway strain of music, Caine felt something crack. He knew it was another piece of the Pyramid fissuring off.

But James remained on the line.

"Wake him, will you?" Caine said. "Tell him it's an emergency."

He was in the process of hanging up the old plastic handle, when the door to the Oval Office slammed open.

Caine's eyes swiveled along with the rest. He stared at the leaning, gasping figure in the door's opening. For a long moment, nothing else broke the tense silence of the room. Everyone watched the man standing there clutch his chest, but like Caine, they didn't move.

"Ethan," Caine said at last. He cleared his throat, recovering. "Ethan. My God. You look terrible. What happened?"

Ethan Wellington, the Vice President of the United States, gripped the door frame, leaving a smear of blood on the white-painted wood. He still breathed in pants, holding his chest with one hand, wearing a trench coat over what looked like bare feet and pajamas.

How in the hell he had gotten there, from the Vice Presidential mansion through security?

Caine's mind grappled with the unexpected development.

Then, in the same set of breaths, he dismissed his lingering doubt.

This might work even better.

Let the whole Cabinet see the terrorist attack with their own eyes.

Whatever Ethan said at this point could hardly matter, when Caine could simply have his seers manipulate the memory of every human in the room.

"Ethan." Caine's voice emerged stronger. "I just called James to fetch you. Are you all right? What happened?"

Ethan gave a half-gasp. It resembled a laugh.

He raised his head to stare at his friend and President, and the expression on his face took Caine aback. A lot more of Terian lived inside that body now.

A lot more.

Caine's infiltrators had been busy.

Turning from Caine, Ethan addressed the others.

"I have ordered the Secret Service to arrest President Caine." He gasped, forced out words. "I've asked for him to be detained."

The Secretary of State laughed nervously.

"What charge?"

Galaith turned. Rogers had spoken, his Chief of Staff.

"Attempted murder." Wincing in pain, Ethan clutched his side. "Conspiring with enemies of the United States." His eyes flickered up like amber spotlights, meeting Caine's. "I'll probably know of a few more things he's done by the end of the day… he's mentally unhinged."

Caine shook his head in bewilderment. "What possible benefit can you see from this, Ethan?"

The question meant more than anyone else in the room could know.

Taking a step towards the door, Caine snapped his fingers at the porter. "What in God's name are you waiting for?" he thundered. "Call for medical help. Now. The Vice President's obviously been hurt!"

Caine walked towards Ethan.

He would just use the Barrier to knock him out.

Before Caine could reach the door, Jarvesch, the Secretary of Defense, inserted herself between them. She approached Ethan's bent form, touching his shoulder.

A kitchen staffer wheeled in their breakfast on a pushcart stacked with silver trays. Caine heard the porter ask for the White House physician over the central speaker as the wheels of the cart squeaked jerkily across the carpeted floor.

The secret service agent by the door clicked his fingers to get the staffer's attention, frowning when the man didn't turn.

Caine only noticed this peripherally.

Tensing, he watched Jarvesch take Ethan's arm, looking into his face.

Then she cried out, opening his coat.

"He's been shot!" She turned to the rest of the room. "He's been shot several times! God, Ethan! What happened?"

The kitchen staffer stood stock still, gaping, holding a towel in one hand and the handle of the cart in the other. He stared at the Vice President along with the others.

Then he turned, facing President Caine.

Before anyone could move, before Caine even glanced at him really, the staffer raised the towel and squeezed off three rounds in rapid succession.

Caine turned towards the sound, but too late.

The slowed-down vision of the Barrier allowed him to witness the last shot, almost as an abstraction.

It didn't allow him to get out of the way.

Smoke came from the gun's end, the hand jerked, and then—

Panicked yells fill the bunker.

Caine is somehow on the floor.

He fights to breathe, but he's got a frog in his throat. He tries to clear it, chokes. He hears them, hears the shots echo in his ears well after the fact, but really all he sees is the towel, the blank look on the man's face, the strange clarity in his eyes.

Caine stares at the Oval Office ceiling.

He wonders that he felt no warning from the Barrier.

He breathes in labored inhales and stuck exhales, breathing as if through water. He hears a struggle, the breaking of glass, but that's far away, too. He wonders how anyone could have gotten past his security, that of the Pyramid more than that of the human compound, although the latter is not inconsiderable, either.

Then he remembers.

Something was wrong.

Something was terribly wrong.

Liego disappeared, and then—

Ethan is there. Ethan kneels heavily, still clutching his own side.

Ethan Wellington, Harvard graduate and decorated soldier, is an entity almost separate of Terian in Caine's mind. Their wives are best friends. Their kids go to the same school. They vacation together, stood up at one another's weddings. As Ethan crouches next to him, Galaith and Caine bleed over as well; for an instant, he believes his friend is there to help him.

Then he sees the gleam in Ethan's eyes, the yellow glow behind brown irises, threads of those other fragments woven into the stable facade of his friend from Massachusetts.

The Pyramid shudders in those eyes.

Caine feels grief. Fewer bodies exist in which Terian can hide. Fragments of his *aleimi* crystallized into darker stains weave in with the rest, look through the same amber irises.

Caine knows insanity lives there. He feels responsible.

Ethan leans closer. Anyone watching would see a concerned colleague reassuring his mortally wounded friend.

"We may indeed prove to be the inferior race," he breathes to Caine. "...But at least we can shoot straight."

Gazing up at the dome of the Oval Office ceiling, Galaith chuckles, in spite of himself.

Emotion overcomes him, brings tears to his eyes.

"Feigran," he chokes through fluid. "Forgive me."

He can no longer see the Oval Office.

Lying on the grass, he gazes up at dense clouds. He is surprised when an opening presents itself there, where for the barest instant, he sees the flames of a blue-white sun. But the sun does not brighten his eyes for very long.

Through that same gap, a glint of asteroids beckon, cold but beautiful. Below, in a room filled with humans, the body Galaith used in this very long life finally gives out.

As it does, the Thousand roll over, claiming him for their own.

I FEEL HALDREN EXPEL HIS LAST BREATH.

A flurry of lines and pulleys unravel as he does, leaving with what remains of him.

I watch the Dreng gather up those fragments.

They pull him into the cold, flaming center of their silver clouds, claiming him as one of their own. I watch his *aleimi*—or soul, or whatever is left of him now—disappear into those dense, metallic strands as they take him away.

I am shocked by a sharp flicker of grief.

His absence leaves a hole at the top of the Pyramid.

The structure loses its silver sheen as the cold of the Dreng's light evaporates.

The giant beings from the silver clouds disappear like inhaled smoke from the physical world, leaving an oddly full silence.

I send up a flare.

I don't have long to wait. Vash and his seers, the Guard and their rebel children, allies from all over Europe, Asia, North and South America, Russia, Africa… they all come. They come separately and together. They come bringing countless lights of their own, beings meditating in caves and working out of seer brothels in human cities around the world.

Revik joins us.

He is battered, beaten up, but he is there.

They greet me and one another, lights combining and recombining in different patterns, creating something new.

I flash the plan, the plan they created, and together we move.

A single goal. A single vision.

Human lights shine with us, too: Jon, Cass, Jaden, Sasquatch, Frankie, Angeline, my neighbor, Sarah, the man at the toll booth on the way into Canada, the couple who stopped outside a diner in Vancouver because they worried Revik would hurt me, the little boy whose bread I stole in Seattle. The people on the Royal Faire cruise ship.

My Aunt Carol. My uncles and cousins.

Thousands more I don't know.

Millions of flickering lights.

Feeling them all there together brings a flash of hope.

Then, in another flash, we disperse.

CHAPTER 51
LOST SOULS

"NO!" Terian screams.

He watches the receding cloud of the Dreng.

He realizes the danger too late.

He feels the shift and struggles to compensate, to weave himself into the void above.

"NO! NO! NO!"

Out of nowhere, seers surround him.

These aren't the seers of the Rooks. These wield a sharp, white, painful light, one that burns everything in its path, everything it touches, ripping through strands and connections that hang dead and lifeless, temporarily inert without the Dreng.

And not just seers… he feels *humans* among his attackers.

The Pyramid fights to reform, to pull him up and out, to align him with the top spot, but the murderers intervene, again and again, burning every thread they touch, disconnecting more and more infiltrators from the structure below.

He feels her. She laughs at the carnage.

Laughs.

Hatred rises in him, a crushing need to kill, even as the last whispers of light connecting him to the Dreng's clouds snap and fray.

The Pyramid teeters.

Terian hears it.

He feels it as cracks build momentum, as fissures grow, tearing through now-dark structures. More and more of them fall, breaking apart like compressed ash, until he can only stand there and watch, unable to believe what he is witnessing.

Thrown clear, Rooks scatter like so many *rik-jum* cards, ripped from their moorings like birds thrown from straw nests. Light from the feeding grounds disperses, dumping power from the Pyramid's base.

The seers of the Rooks begin to panic.

Those still hooked into the network begin feeding off one another, killing one another for light. Terian watches in horror as more pieces fall, crushing panicking seers, tearing abilities and knowledge from the communal pools. Lifetimes' worth of accumulated talent crumble to dust, no longer able to hold to the shared mind of the Pyramid, utterly useless without it.

Terian's own structures begin to fail.

As the feeding pools unravel, he feels it as a drop in power so severe he is sure he must be dying.

Then, it gets worse. He feels the Pyramid detach.

It breaks away, Headless.

Terian feels her again. She laughs happily over the seething dark.

He would kill her slowly, vivisect her, murder all her family in front of her, all for the sheer joy he feels in her light.

He screams into the reaches of the Barrier, calling the Dreng back.

But it is too late.

The gap between the silvery clouds and the creation stretches too long.

The Dreng are nowhere to be found.

I SPIN THROUGH A WAVE OF MULTICOLORED LIGHT, LAUGHING AT WHAT unfolds below. I have never felt so happy. Light dismantles the Pyramid while I watch, tearing it from its broken moorings.

Souls disperse like leaves freed by a warm breeze.

I feel humans on different continents blink, come awake.

Even in their pain, their innocence brings up so much feeling in me. I laugh again, unable to help it. There is no other way to express the sheer joy I feel. Light pours from the Barrier, a cleansing torrent that blasts away the dusty, broken remnants of the Dreng's network.

The lynchpin pulled, I have only to watch.

It is the break in the clouds.

It is sunrise.

Then, I feel something else.

Allie, he says, sharp. *It's time to go.*

I open my eyes, fighting to see through the light—

! AND FOUND MYSELF LYING ON SOMETHING HARD THAT JUTTED INTO MY back. I was in a dust-filled space, colored by light from a small, square window with rose-tinted glass.

I looked around, fought to get my bearings.

Revik's long body lay next to mine.

A low boom trembled the floor beneath my back. It brought down dust. I heard coughing around me, some male and some female. A broken lamp swung from the ceiling, and realized I lay in a stairwell.

Voices grew audible around me.

I heard Maygar first. "Well, we can't stay here!"

"You heard what Eddard said," Jon snapped. "The next floor is completely blocked. We'll have to…" Jon's eyes refocused on my face, then widened. He gripped a gun in one hand. "Allie. Jesus! You're awake!"

I looked over at Revik. His chest rose and fell as he lay on his side on the wooden steps. His eyelids flickered, enough that I hoped he was half-conscious, at least. I fought to sit up, to force myself upright.

When I climbed to my feet, I got hit by a rush of dizziness.

Before I could fall, arms slid around my waist, catching me.

I glanced up, surprised to see Maygar.

"You're back," he muttered. He held me against his shoulder. Plaster drifted down from the ceiling as the building shook, dusting his hair. Maygar looked up as another booming sound rattled the windows.

"Is Cass okay?" I asked. "Where's Cass?"

Her voice rose, shaky. "I'm here." She leaned against the stair's handrail as she peered down at me. "What are we going to do, Al?"

Maygar's voice shifted to the tone of a military report.

His words were directed at me, I realized.

"They're blowing up entrances and exits. I've counted at least twenty inside, most of them on the floor directly below. I can't feel any on the floor above us yet, but it's only a matter of time. They've got seers with them, and the elevators are all down, as well as everything in the building fitted with organics. They've got tranq guns too, Esteemed Bridge, and gas."

Maygar grunted, motioning his head towards Revik.

"Rook-boy taught them well," he added sourly. "Eddard was trying to get us out through some kind of underground tunnel, something Dehgoies told him about before you two went under, but now the stairwell's blocked. Eddard says the tunnel's not on any of the plans, but we don't have enough weapons to get through. They could gas us at any minute. These two…"

He frowned sourly at Jon and Cass.

"…Made us carry you both. It slowed us down too much."

I smiled at him, shaking my head. "You want me to feel sorry for you because my friends wouldn't leave me behind?"

His eyes flinched. "I wouldn't have left *you,*" he retorted.

"Allie!" Cass said. "We have to get out of here!"

I looked at Revik. Remembering Terian's scream of rage, I clutched his arm, sliding into his light to see how he was. He was weak as hell, but most of his *aleimi* had returned to his body. The pressure built behind my eyes as I felt Terian searching for us both.

Cass was right. It was time to go.

"Get him up." I clicked my fingers in Maygar's face. "Now, Maygar! And wake him up more. He's still in the Barrier. Give him some of your light."

Maygar let go of me and crouched over Revik.

After shaking him once, he slapped his face, harder than absolutely necessary, I thought, although it seemed to do the trick. Once Revik's eyes were open, Maygar grabbed his arm, grunting as he hoisted him upright. He slid a shoulder under the taller seer's, motioning for Jon to help by supporting his other side.

Then I saw Maygar's expression turn puzzled. He looked at me.

"Something's different. It feels like chaos. Like—"

"I know." I studied his eyes, startled by his seeming unawareness of what occurred. He didn't seem to remember what we'd done to the Pyramid at all. "We have a window," I told him, keeping my explanation short. "From the Rooks, at least. I don't know for how long. And I don't know exactly how it'll affect them."

"What about the barricades?" Jon asked.

"And those soldiers on the stairs?" Cass said.

I looked at all of them, hesitating. "Yeah. Okay. Maygar and I are going to need your help. You're going to get tired. If it gets too bad, tell us, okay? We'll lay off."

"Allie?" Cass said. "Lay off what?"

I met her eyes. "We're going to be draining you. Taking your light. As soon as things start. I'll take as much as you can possibly spare. Don't ask me to stop unless you're desperate. The main thing is going to be speed. Once we get closer to their humans, I'll switch to draining them." I looked up the stairs at Eddard. "Those charges Revik mentioned wouldn't hurt, either. The more we can distract them, the easier it will be to…"

I trailed when Eddard held up a black bag. He shook it, to show me it was empty, then lifted some kind of hand-held remote device.

Getting the gist, I nodded, glancing around at the others.

I considered saying something else.

Something encouraging maybe, something inspiring or leader-like. Seeing the glazed looks I got in return, I realized we didn't have time for that, either. I motioned for Maygar and Jon to follow with Revik, even as another booming sound brought dust sifting to the stairs.

Already, I can barely see for the light in my eyes.

"Stay behind me," I hear myself say.

I feel Revik react, reaching for me, but only just.

THE FIRST EXPLOSION ROCKED THE WHOLE OF THE PENTHOUSE APARTMENT, raining debris down on the crowd of onlookers standing in the street below.

Windows shattered. Car alarms went off as chunks of metal, plaster, paper, fabric, bits of wood furniture and wainscoting along with broken appliances, powdered glass, and paint showered onto the street.

Military Intelligence, Section 5 Senior Agent, Ronald Clement, spilled his coffee over the front of his shirt when the windows blew, ducking down behind a military van.

He touched his earpiece.

His eyes found his partner, Agent Henry George.

"What in God's name was that?" he shouted. "I thought we had them trapped in the stairwell?"

Henry pointed to the penthouse, as if the smoke billowing out the top floor windows was explanation enough.

Annoyed, Clement tapped his headset pointedly. He felt the other agent click over, and immediately began to speak. "Henry? What happened?"

"Dunno. Where's the head Yank? That's their people, right?"

Another explosion blew out a set of windows on the penthouse floor.

Clement ducked, then watched in disbelief as furniture rained down, including what looked like a four-foot head from a Buddha statue. It caved in the front of a police car as it landed, crushing windshield and bonnet neatly into the asphalt.

Clement barely had time to be grateful no one sat inside when the muffled sound of gunshots grew audible once more.

Assault rifles. Full automatics.

Henry motioned Clement to follow him behind a row of vehicles out of range of the falling debris. A woman in a dark, civilian suit stood there, drinking from a cup that came from a gourmet coffee chain down the street. Henry watched her nod to a man wearing the black Kevlar uniform of SCARB ground patrol. She didn't stop speaking as they approached, although Clement saw her glance at them.

"Director Raven?" Henry asked.

"...I don't understand it, ma'am," Clement heard the SCARB agent saying to her. "Our people... half of them just collapsed. They won't fight. The other half are completely out of control. They won't listen to orders. Some even started shooting one another…"

The woman took a drink of her high-end coffee, her face unperturbed. "Gas the building with cyanide. If that doesn't work, we'll nuke the damned thing."

Henry and Clement gaped at her, then at one another.

The SCARB agent blinked. "Sir?"

"Kill them," she snapped. "Do you hear me? This is no time to play footsie with her, not after what that bitch has done! Kill *all* of them!"

The man wearing the SCARB uniform saluted. Right before he turned to walk away, his face seemed to crumple strangely, turning almost childlike.

"How could this have happened?" he asked the woman. "What will we do, now that we no longer have—"

"Pull yourself together, Agent," she hissed. "Or you'll join her."

"Director Raven?" Henry pressed, louder.

Clement gave Henry an irritated look, mainly for interrupting his eavesdropping.

The woman, Raven-something—or perhaps something-Raven, Clement wasn't sure—turned. Her blue eyes glinted, shockingly light in an Asian-featured face. She stood taller than Clement remembered, at least an inch taller than he did. She wore her hair long, unlike any other breed of agent Clement could recall. It hung in a dark curtain around her oval face, jet black in color, sleek and straight.

Her high cheekbones and odd-colored eyes hinted at her seer blood, but apart from her height, she could have been human.

A really stunning, beautifully put-together human.

On her index finger, Clement saw a ring glint in the few wisps of sunlight.

Its design showed a six-pointed cross.

"I think you understand what needs to happen here, soldier," she said to the SCARB agent, still staring at Clement. "It's time to clean up. That means our side, too."

The agent nodded, his eyes still holding that dense, childlike grief.

Clutching his helmet in one hand, he wandered back towards the building, as though lost.

Director Raven smiled at Clement, her shocking blue eyes still holding that odd focus. She held up the paper cup in a kind of salute.

"Coffee?" she asked politely, raising a charcoaled eyebrow.

A chunk of cement hit the street, flattening a letter box. A larger piece crushed a yellow fire hydrant, sending up a plume of white spray.

Clement glanced over at Henry.

His partner stared at nothing, his expression frozen, his face drained of blood. Turning away from the woman and from Clement himself, he clutched his earpiece as he listened.

"Can you repeat?" he shouted.

His mouth hardened as he listened.

"So it's absolutely a sure thing? He's really dead?"

"Who?" Clement asked. "Who's dead?"

"Ron!" Henry shouted, not hearing him. "They shot the U.S. President! Gunned him down in their own White House! Looks like the V.P.'s not going to make it either!"

"What?" Ronald Clement stared at his old friend.

Behind him, another explosion rocked the white building.

He and Henry both ducked.

When Clement turned, looking for the person who'd been standing there, drinking her designer coffee and smiling at him with that striking face, he couldn't find her. He scanned the nearby crowd, looking past uniforms into the crush of onlookers gawking from the first set of barricades.

But Director Raven was gone.

CHAPTER 52
BRIDGE

A few blocks from Eaton Place, a manhole cover lifted softly from its resting place flush with the asphalt, revealing pale but dirty hands.

As the cover rose higher, an equally dirty face grew visible.

The hands pushed the manhole cover to one side, planted themselves on the cement and hoisted up a muscular torso.

Maygar sat on the lip of the hole just long enough to get his balance.

He pulled up his legs behind him, then immediately reached back inside, clicking his fingers impatiently for someone to hand something up to where he could reach it. He glanced around as he caught hold of the clothing, then the arms of another, taller man and dragged him through the opening.

He pulled him clear, then laid him down on the asphalt, frowning.

Bending over his inert form, he slapped him sharply on the cheek.

"No sleeping now, Rolf. Wakey-wakey." He slapped him harder, and the other man's eyes flickered open. Once the clear irises could focus, the other man frowned.

"That's right." Maygar smiled. "It's me, dickhead."

"Oh, give it a rest, will you?" The girl climbing out of the hole had a long scar splitting her face and long black hair dyed crimson red at the ends. She was helped up the last rungs by a blond man in a very dirty but expensive-looking jacket.

After them, a middle-aged man with thinning hair and wire-rim glasses climbed out of the hole, his face smudged with smoke.

Behind them, another woman followed. She looked exhausted.

"Do we know where we are?" Cass asked.

Maygar said, "No. But we'd best assume—"

"Wait," Jon said. "Look."

They all watched the woman who'd climbed out last.

Allie walked out into the middle of the street, aiming her feet towards a stretch limousine that had just turned the corner onto the small cul-de-sac where they stood. She held up a hand, staring at the approaching car without slowing her steps.

The car came to a screeching halt.

The others exchanged looks, but barely hesitated before they picked up Revik and ran for the car. Maygar handed him off to Jon once they reached it, walking around to the driver's side door. Sitting in the front seat, a man in a black suit and cap stared up and around at all of them, fear and confusion in his eyes.

"What the bloody hell—" he began.

His eyes went dead, like the power had been cut.

"Get out," Maygar said.

The man obeyed.

Maygar, Eddard, and Cass slid into the long front seat. Jon climbed in the back with Allie and Revik. Putting the car in drive, Maygar wrenched the wheel around sharply and hit the gas. He began the wide turn to get them flipped around and headed out of the dead-end road.

Before he could complete it, a London police car pulled up.

It parked sideways, blocking the cul-de-sac's entrance.

Two cops climbed out of either side of the parked vehicle, holding guns.

To Maygar, their eyes looked completely crazed.

He hesitated before craning his neck to look at Allie.

"Two more, boss," he said. "They've blocked the road."

Allie glanced in the direction of the police car.

...and both officers fell to the ground.

Maygar stared, bewildered by the efficiency with which she'd done it, and to two seers, no less. Dehgoies couldn't possibly have had time to train her so well.

He'd heard mates could sometimes take on one another's skill sets.

Maygar pushed the thought from his mind, but not before it tightened his jaw, bringing a low surge of anger.

"Can you just knock it out of the way?" Allie asked him.

He continued to stare at her.

"The police car, Maygar," she said. "Can you knock it out of the way?"

Maygar turned back to face the road. "Aye, aye."

He jammed his foot down on the gas.

The limo leapt forward, accelerating fast enough for Maygar to feel a little reckless. He slammed the front end of the luxury vehicle into the parked cop car, hard enough to push the other vehicle out of the way, crushing in the limo's right fender and losing a long gouge of black paint in the process.

Allie said, "Guns only. At least for the next few hours."

They all gave the woman in the back seat a nervous look.

"Sure thing, boss," Maygar said, clicking in dark humor.

I GRIPPED THE ARMREST OF THE LIMO WE'D STOLEN AS MAYGAR BEGAN TO wind his way through roads and turnpikes leading out of the city.

Funnily enough, I didn't think much about the stealing part until then. It hit me just how indifferent I'd gotten, even as I wondered whether the minibar had anything to drink in the refrigerated compartment.

"Where are we going?"

The voice asking was deep, with a German accent.

I glanced up. Revik was watching me. All of us had taken turns giving him light, but his eyes still looked glazed, faraway-seeming.

"India," I said. "For now." Remembering the others, I looked between Cass and Jon, who sat in the front and the back of the car. "I have enough on my ident to send you both back to San Francisco, if you want." I saw

Cass's eyes go flat. I glanced at Jon. "...Only if you want. You can go anywhere."

Jon shrugged, his voice neutral.

"Anywhere but with you. Right, Al?"

I looked between them. *"Gaos!* Fuck off, both of you! You know why I said that. You'd think I was the Antichrist for not wanting to see either of you hurt again!"

Watching Jon's mouth tighten as Cass gave me an outraged look, I exhaled.

"You *really* want to come with us? Hang out with a bunch of terrorist seers at the ass-end of the world?"

Cass grinned. "What do you think?"

I looked at my brother, who only nodded. Seeing me beginning to relent, he leaned over to shove at my arm playfully.

"Besides. Brother of terrorist. Hello? They'd put me in jail."

"Me, too," Cass said cheerfully. "I'm a sympathizer."

I exhaled in exasperation.

That time, it was mostly for show.

"Okay. But just so you know... Seertown smells bad. I mean open sewer bad. The water's not right. No matter how many showers you take, you never really get clean like at home. It gets really cold, especially at night. It rains all the time." Feeling their mutual dismissal of my words, I added, "I can't promise we'll be doing anything but hiding, either, so don't expect *this* kind of excitement on a daily basis. And wait until you try seer food."

I couldn't pretend I wasn't relieved though, and Cass laughed.

I glanced at Revik. I wondered how he'd take to the idea of my friends coming along, but he wasn't looking at my face. As I leaned down to open the refrigerator, the chain I wore fell out of my shirt. I followed his eyes down to the silver ring that dangled there.

I felt my face warm.

After the barest pause, he reached for it.

I watched him cup the ring in his hand.

There was a silence as he fingered it.

I took a breath when he didn't speak.

"Terian gave it to me," I said. "To convince me you were dead, I guess."

Hesitating another beat, I reached back to unhook the clasp. Before I could find it with my fingers, he caught my wrist, stopping me.

I glanced up. When I saw his face tighten, I swallowed.

"Don't you want it back?" I asked.

"No." His eyes left the ring, meeting mine. For a moment he only looked at me, then he gestured vaguely, clearing his throat. "It was my mother's. My real mother's."

He paused again, as if unsure what to say next.

"I'd like you to keep it," he finished.

I processed that information, feeling another whisper of pain when his eyes didn't leave mine. Embarrassment reached me, but I couldn't tell if it was his or mine, or both of ours. Maybe it was just an inability to deal with him that close, looking at me the way he was.

He let go of my wrist.

Forcing my eyes away from his, I focused back on the small refrigerator, fighting to catch my breath.

"Do you want anything to drink?" I asked him. "You should eat something, Revik. It'll help replenish your light."

"Yes." A second later, he reconsidered, gesturing negative. "...No, Allie. Not right now."

"No?" I glanced back. "Are you sure? They probably have something in here you can eat. Even if it's just juice, or peanuts, or..."

I trailed when his arm coiled around my waist.

Gently, he pulled me upright, then back into the corner of the leather limousine seat by the door. Leaning over where I sat, he half-trapped me there with his arms, turning his body to shield me from the rest of the car.

For a long moment, with his light encasing mine, it felt almost like we were alone.

He just looked at me, his colorless eyes clear.

"Are you all right?" I whispered.

He shook his head. "No."

He looked like he wanted to say more. He lowered his mouth to my ear.

"I missed you, Allie," he murmured. "...so much."

Fighting a tightening in my throat, I braced against a sliver of pain that hit at my chest. I felt it in my fingers.

I fought with what to say.

Warmth pulsed off his light, but I felt him pull it back, restraining it.

I felt him wanting to say more. Finally, he caressed my face, his fingers gentle as he brushed hair out of my eyes.

"You saved my life," he said. "Again, Allie." His jaw tightened. "I don't know why. I heard you. With Galaith. You have no idea how wrong you are... about what I think of you. You were fucking wrong, Alyson. About all of it."

Glancing up at him, I smiled a little.

"Just a little slow, right?" I said, my voice teasing. "A little worm-like?"

He gripped my hair. "You saved my life. Again, Allie."

My smile faded as I looked at him. I watched his mouth harden, felt his fingers tighten on me as he searched for words.

"You're all I've thought about," he said. "Even before."

I didn't ask him before what.

We looked at each other, silent.

Reaching up, I let my fingers trace his jaw. When he didn't move, I slid them into his hair, then down to the back of his neck. I caressed his throat, tracing the line lightly where he was burned. For a long moment, he didn't move, letting me touch him as he held me against the seat. I caressed his chest, sliding my hand under his shirt, before going back to his face.

I didn't hide my reactions to how thin he was.

I didn't hide my reactions to any of it.

His *aleimi* flared around me as I felt his breathing change. I felt his light grow hotter, then coil deeper into mine as he lowered his mouth. My hand tightened in his shirt as his lips touched my throat. I jumped when I felt his tongue glide over my skin.

He raised his head, his eyes glassed.

He swallowed, staring at me.

I met his gaze, fighting disbelief. That kiss in his apartment felt far away, like a distant dream. This felt a lot more real.

"Are you going to leave me?" he asked.

His German accent came out thick. I heard grief in it.

I stared between his eyes. Clearing my throat, I shook my head.

"No," I said.

I saw tension leave his face. I could feel him wanting to say more. It hung there, between us, as he thought through words, as if practicing different ways to say it.

In the end, he seemed to give up.

He leaned closer. His lips brushed mine, a near question.

I held my breath as he kissed me again. His light remained cautious, around his body, away from mine. I felt him feeding on me still, too, probably in reflex since he was still low on light. At my thought, he took my hand, placing it on the center of his chest. For a moment both of us just hung there as he pulled light through my fingers.

He made a low sound, lowering his mouth to mine.

We were kissing then.

I felt nothing but restraint on him at first, a near caution as his fingers touched my face. I was holding back, too, I realized… but when the pull grew stronger, I found myself opening to him. I'd barely touched my tongue to his when I felt him react. He kissed me again, parting my lips, gasping a little against my mouth.

I opened my light more, and he groaned.

He closed his eyes, leaning into my hand, sliding his fingers into my hair.

Then he had me pinned to the seat.

He kissed me harder, leaning his weight on me.

When I slid my hand inside his shirt, he groaned again.

I felt him asking me then, felt everything about him grow soft, melting into my light, against my body. Pain slid through me from him, almost debilitating, and he let out a heavier groan, his hand clenching on my hip.

He kissed me again, using light in his tongue.

Images flickered through his mind. His intent grew harder, more focused, and I felt restraint behind that, too. He wanted to fuck. That part was unambiguous. He wanted us to go somewhere and be alone so we could fuck for a while. He wanted to know what I liked… or maybe what he could get away with… or maybe how much he could tell me about what he liked… I honestly wasn't sure which of those things felt most true.

He wanted to go down on me.

He wanted to watch me give him head.

I flinched at the intensity of each want, each flicker of intent, each image.

I realized he was hard, pressing against me. His hand wrapped around my thigh. He started to open for real, to unfurl his light—

"Hey!" Jon thumped Revik on the back.

Both of us jumped.

"Chill out," he said. "You guys are like teenagers, I swear." He punched Revik's arm. "That's still my sister, man. Married or not… no way am I going to watch you two go at it in here. No way."

I let go of him at once and Revik raised his head.

His eyes were out of focus, almost drugged, but he nodded to Jon's words. I felt another set of eyes on me and glanced forward as Maygar looked away from the rearview mirror.

Only then did I realize how quiet the car was.

My eyes found Cass's and she grinned at me, shaking her head. The scar pulled at her face when she smiled, changing its shape.

Even Eddard looked faintly amused in his one glance backwards.

Jon patted Revik on the leg. "Sorry, man. Just wait until we get somewhere, okay?"

When the silence stretched, Maygar cleared his throat, leaning down to punch in the car's audio feed.

"…This just confirmed," the announcer's tinny, avatar voice blared in an English accent. "The President of the United States is dead. The White House physician issued a statement minutes ago, outlining how a series of gunshot wounds in the Oval Office proved to be fatal. The unidentified attacker first broke in and shot the Vice President, Ethan Wellington, in his state room at the Vice Presidential mansion, leaving him for dead before…"

I glanced over to see Cass gaping at the radio. Jon, on the other side of Revik, wore an expression that mirrored hers. Then all five of them were staring at me.

Maygar was the first to break the silence.

He snorted, glancing at me in the mirror.

"It was him, wasn't it?" he said. "Galaith. *El Presidente.*" Reading assent in my silence, he focused back on the road. "I don't know what scares me more. The idea that you're on my side… or that you may not always be."

"I didn't kill him," I warned.

Maygar laughed. "No. You just made sure every seer who wanted him dead knew exactly where he was." He muttered, "Brilliant, really. I'd have thought more would be loyal."

"Some *were* loyal," I said.

"Well at least *one* wasn't," Maygar retorted.

I glanced at Revik. He reached into my lap and took my hand, clasping my fingers tightly.

"You did the right thing," he said.

I looked down at our entwined fingers.

Then I glanced out the window. The sun slanted down through an overcast English sky. Even through thick pollution and clouds, columns of fogged gold cascaded down to illuminate discrete pockets of humanity and green lawn.

I thought about going back to that high perch in the Himalayas, with the monkeys and chai, golden eagles floating over strings of prayer flags and snow-covered mountains. I thought about being there with Jon and Cass, hiking with them and hanging out in the markets, going swimming and exploring, making friends with the other seers.

I thought about being there with Revik, and I smiled.

When I glanced up, he was staring at me.

He touched my face when I averted my gaze, and I felt a pulse of warmth off him, affection that slid into something else, that grew almost tentative as it expanded soft tendrils through my chest. It strengthened as I gripped his hand, until I was sending the same back to him, tugging gently on his fingers.

He pulled me closer, letting me into more of his light.

I could feel it by then, what he'd wanted to tell me.

That time, when he stared at me, I didn't look away.

EPILOGUE

ETHAN

Ethan Wellington stood on the steps of the U.S. Capitol Building.

A crowd of thousands—likely tens of thousands—flooded down the steps and onto the parkway below, for as far as his physical eyes could see.

He saw them hanging from streetlamps, crowded together on curbs. They stood on the street, on the Capitol steps, in parking lots, on the footpaths, on the grass. They filled every spot not taken up by another physical object, or cordoned off by the legion of Secret Service, Homeland Security, SCARB, and other military branches who blanketed the city in the wake of President Caine's assassination.

The vast majority of those in the crowd were human, of course.

Still, he'd received well-wishes from several of the seer delegations prior to his arrival for the ceremony. They apologized for their inability to come in person, but Ethan understood better than anyone why no recognizable seer would be safe on the streets of D.C. today, or perhaps the streets of any major city in the United States.

Three weeks had passed since his friend, Daniel Caine, had died.

Since the assassin was identified as a seer who did contract work with the Chinese, the country had been in an uproar.

The Chief Justice of the Supreme Court stood opposite him now, wearing full dress robes.

She was only newly appointed to the role. Caine had chosen her, of course. There'd been some lingering controversy in the wake of his assassination, given where his loyalties were now believed to have resided, and how recently she'd risen to the country's highest bench.

Wellington assured everyone she was in no way involved, however.

He further cautioned that they couldn't very well go back and question every decision Caine ever made while president, not without due cause.

Of course, if they'd known Chief Justice Novak was no longer the same person who had been nominated to the Court three months previous, it's likely they would have been even more alarmed. The few who knew her well—on a personal level, that is—appeared to all be mysteriously unavailable for comment, however.

It was one more advantage to the image ban in place for public figures.

A few well-planned eliminations, some reconstructive surgery, a number of more thorough mind re-patternings, and no one asked any questions.

When the Chief Justice looked up, Ethan smiled, meeting the older woman's eyes.

Hey doc, he thought at her with his human mind. *What's up?*

Xarethe's expression did not flicker.

"Sir," she said. "Please raise your right hand."

Ethan did as he was told. His left hand, which still poked from the end of a dark blue sling, the color of which perfectly matched his suit, he placed on a King James Bible.

The Chief Justice, still wearing her outdated glasses, flashed the slightest bit of warning from her reptilian eyes. All trace of the German accent evaporated.

"Are you prepared to take the Oath, Mr. Vice President?"

Ethan glanced out over the crowd as they burst into cheers of ecstatic applause. He'd broken a conspiracy in the heart of the White House, even tried to save Caine's life as he lay dying on the Oval Office floor. The applause grew more frenetic, more emotional.

It was amazing how quickly they forgot.

But humans loved a good story.

Like Caine before him, Wellington was more than happy to provide them with one.

"I am," he said. "…Ready, that is."

She smiled, raising her right hand. "Very well, sir. Please repeat after me…"

He only half-listened as he intoned the phrases after she spoke them.

His eyes scanned faces in his nearer audience, where his wife, Helen, stood by a little girl in a purple dress with a stuffed white rabbit clutched to her chest. The rabbit was brand new; its fur gleamed a pristine white. The little girl gazed up at him, oblivious to the screams and cheers of the people flooding the steps below the platform.

"I cannot believe he wanted to do this outside," the Secretary of State muttered to Ethan's right, within the girl's earshot.

The Secretary of Defense stood beside him, wearing a navy uniform covered in medals.

She smiled without turning, flipping long, mahogany-colored hair out of her eyes.

"It plays well for the press," she said. "Especially with him injured."

"Do we know yet, who is responsible? Who is *really* responsible?"

Her well-formed lips firmed. "You know the answer to that, James. We don't *always* lie to the press, you know." She gave him a wry smile. "Wellington's already declared war. Of course, it won't be official until tonight. After he speaks to Congress."

Her eyes flashed a pale amber as she glanced over the crowd, pausing to wink at the little girl before she smiled at Ethan.

"Caine did us a favor," she added, giving her fellow Secretary a wry smile. "If nothing else, it is clear now, what we must do to survive."

"Really?" The Secretary of State snorted. "And just what is that, Jarvesch?"

"Exterminate the enemy," she said. "Before they are strong enough to do it to us."

Beyond them, Ethan Wellington continued to speak into the small but powerful microphone, saying the words that would make him the next President of the United States.

"…will well and faithfully discharge the duties of the office in which I am about to enter," he said forcefully.

"So help me, God," the Justice prompted.

Her hard eyes smiled faintly.

The crowd behind him erupted in emotional cheering. The feed cameras ran, capturing faces and waving hands. In the monitors, Ethan saw tears wiped from the eyes of watching humans, banners waving back and forth as he gazed out over the Washington Monument.

In the distance, tanks could be seen parked at either end of the mall.

Jets flashed in the sunlight overhead.

Ethan smiled, and the cheering grew louder still, more emotional.

"...So help me, God," he said.

WANT MORE REVIK & ALLIE?
Grab the FREE bonus epilogue!

Link: http://bit.ly/BS01-Epilogue

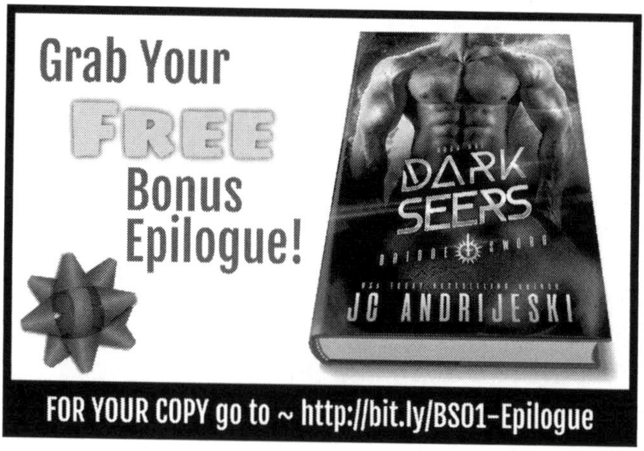

WANT TO READ MORE?

Check out the next book in the series:

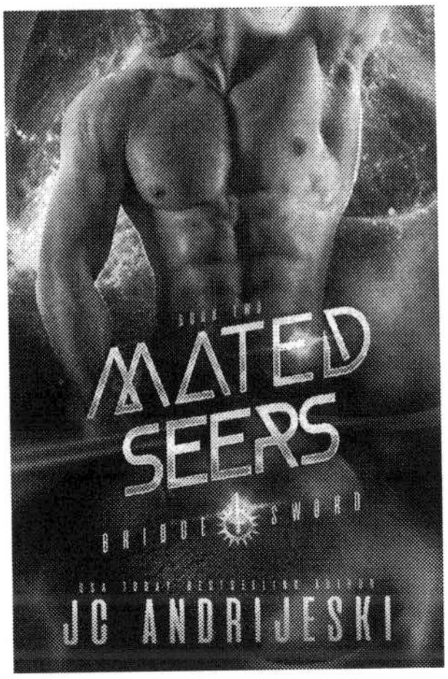

MATED SEERS

(Bridge and Sword: Book Two)

Link: https://bit.ly/Mated-Seers-BS02

"And Death will live among them in the guise of a child…"

They call her The Bridge. She leads them now. The reality of that, of leading a people and culture she barely understands, would be daunting even *without* what the myths say about her.

As it is, they look at her, and see the end of the world.

More unnerving still, they want to follow her there.

She's married now. She's married, but she still doesn't know what that means, not to a Seer, and certainly not to her actual husband, who's never exactly been an easy person to read. A new set of rules around Seer culture and her relationship with the infamous Seer infiltrator, Revik, nearly destroy her marriage before it can truly begin.

Then the boy appears.

A sociopath with all of the energetic markings of Syrimne, a deadly telekinetic who killed thousands during World War I, he doesn't appear to have aged in one hundred years.

Worse, he thinks Allie belongs to him.

*

Psychic suspense. Apocalyptic. The second chapter in an epic, soul-crushing, world-spanning romance that can get dark, dark, dark... but also contains a lot of light.

Slow burn. Fated Mates. Enemies to lovers. Forced marriage. Rejected mates.

Every book ends on a completed arc.

***NOTE: A different version of this novel was previously titled "Shield" (same series name)*

REVIEWS ARE AWESOME

Now that you've finished reading my book,
PLEASE CONSIDER LEAVING A REVIEW!
A short review is fine and so very appreciated.
Word of mouth is truly essential for any author to succeed!

Leave a Review Here: https://bit.ly/Dark-Seers-BS01

RECOMMENDED READING ORDER:
BRIDGE AND SWORD SERIES

The Seer (Bridge and Sword Prequel Novel)
DARK SEERS (Book One)
MATED SEERS (Book Two)
"Le Moulin" (short story) - FREE in exclusive box set when you sign up for my mailing list at https://www.jcandrijeski.com/mailing-list
ROGUE SEERS (Book Three)
Bad Seer (Bridge and Sword Prequel Novel)
SHADOW SEER (Book Four)
"Fireplace" (short story) - FREE in exclusive box set when you sign up for my mailing list at https://www.jcandrijeski.com/mailing-list
SEER KNIGHT (Book Five)
Broken Seer (Bridge and Sword Prequel Novel)
SEER OF WAR (Book Six)
BRIDGE OF LIGHT (Book Seven)
Seer Rising (Bridge and Sword Prequel Novel)
SEER PROPHET (Book Eight)
A Seer's Love (Bridge and Sword #8.5)
DRAGON GOD (Book Nine)
Seer Guardian (Bridge and Sword Prequel Novel)
SWORD & SUN (Book Ten)

THANK YOU NOTE

I just wanted to take a moment here to thank some of my amazing readers and supporters. Huge appreciation, long distance hugs and light-filled thanks to the following people:

Shannon Tusler
Robert Tusler
Amelia Johnson
Joy Killi
Sarah Hall
Elizabeth Meadows
Rebekkah Brainerd

I can't tell you how much I appreciate you!

JC Andrijeski

JC Andrijeski is a *USA Today* and *Wall Street Journal* bestselling author of science fiction romance, paranormal mysteries and romance, and apocalyptic science fiction, often with a sexy and metaphysical bent.

JC's background comes from journalism, history and politics. She also has a tendency to traipse around the globe, eat odd foods, and read whatever she can get her hands on. She grew up in the Bay Area of California, but has lived abroad in Europe, Australia and Asia, and from coast to coast in the continental United States.

She currently lives and writes full time in Los Angeles.

For more information, go to: https://jcandrijeski.com

patreon.com/jcandrijeski
amazon.com/JC-Andrijeski/e/B004MFTAP0
bookbub.com/authors/jc-andrijeski
tiktok.com/@jcandrijeski
facebook.com/JCAndrijeski
instagram.com/jcandrijeski
twitter.com/jcandrijeski

Made in the USA
Columbia, SC
02 July 2022

62635911R00307